Some Luck

Also by Jane Smiley

Some Luck

JANE SMILEY

MANTLE

First published in the United States by Alfred A. Knopf,
a division of Random House LLC, New York,
and in Canada by Random House of Canada Limited,
Toronto, Penguin Random House companies.

First published in the UK 2014 by Mantle

This hardback edition published in the UK 2014 by Mantle
an imprint of Pan Macmillan, a division of Macmillan Publishers Limited
Pan Macmillan, 20 New Wharf Road, London N1 9RR
Basingstoke and Oxford
Associated companies throughout the world
www.panmacmillan.com

ISBN 978-1-4472-7559-6

1 3 5 7 9 8 6 4 2

A CIP catalogue record for this book is available from the British Library.

Printed and bound by CPI Group (UK) Ltd, Croydon, CR0 4YY

V   ooks
a   ; and
                                                                    ters

This trilogy is dedicated to John Whiston,
Bill Silag, Steve Mortensen, and Jack Canning,
with many thanks for decades of patience, laughter,
insight, information, and assistance.

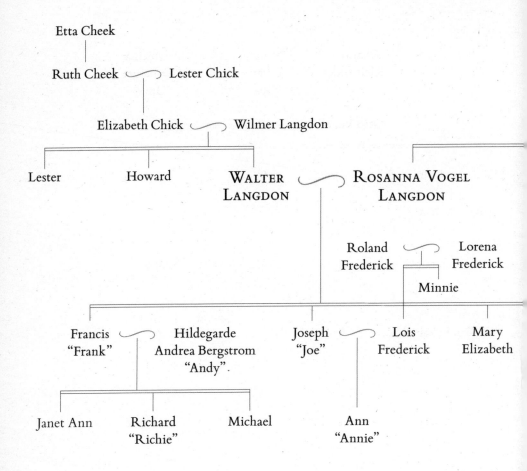

Etta Cheek

Ruth Cheek ⌢⌣ Lester Chick

Elizabeth Chick ⌢⌣ Wilmer Langdon

Lester   Howard   **WALTER LANGDON** ⌢⌣ **ROSANNA VOGEL LANGDON**

Roland Frederick ⌢⌣ Lorena Frederick

Minnie

Francis "Frank" ⌢⌣ Hildegarde Andrea Bergstrom "Andy".   Joseph "Joe" ⌢⌣ Lois Frederick   Mary Elizabeth

Janet Ann   Richard "Richie"   Michael   Ann "Annie"

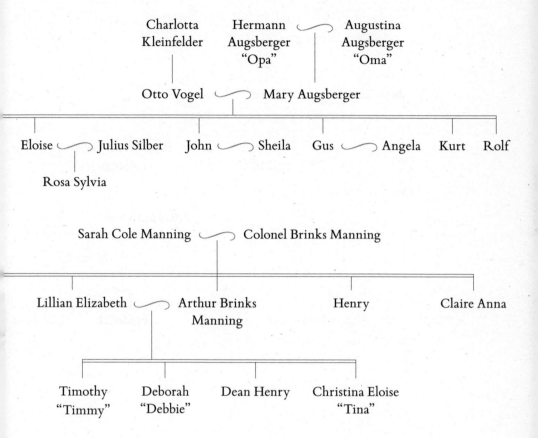

Charlotta Kleinfelder   Hermann Augsberger "Opa"   Augustina Augsberger "Oma"

Otto Vogel   Mary Augsberger

Eloise   Julius Silber   John   Sheila   Gus   Angela   Kurt   Rolf

Rosa Sylvia

Sarah Cole Manning   Colonel Brinks Manning

Lillian Elizabeth   Arthur Brinks Manning   Henry   Claire Anna

Timothy "Timmy"   Deborah "Debbie"   Dean Henry   Christina Eloise "Tina"

The Langdons

Some Luck

1920

WALTER LANGDON HADN'T WALKED OUT to check the fence along the creek for a couple of months—now that the cows were up by the barn for easier milking in the winter, he'd been putting off fence-mending—so he hadn't seen the pair of owls nesting in the big elm. The tree was half dead; every so often Walter thought of cutting it for firewood, but he would have to get help taking it down, because it must be eighty feet tall or more and four feet in diameter. And it wouldn't be the best firewood, hardly worth the trouble. Right then, he saw one of the owls fly out of a big cavity maybe ten to twelve feet up, either a big female or a very big male—at any rate, the biggest horned owl Walter had ever seen—and he paused and stood for a minute, still in the afternoon breeze, listening, but there was nothing. He saw why in a moment. The owl floated out for maybe twenty yards, dropped toward the snowy pasture. Then came a high screaming, and the owl rose again, this time with a full-grown rabbit in its talons, writhing, going limp, probably deadened by fear. Walter shook himself.

His gaze followed the owl upward, along the southern horizon, beyond the fence line and the tiny creek, past the road. Other than the big elm and two smaller ones, nothing broke the view—vast snow faded into vast cloud cover. He could just see the weather vane and the tip of the cupola on Harold Gruber's barn, more than half a mile to the south. The enormous owl gave the whole scene focus, and woke him up. A rabbit, even a screaming rabbit? That was one less rabbit after his oat plants this spring. The world was full of rabbits, not so full of owls, especially owls like this one, huge and silent. After a minute or two, the owl wheeled around and headed back to the tree. Although it wasn't yet dusk, the light was not very strong, so Walter couldn't be sure he saw the feathery horns of another owl peeking out of the cavity in the trunk of the elm, but maybe he did. He would think that he did. He had forgotten why he came out here.

Twenty-five, he was. Twenty-five tomorrow. Some years the snow had melted for his birthday, but not this year, and so it had been a long winter full of cows. For the last two years, he'd had five milkers, but this year he was up to ten. He hadn't understood how much extra work that would be, even with Ragnar to help, and Ragnar didn't have any affinity for cows. Ragnar was the reason he had more cows—he needed some source of income to pay Ragnar—but the cows avoided Ragnar, and he had to do all the extra milking himself. And, of course, the price of milk would be down. His father said it would be: it was two years since the war, and the Europeans were back on their feet—or at least back on their feet enough so that the price of milk was down.

Walter walked away from this depressing thought. The funny thing was that when he told his father that he broke even this year, expecting his father to shake his head again and tell him he was crazy to buy the farm when land prices were so high, his father had patted him on the back and congratulated him. Did breaking even include paying interest on the debt? Walter nodded. "Good year, then," said his father. His father had 320 acres, all paid for, a four-bedroom house, a big barn with hay stacked to the roof, and Walter could have gone on living there, even with Rosanna, even with the baby, especially now, with Howard taken by the influenza and the house so empty, but his father would have walked into his room day and night without knocking, bursting with another thing that Walter had to know or do or remember or finish. His father was strict, and liked things just so—he even oversaw Walter's mother's cooking, and always had. Rosanna hadn't complained about living with his parents—it was all Walter wanting his own place, all Walter looking at the little farmhouse (you could practically see through the walls, they were so thin), all Walter walking the fields and thinking that bottomland made up for the house, and the fields were rectangular—no difficult plowing or strange, wasted angles. It was all Walter, and so he had no one to blame but himself for this sense of panic that he was trying to walk away from on the day before his birthday. Did he know a single fellow his age with a farm of his own? Not one, at least not around here.

When you looked at Rosanna, you didn't think she'd been raised on a farm, had farms all through her background, even in Germany. She was blonde, but slender and perfectly graceful, and when she praised the baby's beauty, she did so without seeming to realize that it reproduced her own. Walter had seen that in some lines of cows—the calves looked stamped out by a cookie cutter, and even the way they turned their heads or kicked their hind feet into the air was the same as last year's calf and the one before that. Walter's family was a bastard mix, as his grandfather would say—Langdons, but with some of those long-headed ones from the Borders, with red hair, and then some of those dark-haired Irish from Wexford that were supposed to trace back to the sailors from the Spanish Armada, and some tall balding ones who always needed glasses from around Glasgow. His mother's side leavened all of these with her Wessex ancestry ("The Chicks and the Cheeks," she'd always said), but you couldn't tell that Walter's relatives were related the way you could with Rosanna's. Even so, of all Rosanna's aunts and uncles and cousins, the Augsbergers and the Vogels, Rosanna was the most beautiful, and that was why he had set his heart upon winning her when he came home from the war and finally really noticed her, though she went to the Catholic church. The Langdon and Vogel farms weren't far apart—no more than a mile—but even in a small town like Denby, no one had much to say to folks who went to other churches and, it must be said, spoke different languages at home.

Oh, Rosanna, just twenty, but with the self-possessed grace of a mature woman! He could see her profile as he approached the house in the dusk, outlined by the lamplight behind her. She was looking for him. Just in the tilt of her head, he could see that she had some project in mind. And of course he would say yes to her. After all, no fledgling had it easy, farmer or crow. Hadn't he known since he was a boy the way the fledglings had to fall out of the nest and walk about, cheeping and crying, until they grew out their feathers and learned to fly on their own? Their helpless parents flew above them, and maybe dropped them a bit of food, but flying or succumbing belonged to them alone. Walter put his foot on the first step of the porch, and felt his customary sense of invigoration at this thought. On the porch, he stamped two or three times, and then slipped out of his boots. When the door opened, Rosanna drew him in, and then slipped her arms inside his unbuttoned jacket.

ON THE FRONT PORCH, sitting up (he had just learned to sit up) on a folded blanket, Frank Langdon, aged five months, was playing with a spoon. He was holding it in his right hand by the tarnished silver bowl, and when he brought it toward his face, his eyes would cross, which made Rosanna, his mother, laugh as she shelled peas. Now that he was sitting, he could also drop the spoon, and then, very carefully, pick it up again. Before learning to sit, he had enjoyed lying on his back and waving the spoon in the air, but if he dropped the spoon, it was gone. This was no longer the case. One of the qualities Rosanna attributed to little Frank was persistence. If he was playing with the spoon, then it was the spoon he wanted to play with. If he dropped the spoon, and she happened to give him a sock doll (the sock doll that her sister, Eloise, had sewn just for Frank), Frank would fuss until she gave him the spoon. Now, sitting up, he put the spoon down and picked it up and put it down and picked it up. Although he much preferred the spoon to the doll, Rosanna always told Eloise and her mother how much Frank liked the doll. Eloise was now knitting him a wool hat. It was her first knitting project; she expected to have it done before October. Rosanna reached into the basket of pea pods and took the last handful. She didn't mind shelling peas.

Frank was a good baby, hardly ever fussy, which, according to Rosanna's mother, was a characteristic of all her side of the family. Speaking of peas, Rosanna and her sister and four brothers were just like peas in a pod for being good babies, and here was Frank, another of the same breed, blond, beautiful, and easy, plenty of flesh but not a bit of fat, active but not fussy, went right down every night and only got up once, regular as sunrise, then down again for another two hours while Rosanna made breakfast for Walter and the hired man. Could she ask for a better baby?

Rosanna finished shelling peas and set the bowl on the blanket, then knelt in front of Frank and said, "What a boy! What a darling boy! Are you a darling boy?" And she kissed him on the forehead, because her mother had impressed on her that you never, never kissed a baby on the lips. She laid her hand gently on the top of his head.

Frank still had his grip on the spoon, but his mother's face transfixed him. As it loomed closer and then retreated, his gaze followed it, and as she smiled, he smiled, and then laughed, and then he waved his arms, which resulted in the spoon's being thrown across the blanket—a first! He saw it fly and he saw it land, and his head turned slightly so he could watch it.

Rosanna laughed, because on his face was a bona-fide look of surprise, very advanced, as far as Rosanna was concerned (though she would have to admit that she had never paid one iota of attention to her brothers and sister, except when they were in her way or in her charge—no one ever said that she enjoyed watching them or had a flair for it). Now Frank's body tilted forward, and all of a sudden he fell over on his side, cushioned by the blanket. Being Frank, he didn't cry. Rosanna sat him up again and handed him the spoon; then she stood up, thinking that she could hurry into the house and set the bread loaves, which should have completed their second rising by now, into the hot oven and be back out in a minute or two. Nothing could happen in a minute or two.

Spoon in hand, Frank saw and heard his mother's dress swish around her legs as she went inside, and then the screen door slapped shut. After a moment, Frank returned his attention to the spoon, which he was now gripping by the handle, bowl upward. He smacked it on the blanket, and though it was bright against the darkness of the blanket, it made no noise, so he brought it again to his face. It got bigger and brighter and bigger and brighter—this was the confusing part—and then he felt something, not in his hand, but on his face, a pressure and then a pain. The spoon jumped away from him, and there was noise—his own noise. His arm waved, and the spoon flew again. Now the spoon was small and didn't look like a spoon. Frank looked at it for a very long time, and then he looked around the blanket for something that was within reach. The only thing was a nice clean potato, into which Mama had cut two eyes, a nose, and a mouth. Frank was not terribly interested in the potato, but it was nearby, so his hand fell upon it, gripped it, and brought it to his mouth. He tasted the potato. It tasted different from the spoon.

More interesting was the sudden appearance of the cat, orange, long, and just his, Frank's, size. Frank let the potato drop as he looked at the cat, and then the cat was sniffing his mouth and smoothing its whiskers across Frank's cheek, squatting to inspect the potato, pressing himself into Frank until Frank fell over again. Moments later, when the door opened and flapped closed, the cat was crouched on the porch railing, purring, and Frank was lying on his back, staring at the ceiling of the porch and kicking his legs—left, right, left, right. Mama picked him up, then arced him through the air, and he found himself pressed into her shoulder, his ear and the side of his head warm against her neck. He saw the cat one last time as the porch spun around him, and beyond that the green-gold grass, and the pale horizontal line of the dirt road, and the two fields, one for oats, a thick undulating surface, and one for corn, a quiet grid of still squares ("There's a little breeze," thought Rosanna; "I'll open the upstairs windows"), and around that, a different thing, empty, flat, and large, the thing that lay over all things.

FRANK UNDERSTOOD the kitchen better now. He had a chair with a table of its own where he sat several times every day, and this seat was perfect for surveying this room where he was never allowed to crawl about. He had just learned to crawl. Almost always, two men entered the room while he was sitting there, Papa and Ragnar. Papa spoke to Mama, and Mama spoke back, and there were certain things they said that Frank felt he understood. Ragnar, however, babbled unintelligibly, and Frank could not understand him even when Mama or Papa was nodding. Nodding was good and was usually accompanied by smiling. Another thing Frank did not understand was that when he himself moved or made noise, there was pain where the noise should be. Pain and noise, both. Now Mama held out her hand. Frank held out his hand in just the same way, and Mama put something hard into it, which, since he was hungry, he brought to his mouth and bit into. When he did so, the pain and noise faded a little. Mama said, "Oh, poor boy. The top ones are always worse than the bottom ones." She slipped her finger under his upper lip and lifted it slightly. She said,

"I think the left one was grown out, but you can hardly see the right one."

Papa said, "Late teethers always fuss more, Mama told me. Les and I got ours at four months."

Ragnar said, *"Ja, ja, ja. Slik liten tenner!"*

Ragnar and Papa lifted their forks and began to eat. Frank had already tasted what they were eating, though from a spoon—mush, some chicken, green beans. Mama set her own plate on the table next to Frank's seat and sat down. She used her fork to place a green bean on Frank's tray. When he carefully put the tip of his finger on the slippery bean, Papa, Mama, and Ragnar laughed, though the bean didn't strike him as funny.

But it was no use. The pain enveloped him again, head to toe, and then the noise.

Ragnar said, *"Han nødvendig noe Akevitt."*

Papa said, "Don't have any of that poison, Ragnar."

The noise increased.

Hands banged on the tray of Frank's seat, and the bean and the crust of bread flew away.

Mama said, "We have to do something. My mother says—" But she looked at Papa and closed her mouth.

"What?" said Papa.

"Well, Ragnar is right. A clean rag knotted and dipped in whiskey. He chews on it and it eases the pain."

The noise grew not louder, but more shrill, and came in little gusts. Frank kicked his feet.

Papa cocked his head and said, "Try it, then."

Mama set down her fork and got up from the table. She went out of the room. Frank's gaze followed her.

For every time Frank looked at Papa, he looked at Mama five times or ten times, even when Papa and Mama were both in the room. It seemed perfectly natural to him. Papa was tall and loud. His mouth was large and his teeth were big. His hair stuck up and his nose stuck out. When Papa's hands went around him, he felt trapped rather than cuddled. When Papa lifted him and put his face down to meet his, there was a distinct sharpness that made his nose twitch. When Papa touched him, he could feel the roughness of his fingertips and palms against the bare baby skin. Papa shrank him. And when

Papa was close, Frank had discovered, there was more likely to be noise. Frank had nothing to do with it. It just happened. Now, in the long moment when Mama was gone, Frank looked away from Papa toward the window.

"All right," said Mama, "I found it in the sideboard. But you've got to put some sugar in the knot or he won't be able to stand the bitter taste." She reached for a cup on one of the shelves, and poured something into it. After that, she lifted the tray of Frank's chair, all the while anchoring him with her hand, and then she took him in her arms and set him gently on her jiggling knee. The noise subsided considerably. But even so, she did put a thing in his mouth, first burning and then moist and sweet, and anyway something to suck upon. Papa said, "Ragnar, the English for that is 'sugar tit.'"

"Oh, Walter," exclaimed Mama. "For goodness' sake."

Ragnar said, *"Sukker smokk."*

Mama said, "I am sure you are telling Ragnar all the best dirty English words while you are cleaning the hog pens."

Frank felt his mouth working, pulling the sweetness through the bitterness. Normally while sucking, he would be looking at Mama, the curve of her jaw and the fall of her blond hair half covering her ear, but now he stared at the ceiling. It was flat, and as he sucked, it seemed to lower itself onto him. The last thing he heard was "Did he fall asleep?"

The jiggling continued.

NOW THAT HE was crawling, Frank found that many doors were closed to him. Most of the time, in fact, he was confined to a space in the dining room that was nowhere near the woodstove in the front room, or the range in the kitchen. Many things were denied him that he once enjoyed, including the quotidian miracle of the flung spoon—he could have a spoon only when he was secure in his high chair in the kitchen (and he now had a strap to tie him in, since he felt no scruples about arching his back and sliding downward beneath the tray in his attempt to find the floor and take off). Things that he picked up, no matter how small, were removed from his grasp before he could give them the most cursory inspection, not to mention get them to his mouth. It seemed that he could never get anything to his mouth that he actually wanted to get there. Whatever he grabbed was immediately removed and a cracker was substituted, but he had explored all the features of crackers, and there was nothing more about them that he cared to find out.

The only thing he had left was standing beside one of the cane-seated chairs in his confinement pen and banging on it with his hands, sometimes one, sometimes the other, sometimes alternately, sometimes together. The cane in the middle and the wood around it presented an interesting contrast. His fist smacked the wood and it hurt just a little, though not enough to matter. His fist smacked the cane and then bounced. He also laughed when he pushed the chair over, but that could backfire if he then fell down—his balance was improving, but he wasn't walking yet. These were seductive feelings, but no substitute for everything else in the house—the staircase, the windows, the basket of firewood, the books that could be opened and closed and torn, the rocking chair that could be tipped over, the cat that could be chased (though not caught), the fringe of the rug that could be chewed. He couldn't even go out onto the porch anymore—when that door flew open, a cold blast shot through it that made him gasp.

Mama and Papa came and went. When he made noise (he now knew where the noise came from and how to make it whenever he wanted to—you opened your mouth and pressed the noise out and there were a variety of noises that produced a variety of effects upon Mama and Papa), she appeared from beyond one of the doors—the kitchen door—and she had a cloth in her hands. She said, "Frankie hungry? Poor boy. Two more minutes, baby." The door closed and she was gone. He pounded his fist on the cane-bottomed chair. The noise he made was "ma ma ma ma ma." The kitchen door flew open. Rosanna said, "What did you say, Frankie?" She stepped into his enclosure and came down to him. She said, "Say it again, baby. Say 'mama.'"

But he said something else, who knew what. It was just noise for now. When she stood up, he did another thing, which was to look up at her and raise both of his arms toward her. It had the desired effect: She said, "You are the most beautiful baby!" And she picked him up, sat down on the cane-seated chair, then opened her dry, hard front to reveal the desired warm, soft object beneath. Frank settled himself into her lap.

It was not the same as it had been, though. There had been a time when her lap was enough, the crook of her arm was enough, the breast itself and the lovely nipple were enough to envelop him in pleasure. Now he was half distracted even while enjoying himself. His gaze rolled around the room, taking in the top corners of the doors, the moldings, the pale light floating up from the windows, the design of the wallpaper, Mama's face, and then around again, looking for something new. Mama absently stroked the top of his head. Her body relaxed and she slumped against the back of the chair. In the quiet of the room (quiet because Frank himself was making no noise), other sounds manifested themselves—the howl of the wind curling around the corners of the house, the clattering of ice against the house (muffled) and the windows (sharp). Sometimes the wind was so strong that the house itself creaked. Just then there was a loud cracking noise followed by a longer, higher sound. Mama sat up. She lifted Frank more toward her chin, said, "What was that?" and stood. They went to a window.

There was nothing more surprising than a window, and you could not get to them on your own. You might have looked out a window many times, and even though the window was right where it was the last time you looked through it, each time there was something different. Sometimes, there was nothing, only flat blackness, but this time there was only flat whiteness. And its smoothness was terrible—when Frank reached out and laid his hand on it, Mama cupped his hand in hers and brought it back to her chest. She said, "Oh, a big branch off the hickory tree. Right into the yard, too. It must be ten below out there, baby boy, or worse. That's cold for this time of year. I hate to think what it'll be like when winter actually gets here." Her shoulders shook. She said, "And more sleet! I hope your papa and Ragnar got all the cows in, I hope they did!" She kissed him again, this time on the forehead. "Goodness me, what a life—and don't tell him I said so!"

They sat down again, this time on the other side of the confinement barrier, in the big chair, and Mama put him to the other breast, the one he preferred, the one with more milk. And then, the next

time he knew where he was, he was in his cot on his back with a
blanket up to his chin, and then he didn't know where he was again.

AFTER THE UNION SUIT, Mama smoothed the socks she had knitted over his feet, sat him up, and lowered the shirt over his head,
carefully avoiding his nose and ears. She buttoned the shirt. Then
she straightened his knees and pushed his feet through the legs of his
pants. The toes of his right foot were bent upward, and he gave a
squawk. She pulled down the pant leg and pointed his toes. Soon she
was buttoning the trousers to the shirt.

Frank felt strangely passive through all this. Once the pants were
on, he went even more limp, so that she could barely slide him into
his heavy, stiff snowsuit, first the legs again, and the suspenders, then,
when she sat him up and he slumped forward. Papa said, "It's going
to take us an hour to get there, and it's nearly five." Frank felt Mama's
grip tighten around his shoulders. It was impossible to get his arms
down the sleeves of the snowsuit, and when she did, they could no
longer bend. She put on his mittens, then situated his cap around his
head and tied the itchy straps beneath his chin. She slipped on his
shoes and tied them. He began to whimper.

But they paid no attention to him. She folded the big flaps of the
blanket he was lying on over his face and said, "Jake is hitched up and
ready, right?"

"He's got his own blanket over his haunches, and the buggy is full
of blankets."

"What's Ragnar going to do for the evening?"

"Stay right here. He's got tomorrow off."

She put him, blinded by the blanket, into Papa's arms and, probably, left the room. A moment later, that blast hit him, and he knew
they were out the front door and onto the porch. He didn't dare move,
and he couldn't move, anyway. Papa paused, then went down, then
paused, then went down, then paused, then went down.

"Oh," said Mama behind him. "Slippery."

"Ran out of salt."

"Be careful, then."

"You be careful. You've got the pie."

"I'm being careful. But there will be plenty of pie."

"Hope so."

"And Frankie's birthday cake. My mother is making her angel food."

"Mmm," said Papa. Now he set Frank in the crook of his arm and gripped him tight around the ankle, and said, "Evening, Ragnar. I'll put Jake away when we get back." Then the door to the buggy opened, and Frank was out of the wind and in Mama's lap again, but he still could not move his arms or his head. He could kick his legs a little. The constriction was strange, or maybe perplexing, in that it didn't require him to make noise of any kind. He lay there and they went on, up and down and forward—he'd done this before and liked it—and he watched things pass on the other side of the pane, everything dark against dark, until he fell asleep.

Now he was propped against Mama's shoulder, looking at Papa as Mama stepped upward. He was still immobilized inside his suit, and hot now, his arms stuck out straight to either side and his head not nestled into her neck, the way he liked it, but sticking up. Papa looked down and said, "Steep steps. Could you hold the rail?" And Mama said, "I'm okay now—the porch is clear." Papa's face was bright, and then they went through, into a bright, loud place, and he was pulled away from Mama, who said, "What a night!"

There was a person here who always said to him, "Here's my darling! Give Granny a smile! That's my boy. Smiles like my father, even without many teeth," and someone else said, "Your father didn't have many more teeth than this baby, Mary!" And then there was laughing, and he was kissed on the cheek, and Granny sat him on her lap and unwrapped him piece by piece.

Now he was sitting up on Granny's knee—she had her hands around him, and he was bending and bouncing and shouting, because all of the light and the smiles were so exciting that he could hardly contain himself.

"One year old!" said Granny. "Hard to believe."

"Just this time a year ago," said Papa, "I looked at Dr. Gerritt and realized that he was drunk!"

"Oh, Walter," said Mama.

"Well, he was. But, you know, he was like a horse that's used to plowing the same field year after year, just did what he knew to do, and everything was fine."

"That was a piece of luck, Walter," said Granny. "But what would we do without some luck after all?"

One of the faces, one he'd never seen before, said, "My goodness, Mary, that is the most beautiful baby. Look at those big blue eyes! And already such hair. You don't see that with blonds very often. My niece Lydia's child is three, and her hair is still as fine as down."

Granny leaned forward to kiss, but she didn't say anything. He walked toward some legs in overalls, and the legs stepped backward. He followed them. Some skirts swished around, too. When he sat down with a thump, hands grabbed him under his arms and stood him up. He headed toward a low table.

Mama had now taken off her coat and carried her pie to the kitchen. She sat down on the sofa, just where he could see her, and said, "Really, he's a New Year's baby, not a New Year's Eve baby. He wasn't born until three a.m." He sidestepped around the table, understanding perfectly well that he was making his way toward her—Frank had no problem with mapping. "Dr. Gerritt told me he came out and then went back in again. Must have been too cold for him. My boy!" She touched his cheek with the back of her finger.

A voice said, "You ask me, any winter baby is a miracle. My sister—" but Mama picked him up as he came toward her and smothered him with hugs and kisses. Another voice said, "Spring fever makes winter babies," and Granny said, "Is that so? No one ever told me that." Everyone laughed again.

It was a wonderful party. Faces leaned toward him and then retreated. Maybe he had never seen so many smiles. Smiles were good. In a rudimentary way, he grasped the concept of universal love. He was the only baby here. He was the only baby he had ever seen.

Now the couch was full of gravelly-voiced stiff ones, like Papa. One of them said, "Karl Lutz lost two cows down that ravine he has there. Break in the fence, and two of them shorthorn heifers went through before anyone realized. Fell over the edge, I guess."

Papa made a noise; then one of the others made a noise. There was head shaking, not nodding. Frank turned around. He had to balance himself with his hand on that little table, but he did it. The women were softer and looked at him more. Right then, Frank generalized from what had been mere habit, and decided that looking at women was just more agreeable in every way than looking at men. He lifted his hand off the table and precipitated himself in the direction of the women. One of them had to catch him a few seconds later, as his body outran his feet, which were slowed by his awkward shoes. He fell into her arms. He had never seen her before.

Granny called, "Supper!" and all the skirts and legs straightened up and moved. Mama bent down and picked him up, seating him in the crook of her arm. He was glad to see her. He put his arm around her neck.

There was no high chair at Granny's, so he sat on Papa's lap, sort of pinned between Mama and Papa. His chin rose just above the edge of the table, and he enjoyed looking around at the bright-colored and flashing dishes—he knew they were dishes of some sort, because there was food on them, and whenever he threw his plate off the tray of his high chair, Mama said, "Frankie, no! Don't throw your dish. That was very naughty." However, sitting in Papa's lap, he could not get his hands on a dish to save his life—Papa's long arm was pinned around him, holding him away from the table. Mama put a green bean in his hand. He held it while she then put a spoon full of something to his lips. He hesitated, but then let it in. It was mush. He was hungry enough to take it.

"Try the pork on him," said Granny. "I cooked it all day. He might like it."

Mama used the thing that was not her spoon or her fork, the thing he could never have, and pressed her plate over and over with it. Then she brought it to him on her spoon. It smelled so good that he opened his mouth, and in it went. "Down the hatch," said Papa, and Frank opened his mouth for more.

"What's in that?" said Papa.

"Just the usual. Some onions and a little fennel seed. Not much of that. Cooked forever."

Mama said, "He likes most things, I have to say. He took a bit of liver the other day. Made a face, but swallowed it."

"Never had a picky eater in our family," said Granny. "You yourself ate asparagus when you were eight months old. Never saw a child just take a stalk of asparagus and gobble it down like that. Slaw. Boiled cabbage. Everything."

"It's the German in 'em," said a deep voice. "*Ja*, it is. I myself liked sauerkraut better than anything when I was a boy. The others were bellying up to the apple pie, and I would ask my mama for another spoonful of sauerkraut."

"Ah, well," said Granny, "what else was there to eat in those days? Got old pretty quick, you ask me."

All this time, Mama was giving him bits of things on the tip of her spoon, many different things, and he was a good boy. He recognized the applesauce and the sweet potato and the crust of bread. He took more of the pork and another green bean. The air was full of conversation, and many words he was already familiar with, though he had no idea what they meant—oats, corn, hogs, steers, barley, harvest, sale barn, threshing, crib, snow, freeze—as well as words that he did understand—sleet, cold, sunshine, spoon, aunt, uncle, no, good, bad, Frank, more, eat, thank you. His eyes roamed from face to face, and then Granny said a word, "Cake," and it went around the room—"Look at that cake!" "Lovely cake, Mary!" "My favorite cake."

All the dishes were cleared from the table, and Papa set him right in the middle, but holding him all the time, and the faces made a noise together—not a bad noise, "Happy Birthday to You!"—and then Mama took him back on her lap, and handed him something soft, and he tasted it, and then he ate it, but only because he was a good eater, and a good boy, and ready for anything. Then Mama took him away into a dark room, and nursed him, and, for goodness' sake, they both fell asleep on the bed, her arm over him and his mouth around her nipple, because, although he wasn't really hungry, his chances to partake of this pleasure had gotten fewer and fewer.

1921

First, Rosanna had arranged it so that her sister, Eloise, would live with them, and it was all going to work out for the best, since they had a better school for her nearby. When she wasn't in school, she could help with Frank, who was getting around the house at about a mile a minute. Then she made a plan with Mrs. Frederick down the road to hatch some chickens in the old henhouse—she cleaned it out before telling Walter a thing about it—thirty to start. Rosanna had grown up raising chickens, and she missed them, and Eloise was used to chickens, and she and Walter both knew without saying a word that if all he did was break even for the year, then there had to be egg money. Walter, she knew, wasn't fond of chickens—their mess got everywhere if you weren't careful, and they could be underfoot—nor did he especially care for eggs, since he had eaten fried eggs every morning for his whole life because that's what his father liked and his mother made. Well, chickens. Then there could be ducks and turkeys. And Eloise would sleep in with Frank, since Ragnar had the third bedroom. But Eloise was happy to come—one baby to take care of was preferable to three brothers. And none of them talkers—Eloise said days could go by without Gus, Kurt, or John saying a word. This was not true of Eloise, as Rosanna reflected when Eloise asked again—was it for the twentieth time?—"So little Frankie didn't get baptized?"

Rosanna was ironing and Eloise was folding. Frankie was down for his afternoon nap. Rosanna said, "Did you go to a baptism, Eloise? No, you didn't. If we had had a baptism, then you would have gone, and there would have been a breakfast after, and there wasn't. Why do you keep asking me?"

"I don't know."

Rosanna took the shirt she was ironing off the ironing board, turned it over, and pressed the tip of the iron along the seam of the collar. It was not quite hot enough, so she took it over to the stove, set it down, and picked up the other one. Eloise said, "Do you think we'll ever get electricity?"

Rosanna didn't say anything. She wasn't particularly in favor of electricity, those wires running who knew where. She said, "Is Mama sending you little notes telling you to keep asking me about that baptism?"

Eloise stared at her, then said, "No."

Then she said, "Not really."

Then she said, "But I know she's worried. Cousin Josie's boy got up one morning and was dead of cholera by the time he went to bed that night."

"No, he—"

"And that boy who was in our school, he was just in first grade, the horses spooked and the wagon wheel went right over him."

"And Walter's brother died when he was two and Walter never got over it, even though he wasn't born yet." She handed the shirt to Eloise, who began doing up the buttons, and took another one out of the ironing basket. Rosanna liked ironing shirts—it was soothing—but she also didn't mind pants and overalls and sheets and pillowcases. If doing laundry was a chore, ironing was its reward.

"I don't think you should laugh about it."

Rosanna spread a sleeve across the ironing board. "Well, I'm not, but they talk more about Lester than they do about Howard, who died in the influenza."

"He was a baby."

"He was older than Frankie."

"So there," said Eloise.

Rosanna bit her lip, and didn't say any more. Either she had talked herself into a corner, or Eloise had won the argument, she couldn't quite tell which, but that was the way it was with Eloise. Even the teacher at school had said to Rosanna, "I had to tell her that she could only raise twenty objections in the morning and twenty in the afternoon. They tend to bring a halt to the educational process."

Rosanna began ironing the back of the shirt, and Eloise went into the kitchen to check on the bread. Of course that was why Rosanna was so careful with Frankie—more careful than Walter liked, and in some sense more careful than Walter knew. If you were a Catholic and you were baptized and you were a child who hadn't had First Communion, then you were not damned to Hell if you died, you went to Limbo, and then, as far as Rosanna was concerned, because she couldn't imagine any truly bad thing happening to one of God's children, you moved on to Heaven and you were fine forever after. Methodists also believed in original sin and infant baptism, but there was a catch, and Rosanna had memorized it—there could be a parent or godparent, but it could not be her unbaptized self, and she could not therefore bring herself to allow the baptism. And so, without even discussing the matter, she and Walter were at an impasse with regard to Frankie.

Why had this not come up at the wedding (a Methodist wedding)? Well, the answer was that Rosanna was headstrong, and had never cared much for religion, and had wanted to marry Walter and get out of the crowd that was her own family. She had assumed nothing else was important. It was only after marriage that you began to think about sin, and if one side of the family (all around, and full of opinions) believed one thing, and the other side (also in and out of the house) believed another, you had to pretend that all beliefs were equally silly and then live with the consequences.

She handed the second shirt to Eloise, who said, "Why did you make six loaves?"

"I said I would make three for Mama, because she's sitting with Aunt Rose this week and doesn't have time to make her own."

"Is Aunt Rose going to get well?"

Rosanna looked at Eloise and put her hands on her hips, then said, "No," because if Eloise was going to ask so many questions then sometimes she had to get a straight answer, didn't she?

"Is she going to die?"

"If she's lucky, since she can hardly breathe and hasn't left her bed for a year."

"Even to go to the bathroom?"

"Eloise, I don't know."

"Why not?"

"Goodness, Eloise, you sound about eight, and you're fifteen."

"Oh."

"Aunt Rose is sixty-eight. She's had a hard life, and her husband left her to go play baseball or something, down in Des Moines, and she never got over it, and that's all I know. I'm sure Mama will have plenty to add the next time we see her."

"Can I take Frankie out? It's not that cold. We can walk down the road and look for wildflowers."

Rosanna picked up the stack of folded clothes and set them in the laundry basket. They smelled starchy and fresh. She said, "That's fine. I saw some bluebells when I was out there yesterday."

She turned toward the stairs. Now she could hear him calling her by name—"Mama! Mama!" The very sound of his voice made her want to set down the laundry basket and run to him, but she maintained her dignity because Eloise was right behind her.

ELOISE WAS THERE at Thanksgiving, and she was looking at Frankie the very moment when he astounded the entire family by shouting, "One two three four five six sedno eight none tin!" Her mother ran in from the kitchen, Rosanna threw up her hands, and even Rolf, who was leaning over his plate in what Eloise considered her brother's usual thickheaded way, looked up and laughed. Opa said, "I'll be!" Frank became the family genius right there. Her mother remembered some aunt who could read at four, and also that Rosanna had said, "I'm very pleased to meet you, sir," to Father Berger when she was not yet two, without any coaching at all. But one to ten at not yet two—well, that was something.

Eloise was less impressed. Now that she had been looking after little Frank for almost nine months, she knew he was far from perfect. The thing he was smart at was not taking no for an answer, but, thought Eloise, no one knew that, because no one ever said no to him other than herself. Rosanna said, "I don't think so, darling," or "Maybe later, Frank, honey," and then Frank wheedled and nodded until Rosanna thought he was so cute that she gave him whatever he wanted, and then she told everyone what a happy and agreeable baby he was. When Eloise said no to him ("No, I will not give you my spritz cookie," for example), Frank opened his mouth and screamed. Then Rosanna came running up the stairs and said, "Why is he screaming?" and before Eloise had a chance to answer, she swept Frankie into her arms and said, "All right, baby. All right, Frankie, let's go downstairs and let Eloise finish her studying." Of course, Frankie didn't get the cookie, but he did get something better, Eloise thought, since Rosanna was still nursing him, just the way her mother and Aunt Helen had nursed every one of the children except Eloise ("She weaned herself at nine months. I never will understand that child") until the next one came along.

Frank didn't ask Walter for anything at all. He sometimes looked at Walter, and he laughed when Walter sat down on the floor and played with the jack-in-the-box and the drum. Or he rode on Walter's shoulders or hung upside down over Walter's arm and laughed, but Eloise could see that Frank was a little afraid of Walter, as who wouldn't be, loud as Walter was.

Every day, Frank attempted with Eloise what worked so well with Rosanna—talking. Just today, when Eloise picked Frank up from the puzzle he was looking at (and chewing on the pieces, not putting it together, where was the genius in that?) to put him in his bed for his nap, he had cried and reached for the puzzle, trying to get down. "Time for a nap," said Eloise. Rosanna was in the kitchen making her pumpkin pies, so there was no help for him.

"Puz!" barked Frank.

"After your nap," said Eloise.

"Puz! One puz!" said Frank, now not crying, but looking at her.

"No," said Eloise.

"One!" said Frank.

"No," said Eloise.

And here was where Frank arched his back and had a tantrum, because Rosanna was always so charmed by Frank saying "One puz!" or "Little later!" that she gave in, and let him have one more minute with the puzzle or ten more minutes before bed. It wasn't at all like living at home with her brothers, who at fourteen, ten, and seven were so used to "no" that, even as their mother was opening her mouth to respond to any request of any kind, Kurt, John, and Gus were making big silent "no"s with their mouths. And then, when Ma spoke, they all laughed and she wondered why.

Eloise's own view was that there was no reason to ask. Years of watching Rosanna, who couldn't help chattering on about all her plans, so that Ma had to have some opinion or other, and Rolf, who just did what Papa told him had to be done, showed Eloise that if you simply went about your business, no one interfered with you, especially in a house where there were six children, sometimes an aunt or a cousin living in, a hired man or two from the old country, and Oma and Opa in and out. You did your assigned tasks in a somewhat ostentatious manner and asked questions until they got fed up with you, then you went behind the corn crib and read your book or drew your picture. And then you put what you were doing under your mattress, and no one ever asked you about it. It was the same at school. If you raised your hand enough times in the front row, they sat you in the back, almost behind the woodstove, and you could finish your work (which was always easy) and go on reading the book you had brought in your schoolbag, entitled *Miss Lulu Bett* (a book that her friend Maggie had bought in a store down in Usherton). She and her friends had all sorts of publications that the adults knew nothing about, including another book called *Tom Swift and His Electric Rifle* and a very fat one called *Little Dorrit,* though none of the girls had been able to get through that one yet. They had copies of *Adventure* magazine; *The Delineator,* which had nice dress patterns that Eloise liked to look at; and four issues of *McCall's.* Each of the girls kept a diary—Maggie had gotten them notebooks, and they had sewn covers out of canvas. Eloise's was tan, with blue embroidery. What, she thought, was so special about a child who could say ten words in a row, just because they had been said to him over and over (as in "One two three four five six seven eight nine ten, ready or not, here I come!")? But now her own mother, the great naysayer, was kissing him all over, and everyone was laughing, and Opa said, "*Ja,* maybe he's smart enough not to buy himself a farm, what you think?"

Everyone laughed as if this were a joke. Eloise thought, "I'm smart enough for that." She glanced at Rolf, who was eating his goose as if he hadn't a thought in the world. Eloise thought, "But Rolf isn't." She picked up the spoon for the mashed potatoes, and served herself another small helping.

"HE ISN'T yet two," said Mama, holding him a little more tightly.

"Ah, he'll like it," said Papa. "Never saw a nicer horse than Jake. You've been on him. I've been on him. Here, Eloise, climb on the feed trough there, and show Rosanna."

It was dim in the big barn, but arrows and sparkles of light pierced the dark walls here and there. Frank knew what the beings were in their separate enclosures—"cows" going in and out over there, white "sheep" with black faces (one two three four five six), a "rooster" perched on a beam above them, and this greatest of beings, Jake the "horse," pale gray, almost white, who now turned his nose and eyes toward Frank and made noise. Frank laughed.

Eloise said, "I have a dress on."

"You're wearing your long johns, aren't you? He's clean. I brushed him before you came out."

They all walked with Jake across some of the dark earth to a place, and then Eloise climbed, and then Papa helped her, and soon she was sitting on the back of Jake, holding his hair, and then Papa put his hands around Frank and lifted him high in the air, and he kicked his legs, and then he was set upon Jake's back, just in front of Eloise, and Eloise put her arm tight around him.

"Oh, goodness," said Mama. "Well, that is cute, in spite of everything."

"I was riding my father's Percherons out to the pasture when I was three," said Walter. "Now, he did not let me ride Uncle Leon's Clydesdales, but the Percherons . . ."

Underneath Frank, the warm, rounded gray surface rippled and moved, and Eloise took both of his hands in hers and put them into the hair, and said, "Hold on, Frankie," and so he gripped that hair. He could feel her through his suit, hard against his back and shoulders. In front of him rose a monumental gray shape that ended in two points, and then the gray shape shifted and they were moving forward. Frank loved moving forward—didn't matter, wagon, buggy, cultivator. He threw his arms into the air, but Eloise was still holding him. Papa's head stayed right there in front of him as the horse moved, but when he turned to look at her, he saw that Mama was smaller, her hands on her hips. All the animals stared—the sheep and the cows and the other horse. The rooster flew down from his perch, lifting his wings and making a squawk. "Good boy," said Papa.

1922

AT THE SUPPER TABLE, Ragnar, Eloise, and Papa sat up straight, and Frank sat up straight, too. Ragnar, Eloise, and Papa never got up from the table during supper, and Frank stayed in his seat, too. Ragnar, Eloise, and Papa never wiggled in their chairs. Frank wiggled in his chair. Ragnar, Eloise, and Papa picked up their forks and knives and cut their sausage. Frank pressed the back of his spoon into his sweet potato, lifted it out, and pressed it in again. "Eat some, Frankie," said Eloise, and Frank inserted the tip of his spoon into the orange mound and lifted it. A bit adhered to the spoon, and Frank brought it to his mouth. "Good boy," said Papa.

"*Ja, jeg elske søt poteter, når det er alt det er,*" said Ragnar.

"Ragnar may not like the rabbit sausage," said Papa, "but I do. Always have. One thing, Eloise, that you should remember is that a farmer doesn't have to grow and sell everything he eats. There's a whole world out there."

"I like pheasant," said Eloise.

"Me, too," said Papa. "You go out into the cornfield after the harvest, and the pheasants are there pecking at the dropped kernels. When I was a boy, we got them with our slingshots, just for fun. And for supper."

Frank put his finger on the bit of sausage and then picked it up and put it in his mouth. It was bitter, not like the sweet potatoes. He made a face, but then he picked up another bit.

"He'll eat about anything," said Papa. "That's a good quality in a farmer. When I was in France, that was a place where they eat anything that moves or grows. I admired that."

"Did you eat a snail?" said Eloise.

"Lucky to eat a snail," said Papa. "Little fish with the heads on, fried up hard. Didn't like that so much. Their animals eat about anything, too. Pumpkins. Turnips. Beer. Saw a man give his horse a beer."

"Do they have beer in France?" said Eloise.

"Up north, where we were, they do," said Papa.

"How long were you there?" said Eloise.

"Less than a year; wished I'd stayed longer and seen some different parts."

Where was Mama? Frank's thoughts returned to this. He thought maybe she was upstairs. Although Frank could climb the stairs and come back down without falling, Papa had blocked them off. He hadn't seen Mama in a long time, though sometimes he heard her voice floating in the air.

Frank said, "Mama!"

"Can't go to Mama yet," said Papa. "But Granny'll be down in a bit."

"Mama," said Frank.

Eloise, who was sitting closest to him, pointed with her fork to his sausage. She said, "It's good for you. Make you big and strong."

Frank gripped the spoon more tightly in his hand, raised his arm, and brought the spoon down on the mound of sweet potatoes. The mound jumped.

"No," said Papa.

"No," said Frank.

"Eat your food," said Papa. "You're old enough to eat what's on there."

Ragnar and Eloise looked at each other. Ragnar cleared his throat. *"Jeg skjønner en tantrum komme."*

"Nonsense," barked Papa. "Frankie, you be a big boy now, and eat your supper."

Eloise looked up the stairs, and then back at Frank. She said, "Frankie, no . . ."

He knew what "no" meant—it was an irritating word, "no." He placed his palms on the edge of the table, both of them, and he took a deep, deep breath, preliminary to a loud, loud noise. He could feel the noise rising from his chair, even from his feet, since his feet were kicking, and as the noise came out, he pushed as hard as he could against the edge of the table, and there he went—the chair arced backward, and he saw the ceiling and the corner of the dining room, and then the back of the chair hit, and Frank rolled out to the side, away from Eloise, and ran for the stairs. Papa's big hand caught him by the collar of his overalls and then grabbed his shoulder, and spun him around. He didn't know where he was, the room was going so fast, though he kept his eye on the stairs the best he could, and there was Granny Mary at the top, or just her feet, he couldn't see the rest, and then there was the floor, and he was sprawled across Papa's knee with his pants down, and every blow included a word: "Don't. Run. Away. From. Me. Young. Man."

Now Papa stood him on his feet and leaned close to his face, and there was that sharp smell again, and the heat and the redness, and the loudness, and Frank closed his eyes and screamed until Papa's hand knocked him down and he was quiet. Everyone was quiet. Frank lay on his back, and he could just see Eloise with her mouth open at the table, and Ragnar next to her. Granny's footsteps came closer and closer, and she sat him up. She said, "I don't know what gets into two-year-olds. It's like your own child has been taken away and this other being left in his place."

Papa said, "Put him back in his chair. He's got some food to eat."

Granny stood up and then picked Frank up and carried him to his chair, which Eloise had set back in place. Frank sat quietly. They were back where they started, everyone straight and tall, no wiggling. Frank was hungry. It had never been about not being hungry. Granny Mary put his spoon in his hand. Frank used it the best he could, but he ate the sausage with his fingers. Papa didn't seem to mind that.

After Frank had eaten three bites, Papa said, "How's Rosanna?"

"Tired," said Granny. "So tired. I wish this child would come. I do."

The room ceased shaking, and Frank took some breaths.

Papa said, "He screams, but he doesn't cry or whine. I'll say that for him."

WALTER THOUGHT he probably grew too much oats, but if you were a Langdon and your mother was a Chick, then it was natural to plant oats, eat oats, feed oats, bed oat straw, and, most of all, enjoy all the stages of oat cultivation. He had talked his brother-in-law Rolf—who had taken over Opa and Oma's farm, though the old folks were still living in the house—into planting forty acres this year, too. Rolf was twenty, but he had as much gumption as a ten-year-old, Walter thought. Rosanna had gumption for both of them.

Walter especially liked binding and shocking the oats—the weather was hot, and grit of all kinds got into your hair and your clothes and your boots and your eyes and your nose, but a field of shocked oats was an accomplishment, and foretold a barn-load of straw and grain that would get everyone, animals and people, through the winter. Oat straw was a beautiful color—paler than gold but more useful.

And Walter also liked the sociability of August—men and boys from all over the county came to his farm, and he went to their farms, and there was plenty to eat and to talk about. It didn't hurt that Jake and Elsa were an admirable team of horses to be pulling the binder—patient, strong, good-looking, stylish grays. Didn't matter who was driving them—a boy could drive them and they would do their job. No running away, like Theo Whitehead's team of Shires did that year, breaking up the binder on the fence line, and slowing the threshing by four days while everything was put back together.

When they came in for dinner, Rosanna had it all organized out back, under the hickory trees. Tables with cloths lined up in the shade, and the bread and the beans and the caramelized carrots and the sweet corn and the watermelon and the slaw all set out, so that they sat themselves down at their places, and out she came with the roasts, two of them, enough for everyone to have plenty, with her own butter in the middle that she made and salted and sold to the store in town—the best butter in the county, everyone said.

In addition to their own two families, there were the Whiteheads and the Lewises and the Smiths, whom Walter and Rosanna only saw at threshing and harvest, everyone in family groups, the men to help with the threshing, the women to help with the cooking, and the youngsters to play—Rosanna set the youngsters up in the side yard, with two different kinds of swings, a tire swing and a bench swing—and the girls were put in the charge of Eloise, who had them turning the crank on the ice-cream churn. Even though Walter didn't grow any peaches, and didn't know anyone who did, Rosanna got some in town—a peck of them—and the ripest went into the ice cream. Of all the families who did their threshing together and therefore their eating together, Walter's family was the only one who made ice cream. The day at Walter's was a long one, because he grew so much oats.

But look at Frank, an advertisement for oats if ever there was one. He was inches taller than the Lewis boy, who was a month older, and he could outrun that Lewis boy, too. What was his name? Oh, Oren. The big boy, almost four, was David. David Lewis was stand-ing facing Frank as Walter passed them, shouting, and Frank was smacking the ground with a branch he'd found. Oren was standing there, looking back and forth between the two of them, and this is what Walter heard—he heard David shout, "Okay, Frank, you stand there, and you tell me what to do." This was enough to make Walter chuckle, and then Frank called out, "David, run to me, push me!" Frank dropped the branch and spread his arms.

When David ran at him, Frank turned his shoulder to the older boy and knocked him down. Then the boys rolled over in the grass. Rough play, and Walter knew Rosanna and Emily Lewis would stop it, but since Frank had dropped the branch, it was hand-to-hand combat—all boys, Walter thought, needed plenty of that, espe-cially Oren, who stood there with his thumb in his mouth. It was his private opinion that he and Howard hadn't been allowed enough shenanigans—when they weren't put to tasks, they were to sit still, do as they were told, speak when spoken to. As a result, he sometimes thought he had never known Howard at all. Walter sped up his step. He was hungry, and he didn't want to hear anything from Rosanna about letting those boys get away with murder.

As soon as Walter washed his hands at the pump, that was the sig-nal for all the men to clean up as best they could and find themselves places at the table.

The first thing all of them did was down several glasses of water, and then the chorus went around: "Hot one! How hot do you think it is? Over a hundred yet? Not so damp, though. Humidity was worse the other day, over at Bill Whitehead's. Down by the river there, always damp." Head shaking. "Got a good crop, though, say that for him." Then, "Try this, Rolf. Rosanna knows her slaw. Nice piece of meat, Walter. Lean, but tasty, I'll say. How many you gonna slaughter this year? I got jars of brisket and sausage bursting out of the cellar, don't know why, just can't eat enough of it, I guess. Didn't have to kill a chicken until May this year. Nice melons, too. Soil around our place isn't sandy enough for good melons. How's your potatoes looking this year? I didn't even plant them in one spot, just covered 'em with manure and straw. Every so often, I grab a plant and lift it up, and look at the potatoes." And then, when they were full, "You can go ahead and grow all the corn you want, Otto, but you ain't gonna make a profit from it unless you feed it to your pigs. More pigs, more profit. Walking dollars is what I call hogs. We got some Durocs this year, from Martha's cousin. I like the Hampshires for the hams, but Durocs are longer in the bacon, her cousin says." Then there was a long conversation about hog breeds. Walter's own hogs were Berkshires, and they liked oats. But what didn't they like? Walter felt happy. There was talk about cars—Bill Whitehead's cousin over in Cedar Rapids had bought his second Model T for $260, but he'd had to pay another forty for an electric ignition. "Least you can get that now," said Ralph Smith. "Cranking that thing before the war, my uncle had his hand broke." Walter cleared his throat but didn't say anything. How a person could have a farm with a mortgage and a car, too, was a problem he hadn't solved, and so he allowed his father's preference for horses to prevail.

Here came Rosanna with Joe, the baby. Joe was five months old now, and big and healthy. You wouldn't know from looking at him that it had been touch and go there for a bit—though how touch and go, maybe Walter himself didn't know. Small baby, even though he was late, according to Rosanna's and her mother's calculations. And Rosanna's mother thought he looked late: "Like a little old man," she said, "worn out and wrinkled." And then the milk didn't come in the first day, or the second, and there was no denying that she was worried. As for Dr. Gerritt, he was so little help that Mary just sent him away. Walter himself thought that it was the oatmeal that did the trick—Rosanna could keep it down, first with water, then with milk, then with cream, and then with butter. She got better every day, and after that little Joe got better, and look at him now. Walter's mother said what she always did, that he was the spit of Walter himself, plenty of dark hair and fat cheeks. Walter watched Rosanna as she carried him around each table, saying, "Joey, Joey, look at all of our friends come to see you!" Joey had one hand on her cheek, and she held the other hand in hers. Rosanna said that he wasn't as far along as Frankie had been at this age, but Walter himself couldn't remember. A spring baby got out more, was all he knew, so he had more of a sense of Joey than he had had of Frank. Joey was still getting up in the night, but Rosanna didn't mind. She was a little protective of him.

The funny thing was that Frank didn't pay any attention to Rosanna anymore—it was like he couldn't hear her voice. His head only turned when Eloise spoke to him, or Rolf (that was a rarity), or Walter himself. Mary said this was normal, and so did Walter's mother, but Rosanna was taking it a little hard. Her mother said, "Someday you'll have had so many that you won't remember the differences between one and the other."

And Eloise said, "You always remember that I was the worst."

And Mary, not to be outdone, said, "Some things do stick in your mind, miss!"

But there was no denying that what they would do without Eloise Walter couldn't imagine. Now she was doing some of the cooking and all of the bed making and dusting. She pumped all the water and carried it in, and all winter she had kept the fires going because Rosanna was so sick. She didn't mind feeding the hogs and the sheep if Walter was busy. She was big, too—well developed as well as strong. As far as Walter was concerned, she had earned the right to have her lamp on whenever she felt like it—kerosene was little enough to pay if she wanted to read late or do her knitting. She had no talent for sewing, so Rosanna had made her two nice dresses and a coat. Three years and she would be married, no doubt, to one of these boys who were now wolfing down his sweet corn, and what would they do then?

Rosanna said that Walter was a worrier, but there was plenty to worry about with prices so low. You may say that hogs paid the bills, or chickens and eggs and cream. There was a fellow down by Ames who bred draft horses and sent them back to Europe by ship, since so many horses had been killed in the war that they'd lost even their breeding stock, but the thing that made Walter nervous (and maybe this was a result of his own experiences in the war) was the length of the supply line. Let's say that, every hundred miles, some other person got a right to take a nip of the cherry. Let's say that. Then, if you were sending your corn and oats and hogs and beef to Sioux City, well, that was two hundred miles, and Kansas City was 250. Chicago was about 325 or so, and beyond that Walter wasn't willing to go. You could just say that the quarters got thinner or the dollars got paler the farther they came—that was how Walter thought about it. So sending draft horses to France and Germany? That was a strange business, like wheat to Australia. Walter didn't trust it. The wealth was right here, spreading away from this table—chickens in the chicken house, corn in the field, cows in the barn, pigs in the sty, Rosanna in the kitchen with Joe and Frank, Eloise safe in her room thinking her thoughts. Walter looked around. His work crew was revived now, and making jokes—did you hear about the farmer who won the lottery? As if there were lotteries anymore. When they asked him what he was going to do with his million dollars, reported Theo Whitehead, he said, "Well, I guess I'll just farm till it's gone."

Too much oats. Too much oats. Walter wondered why he worried about such abundance.

1923

Rosanna liked the buggy. On a brisk late-winter day when the sky was flat and hard above the frozen fields and the sun was bright but distant, and before all the horses' time was consumed by plowing and planting, it was good to have business in town—errands to do and people to see. Jake trotted along, happy, maybe, that the buggy was so light and there was no soil to drag it through, and Rosanna hardly had to shake the reins at him. In town, he would go to the feed store/livery stable and eat his noon oats after she dropped her basket of eggs and butter at Dan Crest's general store. It was a pleasant outing, and she would be back to the farm before two. Of course, during the week, no one was doing much—the Lewises' washing was hung out to dry, or Edgar French had his sheep grazing along the side of the road—but, whatever anyone was doing, at least it gave you a sense of life and progress.

On a Saturday morning, town was busy as could be. There were three churches in Denby—St. Albans (where her family went), First Methodist (where Walter's family went), and North Street Lutheran. All the ladies from all three churches were busy with this and that, either cleaning the church, or meeting in their quilting groups and sewing clubs, or shopping, or, some of them, having luncheons. If Rosanna went to town on a Saturday (and really, with Eloise going to school, there weren't many other days she could go), she had to dress nicely—something in a new style and nice goods. People knew her perfectly well, so no one would mistake her for a town lady, but she didn't have to look like she was dragging herself in from the farm. At the first houses (the Lynch place, on the north side of West Main, and the Bert place, on the south side), she clucked twice at Jake and shook the whip. Best to make her entrance at a brisk pace. Saturdays were different from Sundays, when they went to church (though in the Methodist church you didn't have to go every week, especially if you were a farmer). On Sundays, they put on their Sunday best, which was sober and dull. On Sundays, she wore a hat and tucked her hair in a tight bun. On Saturdays, she looked her age, twenty-three; on Sundays, she looked like her mother.

Of course it wasn't warmer in town, but it seemed as though it was. Rosanna pushed back the hood of the buggy in the sunlight, and waved to people on the sidewalk (Miss Lawrence, her old teacher; Father Berger, who was friendly even though she never went to St. Albans anymore; Mildred Claire, who had known her mother forever). Waving to Father Berger reminded her of her girlish anxieties about baptizing Frank and Joe. She had been positively loco about it with Joe, and then it passed. She put her head around the hood and looked at Father Berger again. Old man now. Her mother and the other ladies in the altar society complained about him incessantly.

Then that girl, Maggie Birch, who was Eloise's best friend, waved her down and ran over to the buggy. Rosanna gave her such a nice smile, even though she considered the girl a little fast, or, if not that, maybe "sneaky" was the word. But Maggie, too, was wearing a big smile. "Good morning, Mrs. Langdon. I was hoping I would run into you."

"Hello, Maggie. How are you today?"

"Fine, thank you, Mrs. Langdon." She hesitated.

Rosanna said, "I understand from Eloise that you are going in for secretarial school, Maggie."

"Mama says I can, yes. I can go down to Usherton for a course and stay with my aunt Margaret and her husband, Dr. Liscombe. Do you know them?"

"I'm sorry to say I don't."

"They have the biggest house. I'm sure I'll get lost in all the rooms. But . . . I was wanting to ask you."

"What?" said Rosanna.

"Well, did you know the Strand Theater down there?"

"Of course," said Rosanna. Jake snorted and shook his ears—a fly this time of year!

"I would really like to go and see a picture, and my cousin George has an automobile now and says he will take me, but I would like Eloise to come along."

"That's ten miles," said Rosanna. "Thirteen miles from our place."

"Georgie is a good driver," said Maggie.

Rosanna regarded Maggie, and tried to decide whether to ask her the question that came to her lips—was this something she and Eloise had discussed? Of course it was, said the girlish side of Rosanna, and best not to know, said the maternal side. So Rosanna said what mothers had said since the world was young: "We'll see."

A pout passed over the girl's face, and Rosanna realized that the condition Mrs. Birch had placed on the trip was that Maggie could only go if Eloise or someone went along. Rosanna shook the reins and left it at that. If she saw Maggie's mother in town, which she well might, she would speak to her about it.

Ethel Corcoran. Martin Fisk. Gert Hanke. Len Hart. Old, young, old, old. To all of them, Rosanna raised her whip and smiled and called, "Hey!" And then she was in front of Crest's, and she shouted, "Whoa!" to Jake, who had anyway already stopped by the hitching post, where some boys were pitching pennies against the wall of the store, shouting and jumping about. Rosanna got out and tied Jake to the post, right between a Ford and a new Chevrolet coupé. "Coupay!" said Rosanna to herself as she lifted out her crock of butter. Dan Crest came to the door of the store and opened it. He took the crock from her hands. He said, "So sorry we didn't see you last Saturday, Mrs. Langdon. Four—count 'em, four—of your best customers were in here, looking for your butter. You know Mrs. Carlyle? She won't make a pie crust without it."

"I use lard myself," said Rosanna.

"Well, she's French on her mother's side," said Dan Crest.

He set the crock on the counter and said, "I hope there are eggs, too?"

"Only three dozen," said Rosanna. "I candled them all myself, and they are large. I cleaned them again this morning." When she went out to get the crate, one of the boys who had been pitching pennies was petting Jake on the nose. She said, "Rodney Carson, you make sure nothing happens to Jake and I'll give you a nickel." A nickel was equal to one egg, if she took it in trade. If she asked for money, she got four cents. But she got five dollars for the butter, and six in trade. Rodney Carson said, "Okay, Mrs. Langdon. Jake is a nice horse."

"Yes, he is," said Rosanna. It was lovely how even the most elementary social intercourse lifted her spirits. Especially this time of year, when the farm was as dirty as could be, with thawing and freezing and damp everywhere. Just to put on your clean clothes and your clean shoes and your nice gloves and your best hat and drive the buggy out onto the road—well! She said, "I'll be back in a bit, Rodney."

By the time she set the crate on the counter, Dan had the sweating block of butter out of the crock and was weighing it on his scales. Ten pounds. He said, "Well, I'm giving some of the other ladies only forty cents a pound, Mrs. Langdon, but I'll offer you fifty, just because it's in such demand. Of course, the time of year means it doesn't quite have the flavor . . ."

"I think you'll find mine does," said Rosanna, with a discreet toss of her head. "Our cows have very good hay, especially this year." Then she said, "Do you mind?" And she walked away from the counter, toward the back of the store, as if there were something she'd seen from a distance. But there was nothing—she knew what she needed. In addition to the momentary charade of pretending that she was merely considering his offer, there was the pleasure of gazing at his goods, being seen to gaze at his goods, and exercising nonchalance. That was the most important thing. At least outside the farm, she was not going to fall prey to Walter's ever-present state of worry-shading-into-alarm. She was going to comport herself as the town women did, greeting everyone from a bit of a platform, whatever it was, even if it was only that she carefully candled her own eggs so that none of them were ever addled, even if it was only that her butter was rich and delicious, even if it was only that she and Jake made such a pretty picture trotting down the road.

Back at the counter, Dan Crest was waiting on an older woman Rosanna had never seen before, possibly the woman who owned the "coupay." Rosanna stilled her movements and the rustle of her dress, and listened. Dan was saying, "Yes, ma'am. Wonderful fresh butter, right from the farm this morning. And the best around." She couldn't hear what the woman said, but then Dan said, "Seventy-five cents a pound, and I'm proud to say it."

"Goodness me!" said the woman.

"There's a French family in town—this is all they buy."

"Indeed," said the woman.

Only then did Dan's eyebrow cock in her direction.

"Well, I . . ." But he made the sale, two pounds, and she also bought some sausages. When Rosanna returned to the counter, he said, "Sixty-two cents, in kind, and not a penny more."

All Rosanna said was "I see you have some apples left."

"Oh," said Dan Crest, "those are some russets from over to the east. You know the Schmidts over there?"

Rosanna shook her head.

"He keeps them in a cellar dug in not far from the river. I would have thought the damp would rot them myself, but they're as crisp as they can be." And so it began. There were so many things Rosanna could have been besides a farm wife, she thought. But it was not a source of regret—it was a source of pride.

FRANK HAD a special place, and what he did was, when Papa was outside and Joey was sleeping and Mama was in the kitchen, Frank climbed the stairs and went into Papa and Mama's room, and he lifted the corner of the blue-and-green quilt, and he lay down on his back and slid under there. The floor was slick against his back, and he got himself all the way to the far corner, right by the wall, and he put his hands behind his head and stared up at the underside of Mama and Papa's bed. The bed was much more interesting from the underside than from the top. It was like his own house under there, dark and shady, and he could look at things that fascinated him. For example, the legs of the bed had feet that looked like upside-down muffins, and above those, spirals—the back feet spiraled one way, and the front feet spiraled the other way, just like the spirals on the stair banister, one way, then the other way, up the stairs. The wood of the bed, which Frank also liked, was smooth and reddish, and on every side there were pegs sticking out. The best part of the bed from underneath were the ropes

that ran back and forth, making squares. Frank liked to slide his finger along the ropes, outlining the squares, but he never put his finger
between a rope and the heavy thing above it, because he had done
that once and gotten his finger stuck, and it had hurt to pull it out.

There were no toys under the bed—that wasn't why he liked it.
Why he liked it was that there wasn't anything under the bed—no
chickens, no Joey, no Eloise, no sheep, no "no"s. He could lie under
the bed and not be told anything at all. It was so quiet under the
bed that sometimes he had a nap. Mama didn't mind him going under
the bed—more than once she had said, "Well, you can't get into any
trouble down there, at least." Eloise would sometimes come to the
side of the bed and throw the quilt up and shout, "Boo! I see you!"
and that made them both laugh, especially since he knew she was
coming because her feet showed below the edge of the quilt.

But Papa didn't like him under the bed, and if Papa had told him
not to go under the bed, then Papa would be very angry if he found
Frank under the bed. And today was a Sunday, and they were going
to go in the buggy to Granny's for Sunday supper, and Frank was
wearing good clothes—clean pants and clean shirt. He had been told
to stay downstairs and not go under the bed, and as soon as he was
alone, he did the very thing he was told not to do.

It was beyond Frank to understand why he sometimes did the
very thing he was told not to do. It seemed like once they told him
not to do it—once they said it and put it in his mind—then what else
was there to do? It was like smacking Joey. "Don't hit your brother.
Don't ever hit your brother, do you understand? If I catch you hitting
your brother, then I will whip you, do you understand?"

But what was hitting? Sometimes, when Joey was walking along,
all you had to do was touch him and he fell down and cried. Other
times, a good wallop had no effect. If there was anything Frank liked,
it was trying things out. Joey was the most interesting person to try
things out on, especially considering that the cat always ran away,
even when Mama was not saying that the cat was dirty and shooing
him out of the house. It was obvious to Frank that if you had something in your hand, no matter what it was, you had to employ it. If
it was a rock, then you had to scrape it on the ground or on a wall.
If it was a fork, you had to poke it into your egg or into the table or
into Joey. If it was a stick, you had to hit something with it. If it was

a screwdriver, you had to turn a screw, and Papa had shown him how to do that. At Christmas, Mama had given him a box of eight colors (blue, green, brack, brow, vilet, ornge, red, yelloooooo) and a book to color in, but he had to try it on the table and the rug and the floor and the wall and his own skin. Only the wall was really bad—he got a whipping for the wall—but they laughed at the ornge on his legs.

Here came the call: "Frankie? Frankie, I don't see you! Where are you?" He didn't say a word. And then her shoes appeared, and then the quilt flew up, and then she was dragging him out by his arm and standing him up and slapping her hand down over his back, and she said, "I just ironed that shirt, and look at it—covered with dust! I don't know what I am going to do with you, Frankie!" She slapped him down again, and held him by the ear as they walked down the stairs. At the bottom, Papa was looking up at them, and he said, "Where was he?"

"Oh, he was in our room."

"Where?"

"Goodness, Walter, he was just—"

"Was he under the bed?"

"Well—"

"You can't protect him, Rosanna. He knows not to go under the bed, and you told him ten minutes ago—"

"I'll just put a sweater on over—"

Then Papa said, "Frank, son, come here. Stand right here." Papa pointed to the floor just in front of his feet. Mama gave him a little push, and Frank went and stood there.

"Were you under the bed?"

Frank shook his head.

"I'm going to ask you again. Were you under the bed?"

Frank said, "No." It seemed like the only thing to say.

"Frank, you have been disobedient and you have now told me a fib. What do I have to do now?"

Frank stared at him.

"Come on, tell me what I have to do."

Frank shook his head again.

Papa said, "I have to whip you."

Mama said, "We should leave; maybe after—"

"Can't wait. You punish a horse or a dog five minutes after the fact, and they don't know what you are punishing them for. Boy's the same."

Rosanna stepped back.

Walter took off his belt. Sometimes he used a spoon or a brush, because normally he was wearing overalls, but now he was dressed for going out, and he had a belt. He gripped the belt by the buckle, and Frank had to stand there facing the window while Papa took down Frank's pants and opened his union suit. Then Papa gripped Frank's shoulder and the blows began, right across his backside. Frank could count—he got to six before he was too confused by pain to count any further. But he didn't fall down. Partly, Papa didn't let him fall down; and partly, Frank didn't want to fall down. Each time he stumbled forward, Papa stood him up and gave him another one. The tears poured down his cheeks, but he didn't wipe them on his shirt or his arm. He had to lick them away, though, because they were dripping over his lips. Eventually, it was over, the pain and the fuss. He and Papa stood there quietly, and Papa did up his union suit and pulled up his pants. Then he turned him around so that he was standing right in front of Walter's knees, and Walter was leaning forward, his eyes alight.

"Frankie," he said, "why did I whip you?"

"I went under the bed."

"Why else?"

"Fib."

"Say, 'I fibbed.'"

Frank hesitated, then said, "I fibbed," although it had seemed as though the fib just came out of him.

Walter said, "These things don't just happen, Frankie. They are punishments you incur with disobedience and deception. You are a smart boy and a brave boy, and your mother and I love you very much, but I've never seen anyone more determined to have things your own way." Papa stood up and slid his belt back through the loops and buckled it. Mama appeared with Joey, who looked sleepy.

Frank felt like he was all on fire underneath his pants, but he stood up straight and let the tears dry on his cheeks until Mama took his hand and walked him into the kitchen. She set Joey in the high chair, then she dipped a cloth into the pail of clean water and wiped Frank's face and dried it. She said, "I don't understand you, Frankie. I just don't. You look like an angel, so how does the devil get into you like that?"

Frank said nothing. A few minutes later, they all went out to the buggy and got in, Mama carrying a pie and a loaf of bread. She said, "Well, we should be there by supper, anyway."

Papa shook the reins at Jake and Elsa and said, "Should be."

"But they'll ask why we're late."

Papa shrugged. Frank sat back against the cushion.

1924

THE NEW BABY WAS a girl, and she was no trouble at all. Just where her uncommon agreeability came from, her grandmothers could not agree—Walter's mother, Elizabeth, said it must have come from Rosanna's side of the family, and, not to be outdone, Rosanna's mother, Mary, swore it came from Walter's side. She was named after both her grandmothers—Mary Elizabeth. She had dark hair, but blue eyes. Walter's mother said, "My grandmother had blue eyes. Blue eyes come and go in our family." But the Augsbergers and the Vogels, when they all looked at you, it was like looking at the sky on a sunny day. Rosanna stayed in bed for two weeks after Mary Elizabeth was born, not because she was feeling terrible, as she had after Joey, but because it was winter and it was frozen and cold outside and there wasn't much to do, anyway. Her mother stayed a week, and then Walter's mother stayed a week, and all she had to do was nap and nurse and sample whatever the mothers had to offer, all varieties of oatmeal, of course, and that was delicious and so soothing, but also pancakes and dried apples boiled up in apple cider with cinnamon and sugar, or waffles (Elizabeth brought along her waffle iron). The happiest Rosanna was, was when she was sitting up on the edge of her bed, nursing the baby, and watching Frank out her window, bundled up to his eyeballs and playing in the snow fort her mother had helped him build in the side yard—the snow was deep and perfect this year, neither icy nor powdery. It was lovely to have the time just to look at the baby, at Mary Elizabeth, and watch her come alive instead of seeing her as a series of tasks and goals, the way she'd seen Frankie and Joey. Walter, too, was happy that it was a girl this time ("Maybe we'll get a bit of a rest with this one" was what he said). And then Walter's mother was opening the door and saying, "Rosanna, I made a little chicken broth, so warming. Would you like some?"

FRANKIE AND JOEY WERE sound asleep—Joey was even snoring a little, which Eloise didn't think a two-year-old would ever do—but Eloise was awake, listening to Rosanna and Walter in the next room talk about a used Model T, which Rosanna wanted Walter to buy but Walter did not want to buy. They had been talking about it for a week. Walter's position was that he had just spent so much money on seed that, no matter how little the fellow was willing to let it go for, it was too much; Rosanna's position was that she had twenty-two dollars of her own money, and she knew that Walter had thirty, and the car was five years old.

"I grow fuel for the horses. How am I expected to grow fuel for the car? You want to drive it into town, you have to drive into town to get gasoline to drive it into town."

Eloise, who liked to drive to the pictures in Usherton with Maggie and George and had now done so several times, didn't see what need Rosanna had of a car. According to George, a Ford was nearly impossible to learn to operate if you were older than twenty, but Rosanna was sure that she could learn, and in no time, too.

"I could make better use of a tractor, if I had the money," said Walter, and Eloise thought that he was absolutely right. The farm was three miles from town—you could walk there and back on a nice day. But she had to admire Rosanna, who never raised her voice or lost her temper or even wheedled. She just kept bringing it up, and if Walter got impatient, she would lower her eyes and pipe down. But, sure enough, she brought it up again. "Don't bother saying no to Rosanna" was what their mother always said, "because it's not going to get you anywhere." Especially at midnight, thought Eloise, in the middle of planting season. She turned over and put a pillow over her head.

THINGS WERE EXPECTED from Frank now that he was almost five. Every night before bed, he was to lay his clothes for the next day out on the floor, just as if there had been a person in there (himself) and the person had flown away (or gone to bed). Then, in the morning, he had to put them on before he came downstairs to feed the chickens and the horses (Papa fed the hogs and the sheep himself). His coat was by the door, and he put on that himself, too, along with his cap and his mittens. His boots were on the porch. While Papa was putting his boots on, Frank put his boots on. Sometimes he put them on the wrong feet, but if he did, he had to walk out in them—there was no time to change, because the animals were hungry.

First they carried oats and hay to the horses—Frank poured the oats out of the bucket into their feed trough while Papa forked them some hay. Then they got another bucket of oats, and Frank walked around the chicken yard, throwing it to them, while Papa checked the nests for eggs. Sometimes, when there were a lot of eggs, Frank got to carry a few of them into the house, but he had to be careful so that the eggs didn't break. Eggs were food and eggs were money— Frank understood those concepts perfectly well.

When they got back to the kitchen, Joey would be sitting in the high chair, eating whatever Mama had made for breakfast, and Mary Elizabeth would be in her basket on the table, looking up at the ceiling. Frank liked to go over to her and jump up and down. Sometimes that made her cry, but the point was not to make her cry, just to make her jerk her head or lift her hands or kick her feet. Mama always said, "Be nice to your sister, Frankie."

"I'm nice," said Frankie.

"Hmp," said Papa.

Joey just looked at them, his head turning back and forth, Frank to Mama to Papa, back to Frank. Joe never went out to feed the horses or the chickens. That was Frank's job.

Frank got to lead the horses to pasture, too. First Jake. Papa put the thing called the halter around Jake's head, and put the rope in Frank's hand, and Frank stepped forward very straight and didn't look back, and when they got to the gate of the pasture, Papa had already opened it, and he led Jake through and turned him around. Then they stood there until Papa took off the halter, and they stepped back and Papa closed the gate. They followed the same procedure with Elsa. On good days, Papa let him ride Jake, but never Elsa. Elsa was a little "marish" and not completely trustworthy, Papa said. Frank led the horses back from the pasture in the afternoon. This was a job he was especially proud of.

What was fun and not a job at all was sitting on the seat of the Ford and putting both hands on the steering wheel and pretending to turn it—left, right. If he had been going anywhere, he would have had to stand on the seat, which wasn't allowed, but it was more fun to sit and make noises. What made him laugh was to make a noise like they were going over a bump and then bounce up and down on the seat.

For Mama, he had jobs, too. He pulled up the covers on his and Joey's bed, with the pillows under the orange quilt that Granny Elizabeth had made for them, and he picked up his dirty clothes and Joey's dirty clothes and put them in a basket. Joey's dirty clothes were dirtier than his. It was hard not to feel that Joey was a disappointment, since, as Papa said, he was a terrible whiner, and always had to be told to stop. Frank was well aware that he himself never whined. Joe also had nightmares and cried out in the night, so Frank had taken the job on himself, without being told by Mama, to shake Joey if he was having a bad dream and wake him up. Sometimes he shook him pretty hard, but no harder than Papa shook him.

Frank was also learning to read. He wasn't old enough for school yet, but Mama had gotten the book from the teacher, and Frank could read almost the whole thing already. It was easy. And every time he read another page, Mama threw her arms around his neck and said, "Oh, darling Frankie, you *are* going to be president, aren't you?"

WHAT JOE LIKED was a little peace and quiet once in a while. Right now, sitting on the lowest step of the front porch, was about perfect. His tormentor, Frankie, had gone somewhere—who knew where,

and who cared?—and Mama was in the house, changing Mary Elizabeth. She knew Joe wouldn't walk away when he'd been told to stay
put, and so did he. She had given him a box of dominoes, his favorite
box of things, and he was laying them side by side on the second
step, making sure that their corners touched. Mama had counted the
dots for him, showing him that some dominoes had more dots and
some fewer, but Joe didn't care about the dots except insofar as he
thought they were pretty against the black of the rectangle. What
he liked was seeing a whole row or, better, a bed of dominoes, all
flat and straight and with no extras. It was very upsetting to lay out
the bed the way it should be and still have dominoes in the box, or,
worse, to lay it out and run out of dominoes while there was a space
to be filled. He suspected that there was a way of knowing ahead of
time whether it would turn out, but he didn't know what that way
was. He also knew that Frankie came around from time to time and
took dominoes out of the box and out of the row and out of the bed,
and then he would keep them, or throw them so that Joe would have
to find them, or he even put them in his mouth and made them
come out like a tongue when Joe asked for them. Mama only very
rarely caught Frankie doing this. Whenever Joe tried to say something important about Frankie, he was told not to be a whiner. So,
even though he was preoccupied with Frankie and all of the things
Frankie did to him, there wasn't anything he could think of to do
about it.

He stood up and looked at his row of dominoes. It was pretty
long. Joe smiled.

FRANK PRESSED HIMSELF deep into the sofa, hoping to hide sufficiently from Mama so that, when she came down the stairs from
putting Joe to bed, she would not see him and so not put him to bed.
He felt that a great wind was blowing inside of him, and that it would
blow him right out of the bed and back down the stairs if she took
him up there and laid him down. He hid as best he could, and he also
made himself a little rigid—harder to pick up, and easier to protest
that way.

Here she came.

And then she did look, but she only bit her lip and went into the dining room. Frank relaxed, sat forward again, and looked at all the faces. Yes, Granny Mary. Yes, Eloise. Yes, Uncle Rolf. Yes, Grandpa Otto. Yes, Oma and Opa. These and others were perfectly familiar. But in addition to them, there were Tom, who was seven, and Henrietta, who was six, and Martin, who was nine. These were his Second Cousins, according to Rosanna, and they lived very far away, in a city where there were no cows, no hogs, no chickens, and not even any horses, only tall buildings and hard roads and many, many automobiles. The Second Cousins were visiting for Thanksgiving and staying with Granny Mary.

"Oh me," said Opa, "stuffed. How does that happen, I ask you?"

"Opa," said Granny, "you can eat your fill of the goose or eat your fill of the pie, but not both."

"*Ja, ja, ja,*" said Opa. "Still, I am stuck in my chair, never to move again."

Mama, who had come back into the room, leaned down and kissed Opa on the top of his head, where there was no hair.

Papa said, "If we laze about like this, we'll fall asleep. We should play a game."

Granny said, "Something fun for the youngsters, Walter."

Papa looked at him, Frank, and then at Mama, and Mama said, "He can stay up for a little bit." But Frank sat quietly, knowing that Mama could change her mind at any moment.

Then he was at the kitchen table, with all the rest of them, kneeling on a chair, and Martin was on one side of him and Henrietta on the other side of him. He leaned forward, against the edge of the table. In his hand, he had a string, and the other end of the string was tied around a cork. Frank knew all about corks, because he and Joe played with corks in the bathing tub. If you pushed a cork down under the water, it would pop up, and sometimes pop completely out. Corks were fun. All the corks, nine of them, were lying in a circle in the middle of the table, and each cork had a string. In addition to the kids, Granny Mary and Opa and Papa were playing. Papa set the green dice on the table. Frank sometimes played with the dice, too, counting the dots and adding the two numbers together. Papa thought it was good practice for him. Joe could not even count the dots. Right in front of him, Frank also had a little pile of beans—ten beans. Papa had asked him to count them when he put them in front of him. Nothing hard about that, but all the faces smiled. Frank understood easy as you please that these beans were his money, and he wanted more.

Papa showed them what to do—he rolled the dice one, two, three times, and on the third time, he put the pot lid down on the table over the corks. The lid came down fast and made a startling noise, and then Papa picked it up again. Frankie's cork was still there, so he had to give Papa a bean. Martin's cork was not there, so Papa gave Martin a bean. Henrietta gave Papa a bean, and Opa gave Papa a bean, and so on around the table. Frank now had nine beans.

Frank did not like giving up beans, but at first he could not see how to avoid it. Each person rolled the dice, and everyone sitting around the table read the dice without saying a word, and while Frank was in the middle of understanding the numbers, the lid came down or didn't. The bad thing was when he pulled his cork just to be safe. He had to give up three beans that way. Frank felt himself getting mad. But Martin was laughing, Tom was laughing, and even Henrietta was laughing, though she had given away lots of beans. Frank knew that if he cried or yelled or had a tantrum, he would be carried up to bed, so he pressed his lips together and stared at the dice. The lid came down. The lid went up. He had to pay a bean to Granny Mary. It was then that Martin whispered in his ear, "It's always seven, Frankie. Just watch for seven."

Seven, as Frank well knew, was six and one, or five and two, or three and four. The next time he saw a seven, he pulled his string, and his cork fell into his lap. He looked up. Papa gave him a bean. He had had three beans. Now he had four beans. He laughed. A moment later, the dice and the lid came to him. Papa said, "Can you drop the lid, Frankie? I can do it for you."

Frank put his hand out for the lid. Then he knelt up on his chair and leaned over the table. All the corks were in the middle, in a circle, with their strings sticking out of them. Frank gripped the dice in his hand and dropped them on the table. They were wide apart from one another. Six and two. Not seven. He picked up the dice. This time he opened his hand a little, the way Martin had done, and let the dice roll back and forth on his palm. Then he dropped them again. One bounced. Four and three. He brought the lid down on the corks. There was a loud clang.

"Not so hard, Frankie," said Papa. Frank lifted the lid. There were five corks under the lid. Five people gave him beans. He gave three beans away. He did this without being told what to do.

"*Ja, ja,*" said Opa, "he's a natural, this boy. Someday, we will tell him about Uncle Hans."

"There is no Uncle Hans," said Granny Mary. "It took me years to figure that out."

"Who is Uncle Hans?" said Papa, who was standing behind Frank.

"Uncle Hans was the lucky one," said Opa.

"There is no Uncle Hans," said Granny Mary.

"True enough," said Opa, and they all laughed.

There was a Hans, though; Opa had told Frank the story.

One day, Hans left the village and walked toward the dark mountains. As he was walking along, a hedgehog came out of the forest and said to Hans, "Would you like to come with me into the forest? I will give you an enormous fir tree to live in, all your own." But Hans said no. He walked along. A little while later, a fox came out of the ground and said to Hans, "Good morning! Would you like to come with me? I will show you a wonderful cavern all hung with icicles, clear and shining and beautiful." But Hans looked at the foxhole and said, "No, thank you." He kept walking, and a bluebird flew down from a tall tree and said, "I will give you a magic feather, and if you hold it in your hand, you can fly way up in the sky and look down on a beautiful lake with many boats." This tempted Hans, but, the more he thought about it, the more it seemed too good to be true, so he turned away and went on. And then a wolf came up to him, and he had big teeth and long, rough hair, and Hans was very afraid. And the wolf growled, "I have nothing for you! Do you have something for me?" Hans said, in a very small voice, "I have a penny. That is all I have to make my way in the city."

The wolf's eyes glared at Hans with a yellow glow, and he growled, "May I have your penny? I do not have even a penny." So Hans gave him the penny, not so much out of fear, after all, as out of pity. Of all the animals, he thought, the wolf was the only one who had nothing.

Once the wolf had taken Hans's penny he said, "Would you care for a ride?"

Hans nodded, and the wolf knelt down, and Hans climbed upon his back. And then the wolf stood up and galloped away down the road. Hans nestled into his fur and held on tight around his neck, and before he knew it, the wolf had turned into a great prince who lived in a palace. As they galloped up to the palace gate, the wolf said, "Of all my subjects, you are the only one who was willing to give me a penny, and so I give you the name Lord Hans, Lucky Hans, and you will live with me in my castle for the rest of your life." And the gate opened. Frank knew that, whatever Granny Mary might say, for him and Opa, Lucky Hans did exist.

At the end of the game, Mama picked him up. He had eleven beans, which was four more than Henrietta and one more than Tom. Mama carried him up to bed. He was awake enough to push his beans under his pillow.

FROM WHERE Mary Elizabeth was sitting, she could see several new and interesting items in the front room. The nearest of these were her own feet, stuck out in front of her, as they often were, pointing upward, and not appearing to wiggle, even though they felt like they were wiggling. The most she could get them to do was shift slightly, back and forth, but she was able to connect this odd immobility with the fact that Mama had slid them into her shoes sometime before. What was new and interesting about her shoes was that they were bright and eye-catching. She watched them. And then, helpfully, Joey squatted down and said, "May Liz red shoes. May Liz red shoes."

Beyond the shoes, and beyond Joey, was Frankie. Frankie had another of the new and interesting items—it stuck out behind him and dragged against the floor, and it stuck out in front of him. It had eyes and ears and it moved, but it didn't seem to be alive. Frankie capered about the room and it went with him. Frankie waved one of his arms. Mary Elizabeth turned her head and her body first one way and then the other way, just to watch Frankie. Then Joey ran over to him and grabbed the lower end and jerked it upward, and Frankie fell down, and Joey said, "It's mine!" Then the two boys did something that Mary Elizabeth found eternally fascinating—they jerked and pulled, back and forth, until Frankie stuck out his arms and pushed Joey, and Joey tumbled backward and started screaming. Frankie kicked him and said, "Stop whining or I will give you something to whine about!"

Now Mary Elizabeth had pulled herself up, using the same chair she always did—it was the easiest thing in the world, especially with shoes on—and in her excitement, she sidestepped around the chair and laughed and took her hand off the chair and waved it. Joey turned toward her, crying less now, and he lay there and sighed, then sat up. Frankie and the new thing ran into the dining room, and Mary Elizabeth heard Mama call, "What are you boys up to now? If I hear any more screaming, I will tie you together like I did last week, and you can learn to cooperate all over again! Your fighting is driving me out of my mind!"

Mary Elizabeth sidestepped two more steps, but her feet and her shoes weren't working very well, and though her one hand was still on the chair, her other was still waving in the air, and, what with one thing and another, she was beginning to lose confidence in her ability to get all the way around the chair to the table. Yes, she was confused, no doubt about it. She stopped moving and looked at Joey.

Joey had sat up. His legs were crossed and he was staring at her.

And it was true—she had lost her grip on the chair, and both of her hands were waving in the air. It was unprecedented.

Joey crawled toward her, his face bright, then sat back on his heels and said, "C'mon!"

She tilted toward him.

The top edges of the red shoes dug into her.

She bent a knee, the right knee, the knee that knew what it was doing more often.

She did not fall down.

She bent the left knee. She bent the right knee again.

Joey crawled closer and held out his hands.

Her arms waved. She fell into him, and he laughed. She laughed.

Frankie ran into the room again. He said, "Mama's mad at you."

Mary Elizabeth got up on her hands and knees and crawled back to the chair she liked. She pulled herself up.

Frankie and Joey were rolling around on the floor again, hitting and kicking. Mama blew into the room and grabbed them and jerked them to their feet. She smacked both of them across the backside with the spoon in her hand, and then she came over to Mary Elizabeth and picked her up. She said, "My goodness me, how am I going to get through the winter?"

1925

WALTER WAS SITTING in his chair at the kitchen table. It was still dark, and Rosanna was upstairs with Mary Elizabeth. Ragnar was feeding the hogs, and at any minute, Frank would come down, dressed and ready to feed the horses, so Walter was a little impatient for his breakfast. At the stove was Irma, Eloise's official replacement, who might have been five feet tall, but maybe not.

Walter didn't know what to think of this girl that Ragnar had married. She said she was nineteen, which was a good age, but she seemed much younger, and she was clumsy to a frightening degree. She had nice hair and would have been pretty if she had not lost her two front teeth, and although Ragnar had not told him how this happened, Walter suspected that it was an accident. Already since he'd brought her home, she had knocked herself out standing up in the chicken house—she had gone out to gather eggs, and when she didn't return, Rosanna went out to discover her flat on her back, two eggs broken in her hand, and the chickens perching on her. It had taken her two days to recover completely from that. She had also dropped two plates and a cup, and smashed her finger in the door. She was as likely as not to stumble over a threshold. "Oh, my goodness," she always said, "how silly of me!" as if her own clumsiness were an eternal surprise.

Walter couldn't figure it out—her feet weren't especially big for her small size. He and Rosanna had looked forward to her replacing Eloise in the house, but she made Eloise seem like a machine of efficiency by contrast. "It's like having a fourth child," said Rosanna. At least she was an easygoing girl, and not demanding. The two of them lived in Ragnar's bedroom for the time being. Walter thought he could get Rolf and Otto to help him put an addition on the west side of the house in the summer, with its own door. Then Mary Elizabeth would get a room of her own, and Frank and Joe would get something a little bigger, anyway.

Irma said, "Well, the yolk split on one of them."

Walter said, "That's fine, just scramble them."

"You want me to scramble them?"

"Yes, Irma."

She turned and, after a minute or two, managed to dish a mess of eggs onto his plate, right beside his half-eaten patty of sausage. It did not look appetizing. He picked up his bowl of oatmeal and scraped the remaining bits out of the bottom with his spoon. Truly, he wished that Rosanna would go back to making breakfast, but then what would Irma do? She had no skills of any kind—she had not been raised on a farm, and hadn't done well enough in school to get a teacher's certificate. Sometimes, Rosanna put her to cleaning the house, but she was slapdash at that, too, and terribly remorseful when spots and stains she had overlooked were pointed out to her. She said, "Oh, Rosanna, I am meant to be a failure, aren't I? That's what my ma always said." Three weeks it was since Ragnar brought her home.

But Frankie loved her. He skipped down the stairs while Walter was cutting his sausage with his fork and taking another bite. He caroled, "Good morning, Papa! Good morning, Irma!"

And Irma said, "Oh, darling Frankie, there you are. I was just wondering when you would come down and have your oatmeal. See, I've sprinkled brown sugar on it." She glanced at Walter. "Just a tiny bit. Did you have a dream, Frankie?"

"I dreamt that I was sitting up in the maple tree, and the grass was green everywhere, and the limbs of the tree suddenly dropped, and I slid down to the ground."

"That must have been a happy dream!"

Walter thought maybe he had never asked Frankie about his dreams. Surely Rosanna did that. Walter himself had the most prosaic dreams in the world, about trying to turn the planter in the corner of one of the fields and getting stuck.

Frank said, "And Jake was in my room, sitting on a chair in the corner."

"What a funny dream!" laughed Irma. When she laughed, Frankie laughed with her. Frank ate up his oatmeal, and Irma gave him a piece of sausage and a scrambled egg. He ate them and said, "That was good."

Irma said, "Oh, you are a silly boy!"

Walter pushed back his chair. He said, "Look, the sky is lightening. It might be a nice day."

Frankie leapt from his chair.

AS FAR AS Rosanna was concerned, Irma's useful quality was that she was patient with Joey, who did demand a lot of patience. Perhaps it was simple fellow-feeling, since Irma demanded a lot of patience, too. Rosanna had never been especially patient; she felt herself stamping around the house in a state of permanent irritability, and had even written Eloise a letter down at Iowa State, where she was taking home economics (and doing very well—who was surprised at that?), living in a dorm with lots of girls, and learning to play the piano. To Eloise she wrote, "If I never sufficiently expressed my appreciation for your sense of order and your unflagging energy, I am sorry. I appreciate it now." Eloise wrote back, "Can you make me a velveteen dress if I send you the pattern? I'm sure Ma would blanch at the very sight of the pattern! *Très au courant!*" Yes, Ma would, thought Rosanna, but she made the dress. It was an easy pattern, and made her, too, feel *très au courant.*

While she did the hem, she watched Irma and Joe with the everlasting box of dominoes, the box that she had given Joe last summer and that he would not let out of his sight. The box itself was shredding, but he wouldn't let Rosanna replace it. He was also now sporting a bit of tape on his forehead, just above his right eyebrow. There was nothing underneath the tape, but Joey swore that that spot hurt him, and the only thing to ease the pain was a "Band-Aid." The "Band-Aid" was from a packet that Irma had brought with her. Rosanna had never seen one before, but then it turned out that Dan

Crest was stocking them, too. They were good for little cuts, but the only people in the household who needed them were Joey and Irma.

What Irma helped him do was stand the dominoes on end in not quite such long rows, and then knock them down by touching the first one in the line. It was a good game for Joe, time-consuming, and he was getting better at it—he could set up nine or ten dominoes in a row without knocking them over until he wanted to (or until Frankie knocked them over, but Irma was good, and quick, at stopping that, too). Sometimes, she could divert his attention from the dominoes and get him to practice hopping and twirling and riding his hobby horse from Christmas. She was good at creating a circle around Joey into which Frank could not rush with ridicule, shoving, and kicking. This was because (and Rosanna appreciated this and was not jealous) Frankie liked Irma, too. Irma told Frankie stories, and sometimes Frankie told Irma stories. So Rosanna was willing to do a little more work in order to be free of those particular cares that revolved around her two ill-matched sons.

She did not, however, give Irma much leeway with Mary Elizabeth (who could now be heard calling to be picked up after her nap). Rosanna set down her hemming and, when Irma looked up, gestured to her to keep on with what she was doing. Rosanna had waking nightmares of Irma falling down the stairs with Mary Elizabeth in her arms, or Irma bumping the child's head on the edge of the cupboard, or stumbling and falling on her. These worries Rosanna acted upon, but kept to herself.

Mary Elizabeth was not as active as Frankie and not as fearful as Joey. She was willing to try some things, but not everything. Rosanna considered that she had a thoughtful look on her face. Once, before Christmas, when she was—what?—ten months old, she had crawled over to a book and picked it up. As Rosanna watched, she opened the book and began turning pages, carefully pressing her tiny forefinger against the corner of the page and pulling it down, and then taking the page between her thumb and finger, and turning it. She hadn't torn a single page. Now she was standing in her crib, holding her arms out.

Rosanna laid her back down in the crib to change her. She was good about that, too—she had been easy to train (Rosanna always started early and went at it with dedication, because it was better in the end not to leave it too late). Now she took Mary Elizabeth's long johns off. They were not wet, so she carried her over to the potty and sat her upon it. Mary Elizabeth was neither a bouncer nor a wiggler. When she had produced, Rosanna handed her a page from last year's *Farmers' Almanac,* then helped her with it. Really, she was an agreeable child, and she would make a useful young woman, and wasn't that the best kind? Rosanna adored her even though she was a bit plain (Rosanna noticed this but never, ever mentioned it and was always maybe too affectionate). She in fact suited her name, Mary (common) Elizabeth (respectable). Should there be another girl, Rosanna thought, she would name her something more elegant. Dorcas? There was a Dorcas in town. Helene? Was there a Helene? But she was one of the Carsons. She had probably started life as a mere Helen. Mary Elizabeth held out her arms, and Rosanna slipped her into the romper suit she had knitted in the fall. Then she gently gripped Mary Elizabeth around the waist while the little girl slipped her feet into her shoes. Once they were tied, Rosanna walked her to the top of the stairs and held her hand as she stepped her way down them. They were steep, steeper than most stairs, so Rosanna was careful to give all of the children plenty of practice but to watch them (even Joey, nearly three, even Frankie, at five—these stairs were no joke).

Downstairs, Joey was waiting for her with his face alight. He shouted, "Mama, Mama! Look!" and gestured at the line of dominoes.

Rosanna said, "How many are there, Joey?"

Joey looked at Irma. Irma's lips moved, and then Joey shouted, "Sixteen!"

"Sixteen! My goodness, such a lot!"

Joey said, "May Liz! Touch it!"

"Really?" said Rosanna. "You want Mary Elizabeth to knock them down?"

Joey nodded excitedly, and Irma nodded, too. Probably this was Irma's idea. Mary Elizabeth walked over to the table and touched the first domino; they all fell in a row, and it was really quite exhilarating to see how both children enjoyed it. Rosanna said, "Joey, you're a nice boy," and Irma said, "Oh, yes, I think so, too."

THIS YEAR, when the sheep-shearing men came to shear the sheep, Frank had a job. You never knew ahead of time when the sheep shearers were going to come—Papa only had twenty sheep, so the shearers would show up all of a sudden one morning, shear the sheep, stay for dinner, and then go on to a farm on the other side of town that had lots of sheep—a hundred, maybe. Always before when they came, Frank had been told not to get underfoot—he could sit on the fence and watch, but he couldn't climb down into the pen or sneak into the barn, either, in case he got up to something when no one was looking. And it was true that Frank liked to get up to things when no one was looking, even if he did get a whipping for it. But sheep shearing was better than getting up to things. This year, his job was to jump on the wool when they put it into the sack so that they could get a lot in. It was a great job.

On the morning when the sheep shearers showed up, Mama looked out the window and saw they were there, then called to Papa out the back door. It was a sunny day, not at all damp. Papa went to the sheep shearers and talked money to them while Mama found Frank a long-sleeved shirt with a high collar. Before he went out the door, she smoothed his socks up over the bottoms of his overalls and said, "You are going to get a bath today, and I don't want any fuss about it." Frank jumped down the porch steps.

Felix and Harmon took turns. Daddy and Ragnar would catch a sheep, put a rope around its neck, and pull it over to the sheep shearers. Felix or Harmon then flipped the ewe over on her back and put her between his legs. First he clipped the hair off her head, then went all around her neck. Then he started on her belly and clipped from top to bottom in smooth rows. The wool fell to one side like a blanket, and the sheep got quieter and quieter, not even baaing, because Papa said that the sheep were glad to be clipped—if you let a sheep go through the summer with all that wool, it might lie down and die. They looked terribly silly without their wool, though—silly and surprised, Frank thought.

Once the fleece was lying out flat on the ground, Papa or Ragnar folded it together and rolled it up, and then put it in the sack. Here was where Frank came in—he climbed into the sack, and while Papa or Ragnar held one of his hands, he jumped up and down all over the wool. He jumped as high as he could, and almost in one place but not quite. As he did this, the one who was not holding his hand went and caught the next sheep. Frank did not want to rest, because he wanted Felix and Harmon to see what a good jumper he was. At the end of twenty sheep, it was dinnertime, and Frank was warm in the sun, and all the sheep crowded together at the feeder the way they hadn't been able to before. After the sheep shearers left, Mama made Frank take off all his clothes and take a bath in the kitchen. When he was clean and all dried off, she took him to the window and looked him all over for ticks, and she found a few—two on his back and two on his legs and one in his hair. She held a burnt match tip against them, and they backed out. All the time she was saying, "Ugh, I hate ticks!" and Frank was very good about standing still.

EVERY YEAR, Walter said that he was going to rip out or plow up or in some way get rid of the Osage-orange hedge that separated the field behind the barn from the back acreage, and every year, he went out there with Ragnar and scratched his head for a minute and then just ended up trimming it. It was, as his father had always said, "horse-high, bull-strong, and hog-tight," but it limited what he could do with that back field. The problem was that it was dense with thorns, a couple feet thick, and a quarter of a mile long. Every time you wanted to get into the back field, you had to go around it, because, as intended, there was no going through it. It was also a bit unusual for this area—more common down south, Walter had heard, where such hedges had been all the fashion in the middle of the last century (when, Walter supposed—the thought made him smile, it was so ridiculous—all American farmers were going to model themselves on the landed English gentry and farm the same land for generations and also fox-hunt across it). But if you replaced it with barbed wire, you had to keep your eye out for breaks in the fencing, and you had to be there to fix it before any animals got through. No animals got through the Osage-orange hedge. In fact, no animals with a lick of sense went near it. But the thing was so permanent, more permanent than the barn and the house, since it had been planted before they were constructed. Probably old Litchfield, from whom he'd bought the farm, had sited the barn where it was because of the hedge—it meant a quarter of a mile less fence to maintain. As a result, the barn wasn't where Walter would have put it. That was another thing that bothered him about the farm. Rosanna liked the house, though.

Really, it was amazing, Walter thought, as he sharpened the shears, how things about your farm that you didn't mind—or hardly even noticed—when you bought it, came to wear you down over the years. When you first walked onto your place, you were so glad to have it that everything looked good. Or perfect. Then, year by year—it had been six years now, six springs, summers, falls, and winters (mud, heat, harvest exhaustion, snow)—all the extra steps began to tell on your affections. And every wrong thing about a farm involved extra steps: that was what that long, impenetrable hedge represented to Walter.

Even so, Walter knew he was less and less able to imagine any other life. He was thirty now. Ten years before, he'd been working for his father—head down, it felt like, his eyes lifted only as far as the next hill of corn. He'd had skills his father approved of, like planting a cornfield in a perfect grid, or fixing a harness so it looked practically new. And then, not unlike a bomb blast, two years after that, where was he, northern France, if you called Cambrai France (some people didn't, they called it "Kamerijk"), and the grid of corn had turned into acres of blood and mud, and what he noticed wasn't the tanks they'd used there, supposedly for the first time ever, but the fugitive birdcalls in the din and tiny purple berries in the blasted hedges. Except for the tanks and the fighting and the trenches, Cambrai had looked almost familiar, so flat was it, the horizon low against the sky. And then that was over and he had the influenza on his way home, in Georgia, and he recovered, and Howard, on the farm with his parents, did not, though his mother did, and over the years she had said more than once, "It should have been me that died," at which point his father would leave the room and his mother would put her face in her hands. The only thing Walter knew to do was to pat her on the knee.

But here he was, and prices were up, and there was Rosanna, and all his ideas about some of those towns he had passed through—Cedar Rapids, Chicago, New York, London, Paris—had simply vanished. He'd been a farm boy. And now he was a farmer, and no longer a boy, and it was disorienting how quickly Frankie was superseding him as the hope of his own father and mother and wife for something that had nothing to do with Osage-orange hedges and badly sited barns and too many cows and not enough hogs (or vice versa).

Well, the clipping was easy when he got down to it—he could go along one side in the morning and the other side in the afternoon and get the whole thing done in a day, and then there it stood, stiff and solid and thorny—a thorn in his side, but only in his side, since his father wished he had something like it—what drove his father crazy about cows was the way they leaned against every fence, but no cow leaned against an Osage-orange hedge—and Frankie loved to throw the hedge apples at the side of the barn, and Rosanna thought the seeds were delicious, if only you could get at them more easily, and the wood burned slow and hot in the winter. Rosanna liked it, too, because you could split one of the fruits, which were certainly not oranges, and rub it along the baseboards and door and windowsills of the house, and it kept out insects and spiders. Sometimes, Walter even cut fence posts from the stems of the hedge—they were straight and strong. The list went on. Walter pricked his thumb on a thorn, but, then again, you could do that on barbed wire, too, as he'd done so many times.

IF ANYONE REMEMBERED that rearing a child on a farm was dangerous, it was Rosanna. Always her eye was out the window. Always she was stepping to one side to look through a doorway. Always she was making sure the gate across the steps leading down from the front porch to the wide, wide world (and particularly the road) was closed. Always she was putting shoes and boots outside and washing hands, not to mention handkerchiefs and bandannas. Walter had been offered a nice yearling bull for free, but Rosanna wouldn't let him get one until . . . well, she hadn't decided. And no large hogs, only feeder pigs that got sold after a few months. The children didn't play in the barn by themselves and were not allowed in the loft, even though Rosanna's own brothers and cousins had loved sliding and jumping in the oat hay. She herself had loved it, the stalks were so smooth and fragrant, but a child someone knew, somewhere, well, something had happened to him about hay, she didn't know what. What she did know was that some farmers understood that the death of someone around the farm, often a child, was the price of farming.

Sad but true, and in all ways, not only that one, the price of farming was high.

On the day it happened, she was not thinking about these things, but she had been, and later she did again. That day, a Saturday, it was raining. Dinner was finished—a simple meal of leftover potatoes and some pieces of chicken. Ragnar and Irma had gone to town, and Walter was out in the barn, fixing the corn sheller—he and Ragnar thought this rain would be followed by frost, and after that would come the corn harvest. Walter was good at using all his spare moments to get his equipment into shape.

Rosanna was knitting. She had some nice wool, not from their own sheep (which was a little coarse, she thought), but fine dark-gray fiber from a flock of Leicester Longwool sheep that a friend of her mother's had down by Newton. She was making Walter a sweater for Christmas, with cables, and she didn't want him to see it, so she could knit only when he was outside or away. Joey had his box of dominoes on the couch—she had talked him into accepting a new box. She had her eye on Frankie, who had his eye on the dominoes but knew better than to touch them, at least when Rosanna was in the room. To Frankie she had given a deck of cards. At the moment, he was turning them over one by one, but any minute, she knew, he would ask her to play a game with him—they would probably end up playing old maid, which Frank didn't like much but would play. He looked up at her. She said, "Why don't you try building a house? Remember, we did that?"

"That was hard."

"Yes, but it gets easier with practice. Uncle Rolf once used almost the whole deck."

"How many?"

Rosanna turned her work and made something up: "Forty-six cards." This shut up Frank.

Now she turned to Mary Elizabeth, who had been stacking blocks but looked up at a flash of lightning in all the windows, and the subsequent clap of thunder. In fact, all of the children looked at her, but she said, "At least five or six miles away, and moving west." Of course she was afraid of lightning—anyone in country as open as this had to be. But they were inside, that was reassuring, and the house and the barn both had lightning rods. Who was it—

Mary Elizabeth stood up, and the thunder clapped again, and Mary Elizabeth started jumping up and down. She was not crying and didn't seem afraid, just excited, was what Rosanna was thinking as she held out her hand toward the girl, and at that very moment the windows lit up, and Mary Elizabeth went down, flat down, on her back, and she hit the back of her head on the corner of a wooden egg crate, and as the thunder clapped, she was utterly silent and still. Rosanna stared at her, her own hands lifted with her knitting. It was Frankie who said, "Mama, what happened?"

Rosanna threw down the knitting and lunged forward from her rocking chair, but then she knelt beside her baby without touching her. The windows lit and thunder clapped again, and the rain outside seemed to pour down on the roof and the porch as out of a bucket, and Rosanna had no idea of any kind what to do.

Distractedly, she took Mary Elizabeth's hand in her left, and placed her right palm on the girl's forehead, as if there might be a fever, but of course there was nothing of the sort. Rosanna said, "Mary Elizabeth? Honey?"

The lightning and the thunder seemed incessant now. She glanced around the room. Frankie was right behind her, but Joey was staring from the sofa. She said, "I need to—"

But what did she need to do? It seemed impossible to do anything. The lightning and thunder roared again, this time almost simultaneously, and Rosanna put her elbows on her knees and her face in her hands, just for a moment. Frankie said, right in her ear, "Mama? Is she dead?"

Rosanna sat up. Over the din, she exclaimed, "No, of course not. She'll be fine!" and just then, Mary Elizabeth's eyes did open, and then she started to cry. Rosanna slipped her hands under the little girl's body and gently took her into her arms, then stood up and carried her to the sofa. After that, perhaps she sat there with her daughter moaning in her arms for forty-five minutes—at least that—until the storm subsided and Walter came stomping in from the barn, soaking wet and full of news, already talking—"You should have seen— I thought"—until he was standing in the doorway from the dining room and said, "What happened?"

Frankie said, "May Liz fell down."

Walter pushed his wet hair out of his face and stepped toward her. "Is she all right?"

No, she wasn't trying to sit up, though she had said a few words.

"How did she fall down? Was she climbing on something?"

Rosanna said, "I think the back of her head hit the corner of the egg crate."

"She'll be fine," said Walter. "We just need to give her a few hours."

The vomiting began before suppertime. Walter ran out to start the Ford. He took Frankie and Joey with him, to get them out of Rosanna's hair. Rosanna wrapped Mary Elizabeth in a blanket and carried her out into the rain, leaning her own body over the baby's so she wouldn't get wet. Walter opened the door, and Rosanna slid into the passenger's seat of the Ford. The boys sat in the back. All the way into town (past Dr. Gerritt's office and on to Dr. Craddock, who was younger and newer to the area), Rosanna knew it was merely appearance that was moving her forward. Though she was telling the boys that Mary Elizabeth was asleep, so they had to be very quiet, sleep was certainly a thing of the past now.

1926

～⤳

Rosanna read in the paper that Billy Sunday was going to come out from Chicago and do a revival in Mason City—not in a tent, like the old days, but in the theater, and only for two nights. He still came to Iowa fairly often, because that was where he had started out, however many years ago, where he'd played baseball and lived in the orphanage and all, and he still had fond memories of the place and the people.

Father Berger had thought Billy Sunday was the devil, and no one in Rosanna's family had ever seen him. All the time he was most famous, they acted as if he didn't exist. But Rosanna got a bee in her bonnet, and it was to take the boys and go up to Mason City and see the famous man.

What was it now, five and a half months since that day, the crashing, thundering day when Mary Elizabeth, such a good child, had passed out of this world for no reason at all? Not a mark on her, and yet she went from talking and running around to lying in Rosanna's arms to being buried in Walter's family plot in the space of a weekend, and who was to blame but Rosanna herself? Though no one said that; everybody said the very opposite, in fact—what could she have done, such a freak accident, like that time when . . . And here was where Rosanna stopped listening. After a month or two, she had garnered massive praise for not succumbing to her grief, but how could you do that on a farm? Never could you say to the corn, you must wait to be harvested; never could you say to the cows, you must put off being milked; never could you say to the boys, don't get up today; never could you say to the winter weather, I don't want to build yet another fire.

But she had changed. She hardly ever went into town now—Irma took the eggs and the butter to Dan Crest and got whatever she could for them. She was more particular about cleaning and cooking, and it wasn't only the winter weather that kept her inside, just as it wasn't only the farm work that kept Walter out in the barn. If he didn't want to look at the spot where their child had made that passage from life to death, Rosanna didn't want to stray far from it. She felt, as soon as she saw the notice in the paper (not thought—she had no thoughts at all, really), that Billy Sunday might give her some new memory, or insight would enter her the way the sunlight entered the windows. Whose fault had it been? Well, obviously hers, but also the fault of the weather, and, beyond that, the heavens. The room had been so dark and so loud.

WALTER DIDN'T MIND Billy Sunday—he'd been to a revival in Cedar Rapids as a boy, a tabernacle affair, a week long (though the Langdons had only stayed three days). Back in those days, Billy still did his patented slide into the middle of the stage (just as he'd slid into home plate those seasons when he was playing in Chicago for Cap Anson). He jumped around and shouted, and Walter had found it entertaining to hear him exhort the members of the audience to "Get on the Water Wagon!" His mother felt that the Sundays may have been a very unfortunate family, and that certainly life was harder in those days during and after the War Between the States, and you had to make your way as best you could, God knew, and Mary Jane Sunday, who had been a Corey, had done the best she could, but, really, they were not the same sort of people as the Chicks and the Cheeks and the Langdons, and so she was immune to his preaching. As Walter remembered, she had sat primly in the tent, glancing around with a small smile on her face. His father had been more susceptible, maybe because of Sunday's energy and athletic fame, not to mention that his grandfather had been a good farmer over in Story County.

After the revival, he had spent a few months reading his Bible in the evenings. But inertia prevailed—they'd gone back to their former religious habits (just enough participation to be able to say they did it, and to keep up friendships with the other members of the church). They didn't dance (didn't care for it), but they did play cards (euchre and cribbage), and his father didn't think that a drop of whiskey from time to time was a damnable thing. That Rosanna wanted to cart the boys all the way to Mason City and then stay in a hotel there (three dollars per night) he thought was strange, but if it got her through this time, he welcomed it, and so did his mother when he mentioned it in town. She said, "She knows what she wants, though maybe she doesn't know what will work. But if you don't give her what she wants, she'll spend the rest of her life thinking that that was the one thing that might have worked."

Everyone said that Billy Sunday wasn't the draw he had once been, but as they got closer to the assembly hall, Walter had to be impressed by the crowds streaming around him. He carried Joey in his arms, and he was sorry that he didn't have a length of rope to tie around Frankie, because Frankie kept disappearing, if only for as long as it took Walter to begin to panic. Rosanna kept saying, "Frankie, hold my hand!" But she was distracted, too. Walter said to her, half joking, "I should have given him his whipping in advance!" but she barely chuckled. A moment later, when Frankie happened to bump into his legs, Walter grabbed his shoulder and said in his strictest voice, "If you don't stay right with me, they'll make you stay out, and we'll go in, and what'll you do then?"

Frankie looked up at him and said, "Run away!" But he took his hand and stuck by him as they went through the door. Fortunately, just inside the door, a fat man with a handkerchief over his head and his hat on top of that saw Frankie start jumping up and down and said, "Boy, you better be quiet for Reverend Sunday, because he don't like a lick of noise from the audience, and he'll send you right out. I seen it happen."

Frank's mouth dropped open—more, Walter thought, at the man's enormous girth than at the reprimand—but Walter took the opportunity to ask him how many revivals he had been to, and the man said, "This is twelve for me. I go to one each year or so. I went to the first one, up in Garner. First time he ever spoke to an audience. That was history in the making." Suddenly he bent down and stuck his face into Frankie's and said, "You mind, hear? I'm watching you!" To be perfectly honest, Walter was glad he did. Rosanna was staring at the stage and the choir and all the people. He said, "Rosanna?" one time, but she paid him no attention.

JOE COULDN'T STAND the noise. The giant room they were in was pounding with it, so the first thing he tried was to lay his head against Papa's chest, just press his ear into his shirt there, put his hand over his other ear, and close his eyes. That was a little better, but then the noise revealed itself not to be just noise, but also shaking and stamping. It seemed like he could hear it through the top of his head and the seat of his pants. When Joe thought of the loudest noises he had ever heard (thunder, lots of cows mooing all at once, Frankie screaming right in his ear), this was still worse. He shifted around so that his other ear was against Papa, but that didn't work, either. It was a terrible riddle, and it made him want to scream into the noise (he glanced up at Walter's face, then at Rosanna's), but he didn't dare. At least Frank wasn't bothering him. In the back seat of the car on the way down, as soon as Mama said, "Now, you boys settle down and try to be quiet for five minutes," Frankie began with the nail he had, poking it into Joe's side, right behind his arm. When Joe grunted, Frankie made it go back into his hand, so that when Mama turned around, there was no nail. Then, when Mama was looking out the windshield again, Joe would see out of the side of his eye Frankie sticking his tongue out. Joe knew that Frankie knew that Joe knew he was sticking his tongue out, so it was no use to pretend that nothing was happening. Never once did Mama or Papa think to check in Frankie's pockets for his weapons. They just looked at him, and he smiled that smile he had, and one or the other of them said, "Joey, for goodness' sake, quit whining."

THE MAN ON THE STAGE looked a little like Grandpa Wilmer, Frank thought, except that he hopped around and shouted and threw his arms in the air like there was something really worrying him and he didn't know what to do about it. Grandpa Wilmer wasn't like that.

Grandpa Wilmer never raised his voice, even when something bad happened, like that time last summer when the yearling bull put his horn through a knothole in the side of the barn and they couldn't get him out and he broke his neck right there. That had been when they were up there for the threshing, and Frank didn't think he would ever forget it. It was a Devon bull (Papa told him that), red all over with white horns, not like the browny shorthorns Papa had, a beautiful bull, hanging against the side of the barn by its horn, dead. Dead like May Liz was a month later.

The man on the stage stepped back, and other people in white robes, with books in their hands, sang a few songs. There wasn't much sun in this place, and there were so many people that it made Frank feel like he wanted to jump up and down, just jump up and down, but that man, the giant who had told him absolutely to be quiet because he was watching, *was* watching—he was three rows behind and four or five people over, right at the end, so if Frank made noise that man could get up and come get him and drag him out. Frank grabbed the edge of the bench and held it tight, and that kept him from jumping up and down. Right next to him, Joey was crying. He wasn't making any noise, but the tears were running down and his eyes were closed. Frank was glad that at least he himself wasn't doing that.

IT WAS INDEED as Rosanna had expected it to be, crowded and a little frightening, but everyone was friendly, and Rosanna felt it— she felt herself disconnect from the irritations of the boys and, for that matter, Walter. She knew Walter hadn't wanted to come—ninety-some miles and two nights leaving the farm in the charge of Ragnar and Irma. It made Walter nervous. But when Rosanna said, "Then I'll go by myself," even though she hadn't yet learned to drive the car, that made him even more nervous, so he agreed to come for the two evenings and the one day, as long as they got up before five and came straight home Monday morning. What Rosanna said, in order to mask her hopes, had been "Well, it'll be nice to get away for once. Even if it's only to Mason City." And it was. The country wasn't terribly different from their own, but it was fun to go through the towns, if just for the names—Eldora, Steamboat Rock, Ackley—and the signs pointing to places like Swaledale that she knew she would never see. Yes, they were probably just like Denby, but the names were enlivening.

She had thought it would be harsh and scary, since Billy Sunday was known for his hellfire sermons. But most of the people she eavesdropped on had come more than once. Not only did they know what to expect, they were already saved. Coming again and again, Rosanna realized, was like having an account at the bank. Everyone said once was enough forever, but twice would be more secure, and so on. Hearing the hellfire sermon amounted to hearing about what would happen to others, not oneself. Rosanna thought that was what accounted for the crowd's unexpected good mood. It was so simple, not at all the hard and empty road that Catholics would have you believe.

She was neatly dressed, with her hair netted in a bun and a plain hat. She had already made up her mind on her own to give up vanity. Considering the quiet life she now led, it wasn't very difficult. Only this time, when she knew she was going out in public, did her resolution give her trouble. She had prettier dresses and nicer ways of doing her hair and more attractive hats, but that was over for her. And it was a small price to pay. So it was that no one looked at her in this big crowd. That had never happened before, but it was right.

She was grateful to Walter for doing her the favor of holding Joey and having Frankie on the other side of him, so that she could give her attention to Reverend Sunday, who was certainly a dynamic man. There was something reassuring about how he seemed to have seen it all, and these things he was saying were the things he had learned not from books, like Father Berger, but from his own experience. He seemed to be saying that you could do it the easy way or you could do it the hard way, but he was here to tell you that the hard way wasn't worth it in the end. What was that old story, the Parable of the Vineyard? Rosanna had always thought how unfair that was, that the workers who showed up late got in just the same as the workers who showed up early, but she hadn't reckoned with the hardships that the late workers had had to endure before they got to the vineyard. Clearly, a day in the vineyard wasn't terribly easy, but a day outside the vineyard was probably terrifying. She did not exactly listen to Reverend Sunday. It was more that she sat quietly and let his words and actions spark her own thoughts.

It was a show, with singing and a big choir, and other people talking. But that made sense, too. Wasn't Mass a kind of show? She had never thought of it like that. Except that the thing about Mass was that the show was in Latin. A show in English was better at holding her attention. She looked around. That time was starting that Walter's mother had told her about, when Reverend Sunday called out to the audience and people stood up and went forward and presented themselves to be saved, and then the audience got more restive with rejoicing. Walter's mother had said, "Honey, don't get caught up in that. It's not very nice. You can be saved perfectly well without making a spectacle of yourself," and Rosanna had agreed. Now she watched the people moving forward and felt rather sorry for them— there were a couple on crutches, and a boy who was being led by his friend and looked blind. Not everyone was like that—plenty were just normal—but one thing Rosanna was never going to believe in was faith healing. She had to say, though, that Reverend Sunday didn't talk about healing—he talked more about drinking. She sat quietly.

WALTER HADN'T STAYED in a hotel since his return from Europe, and he'd only stayed in a hotel once there. This place in Mason City wasn't at all like that place in Amiens where he had stayed while on leave in France (and didn't know what to do with himself except walk around the town and stare at things that had been there for hundreds of years). And it wasn't that strange place on the park that didn't look like any building Walter had ever seen. It was just a hotel, with a bathroom down the hall, one window looking out onto the street, and two beds. Rosanna had Joey in the other bed, and Walter had this bed to himself. They had let Frankie wrap up in a blanket and sleep on the floor, though not between Walter and the door. Frankie was a wild one, no two ways about that. He made Walter and his brothers look domesticated by comparison.

Probably the street was the reason Walter wasn't sleeping. Cars went up and down the street like you wouldn't believe, all night long, as if these people didn't have anything to do during the day, and maybe they didn't. What did they have to do other than buy and sell the sorts of things Walter produced on his farm—corn and oats, or not those, but pork and chickens and beef and eggs and cream and butter? You walked down the street in a town like Mason City and you wondered what went on there. Walter had become just the sort of curmudgeon he used to disdain his father for being—the farm was the source of all good things, and what you couldn't grow or make there, you didn't need. People in town had too much time on their hands, so they built themselves stores and picture shows and even parks, just to be doing something. But really they weren't doing anything. Just using up stuff. His father's voice went on in his head, but it sounded like his own voice, and it was accompanied by a visceral feeling of injustice that Walter wasn't used to, and probably wouldn't feel if farm prices were higher. Why, for example, was an egg now worth three cents to Dan Crest, but he had to pay seventy-five cents for two boiled eggs for breakfast in this hotel? He didn't know many farmers who went anywhere, but those who did were proud of fixing their own baskets of food, and always said it was better than you could get wherever you were going. And it was. But Walter resented that part of it was that if you were a farmer you couldn't afford decent food, wherever you were going. He fell asleep, and woke up before dawn wondering where he was and what he had to get up and do, but there was nothing. Finally (he could hear by the window), the streets were quiet, but he, of course, couldn't sleep a wink. There were two alternatives for passing the time—worrying about Ragnar and the outside work, or worrying about Irma alone in the house. As dawn broke, it felt like he opted for both.

WHEN FRANK FINALLY WOKE UP and sat up, he said, "What's that?"

Mama said, "That's the town-hall clock, striking eight. You boys slept a long time."

Papa said, "I was up before dawn."

"What time was that?" said Mama.

"Not six, anyway. I heard the clock strike six."

Frank didn't understand time. Mama and Irma showed him on the kitchen clock how the hands went around. If it had been up to him, he would have put the one at the top. He didn't understand why the twelve was there. It was like sledding down a hill—the hand should start with one and go down. When he asked Mama about it, she said that he should think of the twelve as also a zero, even though the only zero on the clock was in the ten. He sometimes sat at his breakfast or dinner gazing at the clock and trying to figure it out. Half of what grown-ups said didn't make much sense, if you asked Frank. For example, he liked stories, but quite often there was some part of the story that just seemed wrong. Irma told him a story called "The Pied Piper of Hamelin." In it, a man comes and plays such a song on his pipe that the rats are driven crazy by it, and they throw themselves into the river. Frank thought that this was just barely possible. The next thing that happens is that the townspeople don't pay him. Frank knew that that could easily happen—Papa talked all the time about whether he was going to get paid for his crops or not. The next thing that happened was that the Pied Piper played a song that made all the children follow him out of town and disappear. Only three boys—one who was lame and couldn't keep up, one who was blind and couldn't see the way, and one who was deaf and couldn't hear the song—stayed behind. It was this part that Frank couldn't accept. What about the boy who just didn't want to? The boy who was contrary? Irma never mentioned that boy, until Frank had spoken up and said, "I wouldn't have gone," and then she just laughed.

"Time to get dressed," said Mama. "The service starts at ten, and I want to walk around for a bit."

"What's for breakfast?" said Joey.

"Plenty of things," said Mama. "Let's go out and have a look."

REVEREND SUNDAY WAS more impatient. He seemed angry, and then it turned out that he was angry at the devil, who was present in the hall and holding people back from the stage. Of course, the devil seemed like a nice enough fellow, said Reverend Sunday, good-natured and whispering doubts in everyone's ears. Simple doubts—my life is pretty good, I like my pleasures, I'm not doing anyone any harm, I've never passed out from drink once in my life, I've got a job or a husband or an automobile or whatever. I'm young—I've got years ahead of me to get this done. The devil always had such a reasonable voice, and so did Reverend Sunday for a while. He said, "I know the devil. The devil is always trying to make himself a friend of mine, and he isn't that, but I know him well." And then his face went dark, and he started arguing with the devil, making the devil tell everyone what Hell was like, how it wasn't a simple place at all, where things were easy enough, it was a terrifying, black, burning place, and you want to talk about having years ahead of you, well, all the years you might waste before you got saved (if you ever did get around to it) were as the blink of an eye compared with those years in Hell—they didn't even have years in Hell, they only had eons. Now he started yelling at the devil, telling him to get out of this room and out of these people and away from Reverend Sunday himself: "Get thee behind me, Satan!" And he turned his back and jumped about, as though Satan were beating him, and then he spun around and raised his arm, and began beating Satan. Next to her on the seat, Joey started crying again, but Rosanna felt she was stuck with her eyes open and her hand on her mouth. The next thing she knew, she was standing up and she had Joey by the hand. As she left the pew, two people reached out for Joey and took him, and a voice said (a kindly voice), "He's too young, ma'am, but you go ahead," and so she did, up the aisle, toward the stage. And Reverend Sunday changed again—after kicking Satan off the stage, he stood in front of them and lifted up his arms and shouted thanks to the Lord for speaking to the people through him.

The crush was suffocating, but reassuring rather than frightening. Men at the end of every row of seats gently guided them and encouraged them, and if someone was stumbling or weeping too much to see where he or she was going, one of these men took the elbow and steadied the person. Up by the stage, there were places to kneel, and then the choir started singing a song Rosanna did not know, but a beautiful one, four-part harmony, and some of the people around her opened their mouths and sang along, knowing the words. What Rosanna said was "Mary Elizabeth, I know you have gone to Heaven now, just now in this last minute, I know you have left my side and gone to Heaven, and that is your home." And for years after that, she remembered that moment when Mary Elizabeth took her arms from around her neck and flew away.

AND SO Rosanna was saved in March—March 24, to be exact— and the baby, Lillian, was born six months to the day and the hour later, September 24 at about eight in the evening, and from the first time Rosanna looked at her (oh, the birth was so easy!), she knew that Lillian was God's own gift to her. Never had she seen such a beautiful baby. Not even Frankie was a patch on her—her mother said so, Granny Elizabeth said so, and Walter just stared at the infant without saying a word. She was a healthy one—plenty of flesh, but not too much, eager to suck, and relaxed in her body. Rosanna had noticed that each baby, even from birth, had a way of being hugged. Frankie's way had been to kick his legs, Joey's way had been to go a bit limp (just a bit, he was fine), and Mary Elizabeth's way had been to remain a little package, allowing the embrace but not yielding to it. These qualities stayed with them. Lillian's way was to relax as if her mother's embrace was just the most wonderful thing she could possibly know. The birth was so easy that Rosanna was wide awake and feeling fine afterward, so once everyone else had gone off to bed, around eleven or so, she sat up, staring at Lillian, who was nestled in her cradle. Walter was bunking in with the boys for the night, so the two of them were alone.

Something no one had mentioned for weeks was that four days would bring them to the first anniversary of Mary Elizabeth's death. Rosanna suspected that at least Walter's mother and maybe a few of the other relatives thought that the brevity of the interval between the death and the birth was a little unseemly, but Rosanna could not possibly see it that way, now that she knew that Mary Elizabeth was looking down upon her and Lillian and blessing them from Heaven. Her cousin had had a baby a year after miscarrying a previous one, and had once said to Rosanna, "Just think, if I hadn't lost that one, I wouldn't have Arne," but Rosanna didn't see this at all like that. She would have had Lillian no matter what, but Lillian would not have been so blessed—she would not have been named Lillian, but probably something like Helen. What happened was that one day in the summer, for some reason, Rosanna kept humming a hymn to herself, it was "God Sees the Little Sparrow Fall," and she paused to attend to the words she was singing—"He paints the lily of the field, / Perfumes each lily bell," and she knew that the baby she was carrying was a girl, and would be named Lillian, even though there wasn't a Lillian to be found anywhere among the Langdons or the Cheeks or the Chicks or the Augsbergers or the Vogels. She never even thought about a name for a boy. Walter didn't say a word when she declared that the baby was a girl, nor did he say what boys' names he liked. And so Lillian had been Lillian—"Lillian Elizabeth"—for months now, at least in Rosanna's mind. Rosanna knew that her mother was superstitious about using a baby's name before he or she was born—she also didn't like this idea of nightly Bible reading—you never did that in the Catholic Church—but Rosanna was finished with that sort of superstition. Lillian was blessed. Mary Elizabeth herself had blessed her.

1927

ოჄჄ

Now that it was January, and Frank was going to school
every day, even in the snow and the cold, he understood many
things better than he had, and it wasn't only ABCs and 123s. The first
thing he understood was that he was taller than the other seven-year-
old boy, Luke Kasten. Luke understood that, too, and stayed out of
his way. He was also taller than the eight-year-old and one of the
nine-year-olds (Donald Guthrie and Matthew Graham). The rest of
the boys (five in number) were taller than he was and stronger, but not
as smart. A couple of the big ones could hardly read, which perplexed
Frank a bit, since reading was the easiest thing in the world. There
were seven girls in the school, all older. The nicest one was Minnie
Frederick, who lived near them and was eight. She sometimes held
his hand if any of the boys happened to bully him. She would say,
"Oh, Frankie, forget them, they're stupid." But Frank wasn't about to
forget a thing—nosirree, as his uncle Rolf would say.

So far, since school started in September, the boys had done six
things to him: Lured him into the coal shed and locked the door on
him. Peeked at him in the privy. Stolen his coat and kept it for the
entire very rainy day. Splashed mud on him by stomping in a pud-
dle. Kicked him. Poured dirt down the back of his pants. It wasn't as
though Frank was the only victim—the big boys had done ten things
to Luke Kasten, nine things to Matthew Graham, and six things to

Donald Guthrie. Maybe those boys were not keeping track, but Frank was, because keeping track was easy for him. Wasn't he already doing multiplication? As for Miss Jenkins, the teacher, she was always peering at them the way Irma had done before Irma got her glasses, so Frank was pretty sure that she couldn't see much of anything. Maybe, like Irma, she didn't know she needed glasses—what Irma said was "Leaves! Birds! I never saw any of those before!" Or maybe she didn't have the money; glasses were expensive, according to Mama, who told Irma that if she lost hers she didn't know how they would afford another pair. Anyway, the boys who couldn't be seen in the back rows or at the far end of the schoolyard were getting up to plenty of trouble, climbing trees and pelting each other with acorns and worse. And then, today, at the end of recess, when Frank was just standing there, Bobby Dugan and Howie Prince had run up to him, pushed him flat on his back, rubbed his face with snow, and run away laughing. Frank was keeping track.

Aside from Minnie Frederick, two of the girls were nothing much to look at, two were big and imposing (they reminded him of Eloise), and two were very pretty. One of these was Alice Canham and the other was her sister, Marie. Alice was nine and never looked at him. Marie was ten and thought he was a pest. The only pretty girl who liked him was Minnie, but she liked him a lot. Her father's farm was on his way to school, big, three hundred acres, and paid off. Frank had heard Mama and Papa talk about "the Frederick place," but the Fredericks were Quakers, so they didn't visit much back and forth. But that was a great thing, to say what Papa said, "free and clear." And Minnie's ma was known all over for her baking. All the farm ladies were proud of their baking, but Mrs. Frederick tried special things—not just bread and pies and pound cake, but drop doughnuts and cookies that Minnie brought to school and shared. When Minnie had a birthday in November, her mother sent a checkerboard cake, where all the slices were laid out on the plate like a checkerboard, chocolate and white. Frank thought this was wonderfully luxurious, but it was just the sort of thing that Mama did not have time for and Granny Mary and Granny Elizabeth thought was silly. And so Frank was friends with Minnie, also because Minnie held up her head and stabbed those big boys with her always sharpened pencils if they gave her any trouble.

Frank stood up, brushed the snow off as best he could, and made his way toward the schoolhouse door, where Miss Jenkins was ringing the bell. She peered at him as he came toward her, then said, "Young Frank, best to develop a habit of promptitude early in your life. You'll never regret it!" As he entered the school door, she followed right behind him, but she didn't say a word about the snow and water dripping off his backside. All through reading and arithmetic, and then when they ate their lunches and progressed through singing and spelling, Frank dried without once shivering, and pondered his plan. This was episode four for Bobby Dugan and episode three for Howie Prince, and that was just counting what they'd done to *him*. All told, Bobby went after someone or other once or twice a week, and Howie helped him at least half of those times. Bobby most often helped an even bigger boy, Dallas Coggins, but Dallas was home with the grippe. Dallas did something to someone almost every day—sometimes his victim was Bobby, in fact. But Dallas was fourteen. Fourteen was two times seven. Frank didn't think he stood much of a chance against Dallas.

The good thing was that Frank sat behind Bobby and could watch him without being noticed. He could also see into his desk whenever Bobby opened it. It was a mess in there. But looking in there gave Frank a perfect idea, and an easy one, too.

When he got home from school, it was still light. Mama was walking back and forth in the front room with Lillian in her arms, watching for him out the window, as she did every afternoon. He only had to walk a quarter-mile on his own, and that was on the road—the rest of the way, he walked with Minnie, Matthew Graham, and Leona Graham, who was thirteen, one of the plain girls. From the schoolhouse to the Grahams' was through the fields, but Mr. Graham took the horses out and stamped down the snow for them. With Minnie, he went another bit, and then Minnie's ma, in her apron, watched him until he was well on his way and could see his own barn.

He stepped onto the porch; Mama set Lillian in her downstairs cradle, opened the front door, and helped him off with his boots. Joe came out of the kitchen, his thumb in his mouth, but didn't say anything. No, he did not want anything to eat. Yes, he had had a good day at school. Frank knew he couldn't express any desire to go to the barn or even to go upstairs; Mama was suspicious of his motives at all times. She said, "You carry your coat through the house and hang it in the back hall, Frankie." It was when he was doing this that he saw it—one he had forgotten—a nice-sized mousetrap, big enough to hurt but small enough to go into the desk, in a dark corner. He looked at it, but he didn't touch it, because Joey was right behind him.

Joey had a way of sensing that Frank was up to something, so, for the rest of the evening, when Frank was in the house, Joe was right beside him. Frank did look for other traps when he was out helping Papa and Ragnar with the cows and the horses and the sheep, but the traps he saw were too big—he could tell just by looking that he wouldn't be able to hide one of them in Bobby's desk. Papa wouldn't let him out of his sight, either, just like the others. Frank was patient. Nobody thought he was patient; someone was always saying, "Hold your horses, Frankie." But he had stores of patience they could not understand if there was something he really, really wanted to do.

It was when he was getting ready in the morning for his walk to school that he managed to kick the mousetrap very gently with his toe. It snapped, the bait jumped, and Frank slipped it into his pocket. He could feel it—the edge of the trap was sharp, and the spring (he could tell by the way it snapped) was a good one. He buttoned his coat, went out on the porch for his boots, and then put on his hat and mittens. Mama stood just inside the door, holding Lillian and keeping out of the wind. She kissed him goodbye. The last thing she did was to look right at him and say, "If you've got some mischief in your head, young man, get rid of it."

Frank returned her gaze and shook his head. Then he said, "I'm good, Mama. Miss Jenkins played the piano yesterday and let me sing the verses all by myself. Everyone else did the chorus."

"Well, stay good, then," said Mama, before slamming the door. But even after she went inside, he didn't put his hand in his pocket. At Minnie's, Mrs. Frederick gave him a sugared doughnut "to keep him warm," and they trotted onward to the Graham farm. It was cold enough so that the snow was hard, but not that cold. Minnie didn't try to hold his hand. Frank was not sure she had seen him get pushed down the day before.

He decided that he had to keep quiet, but not strangely quiet, and he did—he spoke when spoken to and did what he was told, and when something the other boys thought was funny happened, he laughed with them. Already, after only four months of school, he saw that if you didn't laugh when the others laughed, they hated you all the more. So he was required to laugh when Bobby tripped Alice Canham as she was making her way back from the pencil sharpener. Right after lunch, he had a moment alone in the classroom, during which he set the trap and placed it in his own desk, ready for business.

The problem was that Miss Jenkins lined them up and herded them everywhere—into the classroom in the morning, out for recess, back in, back out, back in, then dressed and out the door for home. Yes, she couldn't see much, but she would see him go into Bobby's desk. That night, Frank lay awake in his bed next to Joey, trying to think of something, but he fell asleep.

He had never paid much attention to Bobby Dugan—he'd only tried to stay out of his way—but now he watched him carefully. The first thing he saw was that Bobby rolled and smoked a cigarette with Dallas and Howie during recess, out by the corner of the schoolyard. They did it again after eating their lunches. Frank didn't know anyone who smoked. He also saw Bobby go into the privy and come out after spending a long time there. When Frank went into the privy sometime later, he stayed long enough to look all around. He stood on the seat on his tiptoes, reached up, and felt where the roof came down to meet the wall. He found the box of tobacco and matches pushed to the back of the space there.

First thing in the morning when he got to school, he went up to Miss Jenkins and whispered that he wasn't feeling well, and might have to go to the privy. Since it was a very cold day, could he keep his coat on in class? Miss Jenkins felt his head, and Frank said, "Mama says I don't have a fever."

"No, you don't. Well, we'll see how you feel. If you need to go home at lunchtime, we'll see."

When Miss Jenkins had some older kids at the reading table, Frank slipped the mousetrap into his pocket, then he huddled at his desk for the first hour, all through geography. Just at the right moment, he thought, he staggered out of the room and headed for the privy. He went in and closed the door. He climbed onto the seat, carefully set the trap, and placed it on the box of tobacco, a little pushed back. He coughed a few times and, once back in the schoolroom, staggered to his seat. In the next half-hour, he revived; by lunchtime, he had removed his coat and hung it on his hook.

After lunch, it worked perfectly. Dallas stole Leona Graham's cookie, and instead of eating it, crushed it under his toe in the snow, laughing; then he, Howie, and Bobby set off for their spot, even though Miss Jenkins called after them. Bobby headed toward the privy on the way. Sure enough, moments after he disappeared, Frank heard a yelp and then some bad words. Miss Jenkins went to the door of the privy, and when Bobby came out with his fingers in his mouth, she said that she would have to make a report to his father. Then she saw the box in his hand, and held out her own. He reluctantly gave it to her. She opened it and saw the papers and the tobacco. She started shaking her head. After that, Bobby didn't come to school for a month. Minnie told him that Bobby's dad had him cleaning hog pens the whole time.

WELL, that dog had puppies. Mama didn't find them for almost two weeks, but Joe knew they were there. He had been going behind the barn and watching them for ten days by that time. There were five of them—there had been seven, but two died, and Joe dug a little hole under the Osage-orange hedge, on the far side, where he knew no one would go, and wrapped each puppy in a handkerchief that he took out of the washing, and buried them together. Even Frankie didn't see him or know what he was doing, and for sure, Joe did not want Frankie to find the puppies, so he kept them as the best secret he'd ever had.

The dog was a stray—when it came around during the fall plowing, Mama thought sure it was carrying something, rabies maybe, and she wanted Papa to shoot it, but Papa said it looked like a shepherd of some sort, and then, in the winter, when the sheep were outside, the dog was good at bringing them in. It was brown and white, with one blue eye. Joe petted it on the head when no one was looking, and sometimes the dog swished its long tail when it saw Joe, but the dog seemed to know that their friendship was a secret. He named the dog "Pal," but he never said that name aloud. After the puppies were born, Joe brought the dog things from time to time—half of his sausage from dinner, a hard-boiled egg from breakfast, a piece of bacon. Mama didn't see everything, and neither did Frankie, and that was a fact.

Joe squatted a little ways from the nest the dog had made, with his hands on his knees, and stared. One puppy was almost all white, two were brown and white like the mother, and two were all brown with white toes. Their ears were back and their noses were always pointed in the air, and their tails were very short, like little worms. They whimpered. Papa thought that the dog had gone down the road to find another place to live.

Then one night, Joe happened to kick Frankie in his sleep. Frankie woke Joe up and said, "I know about those puppies. And if I tell, they'll be drowned in the pond, you'll see." But Mama found them on her own—she'd walked around the barn with some shears and a basket, to cut lilacs off the bushes that ran along the fence line. Joe saw her from a distance—he was loitering with his boiled potato in his pocket, waiting for a moment to go see the puppies. But he saw Mama stand up straight and turn her head. She looked up and down and then walked toward the back of the barn. Joe crept along behind her. She set down her basket and went over to the siding where it was broken, and she bent down.

Joe trotted up behind her, and when he saw that she had found the puppies and Pal, he said, "What's that?"

Mama put her hand on his chest and pushed him backward. She said, "That awful cur had puppies. I thought she'd gone off. Well, your papa is going to have to do something about this!"

"Why?"

"Because there's just no telling what those things are crawling with—worms, for sure. I knew letting that dog stay around would lead to no good."

"Papa said she was a pretty good dog—"

"And the next thing you know, she'll find her way into the house. This is something I'm going to nip in the bud." She spun around. "What are you doing?"

"Nothing. I saw you—"

"Joey, you are the sneakiest boy I ever saw. Half the time, Frankie gets up to no good, but at least he's noisy and doesn't creep around, scaring your wits out of you."

Joey apologized.

Mama said, "Here, you can carry the basket. I need to get back before Lillian wakes up from her nap." They went over to the row of lilac bushes, and Joey walked along, holding the basket in both hands, as Mama snipped off the purple flowers with a few of the smooth dark-green leaves and dropped them in. The fragrance floated in the air all around him. As they were working, two cars passed on the road, and their drivers waved—Mrs. Frederick in a Franklin and Mrs. Carson in a Ford. Joey liked cars. Beyond the road, the field of oats was greened over with thick shoots. When she was finished, Mama put the shears in the pocket of her apron and took the basket from him. He said, "I could sell them. The puppies."

"Oh, for Heaven's sakes. Not in a blue moon."

"They are good puppies."

They walked silently for eight or ten steps; then she stopped, turned toward him, and bent down. She said, "How long have you known about the puppies?"

"A long time."

"Did you tell Papa?"

Joe shook his head.

"Why not?"

"Papa will drown them and shoot the dog."

"As well he should. Did you ever touch the dog or the puppies?"

Joe shook his head.

"Should I believe you?"

Joe shrugged.

"Well, that's honest, at least."

Joe turned away and walked toward the barn. He had to, because he was starting to cry, and Mama hated that. He heard her shout, "Don't you touch those dirty things!"

He knew he should have confessed about burying the dead puppies, but he didn't dare. And anyway, he had touched them only with the handkerchiefs and washed his hands many times since that day, which was a week ago.

Back at the barn, Pal was lying in the nest she'd made, and the puppies were lined up along her belly, suckling, brown, white, brown and white, brown and white, brown. He did something he knew he should not have: he said names, though only in a whisper,

"Brownie, Milk, Sugar, Spot, Bill." Frankie would think they were stupid names, but Joe liked them. He squatted there and watched the puppies for the rest of the afternoon, and Mama could have dragged him away by the ear if she wanted, but she never did. The funny thing was that, when Ragnar and Papa came home to do the evening work, they left him alone, too. At suppertime, he went in the house. Nothing was said about the puppies, though Irma kept tsking over her fried chicken and wouldn't look at him. Night came, and some Bible reading, and then bed. He knew that when he got up in the morning and went outside the puppies would be gone, and Pal, too. And they were. A little while later, Mama said that Granny Elizabeth had some kittens, and would he like one? There was a pretty calico with a mark like an exclamation point on her back. Joe said no.

A little while after that, Papa sat down with him on the top step of the back porch. He cleared his throat about six times and then said, "Joey, I knew those puppies were there. I didn't know you knew."

"I knew." Then, "They were good puppies."

"Maybe. Hard to tell. The female might have been useful if she hadn't had those pups."

"Mama hated her."

"Mama didn't hate her. But Mama knows that a stray dog can have something, something bad. Distemper or milk fever, or even rabies or something like that. Even if you or Frankie or Lillian didn't get something bad from the dog, the cows could, or the sheep or the hogs. I don't know, Joey. I don't know."

"Did you shoot her?"

Papa didn't answer.

Joe got up and went into the house.

1928

~~~

After harvest, Walter and Ragnar, with help from Rolf, Kurt, and John, put an addition on the west side of the house, a room for Frankie and Joey, so that Lillian could have their room. Walter couldn't afford a two-story addition—if the boys wanted Rosanna or Walter, they had to go through the front room and call up the stairs—but Frank was eight by the time it was finished and they moved in, and hadn't John and Gus been sleeping downstairs, on the back sleeping porch, off the kitchen of Rosanna's parents' house, since Gus was five and John was seven?

Walter put two windows in the south side of the addition, and a window on the west side, but no window into the north side. He also studded out a future opening so that one day he could install a door, but just the thought of Frankie with a door to call his own made him nervous. He had not spared the rod, and he had not, therefore, spoiled the child, but Frankie was the most determined child he had ever seen, far surpassing himself, Howard, Rolf, and everyone else on Rosanna's side of the family. It was as if, when he saw certain things, his brain simply latched on to them and would not let them go. It wasn't even contrariness. Half the time, Walter could say, "Frankie, don't do that," and Frankie wouldn't do whatever it was, because he didn't care about it. The other half of the time, it didn't matter what Walter said, or even what Frankie said.

There was a bucket of three-and-a-half-inch nails. Walter said, "Frankie, leave the nails alone."

"Okay, Papa."

"I mean it."

"Yes, Papa."

An hour later, the bucket of nails was turned over, and Frankie was sifting through them.

"Frankie, I told you not to touch the nails."

"I wanted to find something."

"What?"

"A longer nail."

"I told you not to touch the nails."

"But I wanted to find it."

"I forbade you."

"But I wanted to find it."

"Did you find it?"

"No."

"Now I have to give you a whipping." And then he took off his belt and grasped the buckle, and holding Frankie by the upper arm, had him take down his pants.

"What did I tell you?" Whack.

"Not to touch the nails." Whack.

"If I tell you not to touch the nails, you are not to touch the nails." Whack.

"I wanted to find it." Whack.

"What do I do if I tell you not to touch the nails and you touch the nails?" Whack.

"Whip me." Whack.

"Why did you touch the nails?" Whack.

"I wanted to find it." Whack.

"Are you going to do that again if I tell you not to?" Whack.

"No, Papa." Whack.

But of course he did. Nails, after all, were not the same as crawling under the front porch, or climbing to the very top of the tree, or standing on the roof of the house, or dropping from the hay loft (where he was not supposed to be in the first place) onto Jake's back. What would happen if they got electricity (that was the rumor lately, especially since they were so close to town; it was expensive but worth it, everyone said), Walter could only imagine. For Frankie, the wires would be a constant temptation just to try this with a screwdriver or that with a fork. It seemed as though Frankie had to be taught every single lesson in every variation. And, yes, Miss Jenkins, over at the school, said that Frankie was the smartest child she had ever seen in her life, and was on to division, not to mention training for the spelling bee at the end of the school year ("And I do not know who is going to give him any competition"). Certainly, he went to school willingly and even enthusiastically every morning, so that was something to be thankful for.

Walter didn't know what to make of his two boys. If you looked at it a certain way, then the one who needed the beatings to toughen him up, namely Joey, never did a thing to earn a beating, because he hadn't the gumption, and the one who got the beatings learned nothing from them. Looking back on his own childhood, Walter saw a much more orderly system: His father or mother told them the rules. If they got out of line, even not intending to, they got a whipping to help them remember the next time, and they did remember the next time, and so they got fewer beatings, and so they became boys who could get the work done, and since there was plenty of it, it had to get done. That was life, as far as Walter was concerned—you surveyed the landscape and took note of what was needed, and then you did it, and the completed tasks piled up behind you like a kind of treasure, or at least evidence of virtue. What life was for Frankie he could not imagine.

What life was for Lillian was color. As soon as the boys moved out of that bedroom, Rosanna drove into town and went to Dan Crest's and bought a half-gallon of pink paint, and then she painted Lillian's walls pink. When the paint was dry, she put up curtains she had made, pink and white stripes with white ruffles all around the edge. Then it turned out that Granny Mary and her sister had spent the whole winter braiding and sewing a rag rug—pink, white, and green, for Lillian's room, an oval ten feet long—and his own mother had crocheted her a pink bedcover. Rosanna then framed profiles of people and animals she had cut out of paper—a farmer, his wife, a cow, a horse, a pig, a lamb, a rabbit, a squirrel, a fox, and a bird—and hung them on the walls. It took her two full days to fix up the room.

For certain, it was now the nicest room in the house, nicer than the front room, even. But this was not for the neighbors. Walter could see that when he stopped at the top of the stairs on the morning the room was finished and watched Rosanna through the doorway, holding the seventeen-month-old Lillian on her hip and going from picture to picture, saying, "And on his farm, he had a what? A pig! Yes! What a good girl!"

ROLAND FREDERICK GOT himself a tractor. It was a Farmall, gray, small, and nimble, with the two front wheels close together, kind of like a tricycle, and Walter could hear it when the wind was right. Two times in the same week, when he was out in the field behind the Osage-orange hedge, he could see it, too, making its compact and noisy way across Roland's western forty acres. The next time he went to town, he got the story.

The Farmall man, coming into Denby, looking around and see-ing who had the biggest house and the nicest barn, had offered to let Roland try the tractor out for a week. He ended up leaving it there for ten days, and, not having heard from Roland, he took a driver out to get it and drive it into town. But Roland was nowhere to be found, and the tractor, sitting in front of the barn, couldn't be turned on—no gasoline—so the Farmall man left Roland a note, saying he would be back the next day.

Sure enough, that very afternoon, Walter saw and heard Roland—moving rather fast, Walter thought—finishing up his planting, and without any horses or help. It was a lot of noise, but Walter was impressed. His own farm was only half the size of Roland's, and he planted much less corn, but he and Ragnar were not more than half done—the wires were up for the last part of the field, but he hadn't drilled the corn yet. After watching Roland, or, rather, the tractor with the minuscule bent figure of Roland sitting in the seat, make its way across the horizon, he went into the barn.

Of course Jake and Elsa were there, and of course they nickered to him (it was suppertime, at least as far as they were concerned). Elsa was fifteen this year and Jake was thirteen—grayed out now, almost pure white. His father had given them to him when he came back from the war, and they were six and four then, strong, handsome, darkly dappled, and well behaved, a prize team. That very year,

Roland Frederick had had a team of young Shires drag his plow into a deep ditch. One of the horses had broken a leg, and the plow had been rendered unusable—Roland had had to borrow someone else's to finish for the year. Walter and his father had considered themselves a little superior to Roland that time, because they had the sense to breed Percherons, and good lines, too. In fact, given Roland Frederick's lack of feel for horses, it wasn't a surprise that he was riding the first tractor Walter had ever seen. Walter went back outside and watched until he couldn't make out anything more in the twilight, and then headed to the house for supper.

He couldn't imagine what a tractor might cost. A thousand dollars? If so, that was a year's income for him, minus the $268 he had spent on putting up the new addition to the house. And even though his father was talking about getting out of the horse-breeding business, Elsa wasn't that old—he could either put her in foal to his father's stallion now, and have himself a horse ready to work in four years, when Jake was seventeen and Elsa was nineteen—or he could buy one or two of his father's colts and raise them. Just thinking about these ideas was reassuring. How long would a tractor last? No one knew. He washed his hands in the pail of water Rosanna had left by the dry sink on the back porch, and kicked off his boots, thinking with satisfaction that he had things figured out.

At the supper table, over Rosanna's meatloaf, he said to Frankie and Joey, "Did you boys see Mr. Frederick's tractor?"

"I heard it," said Rosanna. "Noisy thing! Don't know how he can stand sitting on the seat in the middle of all that racket."

"I saw it," said Frankie.

"How'd you manage that?" said Walter.

Frankie shrugged.

Up in the hayloft, thought Walter, but he didn't press it. He said, "What did you think?"

Joey said, "Is Mr. Frederick going to shoot his horses now?"

"Oh, for goodness' sake," said Rosanna.

"Send 'em to the slaughter, more likely," said Ragnar.

"He's only got two, and they're old," said Walter. "If he buys that tractor, he can turn them out. He's got plenty of grass for two horses in among the cows."

"If we got a tractor, would you shoot Jake and Elsa?" said Joey.

"No," said Walter. "Anyway, I prefer horses. This is what horses do. You boys listening?"

Joey and Frankie nodded.

"Every spring, horses pull the plow and then the planter, and so they plant their own oats. In the summer, they pull the thresher. What's the thresher, Frankie?"

"The thresher takes the oats from the straw. This summer, I'm going to ride the thresher, and make the oats go into the wagon."

"That's right. So, when the oats are threshed, then the horses are fixing their own supper, and when the oats and hay are hauled to the barn, the horses are putting their supper away. Then what happens?"

The boys' mouths had opened a little bit.

Walter said, "In the winter, the horses take their own manure out and spread it on the oat field. What does that do?"

"Fertilize!" shouted Frankie.

"So where do the horses go to get food?"

"Out to the barn," said Joey.

"Right where they put it," said Walter. "Where does Mr. Frederick go to get gas for the tractor?"

This was a stumper.

Neither boy knew the answer.

Walter ate a bite of meatloaf and some potato, and said, "Texas. And, boys, if you have to go to Texas for something, you don't need it."

He of course spoke with a good deal of self-satisfaction. But he knew anyway that that tractor was going to buzz around his head like a pesky fly, and it did, all night long, in and out of all sorts of dreams that otherwise had nothing in common with one another.

ROSANNA KNEW that not only Walter, but Granny Elizabeth and all of the Langdons would be upset when they heard the news, so she didn't exactly tell them. Instead, she got up early that Sunday morning and had breakfast all made by six—a good breakfast, too, pancakes and some raspberries she went out and picked off the bushes, bacon, and oatmeal with sprinklings of brown sugar, because Walter couldn't start his day without oatmeal. Then, while they were eating, she laid out the boys' Sunday best, which she had spent an hour the previous afternoon ironing, and of course they all thought they were heading off to their own Methodist church in town, where all the Langdons had gone forever, the same church that Rosanna had once considered radically Protestant and fearsome. But no, she said, after she had Lillian dressed in a beautiful green dress with a white pinafore (she herself was dressed very plainly, in a flat sort of blue dress, with her hair in a secure bun), they were going a bit farther afield, just to try it out, to the Assemblies of God church in Usherton.

"Usherton!" Walter scowled. "That's—"

"Eleven miles door to door," said Rosanna. "Twenty minutes, and right on the north end of Second Street. We passed it two weeks ago, when we went to the picture show." Walter had wanted to go to the picture show and see Buster Keaton in *Steamboat Bill, Jr.* Rosanna, knowing this was an opportunity to look for the church, had gone along, not said a word about missing their Bible reading for that night. Even so, she wasn't quite sure about the right way to think of pictures.

"Well, I—"

"We need to try it," said Rosanna. "We need to." And she spoke with such a tremor in her voice (not intended) that Walter didn't even finish his sentence.

From the moment Walter started organizing the boys, and then Ragnar, around the prospect of being gone for almost three hours rather than just over one, like most Sundays, Rosanna could feel herself relaxing. The fact was, Rosanna had been feeling in danger lately—more and more every day and week—and her own avid Bible reading did not ease her feeling. She had tried several methods—starting at the beginning and reading, opening at random, looking for familiar stories and starting with the passage Pastor Gordon used in his Sunday sermon. But she always foundered sooner or later. When she began at the beginning, she could not get past the shoals of names and genealogies, because she didn't know if there was more there than met the eye. Opening at random could be enlightening, but more often than not it was confusing—what was she to make of opening somewhere in Leviticus and reading all those rules she couldn't understand? But, then, Jesus did some unaccountable things, too—not miracles, like the loaves and the fishes, but denouncing that tree because it wouldn't give him fruit. Catholics did not read the Bible, were not even allowed to read the Bible, and surely this was the reason. In the Catholic Church, it was all laid out for you in the missal and the progression from one holy day to the next, and everything made sense, but, then again, you were not saved in the Catholic Church—she knew that—so mere intelligibility wasn't enough. Pastor Gordon's sermons were very dry, almost always about either brotherly love or service to the community, and never once about salvation, the feeling of salvation, as if Pastor Gordon hadn't yet experienced that feeling. So—nothing there.

What she needed was for Walter, and especially Frankie and Joey, to be saved, as she had been, and they were not going to get that from the First Methodist Church (never followed by a second one) of Denby, Iowa. But she had overheard Lucy Morgan and Dan Crest talking at the store about the Assembly of God, and the pastor there, Roger Elmore, a personal friend of someone named E. N. Bell, who was famous and important in some way that Rosanna didn't understand but appreciated anyway. "And also a fiery preacher," said Lucy. "Set 'em all alight, even the icy ones!" and Dan Crest laughed. Rosanna knew that that was what Walter needed. And the boys needed to do more in Sunday school than fill in the stripes of Joseph's coat of many colors.

It was a beautiful day, especially for late June, not very hot and with a little breeze. Walter never minded a drive once you got him off the farm—he liked to see that he was further along in his work, or at least that it was done more properly, than at the farms along the way. They skirted their own town, so it was all farms and fields until they got to the Iowa River. It was shady right around there, and a minute or two later, they came to the church. Only then, as they were driving down that street, did Rosanna remember that she knew no one in the church—not even Lucy Morgan, if it came to that, because her mother knew Lucy Morgan, but Rosanna had only ever spoken to her one time. It occurred to Rosanna that she should have told Lucy Morgan that she would like to visit her church.

They parked down the street, and walked back toward the church building, which wasn't terribly big. Lillian insisted on walking and not being carried, but she put her hand in Rosanna's very obediently and asked no questions—she was such a good child. It was as if she knew where they were going, and that she would be welcomed there. Semiconsciously, Rosanna slowed her steps so that Lillian preceded her just a tiny bit, so that Lillian's beautiful and shining face would be the first one someone might see.

Walter caught up with her and said, "Joey, stay with Mama." To Rosanna, he said, "Got a handful back here," and Rosanna could hear that he did—"Where are we going? Is Granny Elizabeth here? I told Granny Elizabeth—Don't hold me, I can walk by myself!" Rosanna looked down and said, "Joseph, take your thumb out of your mouth." He did, but his thumb was pink and wet. An embarrassment. Now they were right in front of the church.

It was so hard to go in. It was a small church—there were only two steps up to the porch, and the double doors were closed, which meant that the service had probably commenced. Besides hardly ever knowing what time it was, Rosanna always underestimated how long it would take to get ready and then go somewhere.

Walter said, "This is it, right?"

"Maybe."

"Well, it says right here that it is." He pointed to a small plaque beside the double doors.

"I'm sure we're late."

"Not that late. Maybe a minute or two late, if the service starts on the hour." He and Frankie went up the two steps, and he put his hand on the door pull. Rosanna felt herself step back. It was like magic, like something about the church was pushing her away. The doors looked terribly closed and forbidding, and as hard as she had tried, the five of them looked like rubes, especially her, dowdy, and as homemade as cornmeal mush. She shook her head and said, "We're too late."

Walter muttered something that she couldn't quite make out, but then she heard Frankie say "Damn it" and was sure he was echoing his father's words.

She exclaimed, "Frankie! What a naughty thing!" Frankie looked up at Walter. Walter stayed still for a moment, then said, "Well, are we going in? We're dressed to the eyeballs here."

Rosanna felt as if something terrifying was about to happen, but she couldn't imagine what—a warm Sunday morning on a quiet street in Usherton, hardly an automobile going by, the maples planted along the sidewalks just trembling slightly in the breeze, leaves rattling the way they did when they got a little dry. Rosanna removed her hand from Joey's and lifted it toward her face; Joey grabbed her skirt. Was her fear zinging to him, or was his fear zinging to her? As a side thought, was this what Joey felt like all the time? That had never occurred to her before. She glanced down at him.

And then both of the doors flew open, and two men in nice clothes stepped out and wedged them. After that, the congregation started emerging in small groups. The first four or five people paused and waited, and then the pastor, Rosanna suspected, came, stood by the door, and held out his hand for people to shake as they wished him a good day. It was then that Lillian dropped her hand and climbed the steps, and the group of people stepped aside and made way for her. She held herself straight. One woman said, "Oh, isn't she cute?" and a man said, "What's your name, little girl?" and Lillian said, "I am Lillian, how are you?" Several people chuckled, and another woman said, "Lovely child," and at that point, Walter stepped forward and held out his hand to the pastor. "Don't mean to get in the way, sir. We were hoping to attend the service," and that first lady said, "And a little child shall lead them," and pretty soon, Walter had ascertained that the next service would begin in half an hour, and they were certainly welcome. Rosanna walked out of her fear as if it were a booth set beside the curb, and her skin tingled with pleasure as she followed Lillian and Walter up the steps.

A young man showed them to a pew about halfway down the aisle, and they sat there—even Frankie was quiet enough—looking around as the congregation entered for the next service. Rosanna had Lillian beside her, between herself and Walter, and Rosanna stared at her blond hair sparkling in the light that poured through the windows. It shook her a little—just a little—to have given birth to this being. She glanced at Walter. He was looking around as if he didn't know what was happening. But Rosanna did know. She did know, even if she had to keep it to herself.

LILLIAN WAS SITTING in her very own chair, and her dolls were sitting in front of her. Each had a teacup, and two of them, Lolly and Lizzie, had saucers. Lillian gave Lolly a cookie in her saucer, and then gave Lizzie a cookie in her saucer. After pausing a moment, and saying, "Thank you, you're welcome," twice, Lillian picked up the two cookies and took a small bite out of each one. Then she set them down again and said, "Oh, deshilus thank you." Now she picked up her tea-pot and very carefully poured make-believe tea into each teacup, one for Lolly, one for Lizzie, one for Mamie, one for Dula, one for Frances, and one for Jewel. Jewel and Mamie had tiny little hands, so she leaned forward and pushed one of their hands through the handles of the teacups in front of them. Jewel's dangled, but Mamie held her cup pretty well. Lillian thought a moment, then said, "And how are you, I am fine. A pig got in the house, but then it jumped out the window!"

Lillian laughed.

Dula, who couldn't sit up very well, fell over. Lillian sat her up again, propped against Lizzie, who was the biggest of the dolls and had shoes. As she propped Dula up, she said, "Don't be sick, Dula." She made a gagging noise and said, "Oh dear, oh dear, you will feel better in a minute." She slid her toe out very slowly and gently knocked Dula over. She said, "Oh, Dula could be worse." Then she leaned forward and picked the doll up and cradled her in her arms. She began to sing her a song—"Laalalala Babybaby." Then she stood up and carried Dula over to the cradle, laid her in it, and covered her up.

She went back to the tea party and resumed her seat. She said, "More tea, oh, thank you, thank you. Have another cookie." She leaned forward and took careful, small bites out of Lizzie's cookie, then Lolly's. "Mmmm, yes, thank you. You won't believe what the pig did."

1929

ONE DAY in February, Irma and Ragnar asked to have three days off in a row. Rosanna suspected that something was up, but Irma was not showing, so the only thing she said to Walter was that she could manage—the cows weren't producing much milk at this time of year, so making the butter wasn't hard, and Joey could gather the eggs—he was good at it, and didn't ever startle the hens. They left on a Wednesday and returned Saturday night, so that Walter and Rosanna would be free to go to church on Sunday. On Monday, Ragnar came to Walter and said that he had found a job at the veterinary school at Iowa State College, and he and Irma would be leaving in two weeks.

Walter attempted to conceal his irritation. Ragnar was—what?—thirty-two now, and his English was pretty good. Walter had gotten used to treating him like a relation, which meant giving him lots of work and little free time. Rosanna had been whispering for a year that Irma was unhappy on the farm, and so none of this was surprising. He said, "What's your job?"

"Cleaning up the pens, for now."

"You can do that here."

"*Ja,* but Irma, she got job, too. Cooking at the Delta Delta Delta house there. I will also be having gardening chores there."

Walter said what he felt, which was "Sounds like the life of Riley."

"*Ja,*" said Ragnar. He shrugged. Walter didn't ask what he and Irma were going to be paid. It was certainly more than he paid them. Two weeks later, they were gone.

A week after that, it was time to plant the oats. Walter had burned off the cornstalks from that field, and disked in the nicely charred remains. His father had always said that if you could manage to burn over a cornfield once it was harvested and the stalks were dried up, the boost you got for the soil was a measurable one—the oats would be plumper, and there would be more of them—but burning over the field depended so on the weather that he couldn't do it every year. This year the weather had been right, and so that forty acres was perfect—flat and smooth, with no ridges. He hitched Jake and Elsa to the end-gate seeder, and as he drove from fence to fence, Frankie fed the oat seed into the hopper. Frankie at nine was big and strong. They did it on a Saturday, March 2, just about perfect. Then Frankie hayed the horses all by himself, climbing up the ladder into the loft and forking down bunches of the still-golden stalks. On the way into the house for supper, Walter said, "You did a good job today, Frankie. It's going to be more work now that Ragnar's gone."

"Who's going to get that room?"

"I can't make any promises."

"Joey kicks all night, and he talks in his sleep, too."

"Maybe you need Ragnar and Irma's bed. That would solve the kicking problem."

"Not the talking problem."

"We'll see. But your mama needs someone to help. She's always had either Irma or Eloise."

"Who would come?"

"Maybe Cousin Berta."

"Who's that?"

"Berta Augsberger, she was. Berta Haas. She's a cousin in Nebraska. Second cousin. Her husband died."

"What of?"

"Tick fever."

"Was he a farmer?"

"Well, they lost the farm, but yes."

"If Cousin Berta helps Mama, who helps you?"

Walter stopped and put his hand on Frankie's shoulder. Then he said, "You do, Frankie."

In spite of himself, Walter pronounced this as if it were bad news. He spoke as if he expected Frankie to scowl and rebel, and maybe he did—not because Frankie seemed to dislike farming or the farm, but because Frankie was rebellious. Frankie looked up at him, then looked around, out past the barn to the fields. All Frankie said was "May I have some new boots?"

Walter laughed and said, "I'll order you some."

AFTER THEY PLANTED the oats, Frank helped Papa spade up Mama's garden, and then he helped plant some good things in it: peas, cabbage, onions, potatoes, carrots; later, tomatoes, radishes, beans, and corn. Frank knew that Papa thought he should mind about all this work, but he didn't. Everybody, including Frank, was well aware that he couldn't sit still no matter how many times he was told to settle down, so being given stuff to fiddle with was better than looking for trouble on his own. You want to get into the hayloft—well, get up there twice a day, or more, and throw down the hay. You want to mess with the horses? Well, learn how to help harness Jake and Elsa and drive them in a straight line across the field. You like to dig holes? Well, dig them the proper depth and put something in them, like seed. You like to shoot? Well, shoot a rabbit, and Mama will make rabbit stew, or shoot that coyote that's trying to get into the chicken house. You don't have anything to do before school, so you are sitting in your chair at the table, kicking the rungs? Get up an hour earlier and help milk the cows. You want fried chicken for supper? Go out and catch a chicken and wring its neck—you'll have to learn sometime.

It wasn't easy, but Papa turned out to be not as remote and gruff as Frank had feared he would be. Now, when he was showing Frank the way to do things, he was patient, and good at explaining how things worked. He showed Frank how he hung up the harness for Jake and Elsa, and that if you hung it up properly, when you took it down the next time, it went over their heads and around their bodies without tangling, and all you had to do was buckle the straps. He showed him how, at milking time, if you took ten minutes to put the bags Mama had made over the cows' tails, you not only didn't get muck flicked into the milk pail, you didn't get muck flicked into your eyes or your mouth. If you then didn't loiter about before carrying the milk pails in to Mama, then no one, cow or boy, kicked a pail over by mistake. If you fixed the fence as soon as you noticed the break, then no hogs ran through it while you were looking for the tools you should have put away in the first place. Frank would not have called it "fun" to work around the place as he was now expected to, but it was less fun to sit around, no matter where you were sitting, whether it was in the schoolhouse or at the table or reading the Bible in the evening. He had to do something, didn't he? And, too, Papa liked to explain things to him about the farm that made the farm an idea and not just a place. Why did Papa plant clover in with the corn? Papa told him about cover crops, and how clover kept the weeds down. Why did Papa let the hogs in with the cows and the horses? Because the hogs rooted through the cowpies and manure piles and found undigested grains to eat. Why did Papa plant oats in one field one year, and then corn, and then hay? Because different crops took different things out of the soil and put different things into it. Frank liked the term he used—"rotation."

ROSANNA WAS HAPPY to have him out of her hair. Now, if only the same thing could be done with Joey, but at seven, Joey was small for his age and continued to be a nervous case, though he had more or less stopped whining. Now he just stared. If Walter raised his voice or Rosanna burned herself with a hot pan and said "Ouch!," Joey looked startled. He did have chores—every farm boy had to have some— but they didn't involve strength or speed, only gentleness or caution, like gathering eggs. He was, in fact, pretty good at taking a turn with the butter churn and kneading the bread. More than once, Rosanna said to him, "Well, Joey, at least you know where supper comes from. Some folks think it just appears on the table."

For that brief time when Cousin Berta had come "for a visit," Joey was good to her. If she said to pull the curtains, he pulled the curtains. If she very soon after that said to open the curtains, he opened the curtains. If she asked him to pump her water while she washed her hands with lye soap, he pumped. If, five minutes later, she asked again, he did it. If Lillian sat down beside Berta on the sofa, she could ask Joey to take her away, and Joey would come over and hold out his hand to Lillian and say, "Lily, let's jump up and down eleven times." Lillian loved to jump up and down and count—that was a game Joey came up with. After Cousin Berta went up to Independence to the asylum there, Joey was the only one who asked after her. So Joey had his virtues, Rosanna knew. But he was a small, unappealing boy. His features were not regular—his nose went just a bit to one side, like Walter's, and his eyes were not level. How a boy with dark hair got such pale eyelashes, Rosanna did not know. His one attractive feature was his big smile. And it wasn't as though all of these wrong bits were from the Langdon side. His eyes were the spit and image of her brother Gus. It was as if God had picked all the worst features of both families and given them to Joey. Such a cross to bear was hard for Rosanna to understand, except by remembering that she had known she needed saving but had not bothered to do anything about it.

Rosanna kept all of these feelings to herself, and prayed over and over to be rid of them—to see Joey as perfect, the way she saw Frankie (if not Lillian—she didn't think she would ever see anyone the way she saw Lillian). She also recognized that, to her own mother and to Walter's mother, Joey was fine—"a sweet boy," "a darling," or, according to Oma, "a diamond in the rough."

FRANKIE WAS a little dismayed by what a gloomy Thanksgiving it was—Papa and Grandpa Wilmer and Grandpa Otto sitting around the table, shaking their heads and talking about "the Crash." Even Uncle Rolf looked gloomier than usual, if that was possible. But when Frankie went out to the back porch to look at the pumpkin pie again (there was a mincemeat pie cooling there, too, but Frank didn't like mincemeat), he found Eloise. She had her back to the door, and when she turned around, he saw that she was smoking a cigarette. She brought it to her lips, took it away, breathed the smoke out into the cool air, and said, "Say, Frankie."

Frank said, "Yeah."

"You're tall."

"I'm as tall as Bobby Dugan, and he's twelve."

"He must be Jed Dugan's youngest brother."

Frank shrugged.

"Is he a bully?"

Frank said, "Used to be."

"Until—"

"Until he got kicked real hard in the side of his knee and had to go to Dr. Craddock and be on crutches for a couple of weeks."

"How did that happen?"

"He was walking home from school and he ran into someone he had punched during recess the day before."

"Do I know the person he ran into?"

Frank nodded.

"But the Dugans live on the other side of school."

"Not that far."

"Not that far if you're a fast runner, right, Frank?"

"You could say that."

"Who else doesn't bully anyone anymore?"

"Well, Dallas Coggins doesn't even go to school now. I think the school gave up on him. Howie Prince tried a few things, but he stopped when the person he was kicking lured him round the school to where Miss Louis was reading a book and she saw what was going on."

"The teacher?"

"Yeah. I guess when he got home he got such a whipping that he couldn't sit down for three days."

"That was smart, what that person did."

"I don't know, it just seemed obvious."

"How did you know Miss Louis was reading a book?"

"I saw her. I thought everyone saw her."

Eloise stubbed out what was left of her cigarette on a saucer she had set on the railing. She said, "Sounds like there isn't quite as much bullying at that school as there used to be."

"I got it seven times by the time I was Joey's age, and he's only gotten it once."

"Who did he get it from?"

"Me."

"Well, I guess I'm not surprised at that." Then she said, "Boys will be boys. But here's the thing, Frankie. Almost everyone sees things, but not everyone notices them."

"I suppose so," said Frankie. Then, "Were you in Chicago?"

"I live in Chicago now."

"Chicago is big, right?"

"You can't imagine. You just can't. I couldn't. I've been to New York and St. Louis, too, and Chicago seems bigger than they are, but New York has more people, they say. I don't know."

"Do you like it there?"

Eloise put her hand on her hip and crossed her ankles. She was fiddling with the packet of cigarettes. She said, "They couldn't drag me out of there. I think the Loop is the most wonderful place in the world."

Frankie said, a little alarmed, "Do they want to drag you out of there?"

Eloise threw back her head and laughed. Her hair, which was shiny, flicked forward, then backward, then forward again. She said, "No, I'm joking." She had beads on her dress, lines of beads that made a V-shape and glinted in the twilight. All of a sudden he said, "That's a pretty dress."

Now she took another cigarette out of the packet and tapped it on the railing. She put it between her lips and lit it, then took it out and picked something—a bit of tobacco?—off the tip of her tongue. She said, "Thanks for noticing, Frankie. What are you, eight?"

"Almost ten. Ten in a week."

"Well, in a few years, you can come on the train to Chicago and visit me. Or you can talk Walter into putting those beef cattle on the train and bringing them to the stockyards himself, and you can come along."

"I think he sends them to Omaha. He doesn't like to send them very far. What do you do in Chicago?"

"I work at a newspaper called the *American*. I write recipes, but next year I might get to write about other things. I might get to go to some swanky parties and write about those."

"Do you like swanky parties?"

"Don't know yet. I like the houses and the hotels along the lake where they have the swanky parties."

"What lake?"

"Oh, Frankie! Lake Michigan!"

Frank felt his ears get hot. It was very unusual for him to say something stupid. He bit his lip. Then Eloise ruffled his hair and said, "You come see me on the train. I'll show it to you."

Just then, the door behind him opened and Granny Mary stepped out onto the porch, but she backed up and closed the door, and Eloise hurriedly stubbed out her half-smoked cigarette. She coughed twice, and then Granny Mary came out again. Both ladies now had those frozen smiles that meant trouble, so Frank slipped through the door, back into the kitchen.

1930

O N JOE'S BIRTHDAY, Papa came home from town just before
supper, and he had a funny look on his face. Mama was busy
fussing over the fried chicken and the mashed potatoes, which was
what Joe had told her he wanted. He was eight now, which was pretty
big. There was also a pound cake, but no ice cream, because Mama
didn't have time to make it, and no pie, because no fruits were in season and they had eaten the last of the apples stored in the cellar. The
icing for the pound cake was something Joey rather liked, though—
Mama took a jar of strawberry jam from the previous summer, heated
it on the range, and poured it over the top of the cake. It seeped down
into the cake and made it smell very good.

Granny Mary and Grandpa Otto brought Opa and Oma for supper. It took two people to help Opa out of Rolf's car (driven by
Granny Mary), and then it took three to get him up the front steps.
He was little and bent over. If Joe stood up straight, he was nearly as
tall as Opa, which was a funny feeling. Opa looked at him very carefully, and then said, *"Wer ist dieser Junge?"*

"Opa!" said Granny Mary. She leaned toward him and said, "This
is Joseph. Today is his birthday."

"Ja," said Opa, and Mama helped him to Papa's chair, where he
very slowly sat down. A moment later, he said again, *"Wer ist dieser
Junge?"*

Granny Mary came over, put her hand on Joe's shoulder, and said, "Joey, dear, show me your cake in the kitchen. When I was a girl, we didn't have birthday cake."

"What did you have?"

"No one cared about a birthday in those days. If you even knew when your birthday was. We had a girl working for us, she never knew how old she was. Opa used to tease her. He would open her mouth and look at her teeth, like she was a horse. Then he would say, 'Callie, you are more than ten and less than a hundred.' Well, she was a poor girl, in the end." Then Granny pressed her lips together, and Joe knew not to ask any questions about what had happened to her.

At the supper table, Opa sat between Granny Mary and Oma, and Oma tied his napkin around his neck, and gave him a spoon to hold in one hand and a piece of bread in the other, but she and Granny Mary fed him. Grandpa Otto tried not to pay any attention to this—he sat between Frankie and Papa and talked about farm prices. Mama set out dishes of food and made sure that they were passed around the table without spilling, and because it was Joe's birthday, he got to pick his piece of chicken. Opa only once said, *"Wer ist dieser Junge?"* and no one answered him.

Once everyone was served, Papa sat back in his chair and said, "You'll never guess what happened when I was in town today."

"Which town?" said Granny Mary.

"Our town. Denby. Population two hundred and fourteen."

"What?" said Frankie.

"Dan Crest's store was robbed."

"Oh, my goodness!" said Granny Mary, and Opa said, *"Was ist los?"* as if he was worried.

"While you were there?" said Mama.

"I was standing looking at the work gloves, and two young fellows who'd put some things on the counter pulled out guns and said for Dan to give them his money, and he did, just handed them about ten bucks, and they turned to run out, and Rodney Carson—you know, that boy who's been working there—he stuck out a broom handle and tripped them up as they headed out the door. They went sprawling down the steps." Now Papa laughed, and Grandpa Otto said, "Well, I'd like to have seen that." Mama said, "Oh dear! They had guns! I swear, it isn't safe to leave the farm anymore." And Papa said, "Turned out the guns weren't loaded, which was—"

"By the grace of God," said Mama.

"Amen," said everyone.

"Couldn't have been more than nineteen or twenty, those boys," said Papa. "Looked pretty hungry, too. If they'd asked Dan for a loaf of bread, he would've given it to them."

"Lots of folks with nothing now," said Granny Mary.

"Going to be more of those boys, I'll bet, with everything that's going on."

"We just have to pray for mercy," said Mama. Then she looked at Joe and put her finger to her lips. "Enough of that now," she said. "Joe's a big boy today."

"Well, I'm not saying what that robbery, if you want to call it that, meant, but it was funny in the end. I guess those boys learned a bit of a lesson."

Granny Mary said, "Didn't they get arrested?"

"Who was going to arrest them?" said Papa. "No one around to do that. Dan got his money back and took away their guns. They went off pretty sheepish."

Mama made that noise with her teeth, and Granny Mary shook her head, and then Grandpa Otto said that he had heard something on the radio.

"What was that?" said Papa.

"Turns out they found a new planet. You boys know what a planet is?"

Frankie said, "The Earth is a planet. And Mars. And Saturn. The planets go around the Sun."

"Now there's another one. Some fellows in Arizona found it, and they're wondering what to name it."

"I think it should have a girl's name," said Mama. "Only one planet has a girl's name now."

"That's Venus," said Frankie.

Joe wasn't exactly sure what a planet was, but he knew what the Sun was. After supper, they ate the cake, and Joe got two shirts that Mama had made him, and Otto gave him a bag of cat's-eye marbles, which Joe saw Frankie looking at more than once. Oma gave him some neatly wrapped molasses caramels with walnuts, and even though he had to share them around the room, everyone said, "Oh, thank you, Joey, but not tonight, I am just terribly full." Only Opa took one. Once Opa, Oma, Granny, and Grandpa had left, and Mama and Papa had taken Lillian upstairs for bed, Frankie gave him a slingshot he had made from a branch of the Osage-orange hedge.

EASTER WAS LATE, as late as Walter ever remembered it—April 20— and the day after Easter, he started planting his corn. He didn't like it one bit. After years of complaining that the fields were wet and he couldn't get into them, or that the rain just came in fits and starts, so that every time he got his equipment ready he had to put it away again and keep stirring the seed corn so it wouldn't get moldy (or would get less moldy), or that because of rain he had to replant some of the lower bits of the fields, this year he and Frankie had the wires strung in the first section before Easter, and the day after, instead of sending Frankie to school, they drilled the corn. The soil was fairly moist—that was the best you could say for it—and once he had worked for a while, Walter started to worry, not about the corn crop, but about the oat crop. The oats looked fine for now—a few inches high, and green—and Walter kept telling himself not to borrow trouble by worrying about it. But there was no wind. The air just stood there, and it seemed like it had been standing there for weeks. Jake and Elsa were sweating by the early afternoon, even though the work was slow.

Frankie said, "What's wrong, Papa?"

Walter wiped his brow. "Not much. Nice day, huh?"

Frankie said, "When we're done, can I go shoot frogs?"

"Down at the creek?"

Frankie nodded.

"I suppose so. Maybe I'll come with you." Walter hadn't been down to the creek in two or three weeks, and he wanted to see how it was running.

But it wasn't running very high, and there weren't any frogs. No frogs was a bad sign.

Rosanna didn't think much of his worries. She and Joey had two flocks of chickens now, fifty hens in each, and she was feeling rich, because a new café in town had made a deal with her and her alone to supply them with eggs and butter. The owner of the café, down from Milwaukee, Wisconsin, was a German man whose real love was pastry—he could make those old-country treats, schnecken and strudel and even baumkuchen, and he said that Rosanna's eggs and butter were as good as any he'd seen in Bavaria. He expected the citizens of Usherton to storm his establishment once he had it going. Joey was good with both the hens and the eggs—he didn't mind candling, which was a tedious business, and of course the hens seemed fond of him. Rosanna had gotten herself a new type of chicken from Canada called White Chanticleers. Walter thought they were a little picky, and they didn't like to be confined, which meant that they were underfoot a good deal, but they had almost no combs or wattles, and were good outdoors even in winter, even when there was snow and ice. The best part about them was that you could mistake a roasted mature White Chanticleer for a small turkey—it would be that big. And the meat was tasty. Dan Crest was paying her four cents per egg, and the German man—his name was Bruno something, Bruno Krause—was paying her five and a half. Walter was delivering eggs every few days, four dozen, and three pounds of butter. So two good things—the corn planted after all, in spite of his worries, and a new source of income with this Krause fellow—and yet he lay awake looking for the worm in the apple, as his mother would have said. Rosanna was even talking about buying them a new bed—not a rope bed, but one with actual springs, so that they wouldn't slide every night into the center and have to hoist themselves out. Walter turned over, and thought that if they got a new bed he would probably find something wrong about that, too.

LILLIAN WAS SITTING in her chair—she no longer used the high chair, because she was three and a half now, and good at sitting still, right where Mama had put her, and eating what was set in front of her. Or she was usually good at that; today, all she wanted was the tapioca pudding and the strawberries. Even though she was wearing only drawers and a loose smock, and had her hair tied out of her face, it was too hot to eat anything else. All the windows were open, and the dust hung in the air. Mama said, "Goodness me, praise the Lord, please give us just a bit of a breeze!"

Lillian yawned, and Mama said, "Well, you can have your nap on the sofa, darling. It's roasting upstairs. I hope it cools off before bed-time; I didn't sleep a wink last night."

She came over, and Lillian held out her hands for Mama to wipe, and then Mama washed her face. The cloth was cool on her cheeks and forehead. Lillian yawned again. Mama picked her up and carried her into the front room. Lillian wandered over to the toy box and picked up Lolly, who was the cuddliest of her dolls, even though her hair had all come out, while Mama laid a sheet over the sofa, and then Mama took off Lillian's shoes and socks and set them by the arm of the couch. Mama smoothed down her smock and took her hair out of its tie. When Lillian was lying quietly, Mama kissed her on the cheek and said, "Just an hour, while it's so hot. Maybe it will cool off later."

Lillian lay on her back with Lolly in her arms, looking up at the ceiling. It was dim at this end of the room, bright at the other end. Sometimes, the shadows of the trees outside quivered on the ceiling, but they only quivered. It was like looking into a pail of water and seeing the surface of the water move. Mama sat down and picked up her darning. She was doing some socks. Lillian heard the squeak of the rocking chair as it went back and forth, back and forth. One thing to think about was King Midas. Mama had read her that story only the day before, and when she came to the end, Lillian had cried, so Mama had said she would never read it again. The picture of King Midas that Mama had showed her looked regular—he had long hair, like Jesus, but also a crown. He looked nice. But he wanted a strange thing, which was for everything he touched to turn to gold. Lillian had seen that this was a bad idea from the beginning—all she had to do was touch her sausage, which was what they had for supper last night, in order to understand that having everything turn to gold at a touch would be horrible rather than wonderful. But King Midas persisted, then changed his very own child, who was a girl like Lillian, into a golden statue. And there was no turning back once it was done—Jesus did not show up to redeem King Midas, because, according to Mama, Jesus hadn't been born yet. So that little girl, whatever her name was, was done for, and that was what made Lil-lian cry. Mama said, "Well, Midas learned his lesson," and stroked Lillian's hair until Lillian stopped crying, and the two of them prayed to Jesus that they might learn their lessons sooner rather than later, and that they would be gentle lessons rather than hard lessons. But Midas stuck in Lillian's mind. Mama said, "Sweetheart, you have quite an imagination, I must say."

Lillian was still awake, or half awake, and Mama began to sing a song: "Fair waved the golden corn, / In Canaan's pleasant land, / When full of joy, some shining morn, / Went forth the reaper band. / To God so good and great / Their cheerful thanks they pour, / Then carry to His temple gate / The choicest of their store." Lillian liked the word "corn." Corn was yellow and sweet. She liked it on the cob and off the cob, and she liked holding a cob out to Jake and Elsa, and having them bite off the kernels and eat them. She also liked the words "joy," "shining," "cheerful," and "morn." The tune went up and down, and made her sleepier. Mama went on, "In wisdom let us grow, / As years and strength are given . . ." Her voice was low and almost tuneless. Lillian fell asleep.

THE MOMENT when Rosanna knew she'd been living in a fool's paradise was the moment she pumped the second basin of water. She had already undressed Lillian and set her into the first tub of water to cool off—it would certainly be a hundred out there, at least—and Lillian was paddling mildly and dipping a couple of spoons in and out of her bath. She was half talking to Rosanna. As she said, "Lolly and Lizzie need a nap," and Rosanna answered automatically, "I'm sure they do, they were up late last night," the water that spurted out of the tap over the sink fell brown and thick into the pail, and then stopped. Rosanna had never seen a well go dry before. She set the pail down into the sink and put her hands on her hips. Her hands were trembling.

The farm had three wells—one beside the barn, this one by the house, and an old one that had been capped some years ago, not far from the chicken house. Rosanna had no idea how deep this well was, or how it compared with the others—sometimes that didn't matter, water could be deep or shallow. She glanced over at Lillian. The tub the girl was sitting in was not at all large—it had a flat bottom and flared sides about twelve inches tall, and Lillian was sitting with her legs crossed. The water, which was clear, came up about six inches. In the hot weather, Rosanna had been letting her sit in the water every afternoon, just to stave off any fevers or heat strokes that might be going around. Walter and the boys had a pail outside, too, in the shade, that they dipped their bandannas in before wrapping them around their heads under their hats, or wrapping them around their mouths and noses to keep out the dust. The other thing Rosanna had taught the boys to do was to dip their wrists in the water and hold them in there long enough for the blood to cool.

Well, obviously, the first thing was to pray, so Rosanna set down the pail and went over to Lillian, and knelt beside her. She said, "Dear Lord."

And Lillian said, in a singsong voice, "Now I lay me down to sleep, I pray—"

Rosanna couldn't help smiling. She waited for Lillian to finish, and went on: "We see that you are preparing a trial for us. The signs and the symbols are all around us—you give us no rain, and now you have dried up our well. Our crops are thirsty, Lord. We dole out little drops of moisture to them every evening, and they drink them up, but still they look yellow and dry." She was thinking of the beans. "We thank you for your past generosity, and we apologize if we have seemed ungrateful, if we have sat down to your bounty without lifting our voices in your praise. We understand that we became proud and flaunted our pride and were punished." Now she was thinking about how Bruno Krause had come and gone—no customers could afford to pay for such luxuries—and she had had to slaughter half of her chickens and given them away, and though at first the experience was a bitter one, it showed her that there were people, and not just bums and vagrants, but people in Denby and Usherton who hadn't the wherewithal to buy a chicken. There were people who were starving in the midst of plenty, as it said in the Bible somewhere. "We know that the trials you send us are proper tests of our faith, and we hope to pass those tests, dear Lord." Now she was thinking that Dan Crest was giving her almost nothing for her butter, good as it was, but he said that people didn't care about quality when they could hardly afford to eat—he himself almost went out of business, and it could still happen if the drought—yes, he used the dreaded word—didn't end soon, he had no idea what was next and neither did Hoover or anyone else. The oat and barley fields were brown, and there weren't many farmers like Walter and his father, who had some from the year before. The corn looked like green sticks thrusting out of rock, it was that dry. She gripped Lillian's hand a little too tightly, and Lillian pulled away. She opened her eyes. Lillian said, "Mama, I'm scared. You scared me," and Rosanna coughed and said, "You pray, Lillian. The Lord will listen to you, I'm sure."

"Pray what?"

Rosanna thought for a second, then said, "Darling, just close your eyes, and say, 'Dear Father, please have mercy upon your children and keep us and protect us. If there is anything we have done to offend you, we give you our apologies.' Say that."

"What are 'pologies?"

"Saying you're sorry—you know, like when you make a mess and Mama has to clean it up."

"Did I make a mess?"

"No, honey, no, you didn't. I don't know who did. But sometimes you have to say you're sorry and you don't know why. Do you understand?"

Lillian shook her head.

"Someday you will. We don't know all the things the Lord sees. Sometimes he sees things that we don't, and they make him sad and angry, and so we have to say we're sorry anyway."

"Okay." But she still seemed doubtful.

Rosanna began again, "Dear Father."

"Dear Father."

"Please take mercy upon us, your children, and help us."

"Please help us."

Rosanna didn't correct her. "If we have offended you by doing something, we are sorry."

"We are sorry. If—if we did a bad thing that we didn't know."

"Darling," said Rosanna, "it might be that someone else did a bad thing, but it's good if we apologize for it. Like Jesus."

"Like Jesus?"

"Well, Jesus never did a single bad thing, but when he was crucified, he made up for all the bad things that other people had done. That's why he was crucified."

Lillian looked at her for a moment, then went back to moving her fingers in the water, and Rosanna wondered if she had gone too far. It was always a shock for a child to find out—to truly understand— what had happened to Jesus. Rosanna remembered clearly her own reaction of brooding over it for some weeks around Easter, and asking questions: Nails in his palms? Nails? He fell down three times and nobody at all helped him? Where was the Good Samaritan? In fact, it was better to have a rather thoughtless child like Frankie, who listened, then forgot about it. Who at ten still sang "Round John virgin" without recognizing that those words made no sense.

Finally, Lillian said without looking at her, "Did you do a bad thing, Mama?"

"Not that I know of."

"Did Papa?"

"Not that I know of."

"Frankie?"

She hesitated, but certainly this was true: "Not that I know of." Then, "At this point."

"Joey?"

"I can't imagine Joey or you, Lillian, doing a bad thing or thinking a bad thought."

"What is a bad thought?"

Rosanna regretted even beginning this. She said, "Hating someone."

"Do you hate anyone?"

"No, and neither does Papa or Frankie or Joey, or you. Lillian, I don't know why there isn't any water, but the Lord will provide if we pray to him."

"Isn't there any water?"

"Well," said Rosanna, "let's see." She stood up and lifted Lillian out of the tub, careful to retain as much of that water as she could—for plants, and maybe even animals. She dried Lillian with a towel and walked her over to the pump. Rosanna picked Lillian up and set her beside the sink, then picked up, not the pail with the muck in it, but a pot she used for boiling egg noodles. She set it under the spout of the pump, lifted the handle, and pushed it down, then did it again. Water—clear water, and cool—spurted into the pan, and she pumped again. Soon she had about three quarts—the pot held four quarts. She realized that she had panicked. Dimly, in fact, she knew how a well worked—a well was a deep hole into an aquifer. Water seeping through surrounding rock and earth filled the hole, and every well had a capacity—a gallon a minute, or two, or ten, or whatever.

But Rosanna had never in her thirty years seen anything come out of a spigot other than water, and so she had looked at the muck and panicked. Lillian was staring at the water, and Rosanna gave in to temptation and said, "Well, darling, it's a miracle. We prayed for the water, and the water came." Rosanna knew that Walter would disapprove of misrepresenting things in this way, but the words just came out of her mouth. Lillian stared at the water and said, "A miracle."

Rosanna took her down from the sink and said, "Let's go find Dula and Lizzie. I think they've been getting up to mischief." As they left the kitchen, hand in hand, Rosanna saw Lillian turn her head to look at the pump. She did feel guilty, a bit. But, then, what was wrong in believing in miracles? Miracles abounded. There were plenty that you could see, and plenty that you couldn't.

PAPA THOUGHT that he could get five cows, twenty chickens, and Jake and Elsa through the winter. As for lambs and hogs, well, the hogs had been slaughtered and turned into sausage and ham, as they were every year, and the sheep had gone away, too. If things looked better in the spring—if there was some snow cover—Papa said they could start again with shoats and lambs. It was not that they could go hungry—not only did Mama have pork and beef and chicken stored in the cellar, there were deer everywhere, and turkeys, too. Papa said that all the animals were thirsty and hungry. In a way, it was a mercy to shoot them, if they were coming around, because they had lost all caution. Better to be shot than brought down by a pack of dogs.

Frank was not worried. Minnie Frederick was not worried. It was true that the Grahams, who hadn't had many animals, only lots of corn and a few other crops, had lost their farm and moved away, before the harvest even, because Mr. Graham didn't "have the wherewithal" to harvest fields that were parched and dead just to keep them neat—Frank and Minnie tramped through those fields every morning on the way to school. Frank wasn't quite sure what "wherewithal" was—probably money, maybe horses, maybe gasoline, maybe someone to help him. At any rate, the Grahams were gone, had not even turned up for the first day of school. There were lots of others at school who were not worried—the worried ones must have left, Frank thought.

It was Papa who was worried, though Frank wasn't sure about what, exactly, and didn't dare ask. There was a word Papa always shook his head after pronouncing—it was "bank." Frank wasn't sure which of the three things that could go wrong at a bank Papa was worried about—the bank "going under," the bank "cutting him off," or the bank getting robbed. Of these, obviously, the most exciting was the bank getting robbed, and everyone at school talked about such a thing happening, because Donald Guthrie had a cousin in Ottumwa, where seven or eight guys had stolen sixty or a hundred thousand dollars from a bank in September. Ottumwa was only a hundred miles from Denby, according to Papa. The same gang had robbed a bank in Minnesota in the summer, three hundred miles away. Frank suspected they were getting closer. What Papa said about it was "Lucky to have a hundred thousand dollars in a bank in Ottumwa in this kind of drought, if you ask me."

Mama said that there was not going to be a bank robbery—the Lord wouldn't allow it. Frank didn't see why not, and Papa seemed to agree with him—he said, "Well, he's allowed plenty of 'em." Mama said that sometimes Satan got away with things and sometimes he didn't, but in Frank's experience, that was true of everyone, even Joey, who hardly ever tried to get away with anything, but had killed a bluebird with the slingshot Frank had given him and gotten away with it—Mama did not allow them to shoot at songbirds. Frank himself got away with so many things that he expected to do whatever he pleased, and he did.

He expected to get away with kissing Alice Canham, and he did. He expected to get away with kissing her sister, Marie, and he did, and when Marie told Alice, Alice wanted another one. Alice was thirteen and Marie was fourteen. Chances were, thought Frank, that he would also get away with kissing Minnie, but he spent so much time with Minnie on the way to and from school that kissing her seemed like maybe not such a good idea, although, on balance, he didn't see how holding her hand could go wrong.

In order to further chase away any worries that the boys and girls in the school might have, their new teacher this year, Miss Horton, who was maybe eighteen and maybe not—Minnie said she was sixteen and had lied about her age because her family had lost their farm and were living in a shack in Usherton and the money Miss Horton got from teaching was the only money they had—was helping them plan the biggest Christmas pageant ever, and she had been trying out all of the boys and girls for singing. There was a piano in the school; Miss Horton was the one who tuned it up and got everyone to sing. And it was Miss Horton who said to Frank, after he sang two verses of "Beautiful Dreamer" and one of "Hard Times Come Again No More" (both of which she taught him), that he sounded like an angel, and Frank said, "No one ever compared me to an angel before," and Miss Horton said, "Well, I can see that, Frank, but you have a lovely singing voice."

When he told this to Mama, she said that all the Vogels and the Augsbergers were good singers, so no wonder, but she agreed to help him learn the songs he was supposed to sing for the pageant. There were three of them—the whole school was going to do "It Came Upon a Midnight Clear," and then Frank, Minnie, one of the plain girls named Dorothy Pierce, and Howie Prince were to do "The Holly and the Ivy," back and forth between verses. Then, at the end of the first part, or "act," as Miss Horton called it, Frank was to sing alone—"I Heard the Bells on Christmas Day." This was a song that Frank did not know, though Mama did. She said, "I think that's rather a sad song, Frankie."

Frankie shrugged.

"Did Miss Horton sing it for you?"

"She said she would do that next week."

"It is not a joyous carol. I would prefer you sang something that affirms your faith."

"Have you sung it, Mama?"

"Well, yes. Granny Mary likes that one."

Frankie left it at that.

On Monday, when Miss Horton kept him after school to sing the carol for him (Minnie stayed, too), he found that he liked it, and he got the tune right away. On the third time, he could sing along with Miss Horton, and after the fourth time, both Minnie and Miss Horton had their mouths open.

Miss Horton said, "You sang that with real feeling, Frank."

"I did?"

Minnie nodded.

Once they were out of the school and on the way home in the

cold, dimming light, she kissed him on the cheek and said, "That's what you get. But don't tell."

"More after the pageant?"

Minnie laughed and poked him in the arm. She said, "You'll see."

Well, there was no snow cover yet, which put Papa in a bad mood. After supper and a short Bible reading (lately, they were getting shorter and shorter), he got up and looked out the windows of the front room, as if he could make the clouds come. Each time he sat back down in his chair and picked up his paper or his book, his scowl got deeper. And for once Lillian was fussy. Mama didn't know why, it looked like. Twice Lillian said "No!"—something Lillian never said. As usual, Joey just sat there. Finally, Frank said, "Mama, you want to hear my song?"

Mama pursed her lips, then said, "Of course, Frankie. I would like to hear your song."

"What song is that?" said Walter suspiciously.

"His carol for the pageant."

"That should be harmless, at least," said Walter. He put down his paper.

Frank stood up and went over to the stove and clasped his hands in front of himself, the way Miss Horton had told him; then he began confidently, "I heard the bells on Christmas day, / Their old familiar carols play, and mild and sweet . . ." Just there, the same thing happened—there was something about those words, "mild and sweet," that was delicious and drew him onward. The way the notes seemed to go more deeply into him as they got lower (at "goodwill," he had to open his throat and chest to get down almost an octave to that note) made him stop seeing his audience. When he was finished, he saw that Mama and Papa were gawking at him. Papa said, "Frankie, you sang that song as if you knew what you were talking about."

Mama said, "After this year, maybe he does know."

They exchanged a glance.

"Good boy," said Lillian.

Mama said, "You know, Opa was a wonderful singer when he was young. He was in a boys' choir back in Germany that sang for the king."

"What king?" said Joey.

Mama shrugged. "I don't know. German kings, who could tell. A Frederick of some sort. Opa had to wear a satin outfit. But when we were children, he sang German songs for us. Then he stopped. I don't know why."

"He stopped because of the war," said Papa.

"Well, yes, of course," said Mama. "That must be it." She sighed. But then she reached out and Frankie gave her his hand, and she said, "If you are given great talents, Frankie, you are to use them in the service of the Lord. Do you understand?"

Frankie nodded, of course, but he didn't understand at all, really.

1931

WALTER WAS DOING a thing that he knew he shouldn't, but since he didn't have many animals to take care of for the time being, he couldn't help himself—he was walking down to the creek just to check how it was flowing. Frankie and Joey were at school, studying about something entirely unrelated to farming, he hoped, and Rosanna was cleaning up after dinner (poached eggs on toast and some fried potatoes). The afternoon was sadly clear and bitter cold, especially brilliant to the west, which was where all things good and bad came from. There was snow, but his boots went right through it. He tried to ignore this.

If you'd asked Walter how many things about the now mercifully passed year of 1930 he'd found shocking, he would have said that nothing shocked him, but that was not true and he knew it. The question was not what was shocking, but what was not shocking. For example, he had been shocked when his corn yield turned out to be thirty-five bushels an acre—the crop had looked so bad that he had expected it to be lower, more like thirty, or less. After ten years of forty to forty-four bushels an acre, maybe he was just spoiled. And then, after the Grahams left, a farm not half a mile away, he and some of the neighbors, hating to see the crop just standing there, had gone to the bank and asked to harvest it and divvy it up. The Grahams got twenty-one bushels to the acre. That shocked everyone, but they didn't talk about it among themselves—bad luck to do that. Walter could see the Graham house now, and the Graham fields. Walter hurried his steps to get out of the sight of those windows, flat and dark against the brightness of the air. Two on the other side had been broken by someone or something—maybe birds—and Walter had gone over and boarded them up, but that made the place look done for, made you want to peep inside and see the sofa and the dishes they had left behind. Even clothes and shoes.

The oat crop had been worse than the corn crop, more's the pity for the horses and the cows, but the real shocker was that, with all the news about the drought (and it was worse to the south and the west) that they'd gotten over the radio, through gossip, and in the papers all year, prices had still dropped. How was that? Walter wondered. A bad crop year was supposed to be good for someone, and yet last year, 1930, had been good for no one. Of course, his father laughed. He could afford to laugh—he owned his own farm free and clear—but, more than that, his father always laughed at farming and what a joke it was on the farmer.

Rosanna said, "So—no one can buy food because of the Crash, but does that mean they are just going to let the people starve? Why don't the churches buy it up? Or some rich people? The food is there, the people need it. Are they going to let it rot in the bins while people starve?" And, irritated, Walter said, "Yes, probably they are, Rosanna." She found the Grahams' empty house an abomination for the same reason. She said, "People are roaming the roads and living outdoors in the cold and freezing to death, and that house is sitting empty." But there was no answer for her that Walter understood well enough to make. She would say, "I gave away my chickens. I even gave away my eggs. Better that they feed someone than get thrown on the trash heap!"

Walter said, "You are a Christian woman, Rosanna."

So he'd paid his mortgage (just barely) and saved enough seed for the spring (just barely), and they could make it through another year, but what were they going to do for shoes for the children (yes, he had thought of rummaging through the Grahams' junk) and bits of harness that broke, and how were they going to hire someone to dig the well by the house deeper? For two months now, Rosanna had gotten hardly a drop out of it—Walter and Frank carried water from the well by the barn, which was still producing, though not at the rate it had been. The Graham farm was just a little higher than his, and he suspected that the reason they left had as much to do with the wells as with the crops—that farm had never had as good water as the farms around it.

He also had no sense at all of how things were going to go in the coming year. His hopes had risen right around Thanksgiving with a pretty good snow, maybe six inches, but ice and rain a day later had washed it right away. Then another rain, and he'd felt bleak until, around the middle of December, there'd been five inches, and then another inch and another—a week of snow, until, finally, there were twelve inches on the ground, which made it hard to get to Frank's pageant, but when they were *at* the pageant, Walter could not believe the exhilaration all around. When Frank sang his carol, yes, he did a good job, but you would have thought he was Al Jolson, the way all the parents in the audience jumped up and clapped for him. It probably hadn't been good for Frankie, but Rosanna was happy, and even though you could almost see Frank's head swelling, Walter had refrained from dampening their pleasure. Well, the snow was still there, hadn't melted, giving the fields a rest and a promise.

Walter came to the creek. The water was about eighteen inches deep, and crusted with ice from the banks toward the middle though right in the middle it burbled along, dark against the pale ice. Maybe the ice and water were six feet across, or seven. Three years ago, the creek had been three feet deep and twelve feet across (though that was in February) and hadn't dried up all summer, and the year Lillian was born, it had stretched bank to bank—you could swim in it if you dared, which he did not. Well, that was the year of the big floods down south, and which did you want in the end? That was another year when it seemed like he would finally get a good price and he didn't, just the same price as always. Something, he thought, maybe stupidity, did not equip him to understand the life that he led.

THE FIRST TIME Frank heard the word "communist" was the day of Opa's funeral, when Eloise came home from Chicago. He heard

Granny Mary tell Mama when they were standing in the kitchen with their backs to the door, "Eloise isn't a communist. It's that boyfriend."

Frank went over to the plate of sandwiches and took another one. He was of course sorry that Opa had died, at least in a way. He, Joey, and Lillian had gotten to say goodbye to Opa only four days before—Mama had kept them home from school and dressed them in ironed shirts and pants, then she and Papa had taken them in the car to Opa and Oma's house, where the bed was in the front room. Opa was lying there, covered up to the chin even though the weather was pretty hot. Opa's head was tiny, and his eyes were closed. Frank could just hear him breathing, but that was about it. Mama had led them to the bed one by one, and had each of them take Opa's hand and say, "Goodbye, Opa, the Lord be with you. I love you," then give him a kiss on the cheek. His cheek was wrinkled and dry, like an autumn leaf. Mama said he was alive, and Frank supposed it was so, but it was a faint sort of life, Frank understood, and ready to be gone.

Frank was an accomplished eavesdropper (though he would not have called it that—he would just have called it "paying attention"), and so he had overheard all sorts of stories about Opa: Born in 1840, before there was even a state of Iowa, came to America on a tiny ship with no windows that he was allowed to see out of, met Oma just after the War Between the States, in Cleveland, Ohio, where, apparently, everyone spoke German just like back in Germany. And then they came to Iowa.

Granny Mary now said to Mama, "Well, Opa always said, better a communist than an agriculturist. But he only said it in German."

"A communist was a different thing in those days."

Frank's ears might have been ten feet across, but he loitered innocently at the table—he had two ham sandwiches and an egg salad, which he liked very much. He reached for a schnecken.

In Iowa, to hear Opa tell it, he plowed his fields on his hands and knees with a spoon, although Oma always tapped him on the knee when he said this and exclaimed, "You had Tata and Mosca, the two best Belgian draft horses in the county!"

"*Ja,* well, they watched me and whinnied to me if I was doing a good job with my spoon!" Then everyone would laugh. Opa started with sixty acres. ("That many! In Germany, no simple man like your

opa ever had sixty acres! He had six feet by four feet, most of the
time.") Eventually, Opa ended up with eighty acres, and was happy
with that, he always said. Uncle Rolf had been farming them for him
for ten years now, Frank thought. He had them in hay some years and
oats some years.

Frank saw Granny Mary start to cry again, and took his plate out
of the room. Granny Mary said, "I was always so glad that he was my
papa. I always was." And Mama said, "We all were." Mama put her
arm around Granny Mary.

Eloise was sitting on the sofa with Lillian on one side and Joey on
the other. She was playing paper, stone, and scissors with them, and
Lillian was laughing. They tapped their three fists on Eloise's knee
and made their bets. Joey opened his fist, Eloise opened her fist, and
Lillian spread her forefinger and middle finger, then pretended to cut
the "paper" produced by the other two. Frank set down his plate and
said, "Can I play?"

Eloise said, "Sure," and Joey scowled. Lillian said, "Frankie hits."

"He does?" said Eloise.

Joey said, "If he's the rock and you have scissors, Frankie says he
can punch you in the arm."

Eloise looked at him. "Is that true?"

"It's not a hard punch."

"Yes," said Lillian decidedly, "it is." Lillian was four and a half
now, but even though she was small, Frankie thought she talked like
a six-year-old or a seven-year-old. He said, "I won't hit this time. I'll
stop that rule for now."

"Okay," said Eloise.

They played four rounds. Frank won one round with paper; Joey
one with rock; and Eloise two, one with scissors and one with rock.
Lillian yawned and leaned against Eloise, who put her arm around
the little girl. Joey reached for Eloise's wrist and looked at her watch.
He said, "It's nine-fifteen already."

"Late," said Eloise.

"So go to bed," said Frank. He wanted to find out what a communist was.

At the very thought of bed, Joey yawned.

Frank said, "I'm not tired."

"Are you ever?" said Eloise.

Frank shrugged. Actually, the answer was no. Even when he went to bed at night, it was because he was told to, not because he was tired. Frank asked Eloise, "Do you miss Opa?"

"Sure. Everyone misses Opa. He was always nice. He's the only person I ever met who was always nice."

"Why was that?" said Joey.

"He said he left his naughty side in Germany," said Eloise. "Standing on the dock, calling to him, as the boat left the harbor. His evil twin. For years, I thought he really had a twin."

"Did he?" said Joey. But Frank knew the answer.

"No. It was just a way of talking." They were quiet for a long time after that, and, just like a miracle, Joey yawned again and got up from the couch, while Lillian, who should have been in bed hours ago, closed her eyes and fell asleep. Frank said, "Eloise?"

"What?"

"What's a communist?"

Eloise only smiled.

"Are you a communist?"

"Not quite. Did someone say I was?"

"No."

"Then why do you bring it up?" She shifted on the sofa and laid Lillian out flat, then took a shawl that Granny Elizabeth had made off the back of the sofa and laid it over her.

"They said your beau is a communist."

Now Eloise laughed out loud.

"Why are you laughing?"

"At the idea of Julius Silber ever being called a 'beau.' He would call himself my comrade."

"What's that?"

"My friend and fellow worker, someone who wants the same things I do. We don't use words like 'beau' or 'fiancé.' They're too French. Julius is English."

"So a communist is someone who doesn't like French things? Grandpa Wilmer is like that."

Eloise pursed her lips and sat back, then said, "Well, Frankie, either you are putting me on, or you're really interested. I can't ever tell with you."

"I want to know. I do."

She blew out some air and looked toward Granny Mary, then said, "Communists are people who see how unfair the world is and want to make it more fair. They see that some people have much, much more than they will ever need, and other people have nothing, and they don't think that there is any special reason for that, like God ordaining it or something."

"Why do you think it is?"

"I think there are a lot of reasons, but the reasons are different here than they are in France, say, or England. Julius was born in England, so he has different ideas from mine."

"How?"

"Well, in England things are *really* unfair, and have been for centuries, and if a person tries to better himself, he really can't, because the system won't allow it; but in America things that are unfair are more changeable, because they've only been unfair for, say, seventy or eighty years, and so—well, and also, the country is so big that if things are unfair in, say, Virginia, you can go to Texas or California and try it there."

"I would go to Chicago."

Eloise, looking just like the image of Chicago that Frank always thought of, in her smooth black dress and short hair that was waved and pressed against her head, patted him on the cheek and said, "I keep waiting for you."

"Are things unfair in Chicago?"

"Well, Julius and I talk about that every day. Let's say that they are less unfair than they are in England, and Julius likes it because he can live there and do what he wants, but it's pretty wild. There are gangsters, you know. But if they repeal Prohibition, I think things will calm down there."

"Are things unfair here?"

"Nothing is unfair here but the weather. However, the weather is pretty unfair lately."

This, Frank knew, was true. He looked at Eloise for a moment, then said, "Can I kiss you good night?"

"Sure." She offered her cheek, and he bent toward her, but her smell was so good that he ended up kissing her on the lips. She pushed him away and said, "Oh, Frankie. Goodness. What is Rosanna going to do with you?"

························

THE CORN HARVEST WASN'T over yet, but anyway Papa put Joey and Frank in the car and left in the middle of the afternoon. He drove them a hundred miles, to a town called Centerville. Joey fell asleep in the car and then was cranky, but they both woke up pretty good when they saw how many people were gathered to listen to a man who was named Christian Ramseyer and was a congressman, though not "our" congressman—too bad for us, according to Papa.

Frank and Joey ran around in the crowd while Papa talked to other farmers they saw. Everyone was dressed in work clothes, not like when you went to church, but when Mama said she wanted the boys to dress properly, Papa said they were making a statement. "Don't make it too loudly" was what Mama said, and then they left.

The farms all the way over looked just like the farms around Denby, but they did drive through Ames and look at the buildings at Iowa State College, where Eloise had learned to be a communist, according to Papa. When Frank said that Eloise said she wasn't a communist, Papa said, "Well, why did she marry that Red Jew, then?" and Frank still hadn't figured out what he was talking about. Anyway, no one was invited to the wedding, and they didn't have a honeymoon.

After everyone ran around for a while, and ate some sausages and corn on the cob, they all went into a building (so many that they were spilling out) and listened to Representative Ramseyer talk about how he was going to save the farmers, and Frank liked what he heard. Representative Ramseyer was older than Papa, but he shouted like a preacher, except that everyone shouted along with him: "We want an honest dollar!"

"Yes!"

"A stabilized dollar is an honest dollar."

"Yes!"

"Farmers will be able to pay their debts!"

"Yeah! Yeah!"

"And buy a few things for their families! Like shoes!"

"Yay! Yes!"

"People would be able to find jobs!"

"Yes!"

"And the banks would stand instead of collapsing! The solution to our difficulties is a simple one, though not easy. But I am working for you!"

"Yes! Yes!"

All the men and boys roared and jumped. Frank thought it was a little like that Billy Sunday time, but not as scary, and on the way home, Papa was as happy as Frank had seen him in months, telling Frank and Joey all about how America worked and communism did not, and that much was clear to every farmer, every hick, every Hoosier, even if it wasn't to big-city types like Julius whatever-his-name-was.

Joey fell asleep, and Frank believed Papa.

But even so, a few weeks later, he heard Papa say to Mama that he only got thirty bushels per acre this year, and he didn't know what they were going to do.

1932

Papa had five Southdown ewes now ("And I don't know why I have those"), and then Grandpa Wilmer gave Frankie and Joe each a newborn lamb from his Cheviot flock for a 4-H project.

Joe said, "Can I name him?"

"I guess so, if it's 4-H. Is Frankie naming his?"

"Patsy," said Joe.

Papa laughed, though Joe didn't know why, and then said, "Well, what about yours?"

"I want to name him Fred."

Papa said that was okay.

The lambs, of course, had not been weaned, so Grandpa Wilmer brought two ewes and two lambs over in the back of his new truck the next day. The new animals had bare faces, which made them look strange, but Joe liked that, too—their faces looked framed by the wool on their necks. Papa put the ewes and the lambs in their own pen, and Frankie and Joe fed them. Joe saw within about a day that Frank was going to leave most of the work to him, but he didn't mind. Every morning, before sunup, he got out of bed and put on his clothes and walked through the dark house, out the back door, through the snow, to the sheep pen, where the two ewes and two lambs greeted him and he greeted them—"Good morning, Fred. Good morning,

Pat, you look perfect today." The ewes seemed happy to have the feed trough all to themselves. They would go back to Grandpa Wilmer's after the lambs were weaned. Joe knew to touch the ewes before he touched the lambs, so he did that for a few days. Since they were Cheviots, he touched them on their faces, and they actually seemed to like it. With Southdowns, you could touch them anywhere, but their wool was so thick you had to wonder if they even knew you were in the neighborhood.

On a Saturday after Valentine's Day, when the lambs (and Papa's five lambs, too) were between two and three weeks old, Papa said over breakfast, "Well, 4-H-ers, today's the day." Joe's heart sank, but Frankie bounced in his chair.

Joey didn't like castrating the lambs and docking their tails when they were only two or three weeks old, but Papa said that he would like the screwworms a lot less—a lamb couldn't feel, or could hardly feel, when his tail was docked, but if and when the screwworm got in there, the lamb could feel it plenty, and it hurt him very much, even if he could be saved, and some could not.

Papa said, "You know, out west, they fry up lambs' testicles and eat them."

From the stove, Mama exclaimed, "Walter! Goodness!"

"Well, the Germans do that, too, and I'm sure the Cheeks and the Chicks have tasted their share. Shall we save some for supper?"

"Some what?" said Lillian, looking up inquisitively.

"Go, go!" said Rosanna, and she shooed them out the door.

The lambs' tails were pretty long—Patsy's came to below his hocks, and Fred's was almost that long.

Papa built a fire in the smithing area beside the barn and set two irons into it. His knives (he had two of them) were already sharpened.

Papa and Frankie herded the seven lambs into the pen, while Joe guarded the ewes in the barn. It was hard to tell who was making more of a racket. Once everyone was separated, Papa started running. Frankie's job was to catch a lamb, throw a rope around its neck, and drag it to Papa. Papa ran to him and helped him; then, at the smithing area, he laid it on its side, and if it was a male, cut into the scrotum, and squeezed out the testicles. By now it was really squealing, but then Papa cut the tail and set the hot iron on it. When it jumped up,

Joe's job was to run over, grab the rope, guide it toward the barn, open the door, and push the lamb inside without letting any ewes out. By this time, Papa was running back to Frankie.

The hardest part was grabbing the rope. Once he had dragged the lamb a couple of feet, it could hear the baaing of the ewes and wanted to go toward that sound. Joe realized that if he kicked the door of the barn very hard a few times, the ewes would back away, and he could push the lamb through. Seven lambs (and Joe was really, really glad that three of them were female) took just over an hour. When they were finished, Papa told Mama that they were very good boys.

When Joe went out to feed Fred and Patsy at dusk, though, he saw that they wouldn't come near him. Papa said, "That's too bad for us, because we'll just have to catch them, and lambs are fast. We've got to put ointment where we cut them or the screwworms will find those wounds and get started. So now you know, boys, that animals are always a pain in the neck."

But Fred was waiting for him the next morning, early, in the dark, and he let Joe stroke him on the face.

NINETEEN THIRTY-TWO WAS when Walter switched parties. He did it early in the year, even though Representative Ramseyer was a Republican and no one knew who the Democrat would be. But Walter was fed up with Hoover, whether he was from down in West Branch or not, and anyway, he left West Branch and went to Oregon when he was eleven—though, to hear the Republicans around Usherton talk about it, you would think he had dinner with farmers every day, then went home and plowed the back forty. But Hoover had gone to Stanford and then all over the world, and maybe, as far as Walter was concerned, he didn't have dinner with farmers ever. So Walter switched parties.

Rosanna was not amused. Their pastor said that the Democratic Party had a greater proportion of sinners and atheists than the Republican Party, not to mention Irish Catholics (as opposed to German Catholics, who were more responsible), which meant not only that they were unredeemed (many in both parties were unredeemed) but unredeemable. She said, "What am I going to say at services when the election comes up?"

"Don't say anything."

"Then they'll know something is wrong."

"Plenty is wrong, they know that already—they just have to look around." Actually, by the first of June, not so much was wrong anymore. The rains had been pretty good, if not great, and the oats were tall and green. The corn was in, and the clover crop also looked fine. It was okay, in the end, to be down to five ewes, seven lambs, five milkers, two horses, twenty shoats (who looked to be about a hundred pounds already), and twenty-five chickens. Dan Crest was paying four cents per egg and about as much for butter as he had before the Crash, and the boys were doing fine with Patsy and Fred. It looked like they were going to get electricity at a good price—the electric company had told Roland Frederick that if they were going to connect Roland's house, they had to connect a few others, too, so Roland would pay, and Walter could pay him back over the next few years. And, of course, Rosanna was now four months along, and everyone liked a Halloween baby—the harvest was over, the house was cozy, and Lillian would be in school along with the boys. Walter's mother thought six years was a long time to go between babies, and even said so, but Rosanna was mum about what she thought might have been a miscarriage, or even two of them. Drought years, hard times, but now that Walter was a Democrat, he wasn't so bored with everything. The candidate he liked was Governor Reed, from Missouri these days, though he'd grown up in Cedar Rapids and gone to Coe College there. He was an honest man. Blaine, from Wisconsin, he didn't like, and John Nance Garner, from Texas, he thought was too much of a character. But everyone said it was going to be Roosevelt, and that was fine with him. He said none of this to Rosanna, or even aloud (and maybe that was superstition), but it made him feel good. Had he ever had a secret in his life? Did anyone he knew? (Probably Frankie, when you came to think of it.) The way their family, their town, and their church went, there was so much gossip that, in all the things they said about one another, something had to be correct. So Walter looked at his wife and his children and his crops and the future, and thought that one good thing about bad times, like the last couple of years, was that regular times looked pretty good by contrast, and the truest sign of regular times was a good rain.

ON THE FIRST DAY of school, which was the day after Labor Day, Lillian was ready in more ways than one. Of course, she dressed herself carefully in the yellow dress Mama had made for her, and some new shoes that she had been saving, and the blue sweater with yellow flowers around the neck that Granny Elizabeth had knitted. Of course, she brushed her hair, and Mama, who now could hardly move, her belly was so big with the new baby (whom Lillian had decided to name "Cindy," because she didn't think Mama would go all the way to "Cinderella"), braided it for her, and she stood absolutely still, so that the braids would lie flat and heavy down her back. She had a hat, too, a straw hat with a yellow ribbon. Frankie went on ahead, but Joey walked with her, and showed her the way—first down the road toward the Fredericks' farm, where Minnie and the baby Lois lived (Lillian liked Lois, and went to play with her sometimes, even though she was only two), and then across the fields, past the falling-down house where a friend of Joey's named something Lillian couldn't remember had used to live, and then over two fences and across a little road to the school. The school was tall and white, and had two front doors, and the first day, after they raised the flag and said Pledge of Allegiance, the girls lined up and went in one door, and the boys lined up and went in the other. The teacher was named Miss Grant, and she had red hair. Lillian whispered "Miss Grant" to herself, the way Mama had told her to do, and by the time she sat in her seat, she knew she would never forget it.

Her desk was in the front row, between Rusty Callahan, who was seven, and Rachel Cranford, who was six. Rachel looked scared, and Rusty picked his nose. Lillian kept her feet together under the desk, and clasped her hands in front of her on its surface. She never took her eyes off Miss Grant's face, in the first place because Mama had told her to pay attention, and in the second place because she thought Miss Grant was beautiful, and she had never seen hair like hers before in her life. It was curly, and it sprang about as Miss Grant stepped here and there and turned her head and told the children what to do. Lillian thought it was entrancing.

In the late morning, Miss Grant sat down with five of them around a table—Rusty, Rachel, Jane Morris, Billy Hoskins, who was big (nine), and Lillian herself. She handed each of them a reader, and demonstrated how they were to set the books on the table and open them flat. The books had pictures, and the print was very big. The first page had one word, "Dick." The page beside it had five words, but most of them were the same words—"Dick," "see," and "go." "See Dick go. Go, Dick, go!" Lillian was entirely familiar with these words—she had been reading them for years in Joey's books. She flipped the page. All the words were familiar.

Lillian looked around. Rusty and Billy were peering at the books in surprise, Rachel was chewing on her braid and looking out the window, and Jane was looking at her, Lillian. Lillian smiled. Jane smiled.

Miss Grant said, "Try again, Billy."

Billy said, "See Deck go. Go Deck go."

"Billy, do you know anyone named 'Deck'?"

"No."

"Do you know anyone named 'Dick'?"

"No."

"No one?"

Billy shook his head.

"Richard?"

Billy shook his head.

"Well, 'Dick' is a name. It's the name of this boy in the picture. Dick."

"Dick," said Billy.

Then he said, "Go, Dick. Go."

"Okay, turn the page. Jane? What does that say?"

Lillian looked at her page. It said, "Run, Jane, run." Jane said, "Run jump run."

"No, Jane. Look again."

Jane looked again; then Lillian saw her face turn deep red. She muttered, "Run, Jane, run."

"Better," said Miss Grant. "Lillian?"

Lillian smiled her nicest smile, holding Miss Grant's gaze as she turned to the back of the reader. Then she looked down. There were lots of words on the page. In an even and steady voice, Lillian said, "Oh, look, Dick. Here comes Spot! Run, Spot, run! What a good dog you are, Spot! Sally sees Spot run. Jane sees Spot run. Dick laughs."

At lunchtime, Lillian shared her apple turnover with Jane, and Jane held her hand. The next day, Miss Grant put Lillian in a higher reading group, but Jane was now her best friend.

ROSANNA WAS SURE the due date was after Halloween, but on October 14, she was standing in the kitchen, doing the dinner dishes, when her waters broke—just rushed out of her and splashed on the floor—and when the first pain came, it was a sharp one, a real contraction. She was to the door between the kitchen and the dining room when the second one came, and at the foot of the stairs for the third one. There would be no climbing the stairs.

So she went into the boys' room and looked at the beds there—she'd been too exhausted to change and launder the sheets for a couple of weeks, and it was harvest, and both boys were picking corn all day long instead of going to school—they were out there now, in a howling wind, along with Walter and Gus, who was helping them for a day. She paused for another contraction, then went to Frankie's bed, which was the largest, and flipped the quilt so at least the cleaner side was up. Then she held on to the bedpost for another contraction. But her mind was working like a radio, telling her what to do with absolute clarity.

There were towels, clean ones. She made her way back to the kitchen and got two of those, and the rest of the water she had heated to rinse the dinner dishes. She also got a shoelace—her mother had told her about that years ago, about all the ladies who gave birth at home, and they always tied the cord with a shoelace until the doctor or the midwife got there to cut it. So Rosanna had a clean, new shoelace she'd kept wrapped in a drawer.

It was hard to carry the pot of water, but, slowly, she did. She went into the boys' room and closed the door, and opened the window, just in case one of the boys or men walked by and she could call out to him.

She laid one of the towels on the bed, and bunched as many pillows as she could up by the headboard. When she lifted her dress, she could see her belly tightening and shrinking. Seeing it was more frightening in a way than feeling it. She said, "Angel Mary Elizabeth, look down on your mama and your new brother or sister, and help us make it through this, Lord preserve us, oh, my God!" After that contraction, she crawled forward onto the bed and knelt with her face in her hands. The door did not open, the wind howled through the window, no rain, thank Jesus, and the cold was good, for now—it kept her from passing out. She keeled over onto her side and tried it—she called out, "Walter, Walter! *Ahhhhh!*" But the wind just rose with her voice. They were far away—she would be shouting to the west and the south, and the cornfield was to the east. She felt tears running down her cheeks, but, really, there was no time for that; the contractions were rhythmic, deep, and quick, and Jesus said to roll over onto her back and arrange herself sitting up on the towel, with the other towel in her hands, and she did. Her belly looked as though it was shivering and rippling, but, then, so did the curtains, and so did the ceiling, and she felt herself pushing—it only took one, and then she put her hand between her legs and felt the crown of the baby's head and moist hair there, and she pushed again, and here was the whole head and face, and then the right shoulder and the left shoulder, and a boy slipped out onto the towel.

The labor had been so quick, the pains so sharp and definite, that she wasn't at all exhausted, and the sight of the baby's face was so enlivening that Rosanna simply did what she had seen others do, whether with babies or lambs or kittens—she gently wiped the mouth and eyes and nose, and then she picked up the shoelace that she had dropped on the bed, and she tied it around the cord, about six inches down from where it attached to the baby, and then she cradled it—him—in her arms. He was big—seven pounds at least, and blond. Rosanna said, "Henry, Henry, Henry, Henry Augustus Langdon. Wait till they see you!"

She was looking at Henry's face. Henry had tried nursing and found it good—God be praised. He latched on like a trouper and got a good dose. Since he was big enough to be due after all, she must have calculated wrong, and she was thinking back when Joey opened the door—sent in for a handkerchief, he was sneezing so much with the harvest.

It was a blessing that it was Joey, given that he didn't care about mess and liked baby animals—Frankie was more particular and was always complaining that Joey didn't straighten up his things. Joey's face lit up as if nothing strange had happened, and he said, "Mama! Is it a boy or a girl? I'll run tell Papa."

"Yes," said Rosanna, "tell him that Henry Augustus is here and wants to meet him."

Joey was out of the room and the house in about two seconds, and even over the wind, Rosanna could hear his shouts.

Henry, Henry, Henry, he was Lillian all over, a blessed boy for sure; if they had been twins, they could not have been more similar. Rosanna stroked his crusted hair and stared at his blue eyes. His head wasn't misshapen at all, and all his little parts were perfect. A prayer just came out as she touched each perfect part—the nose, the eyebrows, the fine threads of hair, the fingers, the toes, the two little heels, which struck her as especially strange and miraculous. Thank you. The silent ecstasy with which she gave thanks reminded her of all the thanks she had given over the years while half thinking of other things or, sometimes, even when she didn't really feel thankful. The curve of his ear, which she ran her finger along.

LILLIAN WAS WALKING with Minnie, as she did every day, back and forth to school, down the road toward their house, when Papa passed her in the car, and Granny Mary was in the passenger's side. Lillian, who had her hand on the back of Minnie's coat, which Minnie didn't mind, looked up and said, "The baby is born."

"You think so?"

Lillian nodded, and five minutes later they were standing on the front porch. Frankie came out and said, "It's a boy. His name is Henry."

Lillian was only momentarily displeased; obviously, it was a very good baby, because everyone had on such big smiles. She walked through the front room without taking off her coat, and straight into Joey and Frankie's room, where Mama was leaning back in the bed, and Granny Mary was walking around with Henry in her arms. Lillian heard her say, "My land, cut the cord with the kitchen shears— well, I hope he boiled them first! Might as well be the Dark Ages around here," and then they saw Lillian and zipped their lips, as they so often did. But Granny Mary said, "Come here, child," and sat down on the corner of the bed with the baby.

He yawned. His fists clenched and his mouth opened wide and he even made a noise, and then his mouth closed and he looked at her a bit cross-eyed, and Mama said, "He can't see anything yet."

Lillian said, "His eyes are open."

Mama laughed. "Well, it's not exactly like kittens, sweetheart."

Lillian gazed at Henry's face, and he seemed, she was sure, to return her gaze. She lifted her hand and moved it toward the baby— Henry. Granny Mary said, "Are your hands—"

But Mama said, "It's fine." And Lillian put her hand on Henry's forehead, which was as soft and warm as anything she had ever touched. She said, "I love you, Henry." And she did.

1933

I f you had told Rosanna that having Henry the way she did would have tossed her down such a deep dark tunnel as it seemed to have when she looked back on it from, say, mid-January, she would not have believed you. Faultless baby, but a despair no amount of prayers could relieve, even a visit by her pastor, all the way from Usherton. Nothing Granny Mary could concoct by way of teas or tonics or even cookies or cakes could lift her spirits. She looked out the window (Oh, the wind had poured in the windows, so cold and shrill. No one could hear her, it was terrifying), she looked down at her own feet (Her own belly looked like a rock, as hard as that, pressing that poor baby out, no matter what she wanted or thought best), she looked at the walls (The walls had shivered and waved as if they might collapse on her), she looked at Henry, and every adorable curl of his hair, every delightful smile, every clenching of his little fist or kicking of his legs, was something that might not have happened if events had gone another way. The sun went down, and she turned on one of the new electric lights; somehow their stark yellowness and the odd shadows seemed ominous. She wept.

Without knowing it, she had been perched on the point of a pin, balanced there between life and death, between what happened to Mary Elizabeth and what happened to Lillian, and she had blindly stumbled forward, and, yes, everything had turned out well—better than well—another beautiful, happy child—but she had been on the head of that pin before and had fallen into the abyss, and then the six years after Lillian's birth had simply been a cloud of ignorance. She had thought such a thing could never happen again, but it happened all the time! Hadn't Walter's brother Lester, whom he had never known, died of measles when he was two? Yes, said Granny Elizabeth, but— Rosanna didn't listen to the "but." Hadn't Oma's sister back in Ohio fallen down the cellar stairs? Granny Mary had never heard that, but Rosanna was sure it was true. Grandpa Wilmer had gotten scarlet fever as a boy and almost died, and Granny Mary herself had gotten lost among the cows when she was three and they hadn't found her for almost a day. Only an hour, and how did Rosanna remember all of these things, said Granny Mary—they were best forgotten, or you couldn't go on, especially as a farmer. Granny Mary didn't even read obituaries anymore. She thought Rosanna should make herself think good thoughts, but good thoughts were the worst, because all around the good thoughts, bad ones clamored for her attention, and the better the thoughts (how darling Henry was, and how helpful Lillian was—not jealous at all), the louder the clamor of the bad thoughts.

Even after she was up and around, and all the bedclothes and towels were laundered, and she was engaged in the routine that she knew so well—cooking, cleaning, nursing, napping, changing—the very corners of the house itself, the walls and the doors, were stamped with the feelings and sights and sounds of that day—she could be stirring oatmeal at the stove and thinking nothing, and the sound of the wind rising around the corner of the house made her heart flutter and her spirits sink—why was that? Oh, the next picture that came into her mind was the boys' windows from the bed, open to the October breeze.

Praying, she came to feel privately, was worse than useless, because every time she articulated that thing that she wanted relief from, it flooded her; the very word "Jesus" began to make her nervous. Then she tried reading the Bible, but there were lots of terrifying things in the Bible—episodes she had read through blindly before, and not just the Slaughter of the Innocents—that she now saw much more vividly in her mind. You could cry over Noah's Ark if you were in the mood. It was not helpful for her mother, or Walter's mother, to say they'd known new mothers who had just the same thing happen to them, though neither of them, thank goodness . . .

Now I know, Rosanna thought. I'm almost thirty-three. I really know what it means to be alive. And she wept again.

LILLIAN COULD REMEMBER one time, it was before she went to school, maybe she was four or three. Anyway, she was sitting talking to Lizzie about being a grown-up, and Frankie came onto the porch with his shotgun in one hand and a dead rabbit in the other—Lillian remembered that, because she didn't like guns, so she had turned Lizzie over to hide her eyes—and Lillian had looked up from her doll bed and said, "When I grow up, I'm going to marry Mama."

Frankie stared at her, which was the first thing that told her she had made a mistake, and then said, "You can't marry Mama. You have to marry a boy, and somebody you don't know."

Lillian had felt genuinely surprised by this new rule, but of course, if it was a rule, then Lillian would certainly follow it. With greater age and sophistication, she had come to understand that what she'd been saying to Frankie was that she loved Mama completely, better than anyone in the world. However, now there was Henry.

The only other baby Lillian knew at all well was Lois, Minnie's sister, who would soon be three. Lois was much more interesting to Lillian than she was to Minnie, or, apparently, to Mrs. Frederick, who didn't like her to get underfoot and when she set her food in front of her said, "Eat it or starve, my girl. It's your choice." It was true that Lois usually ate her food, but Lillian was sometimes afraid that she wouldn't. Occasionally, Lillian had been at the Fredericks' when Mrs. Frederick was doing something and looked up and said, "Goodness, where's the baby gotten to now?" One time, they looked all over for her and found her in a closet. From all of this, Lillian gathered that Lois was not an especially valuable child, though to all appearances she was perfectly adequate—she walked and talked and didn't cry all that much, and she never had a tantrum that Lillian had seen, though Minnie said there were some. Perhaps that was the key—tantrums? Lillian herself had never had a tantrum, and they were obviously indulgences to be avoided.

Lois was a puzzle that was to some extent solved by Henry, because Henry was so wonderful and delightful a child that clearly it was the case that some were better than others, and you were fortunate to get a good one. Even though Mama was sad a lot of the time now, which seemed to be the way you got once you'd had a baby, she never looked at Henry without a smile, and she picked him up and took him in her arms as if she could not help herself. Lillian felt the subtraction of attention from herself not as a loss, but as a bit of newfound freedom and as a recognition that nothing was more valuable than a baby, if it was a very good baby.

She stroked his head, and she encouraged him to hook his fingers over her finger, and she drew pictures of him at school, and she sat next to his cradle and talked to him. She sat quietly on the sofa, against the back so that her lap was as big as it could be, and Mama put him in her arms. She practiced holding him and jiggling him the way Mama did, and her reward was that sometimes, when Mama was busy, she got Henry in her arms if he was fussy, and she would jiggle him and he would stop crying. As he got older, she made faces at him that got him to laugh, and once he was sitting up, she showed him how to clap hands and to look up and down and from side to side. Really, there was no one more fun to play with than Henry. By contrast, Papa, Frankie, and Joey were intensely dull, because they talked all the time about what they were doing and what they wanted and what they thought, topics that Lillian could not care less about. With Henry, you had to watch carefully, and guess what he was thinking, and then do something that showed whether you were right or wrong. Mama said he could only be thinking about whether he was hungry or tired or wet, but Lillian did not agree. She thought he was thinking about a lot of things, like the shadows on the floor and the raindrops hitting the windows, and Mama, of course, and Lizzie and Lolly and the hand-me-down rocking horse some Vogel cousins had brought when they came at Christmas to see the baby. Possibly about Little Red Riding Hood and the Big Bad Wolf—Lillian had told him, not the version that Mama told her, where the Wolf ate Little Red Riding Hood, but the version Granny Mary told her, where the Wolf was going to eat her but since he had eaten the Grandma he wasn't very hungry, so he tied a string to her wrist and fell asleep; once he was asleep, Little Red Riding Hood tied him to the bedpost and ran and got the Woodsman, who came in with his ax and slit the wolf from his throat to his belly button and let the Grandma out. She also sang songs to him—there were plenty of those, and Lillian had a good memory for them. At school, she learned "America the Beautiful," at church she learned "I'll Fly Away," from Frankie she learned her favorite, "Hard Times Come Again No More," and from Granny Mary she learned a song about a girl named Laurie who sat on a hill, "Her golden jewelry sparkles as she combs her golden hair." From Granny Elizabeth, she learned a song about a silkie, which seemed to be a monster, that she didn't understand, but sang to Henry anyway, and from Mama she had learned the saddest song of all, which was "Banks of the Ohio," but she didn't sing that one for Henry, she only hummed it from time to time.

Almost every day, Mama walked past her and saw her playing with Henry and said, "You are a good, good girl, Lillian. A pure angel, and, truly, you are my salvation. Do you know that?"

And Lillian said yes, because that was what she was supposed to say. But she hardly heard Mama say these things, because she couldn't take her eyes off Henry.

PAPA AND FRANK mostly stayed out of the house—that was the easiest thing. Once in a while, Papa said, "Well, son, your mama cannot be pleased, and that's the way women get to be sometimes. You have to make up your mind to put up with it, and go about your business." The outside work could have been worse—had been worse. At least this year there was almost enough rain, and the crop looked pretty good. When the sheep shearers came, Papa gave Joey all the wool, because he said that Frank had hardly done a thing for those 4-H lambs—if they had been left to him, they would have starved to death. But so what if Joey got a few bucks for his wool? Frank had stretched his rabbit skins from the winter on the south side of the barn, and then he had taken them to Dan Crest, who found a man from Des Moines who bought them for a dollar apiece—that was twenty-two dollars—and said they were good quality and "the ladies'll love 'em." He said what he was really looking for was fox, though. No one could resist fox. So one thing Frank did to stay out of the house was roam down by the creek and through the fields, scouting fox burrows and keeping his eyes peeled for other possibilities. Papa said that this was very "enterprising."

Of course, he did all of his other work, too—feeding the cattle and Jake and Elsa, working the fields, fixing fence, and planting. Pruning the Osage-orange hedge had fallen to him, too, and he had hated it until a new boy at school, from out of state somewhere, had told him you could make a good bow and even arrows from the branches of the hedge, and he spent part of the winter doing that. Papa complained about all the farm work, especially now that Elsa was almost twenty and Jake was not much younger. A plan he'd had of raising a foal and getting another one had come to nothing. Grandpa Wilmer had gone out of the horse business; what were they going to do? Maybe Elsa would last through the year, and maybe not. Papa said, for the hundredth time, as he was putting them away and Frank was hanging up the harness, "Well, we'll see what happens. Maybe Roosevelt will send us a couple of good horses, now that he's been inaugurated," but Frank didn't consider himself a horseman, he considered himself a tractor man. He kept his eye peeled for tractors. There were three—two on the other side of Denby, owned by the Marshalls and the Larsens, and one about two miles north of the school, owned by none other than the Dugans. The Dugans' tractor was a John Deere, green as a stalk of corn and with yellow wheels, and Frank thought it was much better-looking than a Farmall, but he did agree about how the Farmall was more like a tricycle, and easier to steer. Both of the tractors on the other side of Denby were Farmalls, black.

Grandpa Wilmer was not going to be the one to get the first tractor in the family. He was out of the horse-breeding business, and had sold his stallion to a breeder down in Missouri for next to nothing, a fellow who had imported some giant donkeys from France after the war and was trying to develop a new type of hinny. But for what, Frank wanted to know? Better to have a tractor.

Mama and Papa were already arguing about whether Frank should go on to the high school. It wasn't that he couldn't do the work—everyone knew that he could, and would—he liked the work. Miss Grant said that she had nothing more to teach him—he knew everything she knew already, and a lot of things she didn't, and so she had him teach the younger boys, though he was not allowed to smack them if they made mistakes. The high school was a ways— three miles—and without any help on the farm, Papa didn't see how he was going to afford anything about this. If Frankie walked, it would take him an hour (a half an hour, thought Frankie, because he could run the whole way), and the hack was slow, too, since it had to wind around to several other farms to pick up other youngsters. But how was Walter going to afford the gasoline to take him, and who would drive? And the school day at the high school was a long one, especially with the going back and forth. "Your smartest child!" shouted Mama. "You want to bury him on the farm for the rest of his life. You think this place is the be-all, end-all, and it isn't!"

Frank's solution was a bicycle—he'd seen one for sale at a second-hand store in Usherton, cruiser style, not very old, fifteen dollars. He knew Papa was going to object—that was always his first response to anything—and maybe it would be hard to pedal on the dirt roads sometimes, but the roadbed curved upward, and he was sure he could pedal fine if he went straight down the middle and watched for ruts. Not to mention snow and ice. The thing was to get to Usherton, and to do that he would have to take the car.

What you did when you wanted to get away with something was not to plan, but to look for an opportunity. Frank didn't think that bicycle was going anywhere—fifteen dollars was a lot of money with everyone out of work and half the shops in Denby and Usherton boarded over—so he waited. A few weeks passed, and the argument went on about high school—Mama now wondered why a man who planned to have a family would buy a farm "off away from every-thing," and Papa asked her if she understood the first thing about soil fertility and wells and taking what you could get, and Mama said she understood all of that perfectly well, thank you, then burst into tears again. Papa said Frank had eighth grade left to go, why not worry about it later, and Mama said, "He's teaching the younger boys! There's nothing left there for him."

The opportunity came one morning after a not so big blowup at the breakfast table. Joey and Lillian had fled, saying they had to be at school early, and Frank was lingering behind the barn, wondering if maybe hooky wasn't a nicer thing to do on a lovely day than sitting in that stuffy schoolhouse. Grandpa Otto drove up in his truck, and Papa wiped his hands on his overalls, ran out to the road, and got in without shouting goodbye. There had been nothing said about this at breakfast, so Frank didn't know why Papa was going to the other farm, but so be it. Frank circled the barn and then the back of the house, until he could look into his own window. His room was empty and still, the door to the rest of the house closed. Frank pushed on the screen and climbed in to get his money.

He did know how to drive—Papa had taught him, in case of emergency. Mama had never learned; someone had to. But he hadn't driven by himself before. Backing the car out was no problem—he just released the brake and let it slide. Once he reached the road, he started it up, backed around, and drove away without a glance. If Mama was waving at him from the porch, he would find out about it later.

He sat up as straight as he could and looked carefully at every intersection for any other vehicles. But what vehicles would there be? It was a clear day—everyone was in the fields. After maybe a half an hour, he went through those woods and over the river, which had risen almost as high as the banks, and into town. Now was the confusing part—how to get to the shop, which he had seen when he was in town with Papa a few weeks ago. But there were plenty of cars and trucks, and he just did what the ones with dirty wheels did, headed toward the farm-supply store. Probably it took him longer to get there than it would have taken Papa, but he recognized the way as he passed. As for driving, he kept to the right, used his hand signals, and maintained the same speed as everybody else, and there it was, the Back for More Store, and right in the window, the bicycle. For- tunately, no one was parked in front, so all Frank had to do was pull over, glide to a stop, and turn the car off.

The woman in the store was glad to sell the bicycle. She said, "Oh, it's so nice when a young person has a chance to see the countryside, and this is a lovely Columbia, hardly used." She smiled at Frank's fifteen dollar bills, and held the door for him as he wheeled the thing out. She said, "Is your father—?" But Frank just pretended he had nothing to do with the car and got on the bicycle and rode it around the corner. It was harder than he'd thought it would be, but, then, the streets were paved, so it was easier in that way. In all this planning, he'd forgotten that he'd never actually ridden a bicycle.

It took about an hour, weaving and winding down the streets of Usherton, some a little busy and some nice and empty. He even waved—to Pastor Elmore as he passed their church. He heard Pastor Elmore's shout following him. Back at the shop, he saw the sign on the window—"Closed for Lunch"—and he hurriedly opened the passenger door and slid the bike in, in front of the back seat, lifting the wheel a bit and twisting it so the thing would fit. Then he got in and drove home, which took a little longer because he was so excited that he kind of forgot how to shift and stalled out a couple of times. He did remember to buy some gas—he'd brought along a dollar for that. He got almost six gallons, which was pretty good, he thought, and would go some way toward pleasing Papa in spite of himself. He also put some air in the tires of the bicycle.

Well, they were waiting for him when he got home—turned out that Papa was only at Grandpa Otto's for an hour or so, and Mama did remember seeing the car drive away, and Papa went over to the school to see if Frank was there. Maybe they were all sitting on the porch because it was a nice day, and maybe they were waiting to see what was going to happen. As he drove in, Papa stood up, came down the steps—he looked pretty mad, though he wasn't undoing his belt. Without glancing at him, Frank went smartly around the back of the car, opened the door, and eased the bicycle out. He heard Joey say, "Oh boy!"

Papa met him and the bicycle at the edge of the grass. He snapped, "What's that?"

"It's a Columbia Cruiser. I think it's about a year old, not much more. . . ."

"How did you get it?"

"Well, I took some of my rabbit-skin money, and I bought it for riding to the high school. I estimate I can get there in a half-hour or less, faster than the hack. . . ." His voice was getting too quick. He glanced at Papa.

"Who gave you permission to take the car?"

"No one."

Mama had Henry on her hip, standing on the top step of the porch, and Frank knew what to do—he smiled at her. And then she said, "You're always talking about enterprising, Walter. That's enterprising."

He made his voice level and businesslike. "I can start high school in the fall and graduate when I'm seventeen." Then, "I put a dollar's worth of gas in the car."

Walter said, "Oh, good Lord. Well, your punishment is to wash the car, inside and out—got me?"

Frank knew he could get Joey to help.

"Thank the Lord you're back safe," said Rosanna. "My heart was in my throat." But she couldn't hide that she was pleased.

ONE DAY at the end of August, Papa came home from the county agent's office in Usherton and said, "I guess we're going to buy a tractor." Joe hadn't seen a smile on Papa's face in a long time—not even during the oat harvest, even though the crop looked pretty good—and Joe had heard him say to Mama, "Five years ago, I knew I could sell the oats for a bit more than I put into growing them, but if I fed them to the hogs and the cattle, the animals turned those oats into real money, and I have to say, I thought I knew what I was doing. But now I can't get six cents on the dollar for what I put into them, and hog and cattle prices are so low that, the more oats that pass through the animals, the less they are worth. I don't know which end is up anymore."

And Mama said, "Did you hear that the Larsens are heading to California?"

"Up past Denby there?"

"They shouldn't have bought that tractor. I don't know what got into their heads."

But then there was a law—Roosevelt got it passed—Papa got money for not planting half the corn crop. "And why should I plant it?" said Papa. "Forty-two bushels per acre, but only seventeen cents a bushel—what's the difference between that and nine bushels an acre at eighty-five cents a bushel? Exactly none, except that those forty-two bushels cost the soil something. So, next year, I'm planting clover on half of it and then plowing it under."

The day when Papa and Frank went off to get the tractor was the day when Eloise came for a visit with her husband and her new baby.

Joe was carrying water to the sheep (down to four now) when he saw the car drive in, a Plymouth with a rumble seat. It was a beautiful car, and when Eloise got out of the passenger side with the baby in her arms, and a tall, thin man got out of the driver's side, Joe ran to the well and washed his hands and face under the pump. By the time he got inside, Eloise and the man were sitting on the sofa and Mama was in her rocking chair with Henry on her knee. Lillian was cooing over the baby, who looked just like the man, Joe thought, if that was possible in a baby.

Mama said, "Joey, look who's here! Eloise has a baby girl named—"

"Rosa!" cried Lillian. "She's five months old. Guess what! She was born on your birthday!"

"Yup," said Eloise. "March 13."

The man had his hands on his knees, and he was looking around.

Eloise said, "Rosa Sylvia Silber. I plan for her to be a heroine of the people. Joey, this is Mr. Silber. He's my husband. Your uncle Julius."

Joe did what he had been told to do, which was to look Mr. Silber straight in the eye and hold out his right hand to be shaken, then say, "How do you do, Mr. Silber?"

The man said, "Pleased to meet you, Joe." His accent was musical, his hand enormous, but long and thin. He had nice fingernails.

Mama said, "Mr. Silber is a writer. He writes things for a living."

"I do, too," said Eloise.

"Well, I—" began Mama.

Lillian held her arms out for the baby, and the baby held her arms out for Lillian. Rosanna gave her first good smile that Joe had seen. Eloise hesitated for a moment, then let Lillian take the baby. Lillian, as always, did a good job and was stronger than she looked. She put one arm under Rosa's backside and another around her waist and held her close. Mama said, "Lillian is a real little mother. Must come from Walter's side."

Eloise laughed.

Joe said, "Papa's buying a tractor today."

"Indeed," said Mr. Silber. He looked around.

"Yes," said Mama. "He got a check from the Agricultural Adjustment Act. And then there was a family who went to California. He got it much more cheaply than he might have."

Mr. Silber said, "We read about the Farmers' Holiday Association."

"Oh," said Mama, "Walter can't stand them. They torpedoed a train."

"That's just a rumor," said Mr. Silber. "But they've accomplished a few things that needed to get done. Farmers need to understand that they are workers, too. They have more in common with other laborers than with great landowners."

Joe liked hearing Mr. Silber speak.

"Maybe so," said Mama. "Maybe so. Maybe so. Care for some lemonade? Hot day."

Mr. Silber leaned forward. "Solidarity is the *most* important thing. The bosses and the bankers have it. We have to have it, too."

Mama's face hardened. She said, brightly, "I'm sorry. I would have to disagree. The *most* important thing is getting right with the Lord, and then he will provide." She cleared her throat. "As with the new tractor, for example."

"Well," said Eloise, "perhaps it would have been better if you and the Larsens, is it, had shared the tractor. Possessions often possess us. I was reared on a farm. I know what that means, don't I, Julius?" She turned back to Rosanna. "I remember full well, when we were children, how nobody had all the right equipment, and so, at harvest time and butchering time, people went around to other farms and helped. That's all I mean. That's the basis of a cooperative movement."

"We still do that. Make big suppers and all. Mama was here with all her friends for the oat harvest two weeks ago. It's enjoyable."

Everyone seemed relieved.

Eloise turned to Mr. Silber and said, "In fact, Rosanna always served the best ice cream. I made the kids turn the crank."

Eloise and Uncle Julius were gone by the time Frank and Papa got back. The tractor was a black Farmall with red wheels. You started the engine in the front with gas, that was called the pony engine, and then that started the real engine, which ran on diesel. Frankie thought the tractor was the greatest thing since his bicycle, but Joe thought it was noisy and ugly, and he didn't like the idea of Jake and Elsa never doing anything again—that might be a step toward Papa's deciding that they had no use anymore and sending them to the slaughterhouse on the other side of Usherton. Joe knew perfectly well that it was one thing for Papa to say that Jake and Elsa had been good horses and would always have a home, and quite another for one of them to step in a hole and break a leg and Papa to decide that it wasn't worth calling the vet to save him or her. When he grew up, Joe thought, he was going to have a dog, and no one would stop him.

1934

⤳

FRANK WAS FOURTEEN, but he looked sixteen and acted eighteen. He got up every morning and did his work around the farm first, then he cleaned up, got on his bike, and was out of the house before Mama had even come down. He could get to the high school in fifteen minutes, depending on the condition of the road and the strength of the tailwind. This year there wasn't much snow, and what there was was light and dry and blew away almost as soon as it fell. When he got there, Frank parked his bike and cleaned himself up again. The high school was fairly new, a big brick building with white-framed windows and high ceilings. It had been in session for three years, but already there was a social divide between the farm boys and the town boys—even if they were from the "town" of Denby, or the "town" of Randolph, which was five miles north of Denby, and even smaller. The nicer part of Usherton was south of Main Street, and kids from down there went to another high school, but the Usherton kids at North High were happy to put on airs around the farm kids. Though not around Frank.

Frank had never enjoyed anything in his life as much as he enjoyed the high school. He enjoyed the Roman Empire, he enjoyed pistils and stamens, he enjoyed $a(b + c) = x$, he enjoyed *Treasure Island,* he enjoyed shop class, he enjoyed chorus, he enjoyed sauntering down the hall as if he had all the time in the world, he enjoyed smiling at the girls and laughing at the guys (or with the guys—the key was that they would never be able to tell the difference). He enjoyed being tall, he enjoyed being broad-shouldered, and he enjoyed the looks he got as he made his way. Yes, everyone knew he was a farm kid—he didn't lie about that—but he made sure that he never had any shit on his shoes and that he always looked smooth and relaxed. His smile (he worked on it) was slow, and he never said yes or no, he always said "Maybe," as in "Did you do that assignment?" "Maybe." "Have you seen *Broadway Bill*?" "Maybe." "Are you going to Freddie Haywood's Christmas party?" "Maybe." There was a lot you could do with "maybe"—yes, no, I don't care, I'm not telling you, I haven't made up my mind. It was exactly the sort of word that Walter and Rosanna hated most. And the very best thing about being at the high school was that Minnie and Joey hadn't come with him. He rode his bike three miles, and he got away from everyone he knew, just about. It could not be said that he had friends at high school. But he didn't want friends—he wanted pals and associates, the sort of teachers and kids who didn't ask questions and let you do what you wanted. Of course, there was a price to pay, and he paid it every day—pedaling home with the afternoon wind in his face, blinding him with tears even if his muffler was wrapped up to his eyes. Fifteen minutes to school was thirty minutes home. But he just gritted his teeth and pedaled harder, rain or snow. Mama worried and Papa was impressed; best of all, they left him alone.

ROSANNA FOUND Henry to be a mysterious child. One morning in March, not yet a year and a half old, he refused the breast. There was a look on his face that she had seen before on him—skeptical. If you handed him a toy he didn't care for or showed him a book he wasn't interested in, he got the same look. Now it was her breast. She closed the front of her dress with some sense of embarrassment, as if it were she who had gone too far. Downstairs, she had the distinct feeling, as she set him in the high chair and scrambled him an egg, that he had come to a decision—enough of that—and he would never look back. It was not as though he were universally hard to please—he ate up his egg and some oatmeal and a spoonful of applesauce that Granny Elizabeth had made in the fall; he loved Lillian (as who did not?), and he laughed readily at games and antics—but he was discriminating. Rosanna had never had a discriminating child before—whiny, yes; picky (Granny Mary had said Lillian was picky when the girl wouldn't wear that hideous green sweater Oma had knitted for her), yes; hard to understand, yes—but there was something rather impersonal about Henry. He was built in a certain way, that was all. Rosanna was both intimidated and intrigued. When she was away from him, she didn't imagine him the proper baby size—always bigger. The other thing was that, even though he looked just like Lillian, she never thought he was beautiful or alluring in the same way that Lillian was, and that, she thought, was because he was so self-contained.

All day long that day, Rosanna kept her eye on him, followed him, handed him a toy or two. He played quietly, looked out the window, ate his dinner, went down for his nap, made no trouble.

And then Lillian got home. Rosanna was in her own room, folding laundry, when she heard Joe's and Lillian's steps on the front porch, and it wasn't more than a moment after that, before Lillian even called out or opened the door, that Henry shouted, "Mama! Up!" Normally, she would have finished what she was doing before going in, but, just to see with her new eyes, she dropped the socks she was balling together, went to the hallway, and peeped into Henry's room. He was staring at the door, a big smile on his face. So she went in. His face fell. She said, "Want to see Lillian, Henry? She's home from school." His face lit up again. Well, she thought as she carried him down the stairs, things could not be clearer than that. But she was oddly unmoved—or, at least, she recognized repayment when she saw it. She, who had always had a favorite, no matter how hard she tried to love them equally and for themselves, as Jesus loved all the little children, was now not the favorite. She thought of a phrase from the Bible—where, she did not know—"In all that has happened to us, you have been just; you have acted faithfully, while we did wrong."

At the bottom of the steps, Lillian was looking up at them. She said, "Mama, Mama! Guess what! Jane has a new sister! They named her Gloria."

Rosanna stepped off the bottom step and set Henry on his feet. He put his hand in Lillian's. Rosanna said, "How wonderful. 'Gloria' is a good name."

"Can we make up a box of clothes and toys for her?"

"Goodness, child, everything we have is for boys, and old and patched. If Frankie didn't wear it first, then Joey did, then you, then Henry."

Lillian kissed Henry and then gave her mother a serious look. She said, "I don't know if they have anything, Mama."

It was true that Jane was a ragged child, though loving and sweet. The Morrises went to some tiny church somewhere, the sort of church where there wouldn't be any old clothes or hand-me-down dolls. She said, "We can ask Granny Mary to look for some nice things at the Catholic church. But when we wrap them up, don't you say where they came from, all right?"

"A secret?"

"Your secret and my secret."

Lillian nodded. Then she said, "Oh, my goodness, Henry, I have a whole new story to tell you! About a cat this time, named Petie. He wears boots!" They walked over to the sofa, and Lillian helped him crawl up onto the cushion.

THIS YEAR, because of the tractor, Walter had planted the corn in a new way—not drilling in a grid, but in long rows. And he only planted twenty acres, enough for seed for next year and for their own animals. The government was paying them not to plant, but, as Walter pointed out to Rosanna, it wasn't paying them enough to buy someone else's corn. He did buy a lister—a Go-Dig lister, and it cost him ten dollars, which seemed like a little but was actually a lot. He had thought that maybe he could make some of the machinery he had used with the horses work with the tractor, if he modified it a bit, and that had worked with the oat seeder, and he thought it might work with the oat threshing. But he couldn't resist the lister. The fact was that, if the rain was going to hold off, then he had to plant the corn deeper—not two or three inches, but five or six, down where the soil was still moist. And the fact was that he was going to know that that plume of dust was lifting behind him and swirling into the sky, and he was not going to turn his head to look at it.

The lister did a thing for corn that Walter had never seen before—you set the disks one way the first time you cultivated the field, and they turned the dirt toward the middle, between the rows, making a little mound there, and letting the corn shoots, planted so deep, make their way to the surface. And then, a few weeks later, when the cornstalks were taller and thicker, and in danger of falling over, you set the disks of the lister the other way, and they piled the soil against the row of stalks, supported them, and protected the ground moisture (as if there were ground moisture). Walter couldn't help liking it. And the whole operation took a couple of days each time—none of that struggle, especially on hot days with the horses to get a few rows done, bringing buckets of water for them, swatting the flies, worrying about them when you saw their flanks heaving and their nostrils flaring, just from the sun and the humidity. Walter hadn't realized how taxing it was to worry about Jake and Elsa. He had said they were work animals and prided himself on knowing that their value lay in their productivity, no different from a pig or a chicken, but, unlike the pigs and the chickens, they had names. The tractor had no name, except "Farmall." It was a relief.

But it was no secret to Walter as he drove the tractor from one end of the twenty-acre cornfield to the other that a tractor was a pact with the devil. How could it be that when they woke up one morning they found dust caked on the west side of the house, and the air so thick you had to wear a wet bandanna outside, keep all the windows shut, and wipe the inside sills anyway? Iowa had prided itself on not being Oklahoma, but how much of a sign did they need? Of course, he did not reveal these thoughts to Rosanna. So he finished planting in a quarter of the time it normally took—that meant that he was looking to plant more, he was looking across the street at other farmers' fields, wondering how much they were planting, and how that was going to depress the price of corn if they were all using tractors to plant. There could be a lot of farmers with horses, but not so many farmers with tractors. That much was evident right off the bat. And yet. And yet, with the lengthening days, Frankie stayed longer at the high school, learning about girls, no doubt, but also about kingdom, phylum, class, order, genus, and species, and also about the French Revolution and the English Revolution and the American Revolution and the Russian Revolution and the Industrial Revolution and the revolution of the Earth around the Sun and all the other revolutions there had been and would soon be, all kinds of things that

Walter didn't know much about, and all of which would draw Frankie like a moth to the flame, because if there was anything Frankie loved, it was making chaos his business. A tractor was what he and Joey needed to get their work done, and so be it, and perhaps, as Rosanna said, the Lord would provide, as he had all along, and didn't Walter know that he was just a worrier, always a worrier? So did driving a tractor make more worry, or less? Yes, the horses were not suffering, and you weren't as close to the dry dirt, but you were driving into the unknown, and at a pretty good clip.

WALTER HADN'T BEEN to the state fair since before Rosanna came along, and Rosanna had never been—the oat harvest was in August, and there was too much farm work to do. But with the tractor this year, and Walter harvesting the oats with Bob Marshall's combine in three days, with help only from Frankie and Joey—well, there they were, with free days in August, and Joe got to take his ewe to the fair after all (Walter had been saying, "We'll see," all along, and this time they saw something good rather than something disappointing).

It made Rosanna a little nervous. She was used to Usherton, and had been to Des Moines when she was a girl three or four times, but Frankie would be clamoring to go on all the most dangerous rides, and it would certainly be hot, and how would they get the ewe there? But it turned out to be easy after all. Roland Frederick was taking his truck—and he would take the six-month-old ewe and Joey. His brother, who lived in Cedar Rapids but had grown up on the family farm, had agreed to come for three days and feed both the Frederick animals and Walter's, because Minnie and her mother were both entered in the pie contest—Lorene with peach and Minnie with blackberry. Lois would go in the car with Walter and Rosanna; Lillian promised to read the two children stories all the way down and all the way back. Frankie had fox money left from the winter (five skins, three dollars apiece), and he promised to give Joey a dollar for the midway. And so, said Walter, if they couldn't afford it, they would worry about it later, because the chance had presented itself, and were they really not going to give Joey the opportunity to repeat his county-fair victory? They both knew that Joey needed all the encouragement he could get.

The ewe, named Emily, was a Southdown. Joey had told Rosanna that he preferred the bare-faced Cheviots, "but they're not in fashion, so you're not going to win with a Cheviot. When I grow up, though, I'm going to have all Cheviots." And all shorthorns for both milk and beef, and all Percherons and all Chanticleers. Rosanna hoped that what Walter sometimes said to her wasn't true—that here Joey was, only twelve years old, and already the world had passed him by.

Rosanna put on her most comfortable dress—the one with the short sleeves, and the little jacket in case it got chilly at night—her most comfortable shoes, and a simple hat she borrowed from Granny Mary, though that was a mistake: with that hat on, she looked like her mother, only not as good-natured. But as she got into the car, she put away the vanities of the world (which was easy enough as soon as she turned around and saw Lillian, sitting with books on her lap between Lois, a very plain girl, and Henry, beaming). Dan Crest had had a lovely length of sky-blue piqué that Rosanna had pieced out into a dress with a little jacket and then embroidered across the bodice. Lillian's hair was to her waist now, and her braids were very shiny and neat. Rosanna decided that maybe Lois wasn't so plain in and of herself, just in comparison to Lillian. She said, "Are you all right, Lois? I like your dress. It's very pretty." She smiled. Lois smiled.

Since it was only fifty miles, and the road led straight there, cutting diagonally across sections, which was rare in Iowa, Walter was soon wondering why they didn't do this more often. Dan Crest did, the Fredericks did, even his folks had been more than once; some people in their church went every year. Rosanna said, "We've got children and business at home, Walter."

"So does everyone. Maybe we're just old stick-in-the-muds. We hardly even go to the movies."

"Most movies are sinful."

"Well, let's try some more out for ourselves. Know thine enemy."

Rosanna made a face, but it was true that she stayed home much more than her mother, who visited someone or other once or twice a week. When her mother told her, just the other week, that she and her father had gone into Usherton and seen a Bette Davis movie called *Of Human Bondage,* Rosanna had been a little taken aback. Now she said, "You were talking to Mama."

"They see a few movies."

"I thought that one sounded horrid."

"But we didn't even see *It Happened One Night*."

Rosanna said, "You know it would terrify me to leave Lillian and Henry with Frankie, my goodness, and Joey. No telling—"

"Minnie would come over."

"I'll just bet." Rosanna knew perfectly well that Minnie had eyes for Frankie—it was embarrassing to look at her. Well, she was a plain one, too, though good in every way, and she would make some farmer a wonderful wife someday.

JOE WAS AMAZED to discover that you didn't have to stay with your ewe every minute. He had more or less expected to camp there, beside her stall, and stare at her for two days, but the 4-H had its own area, and everyone took turns—there was a schedule, and Joe's turn was to be later that afternoon, right before supper, and again in the morning. Of course, you had to come and feed and groom your entry, but the 4-H knew that in this crowd a little peace and quiet off to one side, with not so many people coming and going, was actually less irritating to the animals. Emily was a quiet one, easygoing. Joe put her in her pen, which was clean, and gave her some hay; while he was doing this, Frankie came into the area and looked around for him. Frankie had already seen the midway, and was eager to get over there. He held out his hand and said, "I told Mama I would give you a dollar, but that won't be enough." There were two dollars in his hand. "Just don't pester me, okay?"

"Okay."

"Don't follow me around, and don't call out to me and don't—oh, I don't know—whatever you see, don't tell Mama."

Joe said, "Do I ever?"

"You don't dare."

Joe shrugged.

"Anyway, here." He thrust the money into Joe's pocket and turned away. Joe actually did want to follow him, but he made himself wait, watching Emily, while Frankie loped out of the area and disappeared into the crowd.

"That your ewe?"

Joe looked around. The girl was blonde. She was smiling, and she had a nice sweater on, cream-colored.

"I have a Southdown, too. Yours is nice. I like the way her hind legs are set. She's well proportioned."

"Thanks," said Joe, almost as an afterthought. "She won the class at our county fair." He dug his fingernail into the fence rail. " 'Course, there were only four in the class." He cleared his throat. He knew he was supposed to ask something, then remembered. "Where's yours?"

The girl pointed to a pen across the aisle. "Her name is Poker."

"Mine's name is Emily."

"That's funny. My name is Emily."

Joe felt himself turn red.

"The reason is that my mother had a dog named Emily when she was a girl, and then a horse named Emily, and then me. She says there's no reason not to use a good name as many times as you can."

Joe said, "Your mother sounds like fun."

"She is."

Joe fingered the dollar bills in his pocket and said, "Want to get a root beer?"

Emily nodded. She said, "I bet you're going to win, with that ewe."

IT WAS a cold night, cold enough for a coat, but Frank hadn't brought one. The good thing about it was that he was out on the midway by himself—Papa and Mama had taken Joe and the others back to the room they'd gotten at a boardinghouse, and the Fredericks had left hours ago to have supper with some cousins in Norwalk. There would be hell to pay in the morning—or even in a couple of hours, when Frank tried to sneak into the room without waking anyone up. He had run off just at the very moment when Mama put her hands over her shoulders and shivered, just before she said, "Ah! Well, I guess—" The end of that was going to be leaving the fair, and, sure enough, Frank had watched them from behind the funnel-cake frying stand. They gathered up the family, looked around in vain for him, then gave up and left. If it weren't so cold, it would have taken longer, so that was something to be thankful for.

You couldn't say that the midway was deserted, but in Iowa in

August, you expected it to be seventy-five, so you expected to run from ride to ride and be refreshed as each one spun you around, like the Tilt-A-Whirl, or up and down, but it was freezing at the top of the Ferris wheel, with the wind from the west, so Frank was finished with the rides. In an hour, the exhibits would close, too, and Frank had already seen most of them—the pumpkin that was as big as a hog, the rearing horse carved out of butter, the man with the beard he wrapped around his waist, the man-woman—"How Can You Tell? You Can't!"—and the woman with the fingernails "A Foot Long!" He had watched Joe come third in the ewes and Minnie come second in the 4-H pies (to a mixed apple-blackberry that looked pretty good). He had won Lillian a teddy bear playing Skee-Ball, and impressed Papa (and the man in the booth) by shooting ten duck-targets in a row, until the man said he would pay Frank a dollar to go away, and he did, and Walter laughed for five minutes and said he was going to frame the dollar. They had eaten all kinds of things that made Mama blanch—not only funnel cakes, but candy cotton and hot dogs, and caramel corn and taffy. He had also had plenty of watermelon, and in no order—candy first, meat second, fruit after that. Mama kept her mouth shut, except to say, "Well, pray the Lord you don't get sick." He wasn't hungry, that was for sure.

The girls were just inside the Hall of Machines, huddling together, getting out of the breeze and, Frank saw at the last minute, sharing a cigarette. When they noticed him, Frank smiled. He always smiled at girls. He was taller than both of them, and he guessed that they thought he was pretty old, because they looked at him not like he was a kid. He walked past them, toward the John Deere tractor with some kind of cultivator hitched to it. Deeres were always green, but under the electric lights, this tractor was eye-poppingly green. Frank put his hands in his pockets and stood back from a couple of farmers in overalls who were inspecting it. One said, "I like a Case, myself." Frank did not want to hear this perennial discussion, so he stepped back, and right on the foot of one of the girls. She gave a little scream.

Frank turned around, not taking his hands out of his pockets, and said, "Hey. Sorry. Didn't realize you were standing there." He moved away.

The next exhibit was of a tractor with its own plow, which could lift up at the end of a row. It was a machine that Frank would never purchase, but he gazed at it, cocking his hip to one side, as if it were the most interesting thing in the world. Out of the corner of his eye, he saw the girls move toward the seeders. They stood there for a few moments, then went to the doorway, where they peeked out and drew back in. Frank turned on his heel and did something that he knew Granny Mary would call "sashaying out the door." He went on down past the candy-cotton man and the double Ferris wheel. He glanced around. The girls were nowhere to be seen. But the wind was making his nose run, so that was when he made his big mistake—he wiped his nose on his sleeve, just like a rube would do, and right then, one of the girls, the taller one, with black hair, came around a tree, out of the darkness, and startled him. She was smoothing her dress over her hips. She stopped in front of him and said, "Staring at something?"

"What would I be staring at?"

"Well, I was taking a piss behind that tree, didn't you know that?"

"Nope. Didn't see you." And then he said, "Wish I did." She came up about to his eyebrows, he thought. And she was almost pretty. Eighteen for sure.

"You're a smart kid," she said.

"Who says I'm a kid?"

She laughed and pushed around him, then headed down the midway. He watched her, but she didn't look back. Now he sauntered along, but in two days, he had had a taste of everything, and he had gobbled it all down so fast that it did make him a little sick. At the hotdog stand, he asked the guy frying the hot dogs if he knew what time it was. It was ten-forty-five. Frank yawned.

A few minutes later, he was crossing the campground where all the cars were parked and the tents were set up. The boardinghouse where Mama and Papa were certainly seething with anger was to the left of where the cars were, and he was making his way through all the vehicles when that girl stepped out from behind something black, maybe a Ford. She said, "Oh, there you are."

Frank thought that was a good line. He stopped and tried out one of his slow smiles. The girl said, "How old are you, anyway?"

"Where's your friend?"

"Somewhere. Not here."

"Are you from around here?"

"We drove over from Muscatine."

"That's way east."

"Way east. If you're cold, you can get in our car."

Frank said, "Okay."

When they were in the car, which was actually a Dodge, she said, "So—how old are you?"

"Guess."

"Seventeen?"

"My birthday is New Year's Day." He didn't mention that it would be his fifteenth birthday. "How old are you?"

"Eighteen." Her mouth made a skeptical "o."

The car was not warm, but it was out of the breeze, and with the windows up, he could smell her—a combination of flowers, tobacco smoke, and sweat that was strange. She was sitting by the window. She said, "What's your name?"

Frank said, "Joe. Joe Vogel. How about you?"

"Libby Holman."

He said, "That's a funny name."

"You think so?"

"Yeah."

She stretched her leg toward him, heel first, and said, "Look. I got a run." She took his hand and put the tips of his fingers on the stocking. He didn't know what a run was, and in the dark, he couldn't see anything. He said, "Maybe."

She said, "You're cute."

"My mom says that."

"How about the girls?"

He shrugged, then cocked his head. "I heard they say that."

"Well, you are."

"Doesn't matter to me. I can't look at myself."

"Put your head forward, so I can see you a little in the light."

He leaned forward.

She put his hand back on her leg, and then kissed him, right on the lips. He reciprocated, opening his own lips just a little bit. He slid his hand up her leg, and her leg relaxed. He said, "Where's your friend?"

"Somewhere." And then she rearranged herself for another kiss.

Her jacket and her blouse were open. Her breast was the hottest thing he had ever felt, he thought. She lay back.

In the end, all he did was touch her and look at her. When he came, his thing was pressed against the smoothness of her skirt, and she sat up suddenly and said, "Ugh." Then she pushed him away and lit a cigarette, but she didn't button her blouse or pull down her skirt. She offered him a drag. She said, "How old are you really? Sixteen?"

Frank said, "Maybe."

That got a smile.

THE FUNNY PART, Frank thought on the way home the next day, was listening to Mama and Papa talk about Joey, who was riding with the Fredericks and the ewe. Papa said, "That girl Emily was a very nice girl."

"A little forward, if you ask me."

"Nice animal she had, too."

"I guess she's been in 4-H for years. Her mother said they come every year, and her brother always brought calves. Herefords."

"That right," said Papa.

Frank, of course, was in big trouble, for coming in late, lying, and running off. Mama didn't know what she was going to do with him. He was sitting in the back seat, and Lillian had fallen against him, sound asleep. Henry was up front, in Mama's lap, and Lois had gone in the truck.

Mama said, "I think Joey bought her about five root beers. I don't know why they weren't belching the whole time. I guess they went on the Ferris wheel, too. What was her last name?"

"Stanton. Old man's got two hundred acres by Lone Tree, south of Iowa City there. He said he's looking at less than thirty bushels an acre this year. But I guess they've had more rain than we have."

Mama said, "Well, if she kissed him . . ."

Papa lowered his voice. "Maybe it went the other direction. Maybe he kissed her."

Frank turned his head and looked out the window.

1935

∽

AT DINNER, Henry ate all of his chicken hash and all of his apple-sauce, and Mama said he was a good boy. Then Papa got up from his chair and groaned, but Mama didn't say anything, just kept standing by the sink. When Papa was out the door, Henry slid down from his chair and went over to the sink and held up his hands. Mama pumped some water and wiped his hands and face with a rag.

The room was bright. Henry could see the snow out his window, lots of it, so much that for two days Frankie, Joey, and Lillian had stayed home from school. They had built a snowman sitting in a chair. Henry could see the back of the chair from his crib. It had taken all morning, one of the mornings. Henry liked it. When it was all built, Frankie had sat him in the snowman's lap, and everyone laughed when Henry slid down to the ground.

The house was completely different with no one in it, Henry thought. He went to the toy box and took out three of his books. He opened the one he knew by heart and looked at the pictures while telling himself the story: A man and his wife were lonely. A cat came. More cats came. More cats came. No one had ever seen so many cats in one place before. Papa didn't like cats. Mama said that cats were useful; she shooed them out if they came in the house. Lillian wished she had a cat. Joey wished he had a dog. Henry read the story again, then opened another book, but he didn't know that story. He got up and went into the kitchen. He looked around, but he wasn't hungry. He got up into his chair and got down again. He walked across the kitchen and looked out the window. There was nothing out there, and then there was, something red. Red was a good color. He stared and stared at the red thing in the snow. Maybe it was moving, maybe it was waving. Henry couldn't tell, but he wondered. He opened the kitchen door and put his foot out onto the porch. It was—

"Oh, my goodness!" exclaimed Mama. "What in the world are you doing? I thought you were taking a nap!" She grabbed Henry by the shoulder, and now she whirled him around. "Do I not get a moment's peace? It's freezing out there! You don't have any shoes on, even!" Then she hugged him and started to cry. Out of the corner of his eye, Henry could still see the red thing.

RIGHT AFTER the state fair—all the way to Thanksgiving, maybe— Frank had hardly thought about that girl, Libby Holman. The whole episode just seemed like a little hard bit of a thing that was in your shoe or something. You stopped, shook it out of your shoe, and kept walking. He never told anyone about it (but, then, he never told any- one about anything), and he decided not to think about it, either. He was sure that girl was older than eighteen; when he thought about her, she seemed weird and not like a girl. Whatever sense he had had of being flattered had evaporated as fast as dew in the morning.

Then, at Thanksgiving, a funny thing happened at church (they didn't have the gas to go to church every week, but Mama made sure they went once a month and on special days). At Thanksgiving, Pas- tor Elmore gave thanks for being guided to embark upon a new cru- sade, which was "Nipping It in the Bud." He said, "In these hard times, O Lord, we know that our young people are being led astray by their own thoughts and also by the sinful things they see around them. O Lord, preserve your children from the Jews in Hollywood who infest our world with evil thoughts of bodies and carnality, bare legs, and heaving bosoms. O Lord, you know of what I speak!" And the congregation had said, "Amen!"

On the way home, Frank had heard Papa say, "Now, why did he bring that up?"

And Mama said, "Well, didn't you see that that Mae West picture

came to town? I guess some boys went to see it." Then she cleared
her throat, and Frank knew she was thinking that there were big ears
in the back seat, which there were. Some boys at high school, boys
from Usherton, had been talking about that movie—not about how
naughty it was, but about how it was not nearly as naughty as another
one, called *I'm No Angel*. The boys who were talking about *I'm No
Angel* had sneaked into the theater when the ticket taker went out
back to piss in the alley and thought he had locked the door. Well, he
hadn't.

It wasn't that Frank knew what Mae West looked like or anything
about the movies, even though he had listened closely to what the
boys were saying. But that phrase, "I'm no angel," went together with
Libby Holman and Pastor Elmore, and the thing that was lodged in
his shoe (in his mind, he knew) got bigger and he couldn't shake it
out. If he stayed awake at night and didn't fall right to sleep, he had to
turn on his side, away from Joey, and push his cock down between his
legs, but even then it got bigger. This was called jerking off. The boys
at school talked about that, too. And about whores. Two boys, Pat
Callahan and Linc Forbes, had been taken to whores by their fathers
when they turned sixteen. Frank was wondering if that was the reason Libby Holman asked him his age. Maybe she was a whore, and if
he was sixteen she was supposed to charge him some money.

Of his rabbit and fox money, Frank had kept back eight dollars
and given the rest to Mama. Papa had gotten nothing for the oats and
nothing for the corn after harvest—the cost of planting, when you
factored in fuel for the tractor and a repair that a man had had to come
out and do (and he had taught Papa how to do some repairs himself,
so the money had been worth it, but still they paid him partly in eggs
and butter), had been more than the corn and oats were worth, even
when processed through hogs and cows and sold as milk, beef, and
pork—beef was selling in the winter at under ten cents a pound. Only
Mama, with her chickens and cream, and Frank, with his fox pelts,
were actually bringing in cash, and all of that was going for three
things, shoes, coal, and mortgage. With luck, Papa said, there would
be an early spring and the coal would hold out. And no one at school
had it much better. The two boys Frank knew who smoked cigarettes
were stealing them, and the ones who saw movies were sneaking in.
Every time they went to church, Mama put a quarter in when they

passed the plate. That was fifteen eggs. Frank kept the eight dollars behind a loose board next to the gun case. Since Walter no longer hunted, even deer, Frank was the only person who went near the gun case (and Mama made him store his bullets out in the barn).

But, Frank thought, if Libby Holman were a whore, she wouldn't have seemed so sad after he came on her skirt, but that part made him feel strange, too, both the coming and the look on her face, and the sound of her voice when she said, "Ugh." He had thought that Pastor Elmore was on to something when he talked about his new crusade, but then Mama had made him and Joey go to a class where the man from Des Moines who specialized in all of this didn't say a word that was useful—it was all about kissing girls and magazines and striptease ("It's not worth it, boys, it really isn't," and "Thank the Lord that Iowa is still dry, boys," and "The girls you really like, and who are worth your time, depend on you to keep yourselves and your thoughts clean!"). The night of that class, Frank lay in bed thinking about it, and he couldn't for the life of him make a link between Libby Holman, that cold night in the car, sitting there with her clothes all rumpled and her hair messed up, and the light from the state-fair midway glaring down across her cheek, and what that fellow said. Jackson Clifford, his name was: "Call me Jack Cliff, boys. Wherever you are now, I've been there!"

IT COULD HAVE BEEN colder. Other springs had been, Walter knew. Here he was forty now. Wasn't that something? Walter thought. Been on this farm for fifteen years, and the day he walked through the farmhouse and decided that this was the one he could afford was as clear in his mind as anything. Now he was forty and had a belly and his hair was backing off his forehead, just the way his father's had, and the oddest thing was that his eyes were lighter and lighter blue, as if that was where the graying was taking place, not on top of his head. Walter carried both pails across the barnyard, which was wet but not squelching. Down to four milkers now, which he didn't mind compared with starving to death. He and Joey between them could milk four cows in half an hour. He stepped onto the well cover, which was crisscrossed with bindweed that he should have rooted out, but in fact he rather liked the flowers that would come in the summer. He set the pail underneath the spigot and began working the pump handle. The water came pretty quick—two up, two down. Good well, Walter was thinking.

When the well cover broke away underneath him and the pail fell into the well, Walter threw his arms out straight to either side. The edges of the well caught them above the elbows. Walter looked down. The pail made a splash.

The dark, wet sides of the well dropped maybe twenty feet to the surface of the water. He could just make out the edges of some of the bricks that had been used to shore it up, and he wasn't actually afraid, just startled. Startled at the sight of his own boots hanging there, maybe fifteen feet above the dim shine that would have been his death if he hadn't thrown out his arms. He had never fallen into a well before. It was children who fell into wells.

Of course, he was only preliminarily saved. He had to figure out how to move forward or backward or upward somehow, and for the moment, the instinct that had thrown his arms out wasn't operating. He took a deep breath and looked around. Rosanna was in the house; you couldn't see the well from the house. He had left a barn door open by mistake. He took another deep breath. It was a chilly day. The water would be chillier still.

And yet.

And yet the farm was bust. He had no money, and his land now was worth eleven dollars an acre, maybe. The cows and hogs and Jake and Elsa and the sheep were worth nothing. The tractor was worth less than he had paid for it, not because there was anything wrong with it, but because there was no one who could buy it from him. He dreaded that his father might die and leave him the big farm, even though it was paid for (or probably it was—his father was close-mouthed about all dealings with the bank). He had voted for Roosevelt, and he would vote for the Democrat in '36 if he was any good at all, but it had all come to naught anyway, and so . . .

He looked down again. A single streak of sunlight shone on the surface of the water. The water could be ten feet deep. He would either let out all his breath and just sink, or he wouldn't. He wasn't much of a swimmer, but his father had taught him to tread water. How long could he go?

How long could he hang here? He was a strong man, especially in the shoulders and upper arms.

Would Rosanna miss him? He had to say that he didn't know. She would be furious with him for sure—how could he do such a stupid thing, stepping on the well cover, or not fixing the well cover, or something? And how could he? As in so many things, she was right. That's what he had married her for, wasn't it? That she was smart and self-assured and knew what she wanted. If you didn't have that in a farm wife, then the farm wasn't going to make it. But maybe the farm wasn't going to make it anyway. He looked down again. Experimentally, he let his shoulders relax. They didn't relax. He tried again. They still didn't relax. It was then he knew that the end really wasn't at hand, that his body would save itself, no matter what, and it did. He used his elbows to inch his way forward until his chest was flat against the front edge of the well; then he grabbed the pump shaft below the spigot with his hand and clambered out. He wasn't even wet. The second pail was sitting there on the ground. He stood behind the pump, holding the pail under the spigot, and when it was mostly full, he was careful to stay back from the edge of the well. He got some planks of old barn siding and placed them over the hole. He didn't look at it again, nor did he tell Rosanna, when he went in for dinner, that he'd had a close call, but that was what he decided to name it. It was only a few days later, when he had to fill a bucket at that well again, that he felt the fear, that he didn't want to go near the thing or step on the boards he'd laid across it, though he knew they were sturdy. Once he dreamt about it, too—not about falling into that particular well, but about sinking into a pile of straw so that he couldn't get out, so that the straw got into his mouth and he couldn't make a sound. He woke up in the dark and thought, so he was still afraid of death after all. But when Rosanna turned over and asked what the problem was, he said, "Nothing. Can't remember now."

ROSANNA RARELY LISTENED to the radio, but she did know, if only dimly, about the Labor Day hurricane down in Florida somewhere. Who in Iowa thought about Florida? People in Iowa had problems of their own—maybe not dust storms like the ones out in Nebraska and Oklahoma, and maybe not heat like in Texas, but if you got up in a sweat every morning after barely sleeping all night, and there was no rain for the crops and not much water for the animals, and the children were crying, and when Henry, so beautiful, fell and cut his lower lip and you couldn't afford to take him to the doctor but had to boil a needle and a length of silk thread and sew it up yourself, with him lying on Lillian's lap and screaming, and Lillian herself streaming with tears, well, you had to wonder if a slow demise was preferable to a quick one, didn't you?

But Pastor Elmore knew all about the hurricane, and he saw it clearly as God's will. His cousin was at the work camp there for war veterans, and was lost, presumed dead now, six days later. Pastor Elmore was sweating already before the sermon, given how hot it was, and all the ladies in the congregation were sitting there with their collars open, fanning themselves. Walter had his handkerchief on his head to keep the sweat from pouring into his eyes, and Henry was asleep on her lap—that scar was one he would have for the rest of his life, but after sewing it, she had put bag balm on it and some leaves her mother had, and it wasn't his arm or his eye or his leg, was it? Only Lillian was neat and calm. She was a marvel. Joey and Frankie had stayed home to look after the animals—they were lost to the faith, maybe—but just as Rosanna was thinking that she was too tired to care right this very minute, Pastor Elmore roared out, " 'On that day all the springs of the great deep burst forth, and the floodgates of the heavens were opened!' And why was that, my friends? Why did the Lord see fit to destroy his own creation, like a sculptor who smashes his clay with his fist, or a painter who slashes his canvas? Why, because it wasn't right and good! And does the pot revile its creator for this? And does the painting weep? *No!* And so we must accept that the Lord is getting mighty close to that state of dissatisfaction he found himself in when Noah was six hundred years old. Did you know, my friends, that there is no record of such a hurricane as struck those islands in Florida seven days ago? The first of its kind! *What* does that tell you? And, my friends, look around you. Are your crops thriving and your cattle fattening? *No,* they are not.

"Let me tell you about my cousin. My cousin was not a bad man. His name was Robert, and he was a kind and gentle boy when I first knew him. He was not a boy to tease a cat or trap a bird, but neither was he right with the Lord, and his life was on a downward path. He came home from the war a drunkard, and his mother died of the grief. Nor was he a mean drunk, my friends. If he had a dollar, after spending what he needed to on a pint, he would give it to you, and no thanks necessary. But his wife didn't know him, and his children didn't know him, and he wandered off, from Ohio to Missouri to Texas to California to Florida, hardly a word to his family, only a card from time to time to say where he was, and last spring he was in Florida, clearing swamp, and three weeks ago he was there, too. But the Lord was having none of it. The Lord is just about to that point he was with the Nephilim—sick and tired of the sin. And so he is sending us warning after warning. Did every single Nephilim man, woman, and child offend him? I doubt it. I am sure there were good Nephilim and kind Nephilim like my cousin. They were, it is said, the sons of God, as are you and I. But they were sensuous and irresponsible, and so God saved Noah and his sons and their families, and he saved some animals, and he smashed the rest.

"Now, you are saying that God gave Noah a promise never to do such a thing again, and that is true, but neither did he inundate the whole world—just a bit of it there in Florida. And I am telling you that this is a warning to you and to me. . . ."

Rosanna dabbed her upper lip with her handkerchief, then patted Henry's forehead. Lillian was taking in every word. She was almost nine now. It occurred to Rosanna that maybe Lillian did not have to hear this—she was already careful to be good at all times and in all ways. Did she need to know that being good wasn't good enough? When you came right down to it, Rosanna thought, being a Catholic was more reassuring for a child—it made sense to confess your sins, do your penance, and have a clean slate. Rosanna didn't think about her childhood much—no time for it—but maybe going to St. Albans had been easier than this. If a child thought a priest or a pastor was the voice of God, then at St. Albans the priest droned on every week in the same Latin gibberish and the rules were clear. Here, the pastor was very excitable and full of inspiration—Rosanna knew that he wouldn't have talked about the hurricane or Noah or the Nephilim if his cousin hadn't been killed. She looked at Walter. He had his elbow on the end of the pew and his hand over his eyes. He could make it no clearer that, whatever he said, what he thought was that she had gotten them into this congregation, and it was up to her to get them out.

The pastor boomed out again: "My friends, who can say where it will end? Who can say when the Lord will at last be pleased with us?"

Walter shifted in his seat, and Lillian took his hand. Rosanna saw him squeeze hers. Right then, Henry woke up and coughed. Rosanna knew a sign when she saw it. She poked Walter and cocked her head toward the entrance. Walter took her meaning as if he had indeed been waiting. As one, they got up quietly, and eased out in Walter's direction—thank the Lord, not the center aisle but the right-hand one—and they walked toward the door without looking back or looking down at any of their fellow worshippers. Behind them, Pastor Elmore said, "My friends, I think, humbly and even with thanks, that we should be prepared for just about . . ." The door swished closed behind them, and they were out on the porch.

1936

〜

FRANK WAS SITTING in his seat in the fourth coach (right behind the dining car). Out the window, there was nothing to look at but snow, snow, snow. That was the way it had been all winter—at home, the drifts on the west side of the house were above the roof of his and Joey's room—when you looked out the window you saw a crystalline white wall. This snow was blowing, but it was still utterly white, and Frank could feel the train slow. He had been on the train for three hours, so maybe they were almost to Clinton, maybe not. The last stop, where the stationmaster had put the flag up for some folks who got on and then passed through to the sleeper, was DeWitt.

The reason Frank found himself on the train, the Challenger, the newest and best train on the Chicago and Northwestern line, was that Mama just could not put up with him any longer, though what she said was that he had to go to school, there was no way around it. Maybe it wasn't so important for Joey, but Frankie needed school. The idea that he would go to school in Chicago had rolled across the table as a silly thought at Thanksgiving, when Eloise came home with Rosa and Julius. Already by that time, Frank had missed six days of high school, off and on, because of snow, and Mama was plenty steamed about it—steamed at Papa, it seemed, as if the blizzards were Papa's fault. "Well, send him to me in Chicago," said Eloise, and Mama said, "Oh, don't be ridiculous!"

But between Thanksgiving and Christmas he had missed nine days, four of them because the school itself was closed when the water pipes burst. Grandpa Wilmer and Granny Elizabeth and all the oldest people Frank knew said that they had never seen a winter like this—it wasn't just that there were layers of snow on the ground, five feet in some places, not including the drifts, but it was deathly cold and windy, too. Papa's cows and sheep and hogs hadn't been out of the barn for any reason in two months. "Are we living in Minnesota now?" exclaimed Mama. But Papa said it would turn out fine in the end, because the drought was over. At Christmas, Eloise issued her invitation again—yes, the snow was deep in Chicago, too, but she and Julius had a big apartment a block from the high school. Frank would like it, she thought. And Mama said yes.

The train came to a halt, but there was no town to be seen, even dimly. Frank looked around at the other passengers—there were twelve of them in this car, a family with three kids, two ladies, and the rest businessmen. The ladies kept talking, and the businessmen kept reading their newspapers. Only the kids gawked at the windows. The car was quiet. Frank got up.

The wind in the vestibule was sudden and breathtakingly cold, even though it was surely no sharper than Frank had felt many times heading home from school. As Frank pushed and pushed on the door into the dining car, he felt a moment of panic. In the dining car, there was more news—the locomotive had run up against a huge drift. Crews were coming. No telling how long it might take. Frank eavesdropped on a man asking the porter "whether you expect supplies to hold out." Since he had a glass of whiskey in his hand, Frank figured that was the supply that he meant.

"Yes, suh. I expect they will hold out for a week, suh." The porter was the first black man Frank had ever seen. Mama had told him that he would see plenty of black people in Chicago, and that he was to avoid antagonizing them by looking them in the eye, and that only low-class people called them "niggers," and that that word was another thing they didn't like, so to be careful. They were to be called "colored." But it looked to Frank like it was the porter who was being careful. Frank bought a chicken sandwich from him for a quarter, avoided looking at him, and went back through the vestibule to his seat. It was disconcerting how warm and still the interior of the coach was, compared with how wild and cold the weather was. Frank picked up his book—he was reading *Robbers' Roost,* by Zane Grey. He had gotten it from one of the guys at school, and he planned to send it back before the guy realized it was missing.

The conductor did not say what "held up" the crew, but by the time it was dark, and everyone knew they were stuck at least until morning, things in the coach weren't quiet anymore. Two of the children were crying, and the two ladies were tutting and shaking their heads; one of them said in a low voice (but Frank was used to listening to low voices), "If we make it till morning . . . but you heard about that train in New York. Mumble-mumble frozen to death." Frank could hardly keep himself from looking around, but he didn't dare. If he did, they would lower their voices even further and he wouldn't learn a thing. One of the businessmen kept pushing a button next to the window, but the conductor didn't come. And then the lights went out. Frank set down his book, but still there was nothing to see in the pale, snowy darkness, least of all "crews."

Not long after the lights went out, the conductor did come through with a flashlight, and he had two porters with him. He announced that the Chicago and Northwestern Railway was very concerned about the comfort of its passengers, and that since there were berths available in the sleeper car, it had been decided that coach passengers would be allowed to make use of those berths for the night. Other passengers had chosen to bunk down in the dining cars and the bar car (one of the businessmen laughed at this), and perhaps, given the comfort of the seats in the coach, others would prefer to stay where they were. If so, the railroad would be happy to supply them with blankets and pillows. Crews were ready to get to work before dawn, but the drift was a large one—not so high, but extensive and difficult to clear.

It was one of the ladies who said to Frank after the conductor left, "Son, you better claim one of those berths, because at least you can insulate yourself in there. We heard of a train near Buffalo—it was the coach passengers who froze to death. You come with me." The two ladies led Frank to the conductor, and declared that they wanted upper berths ("because heat rises") and also one for their nephew here. The conductor was in no mood to argue.

His night in the berth was a strange one—maybe he had never

been in anything that felt so much like a hole in the ground. He could open his eyes and see the window, but as soon as he closed them, he sank again. When, in a dream, he thought Joey poked him, he threw out his arm and hit a wall. That woke him up. And then, lying there, he was as sure as he could be that he was going to die—that on this train, unlike the one in New York—not Buffalo, near Rochester, was it—everyone would freeze to death, and it didn't matter that he was perfectly warm. The freezing part seemed to have more to do with being three hours from home and three hours from Chicago, as far as he could be from everything and everyone he knew, than it did with mere temperature. "Hell's bells," he said aloud, "I miss Joey." And he did. His head touched the wall, his feet touched the wall, his hands touched the wall, and only a curtain hung between him and falling out of the berth into the aisle. If it hadn't been for those dead passengers in Rochester, he would have gone back to his seat.

But the train was moving by sunrise, had already, in fact, crossed the Mississippi, a sight Frank was sorry to have missed. They were at Union Station in Chicago by nine, and Frank's breakfast (eggs, bacon, an orange) had been free. He had thanked the two ladies for "saving" him. When they pulled in, he was picking his teeth, something that he saw one of the other passengers do and that he thought looked very urban. He looked out the window and could see Eloise running down the platform. When he got off, the first thing she said was "Frankie! What in the world would I have told your mother!"

"She's seen plenty of snowdrifts," said Frank. And then he said, "Call me Frank."

And Eloise said, "Oh, you are so funny. Are you sure we're related?"

"Only Mama would know," said Frank, and they both laughed. Eloise reached up and ruffled his hair. But Frank was surprised, and maybe a little taken aback, by how happy she was. Maybe those people in New York really had frozen to death.

THE DRIFTS IN CHICAGO were still nearly as tall as the streetlights, but it was the end of March, and you could get around. Which was good for Frank and bad for Eloise, since he was gone most of the time and she had just about no control over him. The thing was, he was so charming. When he came in, he would say, "Oh, I was down at the Y, and they said to say hello to you," and she knew he was at the pool hall or down by the stockyards or the train yards. But she had walked over to the school and talked to the principal about him, and the principal said that he was a very quick student and was making straight A's. And, said the principal, "There is a sweetness about him. A bit of the country boy." Right, thought Eloise.

She had her hands full with Rosa, who was three now, and with her job, writing articles for both the paper and the *Daily Worker,* and, of course, with Julius, who was turning into a Trotskyite, and so was she. But she kept her mouth shut about it and he didn't, and if they expelled him from the Party, she would have to go, too, and then what? Half of her income came from the *Daily Worker,* and all of his came from the Party, since he was in charge of education.

Her worries about Frank only bothered her when she got a letter from Rosanna; she had one in her hand now and wasn't all that eager to read it, but she put Rosa in her high chair, set her scrambled eggs before her, and ripped open the envelope.

Dear Eloise,

Thanks for your reassurances about Frankie. There is no out of sight out of mind with him, at least not for me. I wish he would write more often, and at greater length, but if, as you say, he has lots of studying to do, I understand that. Every word he reads and every math problem he solves is another step away from farming, and that is good, as you know.

Usually, Rosanna was not quite as open about these sorts of opinions. Eloise read on:

If there is more snow in Chicago, even in Chicago, than here, then the end really is at hand, because although now we haven't had a new blizzard in a couple of weeks, we are still digging out. Walter has a tunnel between the house and the barn. You would think that he would be happy, but he says that if the ground stays frozen while the snow melts, it will just run off, and then the floods—I don't like to think.

However, we are all fed, and the snow has insulated us from

the winds, and so the rooms we are heating have been warm enough. I am in a mood to be thankful, because a terrible thing happened to Mrs. Morris, and Lillian and I have been over there twice.

Eloise didn't want to read on, but she did. Mrs. Morris, she remembered, was Lillian's best friend's mother.

Last week, she had a baby, a boy. Her Jane is ten, Lucy is five, and Gloria is two, I think. I guess she's had trouble before. They wanted a boy, but this one, Ralph, they named him, seems to have been very premature. He is tiny. He cries day and night— he even pulls away from nursing to cry. Of course he has to be swaddled because of the cold, and he can't stand that. Mama says that in her day he would have been quietly passed on to the Lord, and maybe he would have been, I don't know, but Mrs. Morris would never do such a thing. I help her a bit with the baby, and Jane stays here for the most part, with Lillian, which is fine, because there is still almost no school. Jane and Lillian read books to Lucy and Henry, and the two little ones don't seem to care that they are hearing about the French and Indian War or the last of the Mohicans. Every time they stop reading, Lucy asks, "How's Ralphie?" My goodness, so sad!

Eloise wished she didn't know how this was going to end. The one thing she and Julius had formerly disagreed upon was procreation— Julius thought they should produce as many New Men and New Women as they could, whereas Eloise shrank from subjecting more children than necessary to the cruelties of life. Now, of course, they disagreed about lots of things, and if Julius were to come back to the apartment this very minute, no matter how many resolutions she made, they would resume their argument about Stalin, the trials, the vilification of Trotsky, solidarity versus truth. He was always manipulating her into the righteous but powerless corner—what was she willing to give up just to hold her own opinions? She was reacting, he was sure, to having grown up Catholic rather than to the needs of the working class. Obviously, it was a bigger leap for her from the Opiate of the Masses to the Dictatorship of the Proletariat, especially since she came from long lines of landed peasants on both sides, but eggs had to be broken, omelettes had to be made.

Her own analysis was that Julius, as the nephew and grandson and great-grandson, etc., of English rabbis, had a love of and talent for rhetoric, and no one else argued with the fine-hewn eloquence of communists. He wanted to stay in the Party in order to disagree with them. And the revolution in Chicago, the founding spot of the Communist Party in the United States, was burbling along just fine. They could afford a little thesis and antithesis. She picked up the letter again, but then put it down and looked at her watch. She said, "Rosa, Nancy is coming over with her mommy, and they are going to watch you while I do some writing, okay?" Rosa shook her head, but she didn't cry. She said, "Nancy pulls my hair."

"Doesn't Mary stop her?" Mary was about Eloise's age, in charge of writing up minutes from meetings.

Rosa shook her head. "She's busy."

Eloise picked Rosa up and set her on the floor, then said, "Okay, honey, listen to me. When Nancy pulls your hair, you take her by the shoulders and look her right in the eyes and say, 'Stop that. Right now.' No yelling, but very firm." She knelt down and took Rosa by the shoulders and demonstrated. Then she said, "Understand? Speak up, but don't retaliate, okay?"

Rosa nodded.

"Now go watch out the window until they come." Rosa walked away, and Eloise picked up the letter again. It was strange to Eloise that Rosanna never complained, no matter how Job-like her life became. But, then, perhaps she didn't know what had happened to her. Eloise was amazed every time she went back for a holiday. Rosanna, who had been so beautiful fifteen years ago, with blond hair so thick that it burst out of her hairpins, brilliant blue eyes, and a sudden, dazzling smile, now looked cadaverous, with hollow cheeks and a flat, controlled bun. She was thirty-six and looked fifty. The turning point had been the birth of Lillian—everything Rosanna had seemed to flow out of her and into the little girl, and no one noticed except Eloise, who had grown up thinking Rosanna was the most beautiful person in the world, and the luckiest, and the brightest. Eloise looked around, and then crossed herself for luck and in thanks for having escaped the farm. Life in Chicago was full of vociferous "struggle," but Julius was right, wasn't he? He had saved her.

FRANK'S NEW SCHOOL was actually new—it was called the Franklin Branch, and it had only been open for two years. It was much bigger than North Usherton, and there wasn't a single farm kid enrolled, unless you counted Frank, which Frank did not. It had a big library, a gymnasium, and a meeting hall where the student body gathered to be told things, and where performances and shows were put on— Frank was pretty impressed when, two weeks after his arrival, the students themselves did some singing, tap dancing, piano playing, and violin playing. The first half was for classical music, and the second half was for popular music, and the last act was eight girls who kicked up their legs and threw their arms around, and eight guys who tossed them in the air. There would be another show at the end of the year, and Frank planned to be in it, but he wasn't going to sing "She'll Be Coming Round the Mountain." "Ain't Misbehavin' " was more like it, but in the larger scheme of things, he was misbehaving, and it was wonderful fun.

He had fallen in with a gang of boys who ranged all over Lincoln Park and the North Side of Chicago, Terry, Mort, Lew, and Bob. Bob was the most accomplished thief—he walked into Woolworth's and even into Marshall Field's in one pair of shoes and came out in another. For his mother's birthday, he had stolen a five-pound roast, walking out with it under his coat. He had also stolen her birthday present, which was a silk blouse. The other boys, and Frank himself, stuck to packs of cigarettes and bars of chocolate, but Bob would try anything. Terry and Mort were the brawlers. When they happened to run into the gang from St. Michael's, who were good fighters because they were Micks, Terry and Mort could do damage if they had to. Lew, Bob, and Frank did some punching, but only for the fun of it. Terry broke one kid's nose—really broke it—and Mort had another kid down and was kicking him as hard as he could, until the kid could hardly walk. Lew was the best talker—he talked a mile a minute, and just like Jimmy Cagney. Lew knew all the stories about the twenties in Chicago, and swore up and down that his dad and his uncle had been bootleggers, but Mort said that Lew's dad and uncle were plumbers and always had been, and so what? Lew had perfected a type of swagger and knew how to get into Cubs games for free, so Frank was looking forward to Opening Day. The boys were going to skip school, as was everyone else. Wrigley Field was about a half an hour from Eloise's place, less on the L. There was a catcher everybody was wild about named Gabby Hartnett. He was called Gabby because he had a big mouth and was funny. His batting average in the last season was .344, and Lew was sure he would end up in the Hall of Fame. Frank didn't tell them he had never been to a baseball game. Even Julius liked baseball games, and they took Rosa.

It was Frank who was good with the girls. The others stood back and gawked at him—he could talk to any girl, and he would talk to any girl. He didn't care whether she was nice or had a bad reputation or was pretty or not. He started by giving the girl a smile—not a dumb smirk or a sideways thing, but a good smile. He made sure she saw it, but he didn't say anything right away. When the girl was used to smiling back, then he would start chatting like they'd been talking all along. It was easy. And, as he tried to explain to the others, though to little effect, it didn't matter if some of them walked away—girls were all the same; you couldn't tell by looking which one you wanted. The other thing was that if you had the girls on your side, then the teachers liked you. Frank didn't know why that was, but maybe that, too, was the smile. One teacher, Mr. McCarron, he thought might see through him—he was a little impatient, and he taught French. But Frank liked French. He was in there with freshmen, since there hadn't been French at North Usherton, but he did his work and practiced his pronunciation and raised his hand and asked Mr. McCarron about all the Louises and the Charleses, and the *ponts* and the *gares*. He imagined Paris to be a kind of better Chicago. He said that his father had spent a lot of time in Paris during the Great War, but of course he hadn't. Yes, Frank had a contribution to make to the gang that was certainly on a par with Lew's, Bob's, Terry's, and Mort's—he was the best liar. He didn't tell stories and he didn't put on any performances, but he got them out of trouble two or three times. Frank liked to think of himself as the brains of the operation.

It was in this spirit that he made himself available to Julius, who was willing to pay him for writing up leaflets focused on Youth. It didn't take long, and by doing it, he learned to type. *Who Is Our Real Enemy?* was the name of one—about Hitler. *What Is Really Going On in Spain?* was another. *Who's the Boss?* was about whether members of the petite bourgeoisie were really free or actually slaves of the system without knowing it. After listening to Julius go on and on around the apartment, Frank could blab away in these leaflets without a hitch. Julius would read them over and correct him, and then when the leaflets were printed up, Frank saw them as a sort of publication, even though his name wasn't on them. Julius paid him five dollars a leaflet, including typing.

But the thing Frank really loved had nothing to do with the gang or school or girls, even; he loved the L. It was Bob who showed him, since Bob had to range fairly widely in his avocation of stealing, so Bob took him south, down to the Loop, all the way to the University of Chicago, and north to Evanston and Wilmette, and west to the cattleyards. The L ran fairly steadily in spite of the snow, and it gave Frank a sense of dazzling speed and mobility, especially when he caught a glimpse of the still, flat, frozen white in the distance. At those moments, even though the L was big and noisy and made of metal, it felt cloudlike, as if he were sailing in a thunderhead over the still plains. The L made him want to fly in an airplane, as Julius had, as Eloise had, as even Bob had, though only to Minneapolis. When he was on the L, it convinced him that he would never return to the farm, never see the farm again, maybe only ever see Mama and Papa and Joey and Lillian and Henry from a great distance, from high in the air or way down the street. He imagined himself waving and them not seeing him, and himself walking on and turning the corner.

SCHOOL GOT OUT later in the summer in Chicago than it did in Usherton, and even the corn was already planted by the time Frank was finished for the year, so Mama said that he could stay with Eloise if he found work of some sort. He didn't, at first, and then he did. A fellow at Party headquarters got him a job at Marshall Field's, working in the stockroom. But three weeks into that, just before the Fourth of July, Eloise received a letter, and that night there was crying, and then, the next morning, Eloise got up at six, when Frank woke up, and she came into his room and sat on the bed, pinning Frank under the sheet. Her eyes were red, and she said, "Frank, something happened."

The first thing that Frank thought of was that Mama had had another baby, but he didn't say anything. Eloise said, "Your uncle Rolf. Your uncle Rolf died." She glanced toward the doorway, and Julius was there. Julius made a noise. Eloise said, "Frank, Rolf killed himself, and so we have to go back home for the funeral, and we're taking the train today. It leaves at ten-twenty."

Frank did think this was shocking, but in comparison to what he had imagined, rather dryly shocking, and strange because Uncle Rolf had finally done something.

When they got to the farm, where Grandpa Wilmer left him before taking Eloise, Julius, and Rosa on to the Vogel farm, Mama was rather desperately glad to see him, as if it were Frank who had been in danger, not Rolf, and Frank felt a stab of fear that he wouldn't be allowed to go back to Chicago, but he sat with her on the sofa, holding her hand, and didn't say a word about that.

Mama kept taking deep breaths and putting her hand over her mouth and looking at him. Finally, she said, "Frankie, did Eloise say what happened to Rolf?"

The windows were all open, and the heat and the dust were blowing through the house. He remembered that later when he thought of this moment, how gaspingly hot it was as Mama said, "Well, Frankie, he hung himself in the barn. He did it late at night, after everyone had gone to bed, so that he was sure he wouldn't be found until morning. Papa, your grandpa, had to cut him down when he went out to milk in the morning. He just thought . . . He just thought that Rolf had gotten up early because of the heat. Then the cows were milling around the barn door, so he wondered . . . but he never imagined . . ." She coughed, and then did an odd thing, which was she put her head on his knees for a moment. When she sat up, she said, "Lillian and Henry only know that Uncle Rolf died. Joey hasn't asked, but I'm sure he knows what happened. To you, Frank, I have to say that any life . . . that this shows me that any life is better than farming. I know he did this because he could see no way out. The drought this year is the worst anyone has ever known around here. The sky gets black and the clouds roll in, and there's even thunder, and then a drop or two, and nothing more. They had this in Nebraska, and we felt for them, but we felt superior, too—it would never get here—but it's here. Every day is hotter than the day before. Your dad thinks that the heat turned Rolf's brain somehow, but it wasn't that. When Opa left him that farm, I saw it in his face—he was trapped. He never said a word about whether he wanted to farm or didn't want to farm. Now he's said his word." Then she leaned forward. "You have a choice, Frankie."

But he knew that farming was not a choice for him.

The coffin was closed, a solid block in front of the altar. St. Albans, which was made of brick, had heated up over the summer like an oven, so the windows were all open, and Frankie could hardly hear the priest say the service. The altar boys were sweating in their robes, and several people in the seats had to get up and go out for a drink of water. When Frank and the other five pallbearers lifted the coffin, Frank thought it was a good thing that they only had to carry it out the side door and slide it onto the wagon that would carry it to the cemetery at the edge of Denby. He knew from overhearing Mama and Papa that Granny Mary had told the priest that Rolf had fallen out of the hayloft, and the priest had asked no further questions. All of the Vogels and the Augsbergers were in the cemetery, and Granny Mary was determined that Rolf would lie next to Opa, who was the one person who could raise a laugh out of him, and that was that. The cemetery wasn't far, and they all walked along behind the wagon. There was the slow clip-clop of the horses' hooves and the intermittent sound of weeping.

The cemetery, which Frank remembered as grassy, was brown and dusty. Little mounds of dirt had blown up against the western sides of the gravestones. Even the picket fence and the gate, which had always been neatly painted, looked dry and brittle. This cemetery had been so well tended that people around town had picnics there from time to time, just to enjoy the flowers, but now it was a place only of death. Frank couldn't understand how Granny Mary could bear to see Rolf be taken there, or to leave him behind—but that's what they did. They used ropes and lowered his coffin into the dry, dry earth, and they tossed handfuls of dust upon it, and said their farewells, and walked away.

....

AFTER THEY GOT BACK to Chicago, where the weather was just as warm but at least they could go to the lake and sit in the water, Eloise and Julius renewed their argument about the farm. Frank had heard this argument a few times since coming to Chicago, but now it was never-ending. Even Rosa, who had been listening to arguments all of her life, put her head down and then moved farther up the beach. Eloise said, "They have nothing! They aren't stupid. They can be taught why they have nothing."

Julius, who was wearing trousers and a shirt even though Frank, Eloise, and Rosa were in swimming costumes, started shaking his head before she even finished, and said, "No, indeed. No, indeed. The peasantry has no political role. They are incapable of it."

"But conditions have never been this bad before. My brother killed himself!"

"Did you not listen to your mother and your sister, darling? If only he'd gotten married. If only he'd gotten off the farm more. He was always so turned in on himself. You have to get off the farm and see the bigger world! You have to meet some girls! They don't have even a basic class analysis."

"Yes, but I'm not saying they understand already, I'm saying that conditions lay the groundwork. Roosevelt's policies aren't working— they understand that. My sister even asked me if things are better in the Soviet Union—she heard that they aren't, but she doesn't know who to believe anymore."

"But, darling, do you mean that your father or your brother-in-law would welcome collectivization? Would hand over their land, worthless as they say it is, to the workers? The cows, the sheep, the chickens? The tractor? Walter took me out and led me around the tractor for half an hour. His theory about Rolf was that he knew he would never have a tractor, and that he was being left behind."

Eloise's voice rose. "They know what they have has no intrinsic value! It's a burden! Why not share it?"

Frank finished the wall and moat he was building out of the sand—he had even dribbled water on the wall to smooth the surface, and then inscribed lines into it to represent blocks of stone. Rosa came over and stood in front of her parents, but they were intent, so she put her hand in Frank's and said, "I want to go down there." She waved her other hand at the surf, which was swaying easily in and out like water in a bowl.

Frank said, "We can't swim."

"Someone could teach us."

Another protest from Julius clattered on the air. Frank squeezed Rosa's hand and said, "The lake is pretty flat."

She led him south along the edge of what he supposed you called surf. Mort and Lew were good swimmers. He thought they might teach him without laughing at him, and if they did laugh, he could just punch them out.

Rosa said, "They're struggling."

Rosa, not quite three and a half and using this word, made Frank laugh, but he said, "All moms and dads struggle. Or fight." Then, "Maybe not about what Eloise and Julius fight about, though."

"What?"

Frank thought for a moment, then said, "Oh, what to buy, I guess. What to do with naughty children."

Rosa gazed soberly up at him, then said, "You do what you want."

He said, "I just do it."

She nodded.

1937

∾

JOE WAS AT SCHOOL, and the light was better in his room, at least
in the afternoon, so Walter took the letter into there to read it.
It was from the principal of that school in Chicago where Frankie
was going, and it was about something Walter didn't want to think
about—and why should he? He wasn't going to have a say in the matter, anyway. The matter was college—should Frankie go, and where.
Walter was suspicious of college, because it was not something any
of the Langdons had ever done, but the Vogels and the Augsbergers seemed to think you couldn't go wrong if you went—look at
Rolf, who had refused to go to St. Ambrose and play the trumpet in
the brass band. Rolf hadn't gone when he had the chance, and then,
twenty years later, he goes out and hangs himself in the barn. That
brass band had seen the world, and if Rolf had gone to college for a
couple of years, Rolf might have been a happier person—that was
how the Vogels and the Augsbergers thought. But if you pointed out
that Eloise had gone to college and that now she was a Red, they
didn't say a word about it.

The letter was addressed to both him and Rosanna, and Rosanna
had already read it three times.

Although I was not quite sure how your son Francis would fit
in here, he has done a wonderful job, not only in his classes, but

in participating in extracurricular activities. Surely you have
heard that he sang at both the Spring Into Action Student Show
last year (I believe it was a rendition of "I Got Rhythm"), and
the Autumn Golden Glee Show ("Ain't Misbehavin'"). I was
especially impressed this fall, when he asked one of the other
boys, a competitive swimmer, to teach him to swim, and the
two boys went over to Lake Michigan every day well into
late October, at least two weeks after I would have considered
the water too cold, so that he could master the crawl and the
backstroke. I bring this up only to demonstrate that your son
is remarkable for the determination that he brings to every
activity. Although last spring I was not certain that he was
spending time with the best and most morally upright of our
boys, my fears in that regard have been put to rest.

In short, I do feel that it would be a betrayal of both Francis's
evident intelligence and his industry to prevent him from
attaining a higher education. I am sure he could excel in any
field, and would bring great pride to his family. From the few
things he has told me, I know that before he came to Chicago,
he was an eager student, and that he was also enterprising in
using his hunting skills to earn money.

It may be that you feel that seventeen is too young to embark
upon a college education, but I do think that if the institution
of higher learning were carefully chosen, Francis would find
himself in upstanding and respectable company, and your
worries could be laid to rest.

Please think about what I've said, and if there is any way that
I can lend a hand to the realization of Francis's ambitions, I am
entirely ready to do so.

The whole prospect bothered Walter, but not in any way that
he could express. It was not, as Rosanna suggested, simple narrow-
mindedness on his part. It was not that he felt that the world would
damage or hurt Frankie in any way, it was much more that there were
plenty of things out in the world that Frankie would learn about, and
that he would then have no scruples at all.

Walter lay back on the bed and looked out the window. Blue sky.
A year ago, this very window was shrouded in snow and ice, and

they had survived. Here it was almost March. They had had a decent amount of snow, and the usual amount of wind, and some sleet and hail. But everything came and went rather than staying and staying. Maybe it was an omen for the spring and the summer. His corn crop in the fall hadn't been the worst—ten bushels an acre better than two years ago—but still not what it was in the twenties. Maybe that was an omen for this year, too. What did Walter want Frankie to do? Rosanna told him that he had written her and said that Eloise suggested he go off to Spain and fight for the Loyalist cause, but Walter thought he was putting Rosanna on.

Walter stared up at the ceiling. One thing was for sure, the boy who had left a year ago was not the man who came home for Christmas—taller than Walter, shoulders like a bull, but lean. Blond as a girl, blond as Jean Harlow, and with those blue eyes. He had learned to walk and stand like a city boy, but one who knew his way around and could break into a run if the cops were on his tail. This thought made Walter smile. Well, maybe it was true what Rosanna said, that Walter saw only the bad side of Frankie and always had. "He was always tough, Rosanna. I knew that, didn't I?"

"You think that's a bad thing! In this world, those are the ones who survive."

He didn't think toughness was a bad thing. He had cultivated it. However, it was easier to see your kid for what he was when you saw him at a distance, and Walter was afraid of what else Frankie was—ruthless, maybe. Thinking that, he looked around the room, wondering if there was a hidden stash of something, and what that would be. Cigarettes? Whiskey? Girlie pictures? Even money? He had always known that, in the hardest times, Joey was giving him all his money, while Frank was holding some back.

Walter stood up. To be honest, was that bad in these times? Take Rolf, again—he was now their example for everything that could go wrong. Granny Mary and Grandpa Otto and Opa and Oma never asked a thing from Rolf that he didn't give them, with all apparent willingness. In the end, it was too much—that's how Walter saw it. And he couldn't think of Rolf now without thinking of himself falling into the well—something he still hadn't told Rosanna about. Maybe the measure of what, over the years, he had kept back for himself was the measure of what saved him, what propelled his body of its own volition to the front of the well and out. The joke was that if he'd killed himself he would have missed the worst year of his life, and still he was glad that he hadn't killed himself.

He closed the door of Joey's room behind him, and just then he could see Lillian and Henry step onto the front porch. He could hear them, too. Henry said, "Let's go look at the lambs."

And Lillian said, "What did you name yours?"

Henry said, "Duke."

Walter opened the door.

IT WAS LILLIAN who arranged it with Miss Perkins. Miss Perkins was their teacher—this was her second year. She was not a young woman; she had taught in lots of schools, including one in New Mexico, which Lillian thought was very exotic, because Miss Perkins had two potted cactuses on her desk, and sometimes she talked in Spanish to them. Miss Perkins had come home to live with her mother, who was very old and demented. They lived in Denby. For a while there were only eight students in the whole school—Joey because he was not quite ready for the high school (and didn't want to go there anyway, he told Lillian, because he would be bullied for sure); another boy, who was twelve, Maxwell; herself and Jane; a boy named Luther, who was ten; Roger King, nine; Lois, who was six, almost seven; and Jane's sister Lucy, who was also six. It turned out that Miss Perkins drove her car to school, and she got into the habit of picking up Lois and Lillian, because they lived on the way (Joey walked or ran, as he always had). One day after Christmas, Miss Perkins saw Henry waving like mad in the front window as they left, and asked how old he was. Lillian said, "He's four, but he can read and write the alphabet, and in my opinion, he should do what he wants and come to school with us."

Miss Perkins let him come on the condition that he sit at a desk and behave himself, and he was able to do that if Lillian gave him either a book or some paper and some crayons, and so he started coming to school. Walter didn't mind because Henry was afraid of the animals, intensely talkative, and worthless on a farm; and Rosanna didn't mind because he cried for Lillian every day anyway. Now he was in the habit of going to school. When Mama asked Miss Perkins how it was going, she said, "Well, he's got the biggest ears! My land, a child can read something aloud or make a remark from across the schoolroom, and Henry offers his two cents if he finds it at all interesting. At least he doesn't correct their arithmetic sums. He's a very forward child."

Mama said, "You didn't know our oldest boy, Frank, but he is the same way. It now looks as though he will go to the University of Chicago!"

"My goodness," said Miss Perkins. "Why not Iowa State? You get everything you could want there."

Lillian, who was standing by the front door of the car, helping Lois get out, said, "I'm going to take Lois home."

The two ladies kept talking, and Lillian took Lois's hand. They walked down the edge of the road, which was clean of snow—in fact, there was only snow in the ditches anymore, and the sun was almost warm. Lois unbuttoned her coat.

Lillian and Lois mounted the steps of the Fredericks' big front porch. The Fredericks' house was a very nice one, and Lillian appreciated it every time she visited. It had come on a train from Chicago—or, rather, all its parts had come, with instructions on how to build it—and she imagined that all houses in Chicago, all the houses Frankie saw when he was walking to school, looked like this one. She and Lois opened the big dark front door with the windows in it and went in. They hung their coats by the fireplace. Mrs. Frederick was just coming down the stairs.

She gave Lillian a welcoming glance and said, "I do think I saw some cookies cooling on the kitchen table. They might have been gingersnaps."

"I hope they were," said Lillian.

"Me, too," said Lois.

Mrs. Frederick said, "I'll go look."

Lillian was very fond of all the Fredericks, and sometimes she lay in bed at night imagining their house, where someone was always making a joke and there was never any fighting. Lillian imagined that they had a secret about that, and she liked to come over and watch them, hoping she would figure out what it was.

....

ONE MORNING, after school was out and the corn planting finished, Joe got up and went to feed the animals, and he saw a mound, pale in the early light, lying in the grassy muck of the east pasture, half under the Osage-orange bush. He knew what it was without even going to look, but he went anyway, and when he got there, he squatted down and petted Elsa for a few minutes, along her neck and the roots of her mane; then he closed her eye. She was a bit of a mess—he hadn't brushed her in a week, maybe, and her coat, now snowy white, was grimy. What was she, twenty-three?

Jake was at the far end of the pasture, standing among the cows. He took a few steps toward Joe, then stopped and flicked his ears. Jake was over twenty himself. The only thing either horse ever did anymore was walk around and eat, sometimes with Henry on board— Jake was better at that than Elsa had been. When Henry kicked him, he would actually speed up his walk a bit and stop putting his head down to eat. He would also turn when Henry pulled one way or another on the lead rope. Joe himself sometimes got on Jake and rode through the fields—easier than walking, and more fun. But Joe hadn't done that in almost a year. He gave Elsa a last pat and went into the barn, where he got a couple of burlap sacks and laid them over the corpse. At breakfast, Mama said, "Don't say anything. Maybe Henry won't notice."

"Well," said Papa, "he'll notice when the rendering wagon comes out to pick her up."

"I think they have a truck now," said Joe.

"There you go," said Walter. "Even the renderer drives a truck. Even the renderer hasn't much use for animals anymore."

A couple of weeks later, Joe came home from Rolf's farm, where he had been cultivating the corn, and Papa stopped him as he walked out of the barn toward the house. He said, "Joey, I sold Jake to someone."

Joe's voice shot out of his mouth, loud, surprised, "I think of Jake as *my*—"

"But he's just standing there. This fellow has a use for him."

Papa spoke sharply, but he had an abashed look on his face, and Joe said, "What use would that be?"

"I guess he has an old buggy he likes to drive in parades. A light thing, nothing to pull for a horse like Jake. He's healthy, he should have a job."

Joe didn't disagree with this, but he was suspicious. He said, "How'd he find out about Jake?"

"I guess the man from the rendering plant told him we had a nice horse."

"Well, I don't want to sell him." Joe pushed past Papa—but gently, respectfully—and headed toward the house. It was suppertime, and he was hungry.

Papa said, "It's forty dollars. That's Frankie's fees for a quarter at Iowa State."

Joe spun around. "I thought he gave that up for a year. He was going to go up to Wisconsin and hunt fox and beaver for his fees."

"Now he doesn't have to."

"What about that 'labor school' Eloise and Julius were talking about? Brook something? That was free."

"I guess it closed."

But Papa was neither asking permission nor seeking advice. The horse was sold, and Papa already had the money—the man would be by to get Jake the next day.

Mama was more thoughtful. She came into Joe's room when he was getting into bed, and sat down. She took his hand. She said, "Lillian is crying, too. I told her, but I think I'll wait till Henry asks. Sometimes children get used to things by not knowing quite what's happened for a bit. But Papa and I understand how attached you are to Jake. Papa is sick about this."

Joe removed his hand from Mama's and pushed back his hair. He didn't say anything.

"Joseph. It's not just Frankie going to school for himself. He's going for all of us. The world is changing, and someone has to go out into it and be prepared for it."

Joe snorted.

"Son, you know that that someone is him and not you. You love the world you live in, and that's good. He loves the world we don't know much about, and that's good, too. I consider myself lucky to have one of each in my boys."

She took his hand again, and patted it, then left. Joe knew that there was no hope for saving Jake, and it was true, he would live longer with something to do, and enjoy himself more with an equine friend—the man had another horse with an old lameness, who couldn't pull the buggy anymore. What drove him crazy was that he couldn't find his way around any of their arguments, never had. His own family left him confused and dumb. He didn't think he was stupid—he could plow a straight row, repair a fence, shear a sheep, milk a cow, predict the weather, even get a robin to sit on his finger. He could mimic the calls of seventeen birds and animals, and often did for Henry's and Lillian's amusement (Lillian would tell the story, and Joe would pretend to be saying the parts in "real animal language"). He thought of Uncle Rolf, whose field he cultivated, whose life seemed to be buried in that very field. But he wasn't Rolf, and would never be, thought Joe. Not in a million years.

FRANK WAS SITTING in the Lincoln Way Café in Campustown, across from the college in Ames, and the man who had just taken his order was, to his utter amazement, none other than Ragnar, Papa's farmhand from years ago—eight or ten, anyway. He recognized Frank, though Frank hadn't recognized him. And now here came a woman—Irma, it would be. She looked slightly more familiar. She rushed up to him, grabbed his hands. "Goodness gracious! Frankie Langdon, welcome to Iowa State! When I saw you last you were Mr. Mischief! Do you remember hammering that row of nails into the railings of the front porch? Oh, your papa was fit to be tied! And now here you are! Where do you live?"

Frank said, "In the freshman dorm. But I want to join Sigma Chi if I can. They have a good scholarship."

"Oh, goodness. Have they told you about the fraternity houses? Since the flu epidemic after the war, everyone sleeps in the attic with all the windows wide open through the winter. The dorms and even apartments are at least above freezing!"

Frank laughed. He said, "Like home, then."

"And how are your folks doing? I was so worried about them."

Frankie stiffened. "Fine. They're fine. Henry was born. He's almost five."

"And darling, I'm sure," said Irma. She squeezed his hand. "Back to the kitchen now. But have the special. Corned beef and cabbage. On the house."

Frank had ordered the chicken soup, the cheapest thing on the menu, but he said, "Thanks." In a few minutes, Ragnar brought him a plate of the corned beef, with not only cabbage but some fried potatoes on the side, and a piece of apple pie. Frank made himself eat it with leisurely deliberation, even though he was ravenous.

Frank had been in Ames for six weeks, and he was sleeping not in the dorm but on the banks of the Skunk River, in a tent he'd gotten at the Salvation Army. He had kept back the dormitory money that Mama had given him, because he wasn't all that sure he wanted to continue at Iowa State, and he didn't want to waste a penny if he didn't have to. Maybe it would be better in Iowa City, but Chicago had wrecked him for Ames. Everyone in Ames was just like the landscape—open, bright, friendly, dull. In Chicago, if you didn't smile all the time, people thought you were normal. Here, they thought you were unhappy and hostile, and maybe he was.

However, he liked his classes. If the students were a uniform breed—say, Herefords, contentedly chewing their cud as they kept to the paths and filed mindlessly to their classes (now he was sounding like a communist)—then the professors were animals of every stripe, caged in their classrooms, making their tweets and roars and whinnies. He listened to their lectures, asked his questions, made his contributions, was getting high marks on tests. The cattle scratched their heads and kept turning the papers over, wondering where the clues were, but Frank did fine. Except he didn't have a friend, and for the first time in his life, he wanted one.

Even here, as he cleaned his plate, he was the only person sitting by himself. Every table was full of kids—Irma was a good cook—and everyone was gabbing and laughing. Frank felt awkward and out of place. Somehow, he'd thought there would be someone from Chicago here, someone who was a little like Bob and Mort or even Lew. If he'd taken those guys back to his tent, they would have been inspired by the daring of it. These kids were so clean that Frank thought they would just find it dirty. So he was a farm kid. But the farm kids here were all like Joey.

He pushed away his empty plate and reached for the apple pie. The crust was good, like Mama's. He thought he remembered Mama showing Irma how to make a crust. The apples were good, too. Sometimes, by the river, Frank shot himself a rabbit, skinned it, and cooked it. He had also caught a couple of catfish and cooked those himself, over a fire. When he caught a fish or bagged a rabbit, he thought maybe his year hunting in Wisconsin might have been a better idea than this—he could have chosen a different college or a different life. He savored the crust of the pie. It was crispy and delicious. He estimated that he had about a month left in the tent. He was sure he would think of something, but he didn't know what.

He left Ragnar a tip and walked out of the café. Then he crossed Lincoln Way and entered the campus. It was dark. The gymnasium was up to the left, and the student union was just to the right. Usually when he was looking for a bike, he walked along the road in front of the union, but this time he decided to try the gymnasium. The key was to remember where he'd found it, and then return it early in the morning. That way, he made use of the bike and also put one over on the hapless twit who had left it there in the first place. He was fond of his old bicycle, the cruiser he'd left on the farm, but this method had its attractions, only one of which was that he got to try out various models.

It took him about twenty minutes to head east on Lincoln Way to Duff, then south to 16th Street, where his very small and easily disguised tent was pitched in some bushes. He had stored other things in two trunks, also purchased at the Salvation Army, and they were pushed even deeper into the thickets (he had checked for snakes and poison ivy). The hoboes weren't down here—they were east of downtown, in a wooded area not far from the Chicago and Northwestern tracks; a few younger ones hid out on campus. He was therefore extremely taken aback when he knelt down, opened the flap of his tent, and discovered someone in there. The person lit a match under his own chin as soon as Frank stuck his head in, and then lit the kerosene lantern Frank used for light. It was a guy about his own age, and someone he had never seen before. He was wearing nice clothes. Frank then remembered having seen a car, a REO Flying Cloud, maybe a 1936, on the bridge.

The person said, "So someone is living here."

"Maybe," said Frank.

The person laughed. He said, "Where do you shower?"

"There's the pool at State Gym. Don't you have curfew?" said Frank.

"Maybe," said the person. "I'm Lawrence Field. Shenandoah."

"Frank Langdon, Denby. I'm not in the seed business." The Fields were famous nursery-and-seed purveyors, and that explained the car.

Lawrence grinned. "Are you in furs?"

"You must have come by before dark if you saw the rabbit skins."

"That's what I first saw—rabbit skins tacked to trees."

"And you decided to snoop."

"Wouldn't you have?"

Frank had to admit that he would have.

Ten minutes later, they were in the car, and fifteen minutes after that, they were passing through Nevada, which was dark on both sides of the street. Frank said, "Nice car," and it was—as smooth as advertised, sleek, cushioned, fast, and quiet.

"REO is out of the automobile business now—that's what I hear. But my dad wanted one of the last ones."

"Where are we going?"

"How about Chicago?"

Frank was a little startled, but he said, "I like Chicago. I lived there last year."

"There's a Cubs home game tomorrow. Against the Cards. The season's about over. They aren't going to get out of second place, but I'd like to see it."

Frank shrugged. They shot out of the east end of Nevada, and the flat road stretched before them, as pale and straight as a string between the dark cornfields. Frank had never been in a car driven by another kid before. He said, "Let's go."

1938

～～

FRANK HAD KNOWN GUYS who did whatever they wanted to, but Lawrence Field was the first he'd met who had the money and imagination to broaden his horizons beyond smoking cigarettes, drinking rotgut, skipping school, trying to feel up girls, and stealing things. Lawrence Field never stole anything—he had class—and was the reason Frank lingered around Iowa State through the first quarter and went back after three weeks on the farm for the second quarter. Frank didn't see Lawrence much of the time, and Lawrence didn't solve all his problems, but he did solve one of them—he found Frank a job, working in the horticulture lab, and so Frank could get himself a room, at least for a few months, until the snow stopped.

Lawrence turned out to be twenty, but he looked younger than Frank. Even though his father had put him to work around the nursery and on the family farm from an early age, he was still "waiting for his growth."

"It'll come," he said. "Everyone in our family lives forever." Frank had been back at school after Christmas for a week when Lawrence showed up. Outside, the Flying Cloud accelerated up the street—its motor had a distinct sound—and then stopped below his window. Frank looked out, put up the sash. Lawrence called, "Wear something nice. I'm feeling restless."

Frank didn't mind hurrying when Lawrence was feeling restless—

he was down the stairs in five minutes, dressed in a suit and a camel-hair coat that he'd found in a pawnshop in Des Moines. Lawrence loved pawnshops. Frank got in the passenger's side, noted that there was no one else in the car, and said, "Back to Chicago?" They'd been to Chicago three times since the Cubs game (a win, 5–1).

"Better," said Lawrence. "Rock Island."

"Rock Island!" exclaimed Frank. "Rock Island is a dump!"

"Just wait. Anyway, I need a drink."

One of the "responsibilities" that Lawrence took seriously as the son of a famous family was not drinking in Iowa, which was still dry.

The Flying Cloud did, indeed, fly—eight cylinders and all of them powerful. Straight through Nevada, on to Colo, then south of Usherton, and through the Indian lands around Tama and the dips—an area of hills that reminded Frank of a roller coaster. Then they angled south through Tipton, and east again, through a hillier and more wooded area that Frank wasn't familiar with—he had never been to Iowa City, though he'd meant to go. The car ran so smoothly that Frank drifted into sleep, and only woke up when Lawrence made a turn. He woke up to a big lighted sign: "Roadhouse." Lawrence turned into the parking lot, which was large and full of cars. The Flying Cloud was the only one of its kind, though. Lawrence pulled up toward the rear of the longish building and opened his door. He said, "Not that cold here. I doubt you'll need your coat."

The building had two stories, four doors, and no windows. Men were entering and exiting through all of the doors, but Lawrence headed toward one of the ones near the center of the shingled wall. Frank jogged to catch up to him. Lawrence said, "This is Little Chicago. Heard of it?"

"Maybe," said Frank. This time he meant it.

The bar was long, shiny, and well stocked. It ran in an elongated horseshoe among scattered tables, and the brass foot-rail glinted in the multitude of lights that both drew him toward the bar and accentuated the darkness. The stools were attached somehow, had red leather seats, and spun. Lawrence settled his backside onto one and leaned toward the bartender like he'd done it plenty of times. Frank, who'd only visited two bars in Chicago the previous spring, imitated him. As he put his elbows on the bar itself, he noticed a metal trough beneath the brass rail, and dipped his head to get a better look at it.

Lawrence said, "You piss into that. I never have, but some fellows don't like to give up their spots." Sure enough, as he spoke, a dark but glistening stream of water trickled past. Lawrence said, "The bartender flushes it every fifteen minutes or so."

Just then the bartender said, "Can I get anything for you gentlemen?" He leaned close to peer, not at Frank, but at Lawrence. Lawrence said, "Old Fitzgerald and soda, I think."

Frank had to admire the ease with which he said this, but, then, Lawrence made every transgression look as easy as you please. The bartender looked at Frank. "You?"

"I'll take the same, but straight up with a beer chaser." Then there was the long moment while the bartender made up his mind. Finally, the drinks appeared. Frank, who had never drunk whiskey before, tossed his shot back the way he saw Gary Cooper do it in the pictures, then held his head perfectly steady as his throat burned. After a moment, he took a swig of the beer. Grandpa Otto gave all the kids beer, so he was used to that. Even so, it was a good thing the place was dark, because his eyes were tearing. Lawrence took a sip of his whiskey and soda, an experienced sort of sip. He said, "You always seem older than you say you are."

Frank said, "I was never young."

"I don't know what that means."

"It means I was always up to something, according to my folks."

"Must've been fun."

"Sometimes."

"Maybe," said Lawrence.

Frank laughed. "How about you?"

"Wasn't up to enough, according to my aunts and uncles. They are all well known to be very industrious. My mother is said to have spoiled me, and I am said to be spoiled. When I flunk out, all of their suspicions will be confirmed."

"How can you flunk out?"

"You are truly asking. That's one of the interesting things about you, Langdon. You have no talent for idleness." He finished his drink, and said, "Let's go upstairs."

"What's upstairs?"

"The women's college."

Each of the whores had a room of her own, but at least some of them were sitting in a large hall at the top of the stairs. As he climbed, he heard one of them say that she had been to Chicago to see a Cagney picture about dancing. When Lawrence got to the top, he walked over to an older woman who looked like the madam, and kissed her on the cheek. She said, "Barney, my boy! Are you well?"

Some of the other whores called out greetings, all of them smiled, and two put down their knitting. Frank wiggled his shoulders to loosen them, then stepped up onto the landing as if he knew what he was doing. Yes, he had lived in Chicago, but as far as he knew, communists did not go in for this sort of thing. Lawrence said, "Hi, Butterfly. I've been missing you."

The madam said, "I'm sure you have, sweetie," and looked Frank up and down. She said, "Who's this?"

Frank said, "Rolf."

"Rolf? Rolf what?"

"Rolf Silber." He thought, There you go, Julius. This put him in a good mood.

He ended up with Pixie. Pixie could not have been called a girl, but she was tall and slender, even without the high-heeled shoes. She walked him down the hallway almost to the end, to what might have been her room, or what might have been just a room. She opened the door for him, and followed him in. The room had electric lights— a small chandelier made of glass flowers hanging from the middle of the ceiling. There was a yellow chair, a green-and-yellow spread on the bed, and a sink over in the corner. Frank had no idea what to do, but he tried to look relaxed. He put his hands in his pockets. She stepped toward him. The surprising thing about that was that, even though she was pretty in her way, he didn't feel very good. It took him about five seconds to remember that girl at the state fair—he sometimes remembered that night, but he never remembered the girl in detail. Now he did—the light across her cheek making her look very sad. Her sigh of disgust. The shine of his stuff on the fabric of her skirt. He must have stepped backward.

Pixie said, "You're a pretty boy to be looking so worried. What are you, twenty or something?"

Frank decided for once to be honest. He said, "I just turned eighteen at New Year's."

Pixie put her finger into his belt. She said, "Take your jacket off."

He did so. She set the shoulders together and laid it over the back of the chair.

"Now the tie."

He pulled the end through the knot of the tie, and she took it out of his hands and smoothed it over the jacket. Then she slipped out of her shoes, went to the sink, and put her foot on the rim. After a moment, she started washing herself. She said, "No, look. You need to watch. You don't have to do anything else."

Frank watched. He was glad she went slowly. Maybe that was what had gone wrong before—too fast.

"You're staring at the wall. Look at me."

He looked at her.

After she finished washing, she took off her top. Her breasts looked strange in the light. His eyes closed. He opened them. She was sitting on the bed with a cigarette between her fingers, unlit. She said, "Look, your friend paid, but he didn't pay for any special thing. Anything you want is fine."

What was that girl's name? he thought. She was from Muscatine. Muscatine was right around here. This thought made him dizzy. He closed his eyes again.

But his cock was hard, and Pixie was touching it. She must have unbuttoned his fly. Then he felt a much stranger sensation than touching, and opened his eyes. The top of her head was at his stomach, and he realized she had his cock in her mouth. Moments later, he came, and she pulled away. She got up and went over to the sink, where she spit his stuff into the drain and washed it away. Frank sat down on the bed. It was late, and he wanted to fall asleep. Pixie said, "You like boys, then?"

Frank looked at her.

"It's no big deal. Some guys like boys and girls. Maybe you don't like anyone so far. That happens, too." She shrugged and put on her top. They waited a few minutes in silence. Frank could hear occasional noises from below, steps out in the hall.

When they rejoined the group at the top of the stairs, Lawrence was still with his whore, but it was okay, Frank thought. It was nicer with more girls. Pixie sat down on the sofa, and patted the spot next to her. One of the knitting girls said, "So—where are you from?"

"Usherton."

"Yeah? I'm from Mason City myself. Lizzie here is from Rochester, Minnesota. But most of the girls are from Chicago."

Frank said, "What about you, Pixie?"

"Who, me?" She licked the tips of her fingers and smoothed her hair back. "I'm from down south of St. Louis. Cairo. It's on the river there."

Lizzie said, "Well, it's nice to have a good-looking fellow like yourself come around. There's not a lot of that." She leaned forward and kissed him hard. He liked it.

Pixie said, "You should come back sometime midweek. It's not so busy."

Lawrence and his whore emerged from one of the rooms. He had his arm around her waist. On the way home, Frank said, "Why do they do this?"

"It's a living," said Lawrence. "There's a Depression on. People live in tents and shoot rabbits. What else are they going to do? Lizzie's dad died of diphtheria, and that was the end of their farm. Some are nymphos, though."

Frank pondered the whores for most of the next week.

AT THE BEGINNING of the third quarter, Frank got a job that paid more, one that would keep him in Ames through the summer. Since he planned to move back into his tent, he expected to save quite a bit of money. His boss, who was an assistant professor in the Chemistry Department, wanted to burn cornstalks in a way that would make them usable for gunpowder. Frank foresaw that when the gunpowder was perfected, he and his boss, Professor Cullhane, would put it to use. But it was not perfected yet. It was an interesting idea, though—a field of corn as a weapon.

Frank saw himself as something of a ghost around the campus. He had given up all ideas of Sigma Chi or Sigma Nu. He didn't mind the kids in his classes and liked walking across the campus with this one or that one—he had retained his habit of being nice to all the girls, and so he always had someone to walk with. He was good at carrying books, or, since he had brought the cruiser back from the farm, riding a girl to the library. There was one girl, Annie Haines, in his history class, who liked to sit on his handlebars and be pedaled around town. She was pretty brave, and once in a while he kissed her, but that was all. She didn't know where he lived, though if she'd looked out of her window in her freshman dorm rooms, she would have seen the rooming house across Lincoln Way where his room was. But it suited him that no one knew where he lived other than Lawrence, and Lawrence was sworn to secrecy. Lawrence kept the secret, too— not because he honored Frank's wishes, but because he liked secrets. The reason Frank didn't try to join a fraternity was that, apart from Lawrence and the girls, his fellow students interested him only for observation.

He wrote two essays for Lawrence. One was about the Russian Revolution and Trotsky, Lenin, and Stalin. This one was easy to write—all he had to do was reproduce Julius's "line" on Trotsky, that while he was out in the field during the last year of Lenin's life, when Lenin was so debilitated by strokes, Trotsky was doing the real work of running the army and taking care of administrative business, but Stalin was back in the Kremlin, extending his influence over everyone in the Politburo. Stalin's betrayal of Trotsky only prefigured his betrayal of his erstwhile colleagues and the revolution itself. Lawrence received an A on the essay, and was told that his thinking was "Very astute. You've been paying better attention than I thought, Mr. Field." In the second essay, "Lawrence" wrote about Richard III. He compared the feuds between the House of Lancaster and the House of York to the feuds in the Communist Party in the Soviet Union, and likened Richard to Stalin, "even in terms of height and looks." He ended the paper with a few remarks about how humans remain constant through the ages, in spite of ever-changing theories of human nature. This essay also received an A. The professor considered Lawrence's argument "unorthodox but intriguing." As a result of these two papers, Lawrence did not flunk out of school, but he did have to retake his physics class.

Frank would not have said that he asked for anything in return, but he appreciated Lawrence's generosity—a meal here and there, another ride to Chicago (though not to Little Chicago), a pair of boots that his mother sent that happened to be too big for Lawrence (and why two sizes too big, Frank didn't ask). The spring progressed from dogwood through lilacs, and Frank enjoyed himself. There were lots of ways to fit into a place like Iowa State College, and one of them was not to fit in at all.

WHEN HE PLANTED Rolf's cornfield, Joe decided to breed a hybrid. Actually, it was a bit of an accident. Papa had saved seed from the fall crop (back up to forty bushels an acre, but what good did that do you when the price was twelve cents a bushel?). When Joe checked the seed, there wasn't enough of it to begin with, and some of what they had was infected with a fungus. Grandpa Wilmer had some seed corn, too, but not much, and of a different variety. What got Joe going was that Grandpa Wilmer's variety would grow taller than what Papa had, so he just filled the seeders—three rows of Papa's, then a row of Grandpa Wilmer's, from one end of Rolf's field to the other. He didn't say a thing about it to Papa, at least until the corn was about chest-high, when Papa noticed the difference between the rows. He brought it up one Sunday in July when all the grandparents were over for Sunday supper. Papa was smiling when he said it, but Joe knew he didn't approve. He looked around the table and said, "Joey's going into business."

"What's that?" said Granny Elizabeth. "Wasn't Frankie good at earning money, too? Those fox skins he had were beauties. When was that?"

"Joey's sort of business is the sort where you pour time and money down a deep hole."

"Oh, Walter," said Mama, "what could you possibly be talking about? Joey does what you tell him."

"We didn't tell him to grow seed corn when we said he could take over Rolf's farm."

"What does that mean?" said Mama, and Grandpa Wilmer said, "I'll buy it."

Joe thanked him.

Grandpa Otto said, "Opa tried that for a couple of years. He detasseled every other row and saved that seed for the next year. Lots of work, nothing gained."

"That's not what I'm going to do," said Joe. "I'm going to detassel the rows I planted from Papa's seed, and let Grandpa Wilmer's seed pollinate those plants."

"What are those rows, four to one?" said Grandpa Wilmer.

"Three to one," said Joe.

"Lotta work. That's a big field."

Joe shrugged, then said, "I bet I can get it done before the oat harvest. I bet I can."

Grandpa Wilmer said, "That was good seed. Pretty high yield."

"What good is that?" said Walter.

"Prices are rising," said Grandpa Wilmer.

Grandma Elizabeth and Oma each said something in German, then Grandpa Otto. Walter said, "Well, tell the rest of us."

Grandpa Otto said, "She said, 'War in Europe raises prices in Iowa.'"

Papa said, "There isn't going to be a war in Europe. They learned their lesson the last time."

Oma spoke in German again, and Mama said, "You can talk English, Grandma."

Oma said, *"Nicht zu diesem."* Then she added, *"Alles, was Teufel will, ist Krieg. Die Engländer können es nicht sehen, aber die Deutschen können."*

Papa said, "What did she say?"

"She said Hitler is bent on having a war."

There was an uncomfortable silence; then Papa said, "Prices will go up."

Joe didn't mind detasseling the corn. He did it at a trot, from one end of a long row to the other. He moved along, yanking the pollen-filled tassels out of the stalks and dropping them on the ground. It was not terribly hot—he did it in a loose shirt and light shoes. The field was full of all sorts of bugs and bees, and he had to watch out for snakes, but it also gave him a chance to pull up the rogue corn plants, and the bindweed, and the lamb's-quarter, and the Canada thistle, all of which smelled rather good. Because of how sharp the edges of the corn leaves were, he had to wear gloves anyway, so he got all of the thistles out of the field. Mama said, "You are such an industrious boy, Joey. Do you remember the way you stacked those dominoes when you were about two? No, of course not. But every time Frankie knocked them over, you stacked them up again." The dominoes were in Henry's toy box. Joey didn't remember playing with them, but he was sure that mindless activity had been his specialty.

His favorite day of detasseling was the last Saturday, when Minnie, who had been teaching at the schoolhouse for the last year (six students, including Lois), agreed to help him. That day, he slowed down.

He was now taller than Minnie, though he wasn't quite sure when that had happened. He hadn't gone to school at all this year, and so he hadn't had her as a teacher, which meant that he could tell her what to do. He said, "Well, too bad you didn't come at the beginning instead of at the end—the corn is a lot taller now. But there aren't many tassels left. This is cleanup."

She set down the basket she'd brought with the clean dish towel tied over the top, and Joey threw his jacket over that. The morning had started pretty cool, but it was warming up fast. The tassels were bright yellow at the tops of the green plants, but you had to reach into the leaves and grab them at the base, or they would break off. After he showed her, she went over a few rows and he could barely see her. She shouted, "Looks like a good crop!"

"Too soon to tell."

She shouted, "That's how I feel about my students!"

Joe laughed. At the end of the row, they sipped some water from the canteen he was carrying. Minnie said, "So what do you hear from Frank?"

"Not much. I guess they have a nice swimming pool there. He likes that. Did you know that he learned to swim when he was in Chicago?"

"He wrote me about that."

"You probably hear more than we do."

"He said he was working on making gunpowder out of cornstalks."

Joe said, "I think that's a joke." The joke was that if there was anything in the world Joe could imagine Frank trying, it was making gunpowder out of cornstalks. And bullets out of kernels.

They made their way down the next two rows, back to the basket. When they were having a sandwich (chicken salad and cucumber—the cukes were sweet), Joe said, "How were your students this year?"

"I had to be kind of strict with Lois and Henry. I think I hurt their feelings. But it's not like when Frank and I were going there—lots of kids, and so lots of distractions for the teacher, and so lots of fun. Do you remember when Frank set the mousetrap for the bullies, where they kept their cigarettes in the outhouse?"

"Never heard about that one."

"He might have been seven at that point. I thought he was so brave and smart. Even though they were bigger than he was, they left us alone after that, because he was as sly as could be. Another time, he put a half-rotted rat in one of the bullies' boots. It was winter, and the kid had to jam his foot in to get it on. We all knew it was in there. Oh my, we laughed. But there's none of that now. I have my eye on all of them all the time."

"I guess, when Lillian and Jane go to the high school, you'll be down to four."

"They might close the school."

She pulled out a small bowl of raspberries, which they ate one by one.

It was nearly noon when they made their way down the third set of rows. Joe wondered what Minnie would do if they closed the school. She had never shown any inclination to leave home, and he didn't know what Mrs. Frederick would do without her.

The last row Minnie walked in front of him, pulling out the tassels that were at her level, and Joe walked behind her, pulling out the higher ones. She had a straw hat on (so did he). He couldn't see even the back of her head, but he could see her hips and her feet. They gave him such a funny feeling that he was a little delirious by the time they got back to the food basket. They drank some water and sat down on a blanket in the shade of the tall corn plants to share the rest of the food. There were more sandwiches, with some sliced sausage, lettuce, and the first of the season's tomatoes on Mama's homemade bread; after that, some of Mrs. Frederick's Linz cookies, with jam in the middle—these were fancy, and she was the only one in the neighborhood who took the time to bake them. The jam in the middle was blackberry, one of Joe's favorites. Minnie said, "I used to hide those in my coat, and then Frankie would tickle me until I gave him one."

Joe must have looked dismayed, because Minnie said, "We were only eight and nine."

"He used to tickle me, too. But it wasn't for a cookie."

"What was it for?"

"To make me pee my pants."

"That's mean."

"That's Frankie."

"Brothers and sisters are mean. Even Jane Morris shoves her sister Lucy, and Jane is the meekest child I ever saw. I think being mean to siblings is the law of the world."

Joe didn't answer. Once again, the discussion had gone past him. He said, "Thanks for helping me. I'll cut you in on the profits."

"Oh, please do!"

They folded up the blanket, and Minnie put her hat back on her head. Joe wondered how much Minnie thought about Frankie. He was pretty certain that Frankie never thought about Minnie.

1939

CLAIRE WAS BORN on Frankie's birthday, but late in the day rather than the middle of the night. Rosanna and Walter had time to get to the hospital in Usherton. Once she was there, under the care of Dr. Liscombe, there were plenty of nurses, all in white uniforms and about nineteen years old. Rosanna could not imagine how she had given birth before, although she could remember it perfectly well. The new hospital had all the latest things—big windows, railings around the beds, linoleum floors, swinging doors, rooms with only two beds in them. After Dr. Liscombe delivered Claire, they took her away, and didn't bring her back for four hours. What a relief that was! The birth was easy—what birth wasn't, after five previous ones, Rosanna would like to know—but she felt she deserved a nap, anyway. Once she'd had one, and they put Claire in her arms, she thought it was the first time she had ever looked at her new baby and not gone nuts.

Claire was a seven-pounder (seven pounds, three ounces—when had she ever known the exact weight before?). She had a down-to-earth way about her. She wasn't an angel and she wasn't a beauty and she wasn't the repository of all of Rosanna's hopes, whatever they were. (What were they? wondered Rosanna.) She was a baby who had Walter's hair and Rosanna's nose and someone else's eyes—maybe Granny Elizabeth? Rosanna smiled at her—who could help it?—and smoothed her dark hair to the side. She put Claire to the breast. She almost said ouch; this was the thing she had forgotten, how much it hurt the first few times. The nurse who had brought the baby said, "Oh, doesn't it ache, though? There was a lady in here last week whose one-year-old was still nursing, and even she winced when the newborn latched on. But I don't need to tell you."

Claire did her job, first on one side, then on the other, and the nurse said "Excellent!" and took the baby away for another four hours. Rosanna, who had forgotten to bring a book along, took another nap.

When the nurses weren't looking, Rosanna got up and walked around, and so she was standing in the doorway when her mother appeared, walking down the white hallway from the far end, where the elevator was. At first she thought her mother was Oma, so slowly did she walk along, with her head down, a little abashed by the grandeur of the stark walls and the tall doors to the rooms. Rosanna couldn't help stepping back and letting the door of her room close, and then looking at her own reflection in its circular window. Too old to have a baby, wasn't she? Thirty-nine, almost, her hair a thin bun. Frankie, now nineteen, had filled her out, given her dimples in her cheeks, made her hair grow an inch a month. Claire had drained her. No more, she thought, and then there was a knock.

Her mother had a bag with her. She set that next to Rosanna on the bed and said, "My dear, you look more like you just went shopping than like you had a baby!"

"Well, it's more like a vacation here than a birth. I hardly know what to do with myself."

"Enjoy it, enjoy it. They're already looking out the door at your place, wondering when you're coming home. Lillian sent you a poem." Her mother handed her a piece of paper, and she unfolded it: "We send our love to Baby Claire, / So far away. If we were there, / We'd kiss your toes and fingers, too, / Just to show that we do so love you." Rosanna said, "Has there ever been such a child?"

"Well, you can say that about any child, really. Each one is his or her own little universe."

Rosanna pressed the button, and, sure enough, a nurse in a white cap and white shoes eased through the door. Rosanna said, "My mother would like to see the child."

This nurse was one of the nineteen-year-olds. She said, "I don't know that we can allow that, Mrs. Langdon. The infants are on a strict schedule."

"I won't feed her, if you—"

"It's not just feeding. They benefit from a clear routine."

Rosanna looked at her mother, then said to the nurse, "What's your name?"

"I'm Wilma," said the nurse.

Rosanna said, "My mother here delivered my second baby. I delivered the last one by myself."

"I'll get in trouble," said Wilma.

Rosanna turned to her mother and said, "How did you get here?"

"Grandpa brought me. He went on to the feed store."

"In the truck?"

Granny Mary nodded.

Rosanna said, "You're bringing the baby back to me at eleven, right?"

"Yes. Eleven o'clock feeding, then a bath, then a nap. When you leave the hospital Monday, we'll give you a schedule and instructions."

Rosanna bit her lip. She said, "Thank you."

When the nurse left, she said, "What time is Papa coming by?"

"He said to call him at the feed store."

"Well, call him and tell him eleven-thirty." She handed her mother the phone beside the bed.

It was the older nurse who tried to stop them. They had gone through the door past the elevator and were starting down the stairs when she ran up from the floor below and placed herself in front of them. She said, "I don't believe you're ready to check out, Mrs. Langdon."

"I am, though. I'm fine."

"You can't take the infant out in this cold."

"Is it going to be warmer in three days?"

"You are being very irresponsible!"

"Taking my own child home to the place where she's going to live?"

"She's two days old! Don't you live on a farm?"

"Look at it this way. She's been living on that farm for nine months. I'm sure she'll feel very comfortable there."

Granny Mary put her hand on the nurse's arm and encouraged her to step aside. After a moment, she did. Rosanna was pretty tired, actually, when they got to the bottom of those four sets of stairs, but there was her father, the truck at the curb, warm and running. Granny Mary opened the door, and Rosanna got in. Her mother got in after her and slammed the door. Rosanna could see a hospital person, someone in a suit, hurrying down the steps and gesturing. Her father checked the side-view mirror and pulled away from the curb. Rosanna said, "I think this is the closest we'll ever come to being gangsters."

"Well," said her mother, "Papa here did make his own beer all through Prohibition." They all laughed.

Rosanna said, "I don't see why all of my births have to be so dramatic."

Granny Mary folded the blanket away from Claire's little face. Her eyes were open, but she wasn't crying. Granny Mary said, "They all have happy endings, though." When they got to the farm half an hour later (they had to go a little slowly because of the bits of four-day-old snow that had drifted over the roads), Walter was out in the barn with Joey, and Lillian and Henry were playing a game with Lois. The kitchen was cold, the range hadn't been lit in three days, and Rosanna suddenly missed the dull luxury of the hospital. But she knew this was her life. Better to be immersed in it than to see it from afar.

AT THE END of winter, when the weather was too cold for them to go out for recess, and they had sung all the songs in the songbook, Minnie taught them to sew. They pushed four of the tables together and laid out some fabric on it that Minnie had gotten from Dan Crest—blue and white stripes, and enough for everyone to make something. The hope was that by the time they were all finished with their projects, spring would be in full bloom, and they would be able to wear what they had made.

Blue and white stripes reminded Lillian of mattresses and pillows, but she tried to enter enthusiastically into the project. She would make an apron for herself, one with ruffles over the shoulders, and a smocked pinafore for Lois—Lois could do some of the cutting and sewing, and Lillian would do the smocking, in red. Minnie whispered, "I know this fabric is hideous, darling, but it was all he would give me. He couldn't sell a yard of it, I'm sure."

Lillian nodded.

Henry decided to make himself trousers and a vest. The stripes would run downward on the trousers and across on the vest. Lillian said, "Don't you think that's a little loud, Henry?"

He grinned.

Jane had decided on a gored skirt, and Lucy on a dress. Lillian thought that everyone was getting a good lesson in making a silk purse out of a sow's ear, which was what Mama said that you would have to do for your whole life if you didn't watch out, so it was never too soon to start.

Lillian helped Henry cut the pattern out of butcher paper that Dan Crest had also given them, and she helped him lay it out when it was his turn to use the pins. At six and a half, he was already pretty good at cutting with scissors. All she had to do was show him how to run the back of the blade along the wood of the table. It took him all of one snowy afternoon to cut out his pieces, but that was okay; Minnie had them sit around him and read their book aloud—it was *Tom Sawyer.*

Mama couldn't believe they were sewing at school, but Lillian defended Minnie. She said, "All the rest of the year, we run around, and she lets everyone climb trees and play baseball, even though we're all girls except Henry."

Mama actually had pins between her lips as she shook her head. She was mending a rip in Papa's overalls that he'd gotten climbing the fence. Claire was asleep across the room, so they were keeping their voices low.

"Anyway, she makes him add up inches and feet and yards and measure with a tape, and poke his pins in straight. And if he drops the pins, she makes him count the ones he's got and find the ones he's lost."

"You're so crazy about Minnie, I must say."

Mama didn't seem to like this. Lillian said, "Everyone at school is. She's fun."

"Reared on cake and cookies," said Mama, pulling the last pin out from between her lips and inserting it into the patch. "Well, there's something to be said for that easygoing way, I suppose."

Mama did agree with her that the blue and white stripes were very loud, but she gave Lillian thread for smocking—navy and red.

In the afternoons, they sat by the west windows of the school, looking out on the snow and the outhouse, and they sewed while Minnie read aloud. Lillian, who had been sewing since she was eight, was finished with her apron in two days. Jane was not terribly straight in her stitching, so she had to unstitch several times, until she learned to pay attention to what she was doing and stop looking out the window. Lucy was slow, but much more careful than Jane, though she occasionally pricked herself with a pin or a needle. Lois, now nine, tended to forget what she was doing and gawk at Minnie, listening to the story. When Minnie noticed this, she would stop and say, "I can't go on until Lois stops wasting time." Lois would go back to sewing. Looking at her seams, Lillian knew she would end up redoing them.

Henry needed help, but he didn't need that much help, which surprised Lillian. He never pricked himself. He sewed with his tongue sticking out of the corner of his mouth, but he was intent, and when he finished the first long seam, the outer seam of his trouser leg, he shouted, "Hooray!" He found it so inspiring that he carried his trousers home on Friday, and worked on them through the weekend. Papa and Joey might have said something mean, but the sight of him on the sofa, staring at the blue and white stripes and sewing, was enough to shut them up.

Mama said, at one point, "So he wants to sew. Opa always knitted. He knitted himself a sweater every couple of years."

Since no one ever said a bad word about Opa, Papa kept his mouth shut. Lillian was glad that Frankie was in Ames. On Tuesday, Henry set aside the trousers and started on the vest. When she finished *Tom Sawyer,* Minnie brought some music from home, not songs for them to sing, but music with swoops and big chords. It was so cold in the school that Jane had to make sure that the stove was stoked at all times, and they had to put socks over their hands under their mittens and three pairs of socks inside their shoes. On the way to school, Lillian had to watch Henry to make sure that his muffler didn't fall down and expose his nose. But after the projects were done and they were sitting once again on the swaying leafy branches of the maple trees, Lillian thought that that week had been the best of the school year, and that Minnie was the sister that she wanted more than anything.

EVEN AFTER the spring came and the weather warmed up, Rosanna left Claire's cradle in the front room. The house had been so cold for three weeks that they had all slept there—Lillian on the sofa, Joe on a kind of camp bed, Henry on the floor, and Claire in the cradle at the foot of the stairs. Walter and Rosanna slept in their room, but with all the vents open and blankets over the windows. At the top of the stairs, you could actually feel a warm breeze if the stove was going strong, but away from the door, it was quite chilly. Well, they survived, and now the daffodils were out and it was only a few weeks until the last frost date and time for the corn to go in. The good thing about having the cradle there was that Walter sat down on the couch when he came in and out of the house and chatted with Claire. And whether that was the reason, or whether Claire simply appealed to him because she was calm but alert, Walter didn't know. Fact was, he liked her. She was his baby.

Rosanna was not unkind to her—her touch was gentle and her look was motherly—but she didn't make of her what she had of Lillian and Henry (and he couldn't remember anything about Frank as a baby or Joey, except that Frank was always throwing things and Joey whining). Walter knew that was because the baby wasn't blonde and looked like a Langdon rather than a Vogel. However, Walter reminded himself, what did it matter to Claire? She was nursed, she was changed, she was carried from place to place. She was set up against the corner where the arm of the sofa met the back, she was given the tiniest bits of mush and applesauce from the tip of a spoon. Lillian sang her songs, and Henry played patty-cake with her, and maybe only Walter noticed a difference. Maybe Rosanna herself didn't even notice a difference.

But that left an opening for him. What he liked to do was sit beside the cradle while Henry ran around the room in his silly striped suit (which he was wearing into rags) and get her to laugh—not by touching or tickling her, but by turning his head away and turning it back, opening his mouth and slamming it closed, sticking out his tongue and pulling it in, putting his hands over his face and pulling them away again. She laughed and laughed, and he said, "Clairy, Clairy, Clairy, she's so merry!" and then laughed himself.

SCHOOL HAD HARDLY even begun when Lawrence showed up at Frank's tent and suggested they go to Chicago for Labor Day weekend. He was bored with his classes.

Frank said, "We've been in class one week."

"I know. But I took a look at the syllabus."

"You're supposed to look at the syllabus and buy the books."

"Well, I try not to."

The Flying Cloud was parked on the bridge. Frank climbed up the bank, brushed off his trousers, and said, "You need to wash this baby." Somehow, though he was two years younger than Lawrence, he had become the older brother. But a nice older brother—no kicks, no slaps, no punches, no yelling, just advice. For example, he had told Lawrence to get rid of Gertie Elkins, and he had. Gertie Elkins had had "gold digger" written all over her, and she had said the same thing of Frank, so Frank had told her, "What you see is what you feel, baby. Whores are cheaper than you." He said, "Is there a game?"

"Not unless we stay till Tuesday. There's a doubleheader Monday against the Pirates."

"I have class Tuesday."

They got into the car. Sometimes Frank thought that his real friend was the car, not Lawrence.

Lawrence said, "Maybe Diz'll pitch."

"Dizzy Dean is done for," said Frank.

"But I like to see him anyway. And—"

"And what?"

"I want to see the communists."

"Julius and Eloise?"

"I miss them."

"They're about to be drummed out of the Party, Julius is such a Trotskyite."

"I would like to see them even if they were only socialists. Eloise is sexy."

"She's thirty-four years old."

"Myrna Loy was born in 1905."

Frank said, "She's too old for you, too."

Julius and Eloise lived in a better place than they had—on the North Side, just south of Evanston, not where the big houses were, but not far from the lake, either. They had three bedrooms now, and he had taken Lawrence to visit them twice already. Anyway, they had plenty of hot water and it was cheap to stay there. Lawrence loved the communists. He had let Julius take him to a meeting and talk to him about world revolution, which Julius was happy to do, even though Lawrence was obviously petit-bourgeois scum and, as Frank said to him, "He will execute you after the revolution, you know that, don't you?"

"Not if I give him the car."

It took about five breezy hours to get there, but Eloise wasn't happy to see them. She took a long time to come to the door, and then went straight back to her typing. The apartment was a mess, and the sheets were sitting folded on the unmade bed of the guest room. The sound of typing stopped, and then she appeared in the doorway, her cigarette in her hand. She said, "A fellow we know from the Party in England was here for a week. He left yesterday morning, but with all these things in Europe, I haven't had a moment."

"What things?" said Lawrence.

"The explosion two nights ago at the train station in Tarnów, Poland, and now this."

"Now what?" said Lawrence.

"The Germans have already destroyed Wieluń, some little town, and they're crossing the border in about ten different places. Julius has gone down to party headquarters to see if there's any news about what Stalin is going to do. Julius is just off the deep end with Chamberlain. He keeps saying that if Chamberlain hadn't been playing footsie with Hitler all spring, this wouldn't have happened."

"What do you say?"

"Well, half the time I say that accelerating the world revolution is our job and we must welcome armed conflict."

"What about the other half?" said Lawrence. Frank thought he sounded truly curious.

"The other half of the time I have no idea what to say." She looked over her shoulder, out the window. It was almost dark. A moment later, there was a knock on the door. Eloise said, "That's Olivia Cohen, bringing Rosa home. Don't talk about this with her, all right?"

But all through supper, Rosa watched Julius cough and groan and put his head in his hands. Finally, he pushed his plate away and left the table. Rosa said nothing, only glanced after him once.

The next morning, Eloise got Frank and Lawrence up, handed them ten dollars, and said, "I want you to take Rosa to the beach, and then get her some lunch, and then take her to a double feature. Julius and I have meetings all day." The lake was calm, and the beach was crowded. Lawrence and Frank looked at the girls while Rosa, who was a good swimmer now, played in the water. When it got hot, Frank stripped down to his trunks, which he had brought along, and swam as far out as he could—far enough out so that the people on the beach and lifeguard's stand disappeared against the bright Chicago skyline. He floated there for a while, his face pointed toward the sky, and then he swam back in. A girl of about fourteen had joined Rosa, and was helping her build something in the sand. Lawrence was asleep on his back with a newspaper over his face. The front page of the paper was full of Poland. Looking at it made Frank's scalp prickle, because, no matter what Lawrence said about this being Europe's problem, and about how maybe Julius, as an Englishman, a commie, a Jew, was taking it too seriously, Frank thought that of course it had to do with him, of course it did. Wasn't it true, as Mama always said, that he was drawn to trouble? And this was the biggest trouble in the world.

AT THANKSGIVING, everyone teased Joe about how now he was rich. Walter had gotten forty-two bushels of corn per acre; Joe had gotten fifty-two. Fifty-two bushels an acre was unheard of. And because of the war in Europe, he had sold it for two bits a bushel, which came out to over a thousand dollars. Since the seed he had hybridized the year before was leftover seed, and this crop was from the seed he had harvested, and since he had done all the work himself, he had cleared almost nine hundred dollars. Papa said, "Well, I'll have to charge you room and board." Mama said, "Oh, my goodness, Walter, don't even mention such a thing," but everyone else seemed to know he was joking.

Frank said he could buy a new Ford for five hundred dollars, and Henry said he could buy a windup handcar with Minnie and Mickey Mouse pumping the handles, and Lillian said that he could buy a horse—Jake—he could go buy Jake back from those people. But Joe knew what he was going to buy—he was going to buy seed, of course.

It wasn't until the next morning, over breakfast, that Joe and Papa got into an argument about it. Papa said, "There's a lesson for you in this, boy."

"Yes, sir," said Joe.

"You know what the lesson is?"

"I don't know if I do." He meant that he didn't know Papa's lesson. But he knew his own—it was to get out of the house in the morning before Papa got up.

"The lesson is, you got to buy seed, because the corn you grew is sterile. What seed are you going to buy?"

"I'll go into town after Christmas and see what they have."

"Better to go out to the corncrib before Christmas and see what you have."

Joe felt his jaw clench.

"Son." Walter smoothed his voice. "You did something good, especially for a kid who was only sixteen at the time. You experimented. You tried something and learned something and you got a payout."

"Yes, sir. But—"

"But your payout isn't what you think it is. Remember four years ago, when your uncle Rolf left that field fallow?"

Joe nodded.

"And then he plowed that clover under? Well, that was his real legacy to you, Joey. Because then you bred your 'hybrid,' and then you saved that seed, and then you planted it and you got fifty-two bushels an acre, but you have to divide that number by three. Seventeen is what you really got."

Joe ate a bite of toast, and then took his handkerchief out of his back pocket and blew his nose. He could hear running around upstairs—that would be Henry. If Henry got down before Joe was out of the house, Henry would want to tell him a story. Joe said, "I understand that."

"You grow your own hybrid seed, and you got to set aside a field for that every year—that's a field that is out of production."

"If I do it every year, then it's only out of production for a year. If I had four fields—Anyway, you grow your own seed every year— you sell most of the crop and keep some. What's the difference? And you switch varieties, so sometimes you have to buy seed, too. I want to try crossing some Hickory King with some Boone. Those Hickory King plants can get eight feet tall."

"You think the price of corn is up and is going to stay up."

"No, I don't. I have eyes in my head. But I think we ought to take advantage when it is up."

"I don't like your tone."

Joe said, "Sorry, Papa." But Walter's voice was loud, too, and Joe wasn't sure what they were fighting about.

Walter said, "You think it's easy now. Fifty-two bushels an acre! Scarcity is your friend, not plenty. What's going to happen to you if everyone gets fifty-two or sixty, or whatever?"

"I'll try to get seventy."

Walter just shook his head.

1940

〜

AFTER CHRISTMAS, Professor Cullhane was assigned another graduate student (in addition to the one he had, Jack Smith, whom Frank didn't care for, partly because he always had his nose in a chemistry beaker and had never actually fired a gun) and two more undergrads, Bill Lord and Sandy Peck. He gathered them in the lab and he said, "Now, gentlemen, as you know, a hundred years ago, gunpowder—or black powder, as they called it—was made from charcoal, sulfur, and saltpeter, though I would call that potassium nitrate. As most of you know, black powder has fallen out of favor, or you might say it's been superseded by cordite and other deflagration explosives. But look around you. Where are you? You are in the heart of corn country, and our job, our contribution to the war effort we see in Europe—and make no mistake, the war effort that we will soon be part of—is to figure out a way to take the materials at hand and forge them into weapons. Our plowshares, you might say, through no fault of our own, must once again become swords." All the others gaped, Frank knew, because they vaguely recognized those words, "swords" and "plowshares."

"Where do we get sulfur? From volcanoes and hot springs. That's not our business here. Where do we get saltpeter? Well, we should be getting it from manure piles, because that's the safest and most abundant source. And where do we get the char? Fellas, that's what this lab is all about. We want black powder without the black smoke, without the corrosion of the gun barrels. We want weapons that fire shot after shot without cleaning the barrels, and we want that from cornstalks." Then he introduced them all to one another, and told them how Frank and Jack had been working on this for a year now, "and we've made progress."

But they hadn't made progress. Frank and Professor Cullhane had tried to reduce the cornstalks to char in fourteen different ways in order to produce a purer, less smoky product. They had taken the char and ground it into powder, milled it into granules of several different sizes, sieved it through a flour sifter and cheesecloth and medical gauze. Professor Cullhane had been careful about where he got his sulfur and his saltpeter—he had even made himself some saltpeter by going over to the vet school and loading wheelbarrows of cattle manure, sheep manure, and horse manure (all carefully separated) into tanks that he purchased. Frank could see that it wasn't going to work, and when, in the fall, they had gone out shooting (supposedly pheasant along the railroad tracks, just to pretend that they were doing something normal), Professor Cullhane had come back profoundly discouraged—the barrels of their guns, new when they started, were already showing the effects, much more quickly than the professor had expected. No modern army would fight with this stuff. Cullhane had said to Frank, "If the Germans invade, we aren't going to hold them off for long with this." Frank had laughed, but Cullhane hadn't been joking. It was then that Frank realized that Cullhane really did think that the Germans might invade. Even at twenty, Frank didn't see how that was possible.

But then the college had come to Professor Cullhane, and given him more money—two thousand dollars—to continue with his "war work," and it turned out that a lot of that money came straight from the army. Frank was happy to keep getting a paycheck, especially since Cullhane, now that they had a larger workforce, wanted to go over every single process they had already tried, just to see if they'd made a mistake. The paycheck combined with the—okay, he could admit it—strangeness of the project and his feelings of luxurious comfort in Ames persuaded Frank to take fewer classes, extend his degree for another year. And, anyway, what else was there for him to do with himself?

After the meeting broke up, Frank took the other two undergrad boys out behind the Chemistry building in the freezing cold and showed them the manure tanks. He said, "We need to scrub those out and fill them again. I suppose we should start right now." Bill, who said he was from a farm over by Sioux City, stepped forward, but Sandy, who was from Des Moines, stepped back, his jaw dropping. That look on his face, that city-boy, frat-boy look, gave Frank the best laugh of his day.

IT WAS AUGUST, no school. Lillian was at Granny Elizabeth's, helping her can tomatoes, beans, and peaches. Joe was cultivating the cornfield behind the barn, and Mama and Claire were taking a nap. It was not a terribly hot day, Henry thought, but it had been so hot all week that he had slept in only his drawers, with all the windows and doors open. Mama told him not to complain—didn't he remember four years ago, when it was over a hundred for weeks on end and the well almost dried up? Mama hated complaining. But Henry didn't remember that. Summer was summer, winter was winter. One was unbearably hot, and the other was unbearably cold.

Papa had to go to another farmer and buy a part for the oat thresher, and he told Henry to come along. As soon as they drove in the lane and pulled up beside the barn, Henry saw that there were boys here. One was a little older than he was—dressed in overalls, no shirt, barefoot. The other was big, at least twelve, and dressed the same way. The minute they got out of the truck, the farmer said, "Well, now, I meant to find that thing and I forgot all about it. It'll just take a second. What's your boy's name? Henry? Henry, you go off with Sam and Hike here. Boys, half an hour of peace, please."

Sam was the younger boy, Hike the older one. As soon as they were out of sight of the barn, Hike kicked his brother in the backside, and then laughed. Sam turned on him and punched him in the stomach. It was Hike who started to cry. Henry slowed down, and the other two got pretty far ahead. They turned around. But they didn't run at him—Sam just called out, "Don't mind Hike. He's just slow.

He can't even read." Henry didn't like to, but he caught up. They were heading toward a field where horses were grazing, and he liked horses. He counted them; there were six, four chestnuts and two blacks. Hike and Sam climbed on the fence, and then Henry did, too. The three of them hung their elbows over the top rail, and Henry said, "What are their names?"

Hike said, "Daisy, Rose . . ." He paused.

Sam added, "Daffodil, Iris, Hawthorn, and Poppy. Ma names them. She likes flowers." Iris and Daisy, two chestnuts with white blazes, came to the fence, and the boys petted their noses. Hike said, "Let's go to the ravine."

"Yeah," said Sam. "There's something there."

"What?" said Henry.

"Another horse," said Sam.

But the horse was dead. Henry could see that from the rim of the ravine. It was lying there, a big white, bulky, fly-covered mound. It was scary and repulsive—the eyes were gone, the hanging tongue was black, and the coat was crusted over with something. Only the tail was strangely graceful—long, pale, and curving across the dry dirt. "Something's going to happen," said Hike.

"What?" said Henry.

"You'll see."

The two boys ran down the slope of the ravine and picked up sticks. Sam shouted, "Come on!"

Henry made his way down, sliding as best he could on his heels. It was almost midday, and the sun, high in the summer sky, was pouring heat into the ravine, which was full of other trash, too. Henry tried to step carefully. The other two boys ran around barefoot, even though there were nails everywhere, and wooden boards broken into splinters, and sharp stones, and parts of all sorts of things sticking up. But they took their sticks and scurried about the horse anyway, poking it and whacking it. Sam shouted, "Get a stick! There's some over there!" He pointed, but Henry didn't do anything, just stood for a minute by the horse's head, then stepped away from there, so that he wouldn't have to look at the eye sockets. Surprisingly, the horse didn't smell very terrible—but it was huge, much bigger than the horses in the pasture. The boys were particularly intent on beating it across the belly, hitting, then poking, then hitting, then poking. There seemed to be a plan, and it wasn't until the horse exploded that Henry understood what the goal was.

Hike had been beating the belly just in front of the back leg, and then he smacked it furiously one time and poked it leaving a hole. The hole made a sound, and then a line along the bottom of the belly ripped open, and gas and liquid leapt out, the belly ripped in another spot, and more gunk poured forth. Most of it flowed, but some of it popped, and bits landed on all of the boys, including Henry himself. It was the worst thing he'd ever smelled, and it was on him in stinking dots. Hike and Sam started laughing and jumping around, even though it was on them, too. Henry thought he was going to pass out and fall down.

Papa's head, and then the head of the farmer, appeared above the rim of the ravine, and the farmer shouted, "Goddamn you boys! I told you to stay away from this dump! I am going to whip the hides off you! I say stay away, you don't think I mean stay away?" He came sliding down the slope, and Sam and Hike ran up the other side, dropping their sticks on the way. Henry could see Papa and climbed up to him. Papa said, "Let's go. Never should have come here. These are lowlifes here. Didn't even have the part, and tried to sell me six other things. That stinks!"

He told Henry to take off his shirt and throw it in the back of the truck. When they got home, he sent him to the spigot by the barn and had him scrub it. Henry did it pretty well, he thought. But he doubted that he would wear that shirt again.

Over supper, Joey asked if Papa had found the part, and when Papa said no, Joey said, "Did you see Jake?"

Papa said "Nope," and Henry said, "Who's Jake?"

"Our horse we had. We gave it to them to pull a buggy. If I'd known you were going there, I would have come along—"

But Papa was biting his lip, and then Mama said, "What, Walter?"

"They had horses," said Henry. "They had four chestnuts and two blacks. The boys were mean boys."

"Not worth talking about, you ask me," said Papa, and that was the end of that.

But when it was dark and Henry was getting into bed, Joey

appeared in the doorway of his room—something he never did, Joey never came upstairs—and he said, "They didn't have a white horse?"

Henry didn't say anything, but he must have grunted without meaning to. Then Henry said, "Something bad happened."

Joey sat on the bed. "Tell me."

"I couldn't stop them."

"What?"

"They were beating the white horse with sticks. He was dead and down in a ditch, and they beat him until—"

"Until what?"

"He didn't have any eyes."

"Until what?"

"Until he blew up, kind of. His stomach. It got on me."

Joey put his hand over his face and nodded. Henry could see that he was crying. Henry had never seen Joey cry. Joey said, "You didn't have to stop them. It's okay, Henry."

But Henry cried anyway. Joey left the room. Henry cried for a pretty long time, then fell asleep. He wished he had taken a bit of the tail, just a few hairs, which he could have given to Joey.

EVERYONE HAD SAID how much Lillian would like the high school. Mama and Granny Elizabeth had sewn her just the outfits she wanted, ones she'd seen in a magazine, and she had cut her hair (putting her braids, which were twenty-two inches long, away in a drawer). She wore a smoother hairdo now, still bright blond, but she had to roll it under every night and sleep on it. She could not say that the girls and the boys were mean to her—in general, they ignored her, didn't look at her at all. An odd thing to know was that she was short, that when she walked down the hall she was merely part of the crowd, that her greatest efforts simply raised her to the level of most of the others. She, who had been told for her entire life that she was an angel and a beauty and a darling, wasn't any of these things—she was one of many girls who were blonde, a little bigger in the hips than in the bust, a girl who had to watch out where she hemmed her skirts for fear that her calves would look unattractive.

And she, whom adults loved, was not the adored of her teachers, either. They considered her a decent student, for a girl, but, according to the ones who remembered him, nothing like Frank. Frank had been a phenomenon—totally ignorant of some of the simplest things, like the fact that London was in England, but totally capable of learning. Once he saw a map of Europe, and England, and London, and read an assigned book, *Oliver Twist,* he could tell you exactly where Oliver started out, where he went, and where he ended up. Yes, he had a "photographic memory," that was part of it, but he understood what things meant, too. That's what the English teacher said, anyway. The chemistry teacher saw her name on the class list and told the class about the time her brother Frank blew a window out of the classroom with a nitrogen experiment of some sort.

Jane was taller than she was now, by half a head, and thinner, too. She had been used to thinking of Jane as "malnourished," as Mama would say, but now that she was in high school, she saw that Jane was rather elegant-looking—dark and flat-chested. All the girls preferred to be flat-chested with slim hips. They liked Bette Davis, of course, but also Barbara Stanwyck, blondes who were not really blonde, and who didn't look at all like they did, farm girls, Iowa girls. Even Margaret Lindsay, who was born in Iowa and had started out as Margaret Kies—wouldn't that be German?—didn't look like any of the girls in the high school. "Jane Morris" was a good name for Hollywood, and their very first semester, she tried out for a part in the play. She didn't seem to be daunted when she didn't get it, either. When the other kids laughed in her audition, she didn't notice, or didn't care. Lillian cared on her behalf, but didn't say anything. Jane did have a way of lifting her head and flaring her nostrils that said, "I'll be leaving this town very soon," which made Lillian laugh.

At the high school, Lillian missed Henry. Henry was eight now, and such a chatterbox. Lillian was sure he was driving Minnie crazy. She wished that Minnie would go to the school board and report that she couldn't possibly teach at the school without Lillian to help her, and then Lillian could go back there and be of some use, instead of wandering the halls of the high school, wondering why in the world she had to grow up.

....

FRANK WAS HAVING lunch in Ragnar's café with Lawrence, Hildy, and Eunice. Frank didn't go to Ragnar's café all that much, because Ragnar tended to watch him from across the room and ostentatiously leave him alone, but Lawrence liked the steak with popovers. Hildy was Frank's girlfriend, a sophomore in his ancient-history class, from Decorah, far in the northeast corner of Iowa. She spoke Norwegian at home (it sounded like everyone in that town did), and she spoke Norwegian to Ragnar, who was charmed by it. But everyone was charmed by her—she was a beautiful girl—great ankles, terrific knees, slim waist, nice bust, broad shoulders, long neck, glamorous smile, eyes so blue that they seemed to spring out at you when she opened them. When Frank and Hildy walked down the street, heads did turn. Maybe she was better-looking than he was—and he considered that a good thing. She was crazy about Frank—they both knew it. He was playing it cool. Lawrence was here with Eunice. Eunice was from St. Louis, Missouri, of all places, and she never let you forget it. How she had gotten to a place like Iowa State, she couldn't imagine. She was a Tri Delt, majoring in finding a diamond ring.

The first time Lawrence put his hand to his jaw was after he took a bite of steak. A few minutes later, he said, "Hey, ouch!"

It was Hildy, not Eunice, who said, "What's the matter?"

"My tooth. My tooth is stabbing me."

They ate a bit more; Frank had the fried chicken, which was exactly like Mama's, but with fried potatoes, not mashed. Finally, Lawrence just dropped his fork on the table and said, "What is happening?"

The Flying Cloud was parked outside, and the four of them piled into it, but Lawrence said he was in too much pain to drive, so Frank drove. In the back seat (he could see in the mirror), Lawrence was sitting up, and then he fell over with his head in Eunice's lap. Frank also saw in the mirror that she looked down with no expression on her face at all, and then cautiously stroked his hair. They drove around Campustown, looking for a dentist.

The dentist they found, somewhere up Hayward, was not working—he was cleaning his office, since it was Saturday, but one look at Lawrence in the back of the car, and he opened the door and stepped aside. They more or less dragged Lawrence in and set him in the chair. The dentist said that he had an impacted wisdom tooth, and that he needed to go to Mary Greeley. That was over on the other side of town, east on Lincoln Way and across the tracks. It was a bright, cold day, almost time for Christmas break. Over lunch, they had been talking about whether they liked to go home or not. Hildy had said that Christmas in Decorah was a real celebration, like Christmas in Norway—candles, that sort of thing. Frank drove the Flying Cloud through the crossing, and up Douglas. He turned in at the hospital driveway.

Well, Lawrence was dead by Monday morning. Eunice told Hildy, and Hildy showed up at Frank's room on Welch before breakfast, and told him. The two of them stared at each other, and Hildy started crying. Frank said, "Didn't you ever have anyone in your family die?"

"Not since before I was born."

"My sister died when I was five. She was jumping around during a rainstorm, and the thunder clapped. She fell down and slammed the back of her head on the corner of an egg crate."

Hildy said, "Oh, Frank!"

"I always wondered if it was me fiddling my heels on the rug that made her lose her balance."

"You did? You did always wonder that?" Hildy sat down in his lap and wept with her head against his chest. "How can you die from a tooth?" she said. "How can God make that happen?" Frank said nothing, but tightened his arms around her. On a farm, you knew that you could die from anything, or you could survive anything. "Why?" was a question that his relatives never asked—they just told the stories, clucked, shook their heads. He said, "Okay, Hildy. We are going to walk up Hayward and find that dentist and ask him. We're just going to do that." Hildy was so distraught that he had to button her coat and tie her scarf. He made her walk down the stairs, out the door, to the left, over to Hayward, up the street. Forthright, warming steps. He put his arm around her waist, but he did push her forward, between the snowdrifts.

The dentist came out as soon as he saw them, and they told him what had happened to Lawrence. Hildy said, "I can't understand it. How—"

"Massive infection. That kind of pain he had was a symptom of massive infection. I think I'll call the fellow who operated. . . ."

And so it went, all the discussions of every little thing. Not even

Eunice knew the truth, Frank thought, the truth of how Lawrence had lain there in that room, the truth that had nothing to do with what the doctor did or the nature of the infection. The truth would have been in that face that Frank was so familiar with—the eyes, the nose, the mouth, the expressions that passed over that face as life gave way to death. Everyone had missed that, that was the betrayal. It was okay to live or die, Frank thought (there was Rolf, for whom it was okay to die), but it was not okay that no one was there to see the passing.

Everything that others found comforting—fond memories of the dead, weeping, analyzing the last doomed decisions, praying, keeping silent, giving comfort, receiving comfort—Frank found pointless and enraging. The hearse drove the corpse away, Eunice went to Shenandoah for the funeral, someone was hired to take the car, Hildy wrote him every day from Decorah. Once he got back to the farm, Frank said nothing to Mama or Papa about the death, and when Eloise asked him how his friend Lawrence was, all he said was "Dead." Which shocked her. But he walked away before she could ask any questions, and he went back to campus two days after Christmas, saying that he had to get back to work.

1941

I T WAS HENRY who asked for a cake for Claire's second birthday. Rosanna, who didn't feel especially well, had let the thought slip her mind. When Henry began looking into cupboards and climbing on chairs, she said, "What now?"

"I'm looking for Claire's cake."

"I didn't make Claire a cake. She's too young for a cake."

"She likes cake," said Henry. "She knows it's her birthday."

"Goodness me," exclaimed Rosanna, thinking of all the beating of eggs and the sifting of flour, but then she felt that particular torment she always felt when she was caught overlooking Claire in some way. She said, "Well, you can help me. Lillian can play with her in the front room."

"Can we have chocolate?"

"We have no chocolate. But angel food is much healthier, especially for a little girl."

Henry scowled for the barest second, until Rosanna said, "You can separate the eggs." They had plenty of eggs, and separating twelve of them would keep Henry well occupied. They had cream for whipping as icing, too, and there was white sugar left over from Christmas baking—thank Heaven for that. "Go tell Lillian." Henry ran through the door to the dining room, calling "Lil! Lil!" and Rosanna found the tube pan. The range was hot—hot enough to warm the kitchen, as always in January—so she had nothing to complain of.

But Claire was Walter's child, and it was true, as much as she tried to hide it, that her own services for Claire were tinted more with obligation than with adoration. What she told herself was not that she did not like Claire—Claire was a very good child. It was that adoration had not paid off—look at Frankie. And as soon as she looked at Frankie, she wondered what motherhood was for. Everyone said you could not ask for a better son than Frank—successful, personable, and so handsome. Even Walter was satisfied with him, at last. But Rosanna knew better. Frank didn't care a fig about any of them, not even her, his adoring mother. But did every child have to be a loving child? When they were your brothers and sisters, you accepted without hesitation that they had reservations about your parents. In fact, in her own very private opinion, her brother Rolf had not had enough reservations about their parents—her father told him what to do all day, and her mother told him how to do it—and look what happened. Rosanna had been more independent, at least more than Rolf. And Eloise was practically a renegade. And then there were the three boys (now all grown up—Kurt worked in Mason City, Gus was married to an Irish girl who hated farming, and John worked for her father). Six children, six different degrees of love and respect for her parents, and occasional discussions about exactly in what ways Mary and Otto Vogel deserved what they had gotten.

Henry came back into the kitchen and went over to the sink and washed his hands. He was good about that, and about doing all kinds of things that Frank and Joe had never cared about, like taking his supper plate to the sink and, for goodness' sake, changing his underwear. Henry did what Lillian did, and Lillian was perfect. But Henry did not look into his mama's eyes and adore her. Rosanna set a bowl on the table in front of him, a bowl with a thin rim, and next to that she set two smaller bowls, and the egg beater. He looked up at her eagerly. She said, "Okay, Henry. Now, remember—what should you remember?"

"Crack them good, so the shell breaks rather than crumples."

"Right."

"Then put the white first in this small white bowl, and then, if it's clean, pour it into the big bowl."

"Okay, get started."

While he was cracking the eggs in his direct but careful way (no wonder he had learned to sew—his hands were amazingly adept; Minnie always complimented his penmanship, too; maybe Henry was the genius she was looking for?), she buttered and floured the tube pan and looked for the old 7 Up bottle that she hung the pan on to cool after it came out of the oven. She said, "What sort of jam do you want to ice it with?"

"Strawberry!" said Henry.

"Claire's favorite," said Rosanna.

"I love Claire," said Henry. Rosanna did not ask why, but she thought of it.

IT TURNED OUT that Eunice was in his English class. Frank saw her across the room the first day, but he came in late and was sitting beside the door—she was in the front row and didn't see him. The professor, a very old man, mumbled on and on about Alexander Pope and a poem Frank hadn't read yet called "The Rape of the Lock." Frank couldn't hear him very well, because the pane of the window next to his seat was rattling in the west wind. It was six weeks since Lawrence's death. Eunice looked as if nothing at all had happened—she was wearing the same green sweater she'd had on the day they drove him to the hospital. As he sat there, Frank felt absolute hatred for Eunice begin to soak through him. And hatred for Lawrence, too, that he'd taken up with this cold fish, this self-important bitch whose body temperature was 88.6 rather than 98.6. Frank dragged his gaze away from Eunice, across the front of the room, the podium, the blackboard, the backs of the heads of the other students, and looked out the window. It was snowing, but not blizzarding—the path across the campus in front of the building had a white dust on it. Hildy and her brother, who was a freshman, had an avid love of snow, and of skiing—any kind of skiing. The smallest hill was fun for them, and the fact that Birger Ruud, of Norway, had won the gold in ski jumping at the '36 Winter Olympics was a matter of personal pride. Hildy's brother, Sven, thought ski jumping was the ultimate sport, way more important than baseball, for instance. It was windy out there—first he saw someone slip and sit down on the pavement, a professor-looking type, then he saw a girl's scarf blow right off her head, and though the girl grabbed for it, it blew away.

Toward the end of the class, Eunice happened to look around, yawning, and to see him. She didn't smile, but she did keep looking. After a moment, she lifted her fingers in a wave.

She was first to the door, but she waited for him, and he couldn't avoid her. Without even greeting him, she murmured, "I came by your room, but you were at work."

"Yeah," said Frank.

"I want to give you something."

"What?"

"Some photos Lawrence took. There are about ten of them. You and him over where your tent is. Dead animal skins in the background. He's in four of them with you. You want them?"

"You know my address. Mail them."

"I can bring them to class Wednesday."

They walked down the hallway, then down the stairs and out the big front door. She turned left, and marched away without saying anything more.

It was lunchtime, so he was going to meet Hildy at the Union. She was standing beside the wall that commemorated the dead from the Great War, and as she turned toward him, he said, "Lot more names coming to this wall."

She said, "Yeah, it's terrible in Norway." But she said "*ja,*" which struck him as funny. "The ones who can't run away are eating their shoes." He glanced at her. She looked pained, not joking. She pulled his arm tight around herself and leaned into him. They went up the stairs and into the dining hall.

"I saw Eunice."

"Oh, poor Eunice."

"I don't think she cares."

"Of course she cares. She's heartbroken. They were going to get married."

"She says."

"Well, they hadn't bought the ring yet." She turned her eyes toward him and then away. Her eyes were always such a surprise. "But they'd looked at them."

"He would have told me."

"Maybe he thought it was private."

"Maybe she thought she'd caught him."

"I don't know why you hate her. She's nice."

"For a buck," said Frank.

Hildy stared at him. "I know you're putting that on. I know you don't mean that."

He took her hand and squeezed it, then said, "But I do."

"Oh, Frankie darling. You don't mean half the things you say. You're a softie in the middle."

He raised an eyebrow. Just then, some of Hildy's friends headed their way. He knew they thought he was a little scary but interesting, an A student, mysterious. Not one of them knew that his father was a farmer from Denby, forty miles away. He thought that was the funny part.

LILLIAN AND JANE HAD a fight. In eight and a half years of school, they had never had a fight, so Lillian was floored, not only at Jane for saying, "You think Phil is a goof; well, he's not, and I'm tired of you being such a snob!" but also at herself for saying, "Open your eyes, Jane, he is a goof!" And he was, but goofy guys were everywhere, and what did Lillian care if one of them had attached himself to Jane? The top of his head came up to Jane's nose, and he was always laughing, ha-huh-ha-huh, and if he ever had a handkerchief, Lillian would be thunderstruck. Still, he was nice enough, she didn't dislike him, and he was in three of her classes. But Jane stood by the flagpole outside of the school when all the kids were waiting for the hack and shouted at her, "Stop being such a snob! Stop being such a snob!" And when Jane burst into tears, Lillian actually looked around to see who she was yelling at, and she saw the other kids looking at her.

The next day was the worst day of her life. It started at breakfast, when she had Claire on her lap, and Claire gagged up some sausage and it landed on her white blouse, which she had pressed the night before; then she argued with Mama about whether you could still see the spot, and flounced up to her room to change, but there was nothing that went with that skirt, so she had to put on an outfit she had already worn that week. While she was dressing, she saw the hack pass outside the window, and so she had to run to catch it, all the way past Minnie and Lois's house, so she was out of breath and her hair was a mess by the time she was sitting in her seat. Lillian knew that she was a perfectionist, and that that was a bad thing, but sitting there, and then after she got down and went into school, she could not stop thinking about the wrong things—her outfit and her hair, and her feeling that she was already late to everything for the rest of the day. One look at Jane, in math class, sitting with Betty Halladay, told her that Jane was still furious with her; both she and Betty stared at Lillian for a long time before turning their gaze away.

It did seem as though no one at all spoke to her all morning, and then, when her geography test came back, she saw that she had missed almost every state capital—eight right and forty wrong—not merely an F. When she looked more closely, she saw that she had misread the pattern of the answers, and filled in the wrong circles—if she had been paying attention, she would have gotten three wrong and forty-five right (and who knew anything about Olympia, Salem, and Carson City, anyway?). She had even gotten the capital of Iowa wrong—she had marked it as Topeka. The paper had "See me" written along the top. For lunch, there was liver. She hated liver, and it didn't help that everyone seemed to hate liver, and two of the boys in her class started throwing all the liver on the floor of the cafeteria, until some teachers ran over and gave everyone detention.

After lunch, she was so hungry that she fainted in English class and fell out of her desk chair, and so she ended up being walked to the nurse's office by Mary Ann Hunsaker, who held her elbow in a tight grip "in case you fall down." The nurse took her temperature, which was normal, and felt her head, and told her that if she felt sick again she should put her head between her knees, which Lillian could not imagine doing in front of the other kids. And still Jane did not look at her or talk to her in their last class of the day, which was Latin, irregular verbs. When she got on the hack to go home, she saw Jane and Betty across the lawn in front of the high school. They were right next to one another, their heads bowed, and they were laughing. The hack was cold, too—they drove straight into a bitter wind all the way home.

Mama was not happy when she got home. Claire had been fussy all day, and Joey, who had been moving the last of the oat hay around in the hayloft, had fallen through the trapdoor and twisted his ankle

("Or worse than that!" said Mama). He was sitting in the front room with his leg propped on a pillow, and every time Mama walked through the room, she said, "Well, we just pray to the Lord that it isn't broken. My land! It's always something on a farm! What in the world do city people do with their time, is what I want to know!"

It was the worst day of her life not because anything terrible happened, like Uncle Rolf hanging himself, but because her whole life seemed to be falling apart in her hands, and she didn't know what in the world was left. She could not imagine what she could do to reconstruct all the things she enjoyed, and she could hardly remember what it was that she had enjoyed. It was only a year since she and Minnie had gotten the other children to use the end of winter to sew and read. That cozy time was turning into her favorite memory. But she could only remember that it was good, not how it felt.

ELOISE ALWAYS WONDERED if Julius and she would have been so surprised at the German invasion of Russia if they had been living somewhere east of Chicago. Sometimes, the entire atmosphere between London and Chicago occurred in her mind like a huge layer of cotton wool, muffling every single communication from the east, and sometimes it occurred like an echo chamber—whatever was being said, you did not know who was saying it or where it was coming from. At one point, Julius suggested that they keep their eye on the Canadians—whatever the Party decided to do up there, they would do that, too. After Trotsky was killed, Julius declared that that was it, he'd had enough, he would never, never raise a finger to help Stalin, the revolution had veered so far off the tracks that world communism was unsavable. For four weeks, they stayed home from meetings, had no contact with any friends. The ones in the Party were not to be trusted, and the two or three like them, who sympathized with Trotsky, were dangerous to associate with—who knew what revenge Stalin was plotting, even in Chicago? But what were you supposed to do with yourself when you saw no one? So they crept back, one friend at a time. But they never, never mentioned Stalin or Russia or the Soviet Union's alliance with the Nazis.

And then it was an alliance no more, and, speaking of Canada, Julius, now thirty-five (he was a year younger than Eloise), went off to Canada to join the war effort; that was what Englishmen living in the United States had to do, especially after the Smith Act, which might have deported him, anyway. A week after he left, which was three days after the invasion of the Soviet Union by Nazi forces, she took Rosa to the train, bought them a last-minute ticket, and headed west. All the way to Usherton, she contemplated keeping going—she had enough money for the fare to Denver, or even to San Francisco, and Ina Finch, who had been her friend in the Party, had moved to San Francisco and would be happy to put her up, she was sure. But she got off at Usherton just as if she hadn't the imagination to go farther, and there she was. She called her mother from the station, and her father came by half an hour later and picked them up. She had told them nothing about Julius's departure. The war was close. The war was very close.

Eloise and Rosanna had joked over the years that maybe John would never get married—he could listen to their father shouting without turning a hair, but every time their mother sighed, he went pale. However, he was married now, not quite thirty and the girl was a plump thing whose eyes closed every time Granny Mary told her to do anything that she didn't want to do. Over supper, she scraped every bit of food out of every serving dish, onto her plate, and complimented Granny Mary on all the food, as if she hadn't had a thing to eat in weeks. She was so talkative that Eloise saw that everyone else got quieter and quieter as the meal progressed. Rosa, who had been excited to get back to the farm, didn't say a word.

In the parlor, her father took a nap (he had been cultivating the cornfields since breakfast) and her mother continued with her needle-point, which was a picture of three trees in a rolling field, with Canada geese flying off to the left. Her mother said, "Well, poor Julius, what a choice to have to make." She glanced toward the door in case Rosa should appear.

"Who's going to avoid that choice, Mama?" said Eloise. "You know we'll have to go in."

Her mother tutted, then said, "Lindbergh says we're better off staying out of the whole thing. It's not our business." She glanced at Eloise, then said, "I'm not saying I know what to do."

Eloise tried to make her voice level. "Lindbergh thinks the Nazis aren't that bad. He's wrong."

"How do you know?"

"What I hear at the paper. What I hear at meetings."

"Oh, meetings," said her mother. Eloise felt her hackles rise. But she and Julius often discussed whether you could believe what you heard at meetings. They discussed that after almost every meeting, in fact. Her mother peered into her sewing box and pulled out a skein of magenta thread, then delicately picked off a length and began to separate the strands. She said, *"Meine Söhne brauchen nicht um ihr Leben zu opfern für die Engländer. Oder die Russen für diese Angelegenheit."*

"I understand what you said." The gist of it was that her mother, normally the most amenable of women, would not allow her sons to die for the English or the Russians.

"I hope you do."

Then Eloise said, *"Ja, gut, haben die letzten Worte an dieser Stelle nicht gesagt worden, egal was du sagst."* She thought she sounded pretty good—only about 5 percent rusty. No, she didn't think what her brothers did would be her mother's choice. She thought the days of choosing this or that were pretty much over.

But it was rather amusing to argue, even about such a serious matter, in German. All serious family disagreements were aired in German and always had been, and quite often Eloise and Rosanna and the brothers hadn't understood much of what their parents and grandparents were saying. This meant that they had improved their German over the years partly to eavesdrop and partly to talk back. More than once, one child or another had surprised Granny Mary and Oma by piping up without being asked. In Chicago, Eloise had asked some of the others in the Party whose parents were first- or second-generation if it was the same in their families, and it almost always was. Only Julius's family argued in both Yiddish and English, but in Yiddish they argued about family matters, and in English they argued about politics and religion. Safely ensconced in Iowa, with Julius in Toronto, Eloise could think that this was the source of their conflict—their common language was English, and so he could never let anything drop until she had yielded, which, of course, infuriated her.

That night, she sat up by her old window after putting Rosa to bed. The western horizon was flat, flat, flat, and the merest pale string of light shone above it, like a steel rim. Above that, the gallery of stars was beginning to shape itself, deep and broad and sharp in a way that you never saw in Chicago, even out in the middle of the lake. Behind her, Rosa's breathing slowed, and now she was asleep. Eloise turned around and looked at her. She was eight. Eloise didn't believe in Freud—that was bourgeois drivel, really. But she did wonder, just then, if Rosa had ever gained entrance to their family romance. It didn't have to be Oedipal, did it? You didn't have to want to kill your mother and marry your father. But probably you did want to attract their attention once in a while.

AS USUAL, Frank hardly went home at all during the summer. Professor Cullhane thought that they had it—or that they almost had it. They had tried out a batch of the gunpowder that they'd processed in June, and it hardly colored the barrels of their rifles at all. Professor Cullhane had grabbed Frank's hand, shaken it up and down, thanked him from the bottom of his heart for sticking with him another year. The rifles were no longer new, but Frank had cleaned them with perfect care, and the barrels had shown almost no effects. The key was to reproduce that batch. Frank's job was to track the characteristics of the char—how old were the cornstalks, what variety, etc.—and of the saltpeter—cow manure, and what had been the diet of those cows. At Iowa State, it was actually possible to do these things, and also to consult the soil analysis for the field where the corn had been grown. It was possible, but it was time-consuming. So he hadn't gone with Hildy to Decorah to meet her parents, nor had he taken her to Usherton. He had said that he loved her, though. Hildy seemed to think that one thing led naturally to another, but Frank did not agree. Still, Hildy had wangled a way of staying in Ames—she had found a job caring for some children. The wife of a professor in the Physics Department had given birth to a little girl; her other children were only two and a half and four. The woman's hands were full, but she lived in a big house and paid Hildy ten dollars a week, as well as putting her up in a third-floor room. Hildy said, "You'd think she'd have known better," but she liked her charges well enough. Her day off coincided with Frank's, and they took the bus to Carr Pool and sat around. Frank liked to swim laps, and sometimes Hildy dived off the high board. She could do both a jackknife and a back flip. All eyes looked up at her. She was a beautiful girl, and maybe he did love her.

He did not remember that Eunice had never sent him Lawrence's photos until he saw her the first day of the fall quarter, across the dining room in the union. He was finishing a late breakfast, and he looked up. The room was churning with people, and resounding with greetings and news. His eye went to her as if on a chain, and hers turned toward him. But even though they were looking at each other, there was absolute nonrecognition. He might have been staring at the back of her head, and she at the back of his.

THE NEXT TIME he saw her was at a Sigma Nu party. Jack Smith was a Sigma Nu, and he liked to have Frank come to the parties for some reason, maybe just to see what Frank would wear. Frank could not say that he had inherited anything from Lawrence, but he had two jackets that Lawrence had helped him pick out at a secondhand store, three pairs of shoes (he especially enjoyed the spectators), and four ties. His inheritance was knowledge of where to go to get the best styles and the best goods, because Lawrence had loved looking sharp. After Lawrence, Frank even knew how to wear a hat, and the difference between a fedora and a Panama. He had one of each. He didn't wear those to fraternity parties, though.

She was talking to one of the boys. She looked up at him and then looked back at the boy, but Frank could tell that she had lost her train of thought. He passed through to the next room and then out onto the veranda—the porch, except that it was big and had columns. On the porch, the guys were downing shots. Frank downed a shot and lit his cigarette. She came and stood next to him. It was in fact difficult to say anything if you absolutely refused to make the slightest effort at being cordial or even at having good manners. Thanks to Walter, Rosanna, and Granny Mary, Frank had good manners. Which meant that he had nothing to say. He was surprised that he still felt absolute antipathy toward her, as if no time had passed since Lawrence had collapsed into her lap and she had paused ever so momentarily before laying her hand on his head. Frank dared her to mention Lawrence's name.

She said, "What does Hildy see in you?"

He flicked the ash of his cigarette into the bushes.

She said, "At least, that was what Lawrence always wondered."

He inhaled another lungful of smoke, blew it out, and said, "Do you come to these parties to pass out and get fucked?"

Her lips formed the barest smile.

After that, Frank knew even then, it was only a matter of time.

The char, of course, didn't work out. Nor did the saltpeter. It got too cold for the tent, and Hildy said that friends of her summer employer would rent him a room with its own entrance. The leaves fell off the trees, and the grass burst out with a last flash of green, and the ducks and geese vanished from Lake LaVerne. It rained. He and Hildy saw *Dr. Jekyll and Mr. Hyde* and *The Maltese Falcon* and *Dumbo*. They talked about the draft lottery, but the war seemed distant and abstract. He was affectionate and chaster than she was, which made her love him even more. Other things made her love him, too—he told her, with real remorse, how he had tormented his brother Joe for Joe's entire life, and now here he was, Joe, making so much money off his crop this year (fifty-six bushels an acre) that he could buy himself a car, a new car—no one in their family had bought a new car in Frank's lifetime. His one regret was how he'd treated Joe. He told her how kind and beautiful Lillian was, and how Henry sewed his own outfit that time and then wore it into rags, and he laughed when Hildy reproduced little bits of funny business that she saw in movies, and he listened when she described her topics for English essays and biology experiments, and he proofread her essays and gave her suggestions that improved her experiments. She said, "Oh, you seem so happy, Frank. You've loosened up. It's because we're better friends." He cried one night in her arms (in his room) about Lawrence.

But it was Eunice that he was thinking of every moment, Eunice that he was seeing—standing in every doorway, sitting at every table, walking ahead of him down every path and street. It was Eunice who said that she would never see him or speak to him again, and who always came back for more. It was Eunice that he told to get out and stay out, Eunice that he looked for and sensed the presence of. He and Hildy had a daily life, with tasks and assignments and weather, days and nights that had names—Thursday, October 16—that measured the passage of time and the growth, or at least the accumulation, of something. Eunice walked around in a blaze that was not a nightmare and not a dream, but was as timeless and separate as that. His feelings for her did not change even as he came to recognize that she was just a girl, just a kid, just someone fixing her hair in the morning and going to class. Whatever she was in that way, to him she was something else entirely—she was the only female he had ever desired. In a way, it was like one of those movies where the man and the woman only say mean things to one another because they'd had bad experiences, and then, in the end, they learn their lesson because one of them is about to die, and you know it's love. But Frank hadn't had any bad experiences, and he didn't care about Eunice's experiences, bad or good. He most especially did not want to know what she had done with Lawrence, and so he got up and walked away whenever she started going on in her semi-Southern Missoura accent about anything at all. More than once, he walked away from her, and returned to find she'd disappeared. But she always came back—or, rather, she always reappeared in the vicinity—and often enough, he got her in private somewhere and got enough of her clothes off to be able to fuck her. He could not have told anyone why his cock went absolutely rigid at the thought of doing her, without any coaxing on his part, but it did. In the course of the autumn, he got to her four times, and he only knew that because he noted it down. If he hadn't noted it down, he, Mr. Organized, who knew every molecule that had gone into that one terrific batch of gunpowder, would not have known the difference between two and forty.

As far as Frank was concerned, the Pearl Harbor attack did not come soon enough. The week after it happened, he finished his remaining essay, took his exams, and then went down to the enlistment office and signed up. When he went home and told Rosanna, she was fit to be tied that he hadn't at least waited to graduate. "All that money down the drain!" And why hadn't he graduated in June? She would never understand Frank. He said nothing at all about what was driving him out of Ames, and Walter commended his patriotism. He did not even drop Hildy a note. He figured Eunice would get to her soon enough, and between them they would put two and two together.

1942

IN LILLIAN'S OPINION, Pearl Harbor wasn't the worst thing to happen that winter. When they started school after Christmas vacation, her history teacher, Mr. Lassiter, had them skip the Civil War for two weeks in order to learn about the attack, and the geography of the Pacific, and the history of Japanese aggression all over Asia since the Russian-Japanese War of 1904. Lillian was surprised by all of that—but, on the other hand, they didn't know any Japs or Russkies, as Mr. Lassiter called them. At home, there was more talk of what was going on in Europe, especially since Eloise came home fairly often now, and had some news of Julius, who was in France, or maybe not France, but England or somewhere like that. They listened to the radio, and it was always something. Frankie was at a fort in Missouri. It was a new fort—that was all Lillian had heard about it.

The worst thing to happen was that Mrs. Frederick had a stroke one day in January, and now all she did was sit in a chair, and everything had to be done for her. In the morning, Mr. Frederick and Minnie got her up (they had moved a bed into the dining room, and that's where she slept); at night, they put her back to bed; in between, Minnie did everything. She had to give up her teacher's job at the school.

Mrs. Frederick could move one of her arms a little bit, and that hand shook up and down almost all the time. She could turn her head, but her mouth stretched off to the left side, and though she opened it and closed it, only sounds came out, not words. Tears seemed to pour down her face. Minnie wiped them away with a handkerchief. Mr. Frederick stayed out in the barn, fixing things, or milking the cows, or getting ready for plowing and planting. Minnie said that he couldn't stand to come in the house, and Mama said that of course he felt guilty about that, which made him stay away all the more.

Lillian did not tell anyone that she thought this was worse than Pearl Harbor, even Minnie—Minnie would have been dismayed to hear that. No one was dead, after all, buried at the bottom of the sea, no one wounded. Around Denby, all was still and cold, and peaceful. Sometimes, Minnie asked about Frank—she would plop down on the sofa after feeding her mother some oatmeal mush, or making sandwiches for Lois, or putting clothes through the wringer, and ask about Frankie. Since Frank had only written home twice, Lillian decided to make things up—he had a friend from Arkansas now, named Isaiah Furman, and they had to get up at 4:00 a.m. and tiptoe through the forests in long, silent lines, carrying packs that weighed eighty pounds, with their rifles above their heads. They had to shout "Hut two tree faw" and salute and wash their own underwear in buckets of water they got from the river, and they also had to eat and drink from their helmets. Minnie listened with interest and seemed to believe Lillian. Frank had written to say, "I got here. The trip wasn't bad. The barracks are pretty primitive, but warmer than my tent, more later." The second time, he wrote, "Don't mind the drilling, it is easy. Lots of complainers around, though. I guess we are headed east. Will let you know, Love, your son, Frank."

Lois stopped going to school altogether—there was too much to do around the house. Minnie gave her reading and writing to work on. Henry had to go with Lucy to the school on the other side of Denby. It was not far from Joey's farm, so Joey drove them there every day in his new car. Since it was winter, Joey was not working in the fields, but he had decided to fix up Uncle Rolf's old house and move in there. Uncle John and the new wife, Sheila, didn't want that house—too small and primitive. It only had four rooms, but Joey said that was enough. He milked the six cows first thing, drove the kids to school, worked all day, fixing the roof and replacing the windows, until the kids were finished for the day, then drove home and milked the cows again.

Lillian was a very shallow person, because the thing that made her saddest of all was how the Fredericks' house, which was still, underneath all the mess, the nicest house she had ever seen, was now a place that looked bad and smelled bad. Minnie could not keep ahead of the mess, because she would always have to stop and do something for Mrs. Frederick. She put some things away as best she could, but she washed the dishes in the sink as she needed them, and the same with the pots and pans. She herself did not seem to eat anything, only to drink tea ("My one luxury," she said, with cream in it that she kept back from sending to Dan Crest). She was thin, and her hair was always hanging down in a tangle. She didn't say much about it, but Lillian knew that she was up and down all night, because Lois told Lillian that Mrs. Frederick cried out a lot and someone had to get up and quiet her, and it wasn't Mr. Frederick ("He's never been a patient man," said Mama). Anyway, when they discussed it over their knitting and sewing, Granny Mary, Granny Elizabeth, and Mama all agreed that the sorts of things that Minnie had to do were not a man's work. Granny Mary said, *"Nun, man weiß nie, was eine gute Sache ist und was nicht. Gott muss einen Plan haben."* Mama said, "But it's not a plan I like very much." Granny Mary said, *"Ja,* well . . . ," and shrugged, then crossed herself. Then they talked about worse things that had happened to people over the years.

WALTER WASN'T QUITE SURE how to think of anything anymore. You didn't think that war was good for anyone, and when you went to church, you prayed for soldiers in the army, and civilians in the battle zones, and the cities being bombed to smithereens, and yet in the fall he had made three times his income of the previous year, and he was supposed to give thanks for that—surely it was bad luck not to. And then there was Frank. Rosanna was livid about Frank's quitting college two quarters before graduating (and with an A average)—he hadn't been drafted by the lottery, so why not hope for the best?—but Walter thought Frank fit the army like "stink on shit," as the expression had gone when he himself was in the army, and Walter hoped Frank got more out of the experience than he had. Didn't he miss him? Well, what was there to miss? Ames or the Ozarks or North Carolina or Europe? For all they heard from him, it was about

the same. And then there was Joe—Joe had gotten a 2-A farm defer-
ment from the draft board, but maybe, for his own sake, he'd be better off in the army, seeing the world. However, there was plenty of
work to do. As Walter sat with Claire on his knee, holding her hands
in his and saying, "This is the way the lady rides, clop-clop-clop," he
sorted in his mind how many fields he, Joey, and John were going to
have to plant this year. "This is the way the gentleman rides, trot-
trot-trot." Claire began to giggle. There was really no reason to plant
much in the way of oats—only some for the family, the pigs, and the
cows, one field—but that was a lot of work for some hay and grain.
"And this is the way the . . ." He paused until Claire cried, "Farmer!"

"Yes! This is the way the farmer rides!" She rocked back and forth,
laughing, and Walter laughed, too. She was three now, and this was
her favorite game. The Fredericks had gotten rid of Lois's old hobby
horse, so often she sat astride that, held a curl in the wooden mane,
and yelled with pleasure.

From the kitchen, Rosanna shouted, "You about ready for supper?"

Walter got up and carried Claire into the kitchen. Henry was setting the table, and Lillian was mashing potatoes. She poured in a little
milk. Walter said, "What are we having?"

"Fricassee," said Rosanna, "but no dumplings. You've had enough
dumplings, and so have I. I've got new peas from the garden, though,
and the last of the asparagus. And these are the last of the potatoes
until the new potatoes are ready, so let's enjoy them."

"Always do," said Walter.

He set Claire in her seat on her cushion, and Henry set the water
pitcher on the table. The door opened, and Joe came in, stepping
out of his boots as he did so. There was a blast of spring air through
the doorway, right in Walter's face, moist and fragrant of mud and
manure as well as apple blossoms and new grass. Walter took a deep
breath. When Joe sat down, he said, "So how many acres we got to
plant this year?"

"Eighty for me, a hundred and forty for you, two hundred for
Grandpa Otto, and I guess Grandpa Wilmer is putting a hundred and
eighty in corn and letting ninety lie fallow. We can seed that with
clover when we get the chance." He paused and looked at Walter.
"Mr. Frederick asked if we would plant his back fifty, along our fence

line. He's had it in oats, and he manured it a year and a half ago. It should produce pretty good."

"Why doesn't he plant it himself?"

"He doesn't feel up to it."

"We'll see," said Walter. "I'll go talk to him about it. Six hundred and fifty acres is a lot. The tractor has thousands of hours on it now, and my father's tractor is older than that."

They let the unspoken question of a new tractor lie unmentioned on the table.

Joe said, "I can do it. The days are getting longer. Mr. Frederick's field is flat and has no fence to watch out for. Should be pretty easy."

In the meantime, Henry was picking the meat off his chicken bones, and Lillian was helping Claire get her peas onto her spoon so she could put them in her mouth. Rosanna was getting up for the pepper, and then peppering her potatoes. It was a family supper; Walter was forty-six years old. Then he looked over at Rosanna, and said, "What day is it?"

Lillian said, "March twe—"

"Oh my goodness, Walter," said Rosanna. "It's your birthday! I'm sorry I forgot!"

"I forgot," said Walter. "Wish it had stayed forgotten."

"How old are you?" said Henry, and then, when Walter said, "Forty-seven," Henry looked horrified. Walter said, "Well, Grandpa Wilmer is seventy-four, and Grandpa Otto is seventy-two."

"Don't tell them that," said Rosanna, and Walter laughed. "And they say time passes so slowly on a farm."

Lillian said, "We don't have any presents for you, Papa!"

Walter said, "Now's the time for me to give you presents on my birthday, not the other way around. Let me think." Walter savored his last bite of mashed potatoes, then said, "I'll be right back."

Upstairs, in the cupboard, he had a box of things he had saved as a boy and a young man. He hadn't looked into it in twenty years or more. Nothing fancy or valuable, but things that had meant something to him at one time. He found it, and found the key, and carried it downstairs without opening it. "I always wondered what was in that," said Rosanna.

Walter inserted the key in the lock, turned it with some difficulty, and then pulled it out. He lifted the lid. He had forgotten there were so few things in it, but there were enough. He gently tilted the box and let them fall out on the table. Henry got up on his knees, and everyone else leaned forward. With his forefinger, Walter moved the objects apart so that they all could be seen.

The first one he touched was a feather, still surprisingly golden. He said, "This is an oriole feather. Orioles in France were different from orioles in America—brighter. They had a beautiful song. This feather was just lying on the stone railing of a bridge I walked across, and I picked it up."

He touched a coin. "This is an Indian-head gold dollar. Grandpa Wilmer got it for his twenty-first birthday, and gave it to me when I was born."

He touched and picked up a tiny withered stem, then brought it to his nose and inhaled the faint but delicious fragrance. He said, "This is a sprig of lavender. I bought it in a market in France." He held it out to Joey, who took a whiff.

He picked up an envelope and lifted the flap, then pulled out a photograph and handed it to Lillian. As she peered at it, he said, "That's me at twenty-two, with my buddies in the army. I'm in the middle, with all the hair, and next to me on the left is Herb Andronico, who was killed about two months later, and on the right is Norm Ansgar, who died in the flu epidemic."

Lillian said, "You were the only one who lived?"

"Of the three of us, yes. That's why I saved the picture."

Lillian passed the picture to Rosanna, who held it up in the light from the window. She said, "You never talked about these two."

"What was there to say?"

The last thing was a tiny handkerchief, clearly not for nose blowing—mostly lace, now yellowed. Walter opened it out. He said, "My great-grandmother Etta Cheek made that, back in England, when she was a girl. Oh, that would have been around 1830."

Now they all looked at the five objects for a few moments, and Walter said, "Joey?" He thought Joey would take the dollar, but Joey took the sprig of lavender. "Lillian?" He thought Lillian would take the handkerchief, but she took the feather. "Henry?" Henry took the gold coin and rubbed it on his shirt. Walter picked up the photo-graph, and Rosanna said, "I would like to save that for Frank." Walter handed it to her. Then he set Claire on his knee, pointed to the handkerchief, and said, "There's a present for you on the table, Claire. It's very old. I am going to write a note to you all about it, and keep it for you. Would you like that?"

Claire nodded and laid her head against the base of his neck. Rosanna said, "I'll bake you a cake tomorrow, Walter."

Walter didn't care about that. But he felt Claire in his lap, pressed against his side, and he looked at the two dark heads and the two bright heads, and then at Rosanna. He sensed the knowledge pass between them that the years represented by these lost objects did not have to end as they had. If he'd fallen in the well, for example, Rosanna would have found the box, wondered what all of these things meant, and never known. A shiver passed over him, and then he saw the same shiver pass over Rosanna. They smiled to one another—a rare occurrence these days.

FRANK WAS SUPPOSED to be in the Corps of Engineers—that's what most of the other soldiers did at Fort Leonard Wood, which was in a forested, closed-in, hilly area that was not like Illinois and certainly not like Iowa. It was green and hot, and there was hardly ever a breeze. Frank's drill sergeant, a man from Texas, had some different ideas from the others, and he got the recruits to play a little game. The game started simply—he took a mess kit, opened it up, and then threw a handful of coins into the dish. After giving the soldiers a minute to look at the coins, he closed the mess kit and asked what was in there. It was easy. Frank knew the first time—four pennies, a nickel, two dimes, and a quarter—and he knew the second time—six pennies, four dimes, two nickels, and two quarters. The second time, he had thirty seconds. After that, the sergeant used other bits and pieces, not coins: Six pebbles, four leaves, and three acorns. Eight kernels of corn, three dried beans, the two acorns again, and four maple seeds. Five .22 shells and three .30 shells. This was not something that Frank had to learn, it was something that he already knew how to do. From what? From counting cows and sheep? From scouting for rabbits? From shooting squirrels? From leaving a trail of corn kernels for the pheasants?

The next thing was that Frank and another kid—Lyman Hill,

from Oklahoma—were given better rifles, new semiautomatic MK1s. Frank had heard of them, but never seen one. They were nice—well balanced, solid in the hand, with very long barrels. With the rifles, which belonged not to them but to the U.S. Army, they were given target practice. Frank was good—he hit the bull's-eyes every time out to five hundred yards, so far that he could really only see the corners of the target, until they were given better sights, sights so finely ground that he could see the bull's-eyes again. But Lyman was better. Lyman could estimate the wind speed and direction, and adjust his shot accordingly. He hit the bull's-eye at seven hundred yards every time.

After a week of target practice, the sergeant was excited, and took them to the lieutenant. The lieutenant was new on the job—he had graduated early from West Point after Pearl Harbor was bombed, and he was just four months older than Frank (though Lyman was nineteen and looked sixteen—he had never in his whole life eaten as well as he ate in the army, and after two months, he had already grown an inch). The sergeant wanted to send Frank and Lyman to Ohio, to Camp Perry, for sniper training, and then ship them to Africa—the Seventh Army was headed for Africa, to fight Rommel, and snipers were going. The lieutenant wasn't sure. But, then, the lieutenant wasn't terribly sure of anything, except what the sergeant, who'd been in the army for nineteen years and would have retired if it hadn't been for the declaration of war, told him to be sure of. They were standing in the lieutenant's office, and the sergeant stepped up to Frank and spun him around so that he was facing out the window. Then he said, "Private Langdon. Did you get a look at Lieutenant Jorgenson's desk?"

"Yes, Sergeant."

"Name the objects on the desk, Private."

"Yes, Sergeant. Sergeant, three pencils, two short and one long. One fountain pen in a holder. One pad of army-issued writing paper. One holster and one Colt pistol. Two quarters and a half-dollar. One lamp. One *Basic Field Manual*. One piece of paper, wadded up. Two sets of ID tags." He paused, then said, "One letter, address side up, and one letter, address side down. One cup of coffee, half full."

"Private. Turn around."

Frank turned around.

The sergeant said, "Private. Look at the desk. Anything you missed?"

Frank said, "Yes, Sergeant. The fly crawling around the rim of the lampshade." He said this with a straight face. The fly dropped over the edge, toward the bulb, and the sergeant's eyes twinkled.

Lieutenant Jorgenson said, "What does this prove to me, Sergeant?"

"Sir, it proves to you that if the army is going to have a few sharpshooters—or snipers, as our English cousins like to call them— we need to comb the ranks for men suitable to the job. Any man can learn to shoot, given enough time and ammunition, but not every man can learn to observe his surroundings."

"I'm not sure, Sergeant, that the army has a use for these tactics."

"Sir, you may be correct, but there is a group training at Camp Perry, and they are being sent to Africa, and we do hear that the marines are for it, sir. And so I don't think we need to waste Private Langdon's and Private Hill's abilities on setting up latrines, sir. Private Hill is a somewhat better shot, but Private Langdon has a better eye for a likely target."

"I'll think about it, Sergeant. You and Private Langdon are dismissed."

As they were walking back to the mess hall, Frank said, "What does a sniper do, Sergeant?"

"Hunts the enemy." Frank's face must have betrayed an interest in this, because the sergeant said, "You wouldn't mind that, would you, Private Langdon? The Jerries do it, and the Japs do it, and the Limeys do it. Myself, I don't see how these kids who are taught to stick to the rules are going to win this war, do you, Private?"

"No, Sergeant."

Of course, the sergeant prevailed, and by the first of May, Frank found himself in Ohio.

AS SOON AS Eloise got to the office, as soon as she heard about the raid on Dieppe, before she even knew that the Canadians had participated, she was filled with a peculiar sort of settled dread that she had never felt before. The previous night, at the time they would have landed, dawn in France, she had been sitting in bed, filing an edge off the nail of her right thumb. She had felt a surge of fear so strong that she had looked out her bedroom window and, she thought, seen a face. Someone standing on the back porch! No one should be standing there, because it had no access to the ground, only to the roof. Eloise quickly reached for the light and switched it off, and as her eyes adjusted, she saw that there was no face in the window, and no head framed against the pale, cloudy sky. She stood up and went to the window. The porch was empty. But the sensation of having seen a face in the window remained with her, and when she heard the next morning that there had been a disastrous raid on Dieppe by the Canadian Second Division, along with some other units—all British, it seemed—that nine hundred had been killed, hundreds injured, and thousands taken prisoner, the two bits of knowledge clicked together. Eloise became silently convinced that Julius was one of those who had been killed—if he had not been, no face would have appeared in her window.

Julius, of course, pure materialist that he was, would have been the first to ridicule this idea, but she could not get it out of her head. A couple of the reporters who were following the war news and keeping track of all the battles were horrified and enraged at this one—the Brits, probably Mountbatten but Montgomery, too, had just funneled their infantry and their Churchill tanks into the German defenses and watched them get mowed down, and for no reason that anyone could see—there weren't any troops waiting to follow on, there was nothing in France for them to do except get sucked into overwhelming forces. Even though a lot of German troops had been sent to Russia, France was well defended, and the Brits knew it. The reporters kept glancing at her across the newsroom (she was working on a piece about Oveta Culp Hobby and the Women's Auxiliary Army Corps). They knew Julius was with the Canadians. Finally, one of the reporters came over and laid the dispatches on her desk, but he didn't say anything. What was there to say?

When she got home from work, Rosa was lounging on the sofa, reading a book. She looked so much like Julius—thin face, deep-set, prominent eyes, curly hair, full lips. She thought she was ugly, but Eloise thought she was going to grow up to look like Paulette Goddard. The perennial question of motherhood, Eloise thought, was how honest to be. I won't buy you that doll because dolls train you to be ready to throw away your life in mindless reproduction? Your father went to war because he hates Stalin more than Churchill, and now the running-dog imperialist Mountbatten has had your father put to death out of sheer incompetence? When your father left us, me, he was glad to be gone and might not have ever come back? It is not merely that your father's relatives repudiated him when he joined the Party, they also have no interest in his communist goyishe German American wife, if indeed he ever married her?

Eloise decided not to say anything about her suspicions, only to ask, "What book is that?"

Rosa showed the cover. It was *Lad: A Dog.*

"I love you," said Eloise.

"What's wrong?" said Rosa, scowling.

"Nothing." That was how honest she decided to be.

1943

⤬

FROM HIS VANTAGE POINT in a rocky dip on the hillside above the pass, Frank could see most of the two-mile-wide breach in the ragged hills, the Atlas Mountains. He was one of the few—maybe a half-dozen—snipers who had been sent away from the main force. He quickly dug a little pocket into a foxhole, set up his tripod so that he could pivot his weapon about sixty degrees, then dug out a bit more with his spade, so that he could press back into it if he felt that he was being noticed from the air. He could see one of the others, but only one. There were three squads scattered through the hills. Frank took a sip from his canteen. The weather, though this was North Africa, was far from hot—it was actually rather pleasant.

Below him, where the mountains made way for the road, several units were digging slit trenches. Mines were being laid, but the ground was stony and dry, so the mines were not being dug in—they sat in the dust in casual piles. His sergeant had told him that Rommel and his army were so tired and so far from their supply depots that he would be a little surprised "if they even showed up for the party." Once the party was over, Frank had been told, they would move forward to the village and take out the nests of German snipers waiting there. Frank thought that he would like that part. When the sun went down, it dropped. Light turned into darkness. There was so little moisture in the air that nothing sparkled or lingered. Everything was or was not. They had been warned not to show light of any kind, and Frank ate his rations cold. The desert stars were so numerous and brilliant that it was occupation enough to try to make out a constellation or two. Frank liked everything about the army so far. How long had it been now, over a year? Longer than his father had spent in Europe, from the time he left until the time he got back. Frank had been to Missouri, Ohio, Virginia, then New York in October, where they'd had four days' leave before getting on the ship and sailing to Casablanca. Three thousand men on the ship, in a convoy of thirty ships, and perfect sailing weather, with a stop in the Azores, a place unlike anything Frank had ever seen. But, then, every place he had been, including this very spot in the Atlas Mountains, was unlike anything he had ever seen.

Frank awoke with the first gust of wind, which was sharp and full of dust. It wasn't yet light. He wrapped his scarf around his mouth and pulled his helmet down. Not hungry. He could both feel and hear armored divisions on the move, and he knelt up from where he had been lying and peered down toward the pass. There was movement there in the slit trenches, but it was too dark to see much.

At dawn, the ranks of panzers appeared, flat from this angle, much lower and maybe even wider than the Shermans the Americans were using. Frank thought they were ugly but frightening, and his job was to shoot them, which he did, with armor-penetrating shells. The American tanks, which had been supposed to engage them, were worthless—that was evident in the first ten minutes. Even Private Langdon could see that if the Sherman had to turn itself around to point its gun at the panzer, then the gun wasn't going to be pointed in the proper direction very often. And it was frightening to watch what the German guns did to the American tanks—they set them on fire. All they had to do was aim at the gas tank and blow it up. The Sherman, and, Frank knew, the crew, were done for. But the Americans, perhaps by sheer luck, got a few hits, and when the German crews leapt from their hatches, Frank did his best to get them. Luckily, in the noise and smoke, the evidence of his presence was easily overlooked. He got two, though one of those was a wasted shot, since the fellow was burning already, and possibly a third—Frank couldn't tell if he hit that one or not, because he had to duck back in his hole as soon as he fired.

The men in the slit trenches didn't have a chance, did they? The panzers went straight for them, driving over them and then turning a bit, and crushing them under the tracks. And the mines did nothing. They weren't even useful as rubble—the panzers ran right over them. By afternoon, the battle in Frank's immediate vicinity was over, and he was stranded in his little pocket. The sniper nearby, Courtney, was shot and probably dead—Frank could see him stretched across the dry hillside, unmoving, making no noise. The wounded always made noise. The others, if they were alive, were as quiet as mice, just like Frank, waiting for darkness. He hoped that the Stukas would decide he wasn't worth strafing, but he had chosen this indentation in the hillside with that very thing in his mind—they could not see him from above or behind or in front, only from below, and now there was nothing going on below. The Germans had moved on, leaving a horrifying mess of armor and bodies strewn across the pass. Frank took out his compass. Eisenhower had been at Sidi Bou Zid that morning, which was certainly where the panzers were headed. Sidi Bou Zid was east-southeast. There was another town, Frank remembered—maybe it was T-something—he had heard it spoken of but of course could not read the Arabic of the name. At any rate, it was north-northwest. Frank put away his compass, then settled into his pocket, and waited for the sun to drop and the stars to blaze forth. The moon was almost full, but it didn't rise until nearly midnight. Frank guessed he had about four hours to get somewhere.

BY THE TIME the newsreels had shown the parade of prisoners after the Dieppe Raid, Rosanna and everyone else knew that Julius was dead, so they didn't have to search the faces of the passing soldiers for a face that they knew. After the Battle of the Kasserine Pass, though ("Another fiasco!" insisted Walter. "Those German boys had been fighting for years, so they sent American boys right off the farm to take it on the chin!"), they did not know where Frankie was, only that he had been in the division, the brigade, and the company that was right in the thick of it, the very tank-and-infantry brigade that had allowed itself to be lured into the trap and destroyed. They knew Frankie was a sniper; that was their only hope, but it didn't seem like much of one. When she saw the newsreel in Usherton,

Rosanna prayed, but thought, Well, if they capture him, they are in for a few surprises. It was a pleasant thought, although it didn't last very long. However, only two days after the newsreel, they had a letter. Frankie had been in the battle, but, suspecting that the Germans would come back after destroying the tank brigades and the infantry emplacements to mop up outlying sitting ducks, he had retreated into the mountains ("Pretty dry and hot. I didn't get far in the middle of the day") for three days. Fortunately, once Rommel had won the battle, he called the operation off ("I guess he thought he'd done us in," wrote Frankie), and so the Americans were able to regroup. Even so, there were thousands of casualties, and their commanding officer, Fredendall, had been relieved of his command ("Big stink," said Frankie). Rosanna was of course thrilled that Frankie had turned up—alive, more than alive, perfectly fine and his usual self. She even baked him a batch of gingersnaps, boxed them up, and sent them off—gingersnaps because they traveled the best, and were often better on arrival after weeks in the mail. She didn't really think they would get to him, but anyone in the army who might open them and eat them along the way would deserve them, she thought.

Walter swore that he had never had any doubt that Frankie would turn up—didn't he always? And he had been worried that Frank would be punished for leaving his unit, but maybe that's what snipers were supposed to do. And he was promoted—he had picked off a German mortar team all by himself. Now he was a corporal. Walter said, "I hope that doesn't mean he's in charge of anything." But he was, according to Frankie. He was in charge of five snipers.

With the letter, he enclosed a picture of himself and a kid named Lyman Hill, whom Frank had known in Missouri and Ohio, and who had not gone over with them earlier, so hadn't been in the battle. Frank expected there to be another battle soon. Rosanna read this line over and over: "We are going to go after those Jerries any day now, and me, I can't wait." Then he wrote, "Love, your son, Frank." He had never replied to the letter in which Rosanna told him about Julius. Rosanna didn't know whether she wanted him to have gotten that letter or not, because she didn't know whether a sense of one's mortality was a good thing or a bad thing in a soldier. In the meantime, her brother Gus had joined up, and what was he doing? He was lying in the bellies of airplanes as they bombed the German industrial cities (though Rosanna didn't know which ones). He was supposed to take pictures showing whether or not the bombs hit their targets. He had stopped writing home, according to Granny Mary, because he didn't want his wife, Angela, to count on his return. Angela had taken to her bed and was talking about going back to stay with her family in Minneapolis, which Rosanna thought would be a good idea.

All Walter and Joey and John did was plant and plant and plant, and then cultivate and cultivate and cultivate. The weather was good. Joey had a knack for growing good seed corn, and Walter had stopped complaining or even telling Joey what to do. Joey told all of them what to do, and they had plenty of money as a result. Enough so that Joey could put an inside bathroom into that poky old house of Rolf's, and even a bow window on the front of the living room. Once in a while, he took Minnie to the movies in Usherton, but if he wanted to do that, Rosanna had to go over and stay with Mrs. Frederick. She didn't mind; she just read a book to Mrs. Frederick, and the poor woman was quiet enough. She was so thin now that Rosanna didn't know how she survived, but it wasn't Minnie's fault—Minnie made her good, nourishing dishes, like hash and creamed spinach, and scrambled eggs with crushed-up bacon, and she made her drink milk with the cream on it, but they did her no good. Granny Mary said it was just like old people: when life held nothing for you, your food went right on through.

Even Lillian had some money, from the job she had taken at the soda fountain not far from the high school. She worked after school and Joey went by and picked her up on the way home for supper. Walter didn't approve of how she was spending her money—on rouge and lipstick (she even had a compact, which she said was silver, though Rosanna suspected that it was only silver-plated). Being Lillian, she wasn't spending all of it by any means—she was saving at least a third and maybe half—but Rosanna completely approved of Lillian's ideas. It was right for a girl, especially a farm girl, who started at a disadvantage, to look as up-to-date and fresh as possible. It was right to look through the movie magazines and see what was the latest thing, and if you had the skills to reproduce this little thing or that—a snood, say—well, why not? Lillian, who had been so unhappy at school, especially after that ingrate Jane whatever-her-name-was (Rosanna knew her name) was cruel to her, had now found her footing, and the boys were looking at her. ("Let them look," said Walter. "They can look as often as they like.")

Only Henry remained mysterious. All he did these days was read. He had read every book that they had at his school, and he held the book right up to his face, as if he needed glasses (though he didn't, the doctor said). His face was still beautiful, in spite of the scar beneath his lower lip (which Rosanna sometimes found herself fixating on), and he was as slender as a reed, but if he was sitting up on the sofa or in a chair, his mouth hung open as he read, making him look half asleep, and if he was lying down, his head tilted to the side and he didn't care if his hair stood on end. Rosanna found it bizarre that such a good-looking child—even a boy—would care so little about his appearance, but all he cared about was *Treasure Island* and *The Black Arrow* and *The Master of Ballantrae*—or *The Hound of the Baskervilles* and *The Sign of Four* and *The Valley of Fear*. If he read one by an author, then he had to get hold of them all, and he pestered everyone until he had gotten whatever there was to be had in attics, storerooms, the Salvation Army shop, and the Usherton library. And all of his favorite writers were English, not American—you couldn't pay him to read James Fenimore Cooper, for example. Just at Christmas, too, he had decided to learn German, so he made Granny Mary and Grandpa Otto *"nein und ja"* him, and even spoke to Rosanna sometimes in German, and would only answer her if she spoke German. Well, he was a smart boy. Strange as the day was long, but smart.

Claire was four and a half, and would start school in the fall. Of all her children, Rosanna would have said that Claire was the only one who was utterly normal. She ate whatever you put in front of her, she dressed uncomplainingly in what was clean, she played with what you handed her. She went to bed when she was told, and got up when you were ready. She had nice dark hair, shiny and thick, and she never wiggled while you braided it. She could count to twenty and spell "cat," "dog," "mouse," and "Claire." She could sing "Alouette," "Are You Sleeping?," and "I'm a Little Teapot." She could recite her bedtime prayer. She often looked out the window, and if you said, "Claire, you are underfoot," she went away. She liked Walter. She went with him out to the barn and talked while he milked cows or fed sheep. She asked for nothing, just received what she was given. Granny Mary and Granny Elizabeth thought she was darling.

Well, that's what a war did for you—it made you look around at your shabby house and your modest family and give thanks for what you had and others had lost. It made you wonder what it would be like, bombs falling through the ceiling, craters in the front yard, nights in shelters, waking up dead, as Henry said once. It made you stop talking about what you wished for, because, in the end, that might bring bad luck.

FRANK WOULD HAVE SAID that he was used to war now—he had been in the army for a year and a half, and in Africa for ten months, but even so, on the night of July 12, he felt as though he had been transported to a different world, although Sicily was not that different from Africa. The dawn crossing had been strange enough; the weather was so bad and the winds were so high that most of the soldiers doubted the invasion would be attempted, but it was, and his sergeant pointed out that if they didn't make it they wouldn't be alive to care, and if they did, the Jerries and Eyeties on the island wouldn't be expecting them. And they weren't—the beaches were clear, and there weren't even any Luftwaffe around, only a few Italian bombers attacking a couple of transport vessels and warships. Even as they made their way across the beaches and inland, they met almost no resistance. They started to the east of the port—Licata, it was called—and then moved toward it. It was a town of graceful pale-apricot stone buildings that looked as if they had been there forever. Off to the east somewhere was Syracuse, a town Frank had learned about in his ancient-history class. And he also remembered Archimedes—there had been a picture in his math book of Archimedes using a lever to lift the world. Archimedes had figured out the value of pi. But Frank doubted that he would get to Syracuse. Licata was good enough for now.

Private Hill was eager to get into the backcountry and shoot himself some Jerries, though some Eyeties would be good enough in a pinch. The rumor was that Mussolini was in trouble, but Frank didn't think that the invasion would necessarily go well because of that. Whenever the generals thought something would work out, Frank was immediately suspicious. He knew, for example (everyone did), that they had sent the tanks and the infantry into the Kasserine Pass without even having a good map of the place. Maybe Patton had more on the ball than Fredendall had had. He hoped Patton had a good map of Sicily, though he wasn't counting on it. Frank himself had eleven kills. He had heard that in the marines there were whole squadrons of snipers who had dozens of kills, but that was the Pacific, where the Japs were dispersed all over otherwise worthless little islands. You had to kill them or they would kill you. All of Frank's kills had been distant ones. That was the point of being a sniper with a precision telescopic sight—you killed them, their buddies looked around for where that came from, and if you could, you killed another one, but if you couldn't, you snuck away. They didn't know you had snuck away, and they started to worry.

Once they had gotten through Licata (by late afternoon), their job was to spread out, past the flats and into the hills. The river was a dry bed meandering through fields, but protected by some vegetation. Frank decided that they would make their way along it, not in it, along the edge. The whole time, they could see the road—who was driving, and who was not looking out for himself. Late in the afternoon, the riverbed diverged from the road, and tilted upward into the pale hills. It was so dry that the six of them were already dusted with white. Murphy and Jones went to the east, crossing the riverbed and following the edges of some fields, and Landers and Ruben went along the riverbank. Frank kept Lyman Hill with him. They stayed in sight of the road. Lyman was itching to shoot something, and shortly before dusk he did—a cat that was itself hunting. When Lyman flipped it on its back with the muzzle of his rifle, they saw that it was a fat cat. Lyman said, "Well, someone in this place is eating, anyway." The residents of Licata, of which they had seen only a few, had been thin and desperate-looking. But there had been no fearsome German nests of snipers in the buildings. His sergeant at Fort Leonard Wood had proved correct: while the Brits and the Americans were wondering about the rules, the Germans were breaking them. The rumor was that the Russians were even worse: they broke the rules of war and they broke the rules of life. If you killed two Russians, somehow four appeared in their place, and if you then killed four Russians, eight appeared. That was what they had heard. When they finally defeated Rommel and took some German prisoners, some had hugged their captors, because they knew that if they got back to their own lines, they would be transferred from Africa to the Eastern Front—to Kharkov, for example, which was worse than Stalingrad. When a corporal Frank knew said to a prisoner, "What if I shoot you?," the fellow shrugged and said, *"Hier oder dort, was ist der Unterschied?"* Frank knew this meant, "Here or there, what's the difference?"

He and Lyman walked along. Lyman was chewing gum. He didn't smoke (Frank had stopped smoking, too—it was dangerous for a sniper to light up), but he needed an endless supply of Juicy Fruit. If he ran out, he got Frank or one of the others to give him theirs. They moved quietly and cautiously, they paused, they avoided twigs, leaves, grass, they surveyed the encroaching darkness. Frank had good night vision, but Lyman's was better, because, Frank thought, Lyman never pondered anything. Nothing preoccupied him—he was like a dog or a fox, an empty head with eyes observing the horizon. Part of the reason Frank sometimes teamed up with him was just to watch him. Lyman had twenty kills.

The bombed-out, barren fields along the river gave way to steep, barren slopes even drier than the fields. Frank and Lyman started diagonally up one of them, staying as best they could against the shadow of the hill. He looked upward and forward; Lyman looked downward and backward. Murphy, Jones, Landers, and Ruben had disappeared, which was exactly what they were supposed to do.

Frank started to look for a spot to bivouac. It wasn't raining, so, even though it would probably get cold, they wouldn't pitch a tent (too much trouble). He found a little ridge in the hillside, and the two of them took shelter there, ate some rations, and set up their tripods in case of something. They hadn't seen much, but you never knew.

Frank was sound asleep when the crash woke him up. Lyman woke up, too, and, like a dog, he was already entirely alert when he looked over the ridge at the road below. The moon had gone down, but against the pale hillside, they could make out what had happened pretty well—a car, a Kübelwagen, had missed the turn where the road angled sharply to the west, and gone over the edge, rolled, and

landed on its top. From the road to where the vehicle lay was a drop
of about twelve feet, Frank thought. He and Lyman were silent, waiting for the thing to burst into flame, but it didn't. In the quiet, Frank
could hear noises coming from the vehicle, not quite terrified yelling,
and something more senseless. Whoever was in the Kübelwagen was
drunk. He ducked down behind the ridge and pulled Hill after him.
He said, "Not our business, Private."

"They are if they get out."

"Maybe," said Frank, but this was, in fact, the case. "I'm sure he's,
or they're, pretty smashed up."

"Don't you want to see? We haven't seen any Jerries since we
landed. Wonder what they were doing."

"Saying goodbye to the girlfriend?" suggested Frank.

This made Lyman stifle a laugh.

Frank said, "What time is it?"

"Two hundred hours. What if someone else comes along?"

"We'll do what we have to do."

But they could not stay down behind the ridge. Watching the car
was like watching a movie or a deer in a clearing—they were there to
do it, and so they did.

A Kübelwagen, like a jeep, had a cloth top, but, unlike a jeep,
the back end of the top was unsupported, and so it lay with the
front wheels tilted upward, resting precariously on its windshield.
There was no easy way for the occupants to get out, and if the windshield were to collapse, they would certainly be trapped. But the
windshield did not collapse, and after a long quiet period, the one
door Frank could see pressed open against the dirt, little by little,
and at last a dark figure wiggled out. It took a long time, and when
it was out (he was out—no reason to believe that this was a woman),
he was quiet for a period and then groaned. Then he started talking,
in German, and Frank understood that he was certainly drunk, and
possibly delirious with pain. Lyman leapt over the ridge, and Frank
called out, "Private Hill!" but in the end, Frank followed him. They
didn't get close enough for the Jerry to see them, and Frank made
Lyman squat down.

The man was lying on his back beside the Kübelwagen, staring up
at the sky. Judging by his uniform, he was an officer, maybe an Oberst.

But if he was one of those, then, like a colonel in the U.S. Army, he would not be driving alone. Frank moved in front of Lyman Hill, pressed him backward, and whispered, "There has to be a driver."

Lyman took this as an order, and began creeping toward the other side of the Kübelwagen, out of sight of the Oberst, who did turn his head, but then looked upward again. A moment after that, he started talking, babbling. One of his hands was on his chest, and the other one was resting on his holster and his pistol, but maybe it was just resting there. Frank didn't think the man had seen him. The door on the other side of the Kübelwagen creaked once and then stopped. The man turned his head in that direction and said a word. Frank thought the word was Heim-something, a name, but he said no more. Frank saw Lyman edge back toward him, not without stretching upward in an effort to see the officer more clearly, but he did get back to Frank without doing anything. He whispered, "The guy's stuck in the steering wheel. I mean stuck, Corporal. Right through the solar plexus."

"Dead?"

"Yes, Corporal Langdon."

Then, without really meaning to, they began to inch toward the officer. He saw them. Frank was certain that he saw them, or saw movement or shadow. His head turned in their direction. His hand folded over the handle of his pistol, and he took it out of the holster. Frank and Lyman Hill drew their service revolvers. But the man, the officer, the Oberst, did not aim at them, or even in their direction. He put his pistol to his head, and then, a very long moment after that, he pulled the trigger.

"Damn me," said Private Hill.

The man gave a loud groan.

Frank felt his skin prickle, and Lyman looked at him. Frank did not quite know what order to give, and the man said, in a clear voice, *"Töte mich. Töte mich, bitte."*

Frank knew what *bitte* meant—"please." And *töte* was "kill," as in *"Ja, ja, es ist Weihnachten, Zeit, um die Weihnachtsgans zu töten."*

"Is he talking?" said Lyman. Frank knew that Lyman would be happy to kill the Jerry—the pleasure would be all the greater at point-blank range.

"He said something."

"What?"

"I don't know."

Lyman believed him.

"I think we have to take him prisoner."

"And do what with him?"

"Take him to the nearest medic."

Frank and Lyman stared at one another.

Lyman said, "That's miles from here."

The man said, *"Bitte, bitte, bitte. Erschießen Sie mich!"*

Frank stood up, walked over, placed the muzzle of his revolver on the man's forehead, and pulled the trigger.

After that, they did what they were supposed to do—they rifled through the man's clothing, and through the things in the Kübel-wagen, and through the pockets of the driver, collecting anything that might provide valuable intelligence. That took about an hour. It wasn't until daylight that Frank saw that he was spattered with blood and brains, bits of bone and hair.

The next day, they made their way farther inland.

1944

FRANK HAD TO WONDER once again whether the generals had any maps or not. He suspected that they merely had compasses, and that they found out which direction was west, and told the troops to go there. Frank was still a corporal, even though he had twenty-two kills now, and had delivered some intelligence from what he and Lyman Hill always called "the accident." For a while, Frank had resented not being promoted, even when his colonel, Drake, happened to say, "So what is it you boys do out there, Corporal?" and Frank had said, "Save ammunition, sir." But once they got to Camino, Frank ceased wishing to be in charge of more snipers. Murphy was shot on December 6. Lyman Hill stepped on a mine on December 17 and had to be carried down the mountain, which took four hours and, because of German mortars, nearly got the rest of them killed— they'd dropped Lyman and hit the dirt four times, but Lyman had lived. Jones had his head blown off by artillery fire on January 4, and Landers drowned in the Rapido River on January 21, though the river was so cold, Frank thought, that it was possible he froze to death before he went under. On the day of the bombing, only Ruben was still with him, only Ruben and he were under orders to attack yet again.

Ruben was from somewhere around New York City. He was short, and better with a pistol than a rifle, but he was exceptional with a pistol. Frank never quite knew if he was joking or not when he said he learned to shoot shooting rats in alleyways "or scurrying from building to building across clotheslines. It was easy to pick them off when they were doing that." Ruben hadn't finished high school—he had, instead, run numbers for a local gangster. He reminded Frank of that kid Terry, in Chicago. He looked tough and he was tough, and there was no trying involved. He had enlisted because the cops had a warrant out on him. He had gotten from New York to Florida, changed his name from something to Ruben, and joined the army. In Florida, he said, they took about anyone. He accepted that Frank was his superior officer, and he took orders as if he had always taken orders, which maybe he had. He was a criminal and he was brave, but he was a born follower.

The abbey was visible from everywhere, even through the curtain of constant rain, and Frank had heard all the arguments—you could see lights, you could see soldiers, you could see artillery, or, if you couldn't, why in the world would any army, especially the Jerries, forgo such a perfect spot for recon? And if they weren't there now, well, give them a day, or a week—they would get there. It was also evident that a thousand guys, or ten thousand guys, or twenty thousand guys, no matter how well equipped, were not going to climb that mountain and storm those walls—in addition to the terrain difficulty, the Jerries had planted every square inch with traps, mines, and wire. Five days before the bombing, after the Italian regiment that stormed up the hill were mowed down, Frank's group was asked to do the impossible again. Some of the boys had taken Lieutenant Martin aside, and they had explained to him their point of view. That Ruben had pressed the lieutenant by the throat to the wall of their emplacement and simultaneously removed the service revolver from the lieutenant's holster certainly accounted for much of Martin's willingness to listen to his soldiers.

Frank would not have said that he ordered Ruben to offer his opinion (and the opinion of all the men) to Lieutenant Martin so forcefully, but he did say that he thought Martin was not only something of a dope, but also of two minds himself. A little persuading was all that was needed. But they did not fall back so far that they didn't experience the night of the fifteenth, when the ranks of Flying Fortresses, Mitchells, and Marauders showed up and pounded the abbey for hours on end, shaking the earth with tremors and the sky with booms, and lighting up all the mountains. Bombs dropped everywhere, it didn't matter where the lines were or were supposed to be—Frank huddled against the earth and wondered again if the generals had bothered with a map. The good thing was that the mountains were so steep and craggy that a bomb had to drop right on you to kill you, and, lucky again, Frank found himself alive in the morning. Ruben, who had whispered prayers all night in some language that was not English, found himself alive, too. Lieutenant Martin did not. But Frank suspected that that was a relief for him more than anything else.

Things were no better at Anzio when their unit was moved there. The Allies had landed months before—right around the time Frank's unit had attacked Monte Cassino the first time—but they had gotten nowhere, and were now drowning in mud. Frank had thought that surely the German army was massed at Monte Cassino, but in fact they seemed to be in the ridges encircling the beach at Anzio, pouring 88mm artillery shells on everything and everyone—it was generally known that they aimed for Red Cross tents. And they had an unbelievable amount of firepower. Day after day, they shelled everything that moved in the marshes below the cliffs, exploding one little stone house after another. Frank saw at once that the Allied plan here was like it had been in Africa, to attack and attack and attack, even though defense forces were superbly entrenched and didn't even bother to bury their own dead. The Allies didn't want the Jerries to dare divert anyone to France, or Greece, or wherever else they might be useful. Every so often, you heard the words "cannon fodder." Well, this was cannon fodder at its most expensive. Frank saw that his job had changed. What use were snipers? You couldn't get around the Jerries, and you couldn't get above them, and they controlled all the buildings. You could do one thing and one thing alone, which was to press them over and over, until—until what? Until, Frank thought (the generals thought), some happenstance turned up. Maybe that happenstance was only this, that it was spring, and therefore freezing cold had been superseded by pouring rain, and they didn't have to cross the Rapido ever again.

Dawn on May 23 was rather nice, if you were only looking at the weather, but when the artillery commenced firing, and Frank began advancing toward the cliffs with the rest of his unit, he thought, and maybe for the first time, You're in the army now. He was in charge of five men. They carried tommy guns, pistols, grenades, and plenty of ammunition. They wore helmets and were, except for the smoke all around them, entirely visible. But they did attain the cliffs. Private Ruben, who was short and quick, managed to take out two machine-gun nests one right after the other, and to get back to their unit, stand on a little promontory, and give everyone and everything around them an exuberant finger. The squad then fought their way through the pass, with only Private Cornhill getting shot, a flesh wound in his left arm that did not, he insisted, even hurt, much less compromise his fighting prowess. Frank let him keep at it through the rest of the day. Frank wasn't as heroic, but he did get six or eight kills. It wasn't until the next day that they realized how hard it had been—their unit was intact, but hundreds of men had been wounded or killed, and dozens of tanks disabled. However, they were off the beach.

Late the next day, they got to a town called Cisterna. Frank guessed that it had once been a nice town—there were the remnants of streets, of parks, of houses, of shops. Their orders were to go house to house, rousting out the last Jerries and shooting them. Ruben was good at this, too, but so was Hernandez, who was from Oakland, California. The both of them actually seemed to relax as they got farther from the countryside. Frank himself got jumpy. Maybe the most disturbing of the Jerries was a fellow in the fourth house they entered, who had barricaded himself in a corner room on what was left of the second floor. He had seen them coming, and shot at them, a fatal error, since Frank had not intended to check that house. They went slowly up the stairs, pressing against the walls on either side of the steps, which were intact. The fellow made no sound and no move until Frank guessed which door he was behind, kicked it open, and ducked. But the Jerry was too frightened to come out, and as they stormed the room, he sat down on the windowsill and was shot from behind by some troops from the Thirty-fourth in the street below. He fell backward out of the window. One other Jerry tried to shoot them but missed, and two simply gave themselves up. At the end of the day, the town was quiet, and the entire German unit wiped out, according to Major Sandler. They bivouacked in the town for two days after that, sleeping most of the time.

The next day, they turned left. Frank didn't know why they turned left, but thought that it was probably, once again, the scarcity of maps. And the rest had done him good. Yes, there was fighting, and Cornhill was injured again, this time shot in the shoulder, so he had to be evacuated. Frank was grazed by a fragment of a grenade; it stung his ear and dinged his helmet. But the Jerries started to evaporate for the first time that Frank had seen, and on a lovely day in June, they marched into Rome. It was very quiet that first day, but the second morning, they woke up surrounded by Italians, and Ruben was talking with them a mile a minute.

THE FIRST GENERAL Frank saw who he thought had any sense was General Devers, and part of the reason Frank liked him was that he oversaw Frank's removal to the south of France. But first they had to gather in Corsica. Corsica was mountainous—as mountainous as Monte Cassino—but there were no Jerries trenched into the peaks and ridges, and at the foot of the mountains were beaches and blue sea. So far, in his war, Frank hadn't cared much for water; every crossing since the one from New York had been harrowing. From Tunisia to Sicily, storms of wind and waves had had him huddling against the side of the transport, trying not to die. The rivers by Monte Cassino were the wildest he had ever seen (but, then, he had only seen the Iowa, which sometimes rose in the spring, only to spread very gently over adjacent fields). The Rapido had been bad enough; the Garigliano, he had been told by troops in the Thirty-sixth Infantry, made the Rapido look like a trout stream in Wisconsin.

The roads overlooking the beaches on Corsica were very elegant and edged by sedate palm trees, under which, in the cool of the evening, whores congregated before their night's work.

Italian whores looked rather different from Illinois whores—younger, older, more desperate, more jaded, and more frightened—and it was a long time before Frank made up his mind to go home with one. They seemed not to live respectably in brothels, but to have rooms and work for themselves. As always, the whores liked him. He was tall, he had put on muscle, and maybe he didn't look twenty-four. Maybe he looked older than that now. He could see in the mirror when he shaved that his eyes were more deeply sunk and bluer, and his cheekbones were more prominent. His nose, too, had changed— had beaked a little. When he walked down the street under the palms, some of the whores shouted, "Hey! Signor Flynn, Look this way! Hey, hey!" He hadn't thought he looked like Errol Flynn—Minnie had said Joel McCrae (and Eunice had said the devil himself). You weren't supposed to be flattered by whores, but he was.

Still, he didn't get around to taking up with one until a few days before they were to set out for Saint-Tropez. Why this girl and not any of the others, why tonight and not any of the previous nights— well, there was no reason for any of it. He had money in his pocket, and an unopened pack of cigarettes, and there was a tall dark-haired girl lounging on the parapet by herself, and he just went over to her and made a gesture with his fingers to his lips, as if he were looking for a smoke. She shook her head, then shrugged and made a sad face. She said, "No, don't got. Sorry."

Frank put his hand inside his jacket and brought out the fags. She smiled and nodded, so he ripped off the cellophane and handed her the packet. She tapped its edge on the parapet, took one for herself, and offered him one. He said, "No, don't smoke," and made a face. "You keep them." Now she laughed. Cigarettes were worth money. She put her arm in his and led him down the promenade. Looking at her face against the background of the bright water and the fading sky, he guessed she was his age. At the end of the promenade, she turned down a side street and then led him to a door. When she opened it, he held back, and she said, "No, you come. You come, Signor Flynn."

Her room was hardly a closet—maybe it wasn't the room she actually lived in. There was only a sink, a bed, a very small window, and a coat rack. She took his hand and drew him through the doorway, then closed the door. She said, *"Parli italiano? Parlez-vous français?"*

Frank shook his head.

She said, "Okay. Okay!" Then she patted his pocket. He pulled out his wallet and threw some money on the bed. She looked at it for a moment, then extracted the ten-dollar bill. She said, "Okay?" Frank nodded, and picked up the rest of the money. When he put his wallet back in his pocket, she put her hand on his cock, which had not yet hardened, but at her touch it began to. She rubbed it a couple of times, and it swelled some more. Frank felt his face get hot. He couldn't help thinking of Eunice. Eunice was the last girl he'd fucked. At the end of the Africa campaign, they'd had leave in Tunis, but they had been sternly warned to stay away from the women in Tunis—the whores, they were told, all had the clap, and the other women all had male relatives, "which is worse than the clap." Since Sicily, there had been no opportunities, and hardly any days off. Once again, for the millionth time, he ordered Eunice out of his head. He looked out the tiny window, and sure enough, there was no room for Eunice against the stone walls or athwart the strip of sky, sea, and mountain that was visible. He let out the breath he had been holding in.

He said, *"Nome?"* He knew that was the word for "name."

"Ah," she said, "Missss Joan!" She pronounced the "J" like "ch." Frank said, "Joan Fontaine?" and the whore nodded. Frank said, *"Rebecca?"*

"Non."

"Gunga Din?"

"Sì!"

"So—we are Errol Flynn and Joan Fontaine?"

The whore nodded eagerly. Frank laughed and said, "Well, let's make a movie." Then she did something Frank knew that whores never did: she traced his lips with her fingertip, and kissed him. It was a kind gesture, and made his cock go limp at once.

But she was good-natured, if not terribly pretty, and he was beginning to feel comfortable. He took off his shoes and sat down on the bed, then leaned back against the wall, which was painted a blue color that coordinated with the sky, and put his hands behind his head. He took another deep breath. The whore pulled out the pack of cigarettes, counted them, took out a second one, and lit it. She sat down on the end of the bed. Frank watched her smoke the cigarette—she seemed to enjoy it very much, taking the smoke deep into her lungs, and then breathing it out through her nose. Yes, she was thin. Her blouse hung on her shoulders, and the waist of her skirt gapped, but her breasts were full, and her calves, too. She wasn't wearing hose; she had drawn seams up the backs of her legs. Frank wondered how many cigarettes equaled a meal. She took another drag. It was a pleasure to watch her. He wiggled his toes, and then she put her hand around his left foot and began stroking the instep with her thumb. Frank had never felt such a thing before. Her thumb moved forward to the ball of his foot, then to the toes. It was relaxing. It almost made him forget what he was there for. His eyes closed.

He felt her weight on the end of the bed shift, and he heard her stub out her cigarette. Only then did her hand begin to move up his ankle, underneath the cuff of his pants. She pushed down the ribbing of his sock, and tickled his ankle, then moved upward to the base of his calf for a minute or two, until his pant leg prevented her from going further. Then she started on the other foot, but she took his sock off first. Frank kept his eyes closed. His cock lay quiet, uninterested. As soon as he noticed his cock, he ordered Eunice to get away from him. He kept his eyes closed. His right leg was now as relaxed as his left. The bed was small. The room was small, the building was small. The town was small. The island was small, and divided from the torture of Europe and the pillage of Africa by a deep sea. In American schools, in Iowa schools, they didn't study Corsica. He knew nothing about Corsica except what he had seen, and that wasn't much. He was Errol Flynn. She was Joan Fontaine. That was maybe the essence of his relaxation.

Frank didn't know that he had fallen asleep until he woke up suddenly. The sun was gone from the window, meaning that hours had passed. The room was cool, too. The first thing he did, in something of a panic, was reach for his wallet. It wasn't there. He opened his eyes with a groan, only to see the whore sitting on the bed beside him. She held out his wallet. He took it and opened it. All the money was there. Frank licked his lips, a little ashamed of his suspicions, and the girl smiled, and then lay down next to him. She stretched her body along his, foot to foot, hip to hip, torso to torso. The top of her head came to about his nose, and she rested it on his chest. She undid his fly. There it was again, so unresponsive, his cock. And yet it was. She tickled it and then stroked it, and it popped, and the moment he realized that he wanted her, she knelt up beside him, slipped a condom over his erection, lifted her skirt, and sat down on him. Her hands were on his shoulders. She began to move, and then she began to undo the buttons of her blouse.

Some things were not comfortable—he could feel a broken bed-spring in the small of his back, and his head hit the wall two or three times—but his cock, in the center of things, was utterly alive, reaching here and there inside her, feeling something like a wall and something like an edge, and something like a hollow—the whole anatomy of her. She squeezed him; he had never felt that before; it was like an embrace. Once she had her bra off, she brought her hands back to his chest, and then, just as he sensed he was about to come, she reached behind herself and tickled his balls. He arched his back and shot into her. He could feel the condom fill and his own semen ooze around the head of his dick. He might have cried out.

It was only now that he recognized how experienced she was—she tilted to the side and rolled him on top of her without letting him come out, then eased off of him so that the condom remained in place. She was good at it. Finally, she got up, disposed of the condom, and washed her hands. The last thing she did was lean over him and smooth his hair off his forehead. No one had done that since he was sick in bed with a virus and his mother was feeling his head for a fever. She handed him a wet towel. It looked clean enough.

Frank wasn't very graceful about leaving her at the same spot where he'd found her. It was late now, after ten. They'd been together for six hours or more, which Frank knew was bad business for a whore, or, yes, a *puttana*—that's what they were called in Italy. He actually tried to kiss her, which some other whores standing around laughed at. She put her hand on his shoulder and pushed him away, though gently. After that, he turned right around and walked away, so as not to see other men approaching her. He had never felt jealous before.

He came back the next day and the next, but she wasn't there. The fourth day, they embarked for Saint-Tropez. On the boat, he listened to Ruben, Hernandez, and Sergeant Koch talk about the whores they had done in Corsica—they expected better ones in France, though Ruben had enjoyed one of his four especially, he called her "the Laugher." She had let him tie her up, and giggled the whole time. One of Hernandez's whores had seen his cock and asked him if he was *"un nègre."*

When they got to France, he also didn't know where the Germans were, but there were plenty of Yanks and plenty of Frenchmen. The day was sunny. Cruisers and destroyers were everywhere, and Frank counted seven aircraft carriers. The planes made patterns as if they were in air shows. The commando raiders had done their jobs. The paratroopers fell from the sky, and even the gliders came floating in. Frank and his squad marched down the ramps of the transports and into the warm, calm water, which hit them about mid-thigh. They splashed onto the beach and spread out. And then they ran inland, and a day later they were all the way to Le Muy.

WHEN THEY GOT TO the Rhine, three months after Saint-Tropez, Frank was a little surprised at how narrow it was. There were rivers and streams all around Strasbourg, and plenty to look at in the town, even though the Allies had bombed it over and over, and the Germans had burned what they could, but the Rhine itself was narrow and flat, neatly confined between built-up banks on both sides, and with quaint old bridges that ran across it. The Germans on the other side were quiet, and Frank suspected typical Jerry treachery—they would be as quiet as rabbits until they had the GIs in their sights, and then they would open fire with everything they had. But Ruben was ready, and Cornhill, who was back in the unit, was, too. They got to the bridge at midnight—an elaborate stone construction—and, step by nervous step, they made their way across. It didn't take long, and there seemed to be no sentries in the German pillboxes they could easily see—even more suspicious. Private Ruben was practically capering by the time he set foot on German soil, but he was short and hard to shoot; Frank didn't know if his immunity was due to quickness, small size, or nothing at all. Frank and Private Cornhill were more cautious, but there continued to be no response. Private Cornhill whispered, "Think they're all passed out, Corporal?"

"We're lucky if they are, Private."

They caught up with Private Ruben, and the three of them squatted down and duck-walked toward the first pillbox, taking cover in darkness, frozen weeds, and a line of leafless trees. When they got right up to it, Private Ruben took out two grenades, but he didn't pull the pins.

Which was a good thing, because the pillbox was empty and cold.

It looked like there hadn't been a soul in there for weeks, if ever. There wasn't even a shell casing or a piece of paper lying around. The Jerries had certainly cleaned up after themselves when they left.

An hour later, they had gone to the next one, which was a hundred yards up the river. No one and nothing there, either. When they walked back toward the bridge, they just strolled along, standing upright, sometimes trotting because of the cold, but never taking precautions—it was the ultimate test. They would get shot if there were anyone at all around to shoot them.

All the patrols reported the same thing—no one. And as the artillery and the engineers and the rest of the Seventh Army massed behind them, Frank began to get excited—Germany tomorrow, Berlin soon after that. It was the end of November. Three years of war was plenty.

By midmorning, when Frank woke up from his snooze, the invasion was ready; the Rhine was theirs. General Devers, inspecting their formations, looked eager. Frank didn't know why the general had been assigned to take his army into the Riviera, and then march it up the Rhone, with only enough action (at least compared with Italy) to keep them sharp. They waited.

The next afternoon, when all the men had found out that they were not going, that Eisenhower himself had refused to let them go, they had several explanations. Cornhill's was that Ike must know that there was a big force of Germans awaiting them in the backcountry across the river—it would be like the Kasserine Pass; maybe Rommel himself was there.

"Rommel is dead," said Frank.

"Do you really believe that?" said Cornhill. "I don't. That's obviously a trick. Ike is being cautious, and he should be."

Ruben took another view, that Ike was so shit-scared of the Germans that he couldn't believe the evidence of his own eyes. They weren't there, but they had been there so often that they had to be there. Ruben didn't like Ike at all—he'd seen his type before, always saying what if, what if. "Is that the kind of guy you want in a fight?" Frank could see that Ruben and Cornhill didn't actually disagree.

Frank simply put it down to another map problem—the army almost never knew where it was going, and they were always surprised when they found what was there. Three years of superior officers had made him 100 percent suspicious of everything superior officers had to say. He trusted only Devers, and why was that? Devers said, "We're going here," and they went there. Devers said, "Expect this and that," and this and that came to pass. But the rumor was that Ike didn't like Devers, and Frank figured this was the reason—Devers didn't have his head up his ass, and everyone else did.

1945

ALL ROSANNA KNEW was that Frank was in France and that nothing in France was good. Did he write? Was he allowed to write? He had written two letters in the summer, from Corsica, and then two more in the fall, one written in a town called Besançon, which was a kind of lace, as she remembered, and another from Lyons. In Lyons, he wrote about some Roman ruins. His letters were masterpieces of saying nothing. That he was alive was her business, what he was doing was not her business. She didn't even know if he was involved in what they called the Battle of the Bulge (though what "the bulge" was, Rosanna could not figure out). She hoped he wasn't, because the Battle of the Bulge was very terrible, and apparently, when the Germans found Americans or other Allies, they just shot them, didn't even take them prisoner. They said they were going to take them prisoner in order to have them put down their weapons, and then they mowed them down. It was a good thing that Rosanna didn't leave the farm much, because every time she went into town, people asked her how Frankie was and where he was, and Rosanna had to say that she didn't know. Yes, her brother had stopped writing for a while after he got over there, but then he had started again, and now he wrote every week, nice long letters about this and that, some of it pretty gruesome. Angela, who had taken to her bed, was up and about now, and was typing the letters for a book. She thought it would be a best-seller, and maybe they would make it into a movie. "That'll be the day," thought Rosanna, but she kept this thought to herself. Every time Angela or, for that matter, her own mother speculated about who would play Gus, Rosanna just said, "That would be good."

In the meantime, Eloise had gotten out of the newspaper business and was working for the WPA in San Francisco. She had rented some kind of duplex there, and Rosa was in a school with all sorts of children, including Negro children and Italian children and maybe even some Japs, though Eloise was very coy about that, and Rosanna had thought that all the Japs were sent away to camps—there was one in Kansas, Rosanna thought she had heard that, but maybe not. No one talked about it. There was a POW camp up in Algona, and another one over in Clarinda, and those POWs worked the farms around there, but Rosanna thought that Joey, John, and Walter were doing fine. POWs in the neighborhood would have made her nervous.

Lillian wanted to go out to San Francisco and get a job when she graduated from high school in the spring, and Rosanna was against it, but not for the reason Walter was, which was that San Francisco was impossibly far away—three days by train. Was she going to sit up the whole way? If not, a berth was very expensive. Rosanna knew that Lillian was not quite ready to tell Walter that she could pay the fare herself. He had no idea how much she had been paid at the drugstore (he would be amazed and a little disapproving—he would certainly not have factored in tips, because Walter thought waitresses only got good tips for flirting). No, Rosanna didn't mind the thought of Lillian having a little bit of an adventure—she would be nineteen this year, for Heaven's sake. Rosanna was married and then pregnant when she was nineteen. What Rosanna minded was the idea that, when Lillian got to San Francisco, Eloise was not going to be the one to take her places where she could meet the right sort of man. Rosanna was sure that Eloise was continuing to consort with Jews and Italians and even Negroes, just as she did in Chicago, and what she would most likely do for Lillian was take her to some low-class neighborhoods and have her hand out leaflets about unions and meet pipe fitters and men like that. Rosanna had no beef with pipe fitters per se—every man she had ever known got his hands dirty every day of the week and most Sundays, and if her father owned a pair of shoes rather than boots, she had never seen them. However, even though Lillian was too good for that life, she was sure to throw herself away, and Eloise wouldn't stop her.

Rosanna had always called Lillian an "angel" and a "saint," and so she should not have been surprised when Lillian turned out to be that very thing, but the result was that she was kindest to all the wrong girls and dated all the wrong boys. Who took her to the Christmas Dance, for example? None other than Otis Olsson, the most backward boy in the senior class, who could not drive and had to be driven by his older brother, Oscar. Why did she go with Otis? Well, she felt sorry for him. The other boys who asked her could date whoever they wanted, but Otis didn't dare ask anyone. And why did they come home early? Well, Otis got carsick on the way over, and threw up beside the road, and that was that. And then there was the Riemann girl, who came over sometimes. Lillian helped her with her homework while the girl gazed open-mouthed at her—adenoidal for sure. Yes, Lillian had other friends, better friends, but these were the ones she seemed to value, and with only Eloise to guide her, she would surely marry someone of just the same type.

Of course, Joey was going to marry Minnie as soon as Mrs. Frederick passed away and Joey could convince Minnie to have him. It was written all over his face and body that he thought the world of Minnie, though she did look used up for her age, twenty-six now, but looking thirty if a day. And Joey not even twenty-three, but every time Rosanna saw him, it was Minnie-this and Minnie-that, and, kind boy that he was, he helped out over there, not to mention that he was practically farming the whole place. Roland Frederick had gone downhill all of a sudden, and couldn't do a thing. Minnie would get the farm, and Joey would marry her, and so he would have the farm, and nothing wrong with that for a boy his age. But it was about as exciting as a hard frost, as Oma used to say.

Probably the best she could hope for with Frank was that he did not bring home a war bride. But she hardly dared think about it.

ON THE FIRST of March, Hildy showed up. Hildy Bergstrom, in a blue Dodge, wearing a navy-blue suit, a stylish white hat with a navy-blue grosgrain band, a beaver coat, and warm snow boots. She parked in the drive just off the road, made her way through the late-winter mud to the front porch, and knocked. When Rosanna spied her through the window, she thought the young woman was lost, or selling something.

She was a beautiful girl, very like Carole Lombard had been (what a sad thing that airplane crash was, still), but with four or five more inches of height, and not quite as square a jaw. She held out her hand and said, "Oh, Mrs. Langdon, I've been wanting to meet you for such a long time. I was in the neighborhood, and I couldn't resist stopping by. I'm Hildy. Hildy Bergstrom. I'm Frank's fiancée."

Well, of course Rosanna's eye snapped straight to her ring finger, but she had gloves on—nice ones made of white cotton with a bit of cutwork around the wrists. Rosanna took her hand, shook it, and said, "Would you like to come in? It's rather cold out here, isn't it? We can have some tea."

The house, of course, was perfectly clean and neat, and not terribly ramshackle. At New Year's, Rosanna had slipcovered the sofa with some nice green chenille, and her best afghan—ivory lace in a fan stitch—was folded over the armchair. Henry had some books around—not even thirteen, and deep into something called *The Woman in White*. Rosanna picked the book off the sofa, turned down the corner of the page, and set it on the lamp table. She saw Hildy glance at it and said, "Frank's brother Henry is an avid reader."

"Oh, I am, too. I love books."

Rosanna left her looking around politely and went into the kitchen to put the kettle on. Making the tea took all of four minutes, just because the range was already hot, and she had boiled the kettle half an hour before. She even had sugar, cream, of course, and some lemon left over from the lemon pie she had baked over the weekend. Rosanna glanced into the windowpane beside the back door. Did she look anymore as though it was possible for her to produce a specimen like Frankie? Not much. She repinned a couple of hairpins and carried the tea and the cups and saucers into the front room. She set them down on the coffee table and sat on the sofa. Hildy gave her a bright smile. Rosanna said, "So—what brings you to our neighborhood? We're a little out of the way."

"Frank maybe has told you that I live in Kansas City now. Anyway, I had to go to Albert Lea, and I thought that I wouldn't have a better opportunity to say hi, so here I am."

"What do you do in Kansas City?"

"Oh, goodness. So many things. I love Kansas City. I'm a buyer for Halls. Maybe you've heard of it. It's part of Hallmark Cards."

"Is there something they need in Albert Lea?" Rosanna poured the tea. Hildy took sugar, not cream.

Hildy leaned forward. "Not on your life. I'm going to visit my cousin. He and his wife just had a baby, so I took a few days off. We've already bought our spring collections, so it's a little bit of a quiet period." She gave Rosanna another big smile, then said, "Frank talked so much about his family and the farm. I'm just thrilled to meet you. I do hope Joe, Lillian, Henry, and Claire turn up."

That was good, Rosanna thought. She did not believe for a moment that Frank had a fiancée—not because he would have told her, but because it just wasn't like him to be so conventional. But the young woman knew something.

"Claire should be home from school anytime now. Henry and Lillian come later."

"I'm sure they're very busy."

A lull settled over the conversation. Both of them took a sip of tea.

Finally, Hildy trilled, "So—what have you heard from Frank lately?"

Rosanna looked at her straight on. "Nothing."

Hildy's smile brightened, then wobbled, then faded. Rosanna said, "How about you?"

Hildy said, "It's been a while, I must say. I was getting a bit worried."

"My brother didn't write his wife for nine months after he went over."

"I know he's in . . ." She hesitated the barest moment then said, "France." But, then, everyone was in France. Rosanna said, "Sometimes he writes to a girl who lives nearby. He's known her since grammar school. She showed me a letter that said he got to the Rhine, and there was no one there, but Eisenhower wouldn't let them go across. Very strange. That was November." Minnie had gotten this letter, the most recent one. Rosanna pretended that she wasn't watching Hildy very carefully. But Hildy wasn't much of an actress. She sighed, and her face fell. Rosanna softened her voice. "When was the last time you heard from Frankie?"

Rosanna expected the girl to say, "Last summer," but she said, "I never have."

"Are you really his fiancée?"

Hildy stared at Rosanna for a moment, then burst into tears. "But I should be!" she said. "I was going to be! If he hadn't left so suddenly, I would be. We were getting along beautifully. He told me everything."

Rosanna took a sip of tea, then set the cup and saucer on the table. She said, "With Frankie, that might be a reason that you would never be his fiancée."

"Why? Why would that be?" Her voice rose. Clearly this was a thought she had had herself.

"Look, Hildy. I'm not saying that I understand Frankie, or ever have. He's not like anyone in our family that we know of. But I do know that if you expect him to do something and he senses your expectation, that's enough to make him not do it."

Hildy had taken off one of her gloves, and now she started twisting it between her hands. Rosanna reached for it, took it, and smoothed it on the table. Hildy, whose crying had subsided, started again. When was the last time Rosanna had seen any of her children cry? Joey, maybe, about some animal's death. But that had been years ago by this point. No one cried at Rolf's funeral or Oma's funeral. Rosanna said, "You're a beautiful girl, Hildy. You need to find someone else."

Hildy shook her head. "I tried. And one of them did ask me to marry him, but I couldn't. I can't forget Frank."

"What does your mother say?"

"She doesn't know. Frank would never come to Decorah to meet anyone."

"There you go," said Rosanna.

"I can't do it," said Hildy.

The one who broke the spell was Claire, who slammed through the front door, saying, "Whose car is that? Hi! Who are you?"

This girl, Hildy, reassembled herself in about two seconds, so quickly that Rosanna would have bet that Claire had no idea of the scene that she had intruded upon. Hildy smiled, reached forward, picked up and slipped on the glove Rosanna had laid on the table. She said, "That's my car. I'm Hildy Bergstrom. I knew your brother in college, and I was passing by. Are you Claire?"

Claire nodded.

"Well, I need to leave if I want to get to Albert Lea at a decent hour." She stood up and put on her coat. Truly, her surface was perfect, thought Rosanna. Her makeup was hardly smudged, which meant that it wasn't makeup—the beauty belonged to her. From a pure breeding standpoint, Rosanna thought, the two specimens of livestock known as Frank and Hildy would certainly produce champions, wouldn't they?

She took Hildy to the door, and Claire walked her to her car. She came back with a box of fudge and said, "She was nice."

"She was," said Rosanna.

ALL THROUGH GERMANY, Ruben made himself a little business, and Frank didn't stop him. In every town and village that they passed through, Ruben went into houses and shops and stole things. It wasn't hard—the Jerries ran off when they saw the Americans coming, and they didn't always lock up behind themselves. Even when they did, Ruben smashed a window or kicked open a door. If there was someone cowering inside, Ruben banished her from the house, then went through the things. Sometimes there was jewelry, but Ruben was more interested in lace and figurines, fancy letter openers, music boxes, ornate picture frames, silver hairbrushes and hand mirrors. He took one or two items every day. What was astonishing to Frank was that the houses did have doors—and windowpanes and roofs and nice things. That Ruben should export some of these nice items to a shop his cousin had in Cape May, New Jersey, was okay with Frank. What Frank saw that he wished he could export was that gunpowder the Germans used—smokeless and entirely unrevealing of the shooter's position. Or those machine guns they had, which fired so quickly that they made one long buzzing sound instead of series of pops, like American weapons. The tanks. The 88s. The Bouncing Betties. The Teller mines. The Russians had more manpower and the Americans had more money, but the Germans had know-how that Professor Cullhane could only dream of.

The slave camp they stumbled across was called Kaufering. All the slaves, who looked barely alive, were bundled into huts dug out of the ground and roofed over. The men (or boys) were like skeletons draped with rags—Frank had never seen anything like them, even in France, even in Italy. It was hard to decide which was more horrifying: the long pile of tormented corpses laid out on the ground, their sticklike arms and legs askew, and their heads angled back as if they were still screaming in pain, or the not-yet-dead, who looked just the same but were still standing (barely) and breathing. They had been employed, apparently, in building airplanes or rockets, but how they could even lift their tools Frank could not understand. Another unit, Frank heard, had come across some of these people being driven by their Jerry captors deeper into Germany. This seemed to be the last thing the Germans wanted to do, the thing they cared most about—shooting their slaves. The slaves were Jewish. Like Julius. Like Rosa. It made Frank feel frozen and horror-struck in a way he had not felt on the battlefield.

They had a look at Hitler's summer residence, the Berghof. Though most of it had been bombed to pieces before they got there, there was plenty to look at, and both the place where Hitler was said to have had tea every day, and another place, higher up, were intact. Ruben made himself busy finding things in the garden, and he did get two items—a spoon that he found under a bush, and a button. He told everyone it was Hitler's own button, the one that popped off his fly when he was pissing himself in fear. But Frank pointed out that Hitler hadn't been there since the previous July. Ruben said, "He knew we were coming." These souvenirs he intended to keep, "unless I get a good offer."

Around the time they got to Berchtesgaden, they began hearing rumors about the Russians—that Ike didn't want to confront the Russians, that the Russians were taking Berlin, that the Russians were coming in hordes from the east and overrunning everything, that the Russians could not be stopped, that their own units had been ordered to meet up with the Fifth Army, which had been making its way up through Italy, so that in case the Russians showed up there would be plenty of them to fight the Russians back to Germany or Czechoslovakia or wherever. There were so many Russians that they could get all the way to western France—this was why no one was being sent home, or even to the Pacific. The next war could easily begin.

Because of Eloise and Julius, Frank was the only one he knew who had any ideas about Stalin, but listening to Eloise and Julius argue all those months in Chicago had done its work—the argument had never been about whether Stalin would kill his friends, only about how close to Stalin you had to be to get it first. Julius always swore that Trotsky's greatest mistake was leaving Stalin back in the Kremlin— he should never have trusted Stalin for a moment. Eloise always said, well, how could he have known, and things needed to be done, and when you were part of a unit, trust was essential. And then there were the trials. Maybe the ones who were executed had done something, said Eloise; no, they hadn't, said Julius. It went on and on. So Frank was pretty sure that Stalin was waiting to get organized, and then he would push to the west, and the next war would begin. But Ruben and Cornhill didn't agree. Cornhill thought that Stalin couldn't care less about Europe, that he would concentrate on rebuilding all those towns—Stalingrad, Leningrad, Kharkov—that the Germans had destroyed. "We can worry about him in ten years," said Cornhill. Ruben didn't care. He thought France and Germany, not to mention Italy, were such a mess that Stalin was welcome to them. "They ain't spending my money to fix up this dump" was what he said.

Frank said, "I didn't think you paid taxes."

Ruben shrugged. "You get my meaning, though. We done our bit. I knew some commies in Jersey City." He rolled his eyes.

JOE LIKED TO THINK of Lillian's birthday as the first day of the harvest—if they were lucky. He kept this to himself, but enjoyed the meals Rosanna always cooked for the birthday. Harvesting was hard work, and he needed a little extra sustenance in the form of, say, a seven-layer cake, to keep him going, especially if the remainder of the cake got sent home with him because Lillian was watching her weight. This year, though, he, Walter, and John got stuck in the fence line in a wet spot at Grandpa Wilmer's, and it took Grandpa Wilmer, who was all the way at the other corner of the farm, two hours to bring his own tractor over and pull them out. Joe knew this was his fault—he should have walked that part of the field. Papa wasn't mad, though, because he hadn't bothered to walk it, either. On the way home, Walter said, "Someday, I will give you a list of all the mistakes I've made, and then another list of all the mistakes my father has made that I thought I would never make. You can compare the two."

Everyone was there when they came in, and it turned out they weren't going to miss anything—not the rib roast or the scalloped potatoes or the crescent rolls. Lois was there—Joe could see her through the screen door, sitting by the table, watching something intently. It didn't matter what, Joe knew; Lois was a watcher—it could be flies on the ceiling. Lillian was up in her room, reading and, Joe knew, pretending that this was a surprise party. Walter blew out some air, threw his cap onto the hook, and started washing up. Joe kicked off a boot, and then heard his mom say, "That is just like him, I swear, saying we ought to hand over how to build an atomic bomb like a doughnut recipe, just to be nice."

Minnie, whom Joe couldn't see, said, "All the scientists say it's easy to figure out. The more we say it's our secret, the more they are going to want it." Minnie sounded rather unlike herself—confident and a little argumentative.

Walter opened the door, saying, "Who are you talking about?"

"Well, who do you think?" said Rosanna. "Henry Wallace. It said on the radio that he told the Senate that we should hand over the bomb to the Russians."

"What do you care?" said Walter.

"Oh, he just gets my goat," said Rosanna. "Always has."

Walter glanced at Joe, made the briefest face, then said, "Why is that, since, as far as we know, you aren't related and he was never a friend of the family?"

"Better for him if he had been. Might not have been telling people how to run their lives since the day he was born." Rosanna scowled. Joe went over and kissed her on the forehead. The argument subsided. Minnie, who had left Mrs. Frederick napping and only come by for a minute, took her plate of food and ran home. Lois and Claire set the dining-room table.

Maybe if Walter hadn't been tired and irritated from the tractor mishap, the argument would have been over, but just at the wrong time, that time when they had all finished their first helpings and were thinking about seconds, when Rosanna stood up, lifted the carving knife and fork, and directed her gaze at the roast, Walter said, "I think Wallace should have been president instead of vice-president. I like him better than Truman. He knows some things, he's thought about things. Truman is a hothead."

"Yes, and if he was from Independence, Iowa, rather than Independence, Missouri, he would be fine with you."

Joe wasn't sure he had ever heard his parents argue about politics, especially with slightly raised voices. He and Lillian exchanged a glance. Henry said, "My science teacher said that they didn't find any radiation at Hiroshima, and that the Japanese lied about it."

"What are you talking about that at school for?" said Rosanna.

"We've talked about it Friday and today. Two girls were crying, so he told them that. He said that there were five buildings left standing and a hundred thousand people died. There was one building pretty far away, and the blast was so hot that the chairs inside the house were scorched through the closed windows. It was five thousand degrees."

"And Henry Wallace wants to let the Russians do that very thing!" exclaimed Rosanna.

Lillian said, "I can't believe telling the girls those things made them feel better. I don't want to think about it, and I'm glad it's not my business."

Henry said, "He said that, even at our age, it's better to know about something than to imagine it all the time."

Joe said, "Happy birthday, Lillian." Everyone shut up, and after a short silence, Claire told about the rabbit Miss Rohrbaugh had at school. It was gray, not white, but it had white tips on its ears. Its name was Paul, not Peter, and each of the nine children at school would have a turn feeding it—in alphabetical order. "I am 'L,'" said Claire.

When he was walking to his place that evening, carrying the remains of the cake, Joe didn't know what to think. His main feeling about the bombing of Hiroshima and Nagasaki had been surprise mixed with a sense of relief. His main feeling about Henry Wallace was more like his dad's than his mom's—someone in Washington had to be a nice guy, and Wallace had that Iowa way of doing it, draft horse rather than Thoroughbred. He looked around. The sky was clear; the corn was certainly drying in the fields, and maybe, if he paused and stood still, he could hear it. But he had seen the picture of the mushroom cloud, and in spite of what Henry's teacher had said, he could imagine it rising above Usherton—a mile high, was it?—achingly bright and loud. Would that be the last thing you would see? Was that the last thing someone like himself on a street in Hiroshima did see? Joe prayed a little prayer—may he not have known what he was looking at, may he have vanished from this earth the very moment he turned his head and said, "What in the world is that?"

LILLIAN WAS WORKING late. It was just about time for the soda fountain to close—she was wiping down the counter—and here he came, in the door, stepping aside for Charlie, who was picking up one of the displays, and then over to her. He had on a camel-hair coat and was carrying a brown leather briefcase. His hat was pushed back a little, as if he were ready for anything. He set the briefcase and his hat on one stool and sat down on another one. His smile was quick. He said, "Where am I?"

"Usherton, Iowa."

"What time is it?"

"Almost ten."

"And who are you?"

Lillian couldn't help smiling. She said, "Who's asking?"

"Arthur."

"Lillian."

"*Lill*ian. How lovely. I expected irises and poppies and a few dandelions, but no *Lill*ians."

"May I get you anything, sir?" She saw Charlie looking at her.

"A cup of coffee and a Coca-Cola."

"Both?"

"You'll see." And she did—he poured some of the Coke into the cup of coffee, and drank that down, then finished the Coke. After the drugstore closed, he asked her to show him the block. The block was nothing special, but he put her hand through his arm, then made up a story about every building as they strolled through the darkness: Was that where the hole in the basement was, the one where the gold bars had been found, that Pretty Boy Floyd had left there? Hadn't she heard about that? In Rapid City, it was all they talked about. Or that place there, didn't she see the faces in the window? Mrs. Lester Tester had twenty-seven children, twenty-six of them girls. "We just wanted a boy," said Mrs. Tester, "so we kept on trying." Lillian laughed and laughed. "What are you laughing at?" exclaimed Arthur. "These are serious matters."

He walked her to her car (Papa's car, which she used when she worked late) and insisted she lock the doors before she drove off. When she came on her shift at noon the next day, he sat down at the counter and ordered a hot dog.

It took two days for Lillian to learn Arthur's surname, and by the time she did learn it, he had already proposed and she had already accepted. His surname was Manning. Arthur Manning. Arthur Brinks Manning. Mrs. Arthur Brinks Manning. Lillian Manning. Lillian Langdon Manning. Lillian Elizabeth Langdon Manning. She wrote them all down on a piece of paper, and then folded the paper into a tiny wad and put it in the pocket of her favorite sweater.

Arthur Manning was driving from Rapid City, South Dakota, to Bethesda, Maryland. He had to be there on October 15. It was now October 13. Lillian sat on her bed in her still-pink bedroom, and looked at the pictures she had never changed, the alphabet, a faded photograph of Mary Elizabeth in a white frame, a picture of some lilies. The pink-and-white-striped curtains. The rag rug her granny had made. The profiles of the farmer, his wife, their cow, their horse, pig, lamb, rabbit, squirrel, fox, and bird. What to take with her? Why was it so alluring that Arthur had not gotten down on his knees, or offered her a ring, just put his chin on her head and said, "You've got me, Lily darling, Lili Damita, Lily Pons, Lily Langdon. I said I would never marry again, but I must, if you will."

"Were you married, Arthur?"

Then he sat her down on a bench, looking at the park, and he said, "Lily Langdon, I was married for two years, and my wife got pregnant, and when she was eight months along, she had a stabbing pain in her back. I was away on a trip, and she was from Alabama and didn't have any friends in Bethesda, so she didn't call anyone. By the time I got back, the bleeding had gone on for two days, and I only got her to the hospital in time for her to die. The baby was already dead."

"What caused that?" said Lillian. Lillian knew she was saying this to give herself time for the sadness of what he was telling her to register. He kept looking at her. She swallowed.

He said, "They told me the placenta broke away from the uterine wall." He put his hands on either side of her face. He said, "Marriage can be a terrible thing, which is why I propose to you in despair."

Lillian slipped her arm under Arthur's and laid her head against his chest. They both took that as a yes.

As she sat on her bed, looking around, Lillian thought that he had suitably terrified them both, and therefore he was just the right person for her. She actually didn't think that Rosanna would dislike him or that Walter would make a fuss. But she wanted him all to herself. So she found a paper sack and put a few things in it—two brassieres and some panties, an extra slip, and her white batiste blouse she had just bought. The twill gored skirt Rosanna had made her. Nothing she was taking was pink, which amused her. Then she opened the drawer of her chest and took out her savings and the golden feather—they were wrapped together in tissue paper. She tucked the packet inside the folded-up skirt. She set a few bits of makeup on top of the skirt— her compact was in her purse, but she chose two lipsticks, a foundation she had just opened, the mascara. Her boar-bristle hairbrush. She folded up the bag and slid it under the bed. Joey would unknowingly drop her at the drugstore at ten, and they would leave from there. She had already written her note to Mama and Papa. She would slip that under her pillow, and leave the bed unmade. Mama would flounce into the room, annoyed that Lillian had not made her bed, and find it. Then—who knew? It gave Lillian a bona-fide thrill to think of it.

1946

~

LILLIAN WOULD NOT have said that she knew a great deal about Arthur, but she only thought about this when he wasn't around. During the day, she tried to spend her time appreciating her apartment in an imposing brick building with white trim that rather reminded her of her high school and the short walks she could take in the neighborhood. She had a small but warm bathroom, reliable hot water, and a deep and satisfying bathtub. She had a gas range, and every time she checked the pilot light, it was still lit. There was a park that ran up to the boundary of the insane asylum, but Lillian preferred the little looping streets and sometimes took the streetcar to different sections—Georgetown and Woodley Park were her favorites—and walked around there. She liked to shop at the Giant supermarket, and she especially enjoyed something called "Cheerios." After nearly twenty years of oatmeal, these Cheerios were a constant pleasure.

In the fall, she had gone to all sorts of sights around the District, first with Arthur, then on her own—the Smithsonian, the Capitol Building, the Memorials—all of them in the howling wind. In fact, the best time they'd had was just before Christmas, when an ice storm coated all the cherry trees along Potomac Drive and then the sun came out and set the ice alight. It hadn't even been cold that day— they'd marched along with their coats open, laughing and glorying in the sparkling blackness of the branches. But now she was nearly four months pregnant, and though she didn't look it, she felt it, so she stayed around the apartment, secretly feeling that the many flights of stairs to their front door, twice a day, was plenty of exercise. What in the world they would do when the baby came and there was a baby carriage, Lillian had no idea, but she had faith that Arthur would take care of it.

She did know that Arthur was the same age as Frank, that he had spent the war in Washington, working for the OSS, breaking codes; that he spoke German and also French; that his mother's family was from New Orleans; that he had gone to Williams College, which was in Massachusetts. Colonel Manning, his father, visited sometimes. He lived in Charlottesville, Virginia. When he came and when he left, he leaned over slightly in order for Lillian to plant a kiss on his cheek, and he always took her right hand in his and patted it three times with his left. Like Arthur, he had a twinkle in his eye, but he didn't tell stories the way Arthur did. Arthur's mother had been a great beauty and had died. Of all the things they never talked about, she was the prime mystery. All Lillian knew of her was her photograph on the mantel. She looked like Greta Garbo with blond hair. Sometimes, Lillian thought that the picture was too much—she, Lillian, would never be that beautiful, and with the baby and all, she was getting less beautiful every day. Her hair, for example, was falling out—she didn't even have to brush it, it just dropped all around her. The first wife, Alice, had been a beauty, too. Her photograph sat beside the mother's, because, Arthur said, there was no one else to remember her but himself. Did Lillian mind?

No, not when Arthur sat beside her on the couch, holding her hand, and having her recite all the names: Hermann Augsberger, Augustina Augsberger, Otto Vogel, Mary Vogel, Rosanna Vogel, Rolf Vogel, Eloise Vogel Silber, Kurt Vogel, John Vogel, Gus Vogel, Lester Chick, Etta Cheek, Wilmer Langdon, Elizabeth Langdon, Walter Langdon, Frank Langdon, Joseph Langdon, Henry Langdon, Claire Langdon. It didn't matter that Walter wasn't yet speaking to her (though Rosanna was), or that Arthur hadn't met a single one of them yet; these were the relatives, he said, that his son or daughter (Timothy or Deborah) was going to have, and there were scads and scads of them. "Have you ever been lonely, darling?" said Arthur. And Lillian always said, "No." But of course she was lonely now, except when Arthur was at home. Arthur banished loneliness.

Every evening at six, she could hear him running up the stairs, and then he threw open the door and took her in his arms. He patted her belly and kissed not only her lips but her neck, on both sides, which tickled and made her giddy. Then, while she was setting the table, he sat in his place and told her what had happened that day at the office—two birds had flown in the window, and Arthur had been assigned to get them out, so they opened *all* the windows, and Arthur ran around with his hat, and then, the most amazing thing, he realized that they were talking, and they had plenty to say. They spoke with something of a French accent, which was surprising, because they were English sparrows—lovely blue color, forked tails—and once Arthur had shown that he was willing to listen to them, they settled on his shoulders as he sat in his desk chair, and told him what they had seen. It was all very important, but, unfortunately, only to birds: the mosquito population is plentiful, but the insects themselves are so small as to be hardly worth eating; there had been a nice harvest of horseflies in Virginia, but every bird in the flock got a little sick afterward; flies outside of grocery stores can be very good; etc. By this time, Lillian was laughing, and Arthur went on earnestly, "I thought they were coming to me—me, Arthur—with information that I could use, but they were just like a couple of blabbermouths on the streetcar, going on and on."

Lillian played her part. "How did you get them out, though?"

"Well, I simply showed them the door, and said that looks aren't everything, and they'd have to come back with something worth my time."

After supper, he helped her with the dishes. He sang songs, like "The Boogie Woogie Bugle Boy" and "People Will Say We're in Love," and he got her to sing along. When they listened to the radio, or he read a book or some papers, and she leafed through a magazine, he liked to lay his head in her lap or hold her against him. Just before bed, rain or not, he put her coat on her and walked her outside around the apartment building, once in each direction, "so you won't get lopsided," and then they were yawning. In bed, he tucked her up against himself and held her until she fell asleep. She thought it was very lucky that she had slept with so many dolls over the years and so was used to sharing the bed.

But where had he grown up? New England. What did he do all day? So boring, put me to sleep to talk about it. Who was on the phone? No one you know, darling. Was there anyone besides his father that he would like to have over or go out with? No one nearby. He didn't resent the questions, he just acted like they were impossible to answer, and like she was far more interesting than he was, anyway. It wasn't until Frankie (Frank!) dropped by on his way home from Europe that she saw even a little of another Arthur.

This Arthur was tougher than she knew. She could see it the moment he opened the door.

But there was Frank. His shoulders had broadened, and his hair and eyes had darkened, and the angles of his face were stark. You would not look at him ever again and say that he was cute. He had the same dazzling smile and the same grace, but he deployed both of them differently than he had—more cautiously, more suddenly. Arthur was clearly struck by him, though Lillian had told him over and over that Frank was a sight to see. Frank was only a couple of inches taller than Arthur, but he looked down on him. It was as simple as that. In the same room with Frank, Lillian felt like she and Arthur were a pair of rabbits. When Arthur stuck out his hand, though, and he and Frank shook, the muscles along the back of his arm flexed. Arthur's chin even jutted out a little, and his voice deepened as he said, "Welcome back, soldier. I hear you've had an interesting four years."

Frank gave her a big kiss on the lips and ruffled her hair, then actually smacked her on the backside. Lillian decided that he had no idea what he was doing. He sat down at the table while Lillian served him some meatloaf and mashed potatoes from dinner, then a slice of pecan pie. He ate as he always had—meticulously and systematically—and Lillian was surprised she remembered that.

When they went into the living room after dinner and sat down to chat, the thing she noticed was that, after he sat in the armchair (which was fine—they preferred the couch), he adjusted it automatically so that the back of it faced a wall rather than a window and the front faced the door. And when a car backfired while they were talking, he ducked. Of course, being Frank, he sat up at once and said, "Joke's on me," and they laughed.

Yes, he had had some odd adventures since V-E Day. Mostly it was beating the bushes for Nazis and herding displaced people here and there—so many had fled from the East that they were camped everywhere, and they were so terrified of being sent back to Poland or Prague or wherever that they could hardly speak. And then there were those, young ones, who didn't know a thing—could hardly remember who they were, and certainly didn't know where they were from. Children who had lived in the forest for years, or in a tunnel somewhere, or a bombed-out house. But there were funny ones, too—a fellow they'd run across in the mountains of Austria who wore a towel around his head, looked into a glass ring that he wore on his finger, and went into a trance. When he came out of the trance, he told them the whereabouts of "Germany's greatest scientist," or "Germany's most important invention," or "the son of Herr Hitler." Always, these desirables were to be found in the next village over. When a squad went to find them, yes, the building existed, and, yes, a machine existed, but it was a coal stove. The son of Herr Hitler turned out to be forty-two years old—Hitler would have fathered him at the age of fifteen. Of course, it was possible, but Frank somehow didn't feel the connection. "This guy sent us on six wild-goose chases. Finally, we found a valuable cache—some woman's collection of fur coats. My buddy Ruben sent the ermine one back to New Jersey as a souvenir."

Frank was good at telling the stories, and Arthur loved them. Arthur had a story, too, it turned out. Lillian was all ears. Did Frank realize that when the Allies invaded Sicily the Germans thought they were planning to invade Greece? That was why there was no one on the beaches, except to the east.

Frank said, "We were surprised."

"We played a trick," said Arthur. "We all helped. We made up a guy, gave him a whole career, a family, papers, ID, monograms, pictures of his dog, 'Duna.' The Brits and the OSS talked back and forth about him and how important he was for a year in a code that we knew they had broken before we let his corpse wash up on the beach in southern Greece, and when it did, it was carrying plans for the invasion of Greece, meeting up with the Russians, all kinds of information. When he died, I rather mourned him. We all did. But it worked."

"It was so quiet there it spooked me," said Frank. "And I was right." Lillian saw that there were plenty of things that had happened in the war that Frank and Arthur were never going to tell her about. Mama would have tossed her hand, clucked, "And rightly so! Less said about any number of things!" But it made Lillian feel startled and anxious, as if a wall of the house had vaporized.

After they went to bed at their regular time, Lillian could hear Frank pacing around the living room until she dropped off. In the morning, he was already up and dressed by the time she had her robe on. He ate his Cheerios and the toast she made in her brand-new Sunbeam toaster, thanked her, and smacked her backside ("behind") again, and when she skipped out of the way, he said, "Bad habit. Sorry, Lil."

"Don't try it with Mama."

Frank laughed.

He went out with Arthur, and they walked together to the train—Arthur to work and Frank to Union Station, then Chicago and home. Arthur was impressed. That night, he said, "We talked nonstop. He's brilliant, your brother, and he has his eyes wide open. If there was anything that escaped his notice in the last four years, I'd sure like to know what it was. We should definitely help him find a job around here."

"I'd like that," said Lillian.

THEY HAD TO POSTPONE Frank's coming-home party at the last minute, and for a sad reason—Mrs. Frederick died, and though you couldn't say it was unexpected, you had to say it was sudden. She had been able to do almost nothing in the last year. They had moved her bed down to the dining room, and she didn't even get out of it to go to the bathroom—Minnie had a bedpan and an old-fashioned slop bucket, and did it all herself, wiping and washing and changing the bedclothes and emptying the slop bucket. That house was the first in the area with indoor plumbing; they could have more easily had her upstairs. But it was strange, Rosanna thought, the little choices you had to make that you never foresaw, such as was it easier to be closer to the bathroom or to the kitchen, did you stow an invalid who could barely move upstairs, where she was out of the way, or did you have her right where everyone who came in would go over to her and take her hand and say hello and then include her in the conversation? Of course, Minnie did the kindest thing, and also never complained about the slop bucket or anything else. Lois was a little put out, though she didn't say it. But Lois was sixteen now, and her childhood had been an utter tragedy. Roland Frederick was a useless man. He stopped doing his farm work and, it was said, roamed from tavern to tavern in Usherton. Lois was pretty enough, but she always looked down in the dumps, and though Rosanna, who had plenty of time, sewed her some nice outfits for school, she didn't wear them with any flair. She let her hair go, too. You could look like a nanny goat, as Rosanna considered that she herself now did, but, still, you ought to be neat and trim.

Frankie didn't say a thing about the party, and probably did not care, but he let Rosanna drag him all around Denby—into Dan's store and the café and the church and every other little place, including the tiny room where Maureen Thompson was now cutting and curling ladies' hair, and everywhere, men and women and kids grabbed him and hugged him and thanked him for his service. Old men sat him down and bought him coffee and asked to hear all about it, and Frankie told them this and that, such as where he'd served and whether he liked Africa or France better, and what the mud was like, and how was his German now, and did he believe this story that they were telling about the Jews and the camps, and what about the Russkies. Frank said what he thought. But he kept smiling and nodding, and after listening in on a few of these conversations, Rosanna realized that the new Frankie was just like the old Frankie—he listened more than he talked, and the other fellow went his way reconfirmed in his opinions, not having learned much that was new.

For the first two weeks, Frankie said nothing about what was next, nothing about a job. He drove the new tractor a few times, and he could still plant a straight row, but he didn't seem to notice the disappearance of the chickens and the cattle—all they had was hogs now, and not many of them. Just corn, corn, corn, everywhere corn. Nor did he take down his gun and set out to shoot any rabbits, though he did move the board in the wall beside the case to find eight dollars, which he split between Henry and Claire. When he wasn't riding the tractor or being shepherded about town, he was gone to Usherton in Walter's car or walking around the farm. He must have crisscrossed the farm ten times. When Rosanna asked him why, he only ran his hands through his hair and said, "Used to it, I guess. Can't stand sitting around anymore, even when moving is pointless."

"You should get out your old bicycle."

"That's a good idea." But he didn't get it out.

He stayed up late with the radio low and got up early. Walter remembered being the same way when he got back from France— lasted for six months. "I was gone for a year. Frank was gone for four, so I guess this'll last for two years."

Rosanna said, "He doesn't seem to be drinking."

"He doesn't."

"Really?"

"Well, Mother, I'm not spying on him. Soldiers drink. That's what they do. A decent, well-run army gives them something to drink, like the Brits."

"Oh, for goodness' sake, Walter!"

"Well, what do you think we did in our spare time in France? Most of us knew how to rig up a still, and there was plenty of wine that needed to be brandy."

"I think he had worse things happen than you did."

"Rosanna," said Walter, "I think he did." They looked at each other, but what was there to say? There was no entry into Frankie's heart, if there ever had been, at least for them. But Walter had answered the letter Lillian sent about seeing Frank in Washington, and Lillian had replied, and Walter had said to Rosanna, "I guess you'd better start knitting a baby blanket." That very evening, sitting in her chair in the front room, Rosanna had brought out the pink, blue, and yellow seed-stitch piece she was working on, and Walter saw that she was already more than half finished. Rosanna calculated, though—if the child was due in July, that was a good time for Rosanna to take the train to Washington, and there would be a lull in the farm work right around then, too, so Walter could just put on some regular shoes and a nice shirt and come along. Had they ever seen the White House? No, they had not. Nor any ocean of any kind. Stuck on the farm like two shoats struggling in a hog pen. The state fair was all very well, but it shouldn't be the last thing you saw in your life. At first you thought of people like Eloise and Frank and Lillian as runaways, and then, after a bit, you knew they were really scouts.

JOE'S EXCUSE for not seeing much of Frank when Frank was around had been that it was planting time, of course. They did have that one day where Frank helped him with the Frederick field, which was a hundred acres now, and as flat as a griddle. Maybe that had been a bad idea, Joe thought afterward. He could see Minnie at the windows, first downstairs, then upstairs, watching the tractor. And she came over twice and sat with Frank. Every time he said anything, she smiled, and when he greeted her by kissing her on both cheeks, she blushed. That wasn't the Minnie he knew—his Minnie was practical and down-to-earth, always happy to see him, but slipping away like a fish in a pond when he tried to put his arm around her. She always said, "That's not for me, Joe. Don't know why," leading him to believe that he was first in line if she changed her mind. But he wasn't first in line.

It was Lois who said, one day when Joe was cultivating that field and went to the house to fill his water bottle and soak his bandanna again before laying it over the top of his head under his hat, "So—tell me one thing. Why is everyone falling all over themselves about your brother Frank?"

"Well, he served in some pretty big battles."

"Yeah, but that's not the reason. They *say* it's the reason. But then they say, 'Oh, Frank. I always knew he would get ahead.'"

"Minnie says that."

"And everything else—he looks like Henry Fonda, he's so tall and strong. He used to be blond, but this is nicer, really." She was good at mimicking Minnie's delivery. "Me, I don't see it. He looks kind of scary to me. I like you better. You're nice."

"Well, you know me."

"Well," she insisted, "you *are* nice. You are nice to us every single day, and I for one know it."

"Well, maybe I can't help myself," said Joe.

"You sound like it's a fault."

That night, lying in bed, Joe wondered if he thought being nice to Minnie and Lois was a fault. Across the room, his collie, Nat, was spread out all over the bed Joe had made him out of an old quilt, and the cats were sleeping in the front room, where they always did— Pepper in the chair by the window and Booster on the heat register. Out in the old barn, he still had two milkers, Betty and Boop, the last in the neighborhood. When they calved, he sold the calves as vealers, but he named them and let them live with Betty and Boop until they were a few months old. This year's pair he had named Harry and Bill, even though Bill was a heifer. He had four rabbits in a hutch—Eenie, Meenie, Miney, and Moe—and no earthly use for them. Rosanna said, "Do you name the houseflies, too?" and Walter always shook his head at the impending doom of naming animals you yourself were going to kill. Rosanna felt that letting the cats in the house was especially horrifying, and she didn't know that Joe let them walk all over the kitchen table and the kitchen counter—was he as bad as Rolf yet? What had Rolf done in this house that had demonstrated his propensity for decline?

After Frank left, Minnie told Joe that she had to get busy now; her mother had died, and maybe she and Lois had better move to Cedar Falls, so that she could at last get her teacher's degree and do something with her life. Lois was in her sophomore year—she could spend the last two years at a school where no one knew a thing about them or their father or their mother, and that would be good for both of them. Best to make up their minds that they were on their own now. Roland Frederick, Joe knew, wasn't violent, but he was unpredictable. He had gone off, no one knew where, but he could always reappear.

All of this sounded fine, and he was so nice, so damnably nice, that he said, "You should do it, Minnie, you should. I think it's the best idea." What was it, sixty or seventy miles to Cedar Falls? Not a distance that he would comfortably travel, with Betty and Boop and Pepper and Booster and Eenie, Meenie, Miney, and Moe waiting for him at home.

IN THE END, Arthur found Frank a job for the government, not in Washington, but in Ohio, near Dayton. What Frank discovered on the job was that he was not alone in wondering what made the German army so good. His job was to go through papers—thousands and thousands and tons and tons of papers that had been uncovered, discovered, recovered by the Allies all over Germany in the last two years of the war. He even had a surprise—a squad from his own Seventh Army had set out from Berchtesgaden, probably on the very same day when Ruben was turning up his button and his spoon, and gone to a cave not far away, the very cave where Himmler had stored all his papers and then dynamited the entrance closed just before the end of the war. The most remarked-upon papers from that cave were the ones about death-by-freezing experiments: If you submerged a man in freezing water, how long would it take for him to get past reviving? The answer was, anywhere from about an hour to just under two hours. And every measurement was taken by the observing scientists as the subjects died—temperature, blood count, urine samples, pulse. Other subjects were successfully revived, by immersion into hot water, Frank gathered.

But the documents he enjoyed reading were not about making cheese in ninety minutes or the effects of "ionized air" or how to make rayon warmer by crimping the threads. He was mildly interested in something called Periston, which appeared to be fake blood, and the fact that a German U-boat was so well insulated and refrigerated that it could travel for months without surfacing to take on drinking water. What interested him the most was an infrared gun sight that had a range of three kilometers, in the dark. Frank felt immediately that he had been viewed by such a sight—maybe many times—that he had appeared as a fluorescent image on a tiny screen. It turned out that the marines in the Pacific had employed the thing once it was confiscated from the Germans, but Frank had never heard of it until now.

Because of the war, Frank's speaking German was pretty good, but he had to work hard at reading the papers. For a while, his main job was just to sort them and box them—he at least knew when one set of papers ended and another set began. Even though others had translated enough to be taken aback, maybe amazed at what they found, there were vast quantities still to go through. American companies of all kinds were waiting for the results; the promise was that everything found would be published and go straight into the public domain. Each afternoon, when Frank left the giant building, formerly

an airplane hangar, he saw rows of men who had read the weekly bib-
liography of patents and procedures, standing in line to buy the documents or to order the ones that hadn't been printed yet.

Otherwise, Dayton was not that different from Usherton, and
Frank was restless there. As a result, he went back and forth to Washington (in his new car, a Studebaker Champion) about once a month—
he could get there in six or seven hours if he drove at night. Arthur
and Lillian amused him, Arthur because he was genuinely amusing
and Lillian because she was so obviously enjoying both Arthur and
Timmy. Timmy, said Rosanna and even Walter (who had come in
September), looked exactly like Frank himself. Sometimes, Frank
squatted down in front of the playpen, watched Timmy, and tried to
make something out about him—what he remembered most clearly
from his own childhood was that lattice of ropes underneath Walter
and Rosanna's bed, that feeling of dim enclosure that was not unlike
the safety of a foxhole, and was a relief from the space everywhere
on the farm—yes, outside, but also out the windows and through
the doors. He could lie under the bed, staring at the woven ropes and
the ticking of the mattress and relax. For some reason, he had not
been allowed to do it very often—he couldn't remember why. The
rest of his childhood was don't touch that and get down from there
and watch out for the back end of that cow and don't let Jake step on
your foot and be careful of the ladder and there's a trapdoor there
and stay back from the planter and don't go near that by yourself and
if you get caught in a thunderstorm, lie flat in a ditch and, yes, in a
high wind, the outhouse could fall over, and careful of the thorns
on the Osage-orange hedge. Only under the bed had he taken deep,
quiet breaths and felt safe. He held out his forefingers to Timmy, and
Timmy grabbed them and pulled himself upward, and then, when he
was sitting, and balancing himself against Frank's fingers, he started
crowing and laughing.

1947

∾

WHEN LILLIAN WROTE TO Rosanna and told her she was
pregnant again, Rosanna wrote back and told her that it was
because she was bottle feeding rather than nursing, which surprised
Lillian a little bit. When they'd handed her the bottle in the hospital
and showed her how to give little Timmy his formula, they hadn't
mentioned that. Nor did they tell her that you had to add sugar
to the formula in order to make sure his BMs were the right consis-
tency. Lillian didn't even mention this to Rosanna, but one of the
best things about rearing Timmy in an apartment rather than on a
farm was that she could take care of him just the way she wished—
she sterilized the eight bottles she would need for the day the night
before, and left them in the enclosed sterilizer on the gas stove over-
night. Then, in the morning, she measured the formula milk, added
the sugar to the boiled and cooled water, mixed the water with the
milk, and divided the total amount into eight equal parts, which she
poured into the sterilized bottles. Just the idea of feeding a baby with
the sort of water they'd had from the well on the farm, even in good
times, gave Lillian the willies. And where would Rosanna have gotten evaporated, processed milk? Yes, Lillian herself had drunk milk
from their cows (with the cream skimmed for butter, of course), but
that she had survived was probably more a testament to luck than
to anything else. And one hadn't survived—Mary Elizabeth. Maybe

Lillian had never known how she died; she certainly didn't remember now, and she didn't dare ask her mother. Possibly, she could ask Frank when he came again. These were the sorts of thoughts that occupied her while she was making Timmy's formula for the day. And, of course, now there was pablum and applesauce and zwieback—he was a good eater. He no longer took a morning nap, but he went down fine in the afternoon, at exactly two, just like the book said, and at seven-thirty for the night, which meant that he was up by five, an hour before he was supposed to get up, according to the book. When she wrote and asked Rosanna about their sleeping schedules, Rosanna said, "Oh, goodness me, down up down up. The only one I remember is Claire, who slept like a rock in the front room. And you, of course. You were perfect. I don't remember a thing before you. There was one time when I put Henry down and he was out the back door after something before I got there. I think he was almost to the barn before I caught him."

Henry was the perfect one now, handsome, neat, a good student, destined never to make trouble. He would be fifteen this year, and already too good for Iowa State. Rosanna thought sure he would go to the University of Iowa and become a doctor.

Every morning, Lillian bundled Timmy into his snowsuit and carried him down the stairs. They had applied for another apartment, on the first floor, but so far it hadn't been vacated. The baby carriage was inside the front door, in the hallway, and Arthur had chained it with a padlock to the banister. It embarrassed Lillian to be seen unlocking the padlock, and then it was rather difficult to get it down the two steps to the walk. The walk sloped just enough so that if she did not hold on to the handle of the baby carriage every second, it would start to roll, and she could easily imagine it gaining speed, bumping down the next two steps to the sidewalk, and rushing into the street (which was rather a busy one—how had she and Arthur not seen all of these dangers when they signed their lease?). But, according to the book, you had to go out—the baby had to have fresh air every day, even in the rain or snow, which was why the baby carriage had a hood. Once she was out, mostly she walked around the streets, or over to the Giant supermarket, where she looked at the rows of baby food and tried to decide which to try next. One particularly discomfiting thing that Rosanna told her was that she herself, Lillian, had loved liver as a baby, calves' liver that Rosanna rolled in seasoned flour and fried in butter until it was just done through. "No one else liked it, but you couldn't get enough." Lillian would never feed Timmy such a thing.

Lunch was baby chicken with peas, or baby turkey with carrots, and a little tapioca for dessert, and then the story and the nap. Usually, Lillian went down, too, but she kept the doors open so she could see the crib, and she taught herself to sleep facing it. Timmy's door was right by the bathroom door, and though he couldn't get out of his crib, and the bathroom door was closed, and the toilet lid was down, what would keep him, really, from waking up, heading for the bathroom, and plunging headfirst into the toilet?

Arthur didn't have these sorts of fears. Arthur had gotten a new job, or, rather, the same job at a new office, and what the name of that office was had gone in her one ear and out the other. Some initials. The best thing about Arthur was that he still ran up the stairs at six and threw open the door, and gave her a great hug, but then he immediately took Timmy in his arms and danced him around, saying, "Who is this kid? Is he that same kid who was here last night? Don't believe it!" Arthur was a tickler and a tosser, and Timmy seemed to love both being laid on his back on the couch and tickled until he was burbling with laughter, and being tossed up and caught like a sack of flour. And he was like a sack of flour, which was a delicate thing. With Arthur tossing, no sack of flour would ever tear and spill, and no baby would ever get hurt.

After Timmy was born, Lillian had caught Arthur crying, and not just one time. Finally, he took her hand and said, "I didn't realize how worried I was, or how dumbfounded I would be. I thought when Laura was born dead that I had just accepted it, but I guess I hadn't." Lillian tried not to think that she loved Arthur for his misfortune, but it did seem to add a deeper color to her love, and it made him a very attentive father. She knew other women with babies now, and their husbands seemed a little put off or frightened by their children, but Arthur was eager for more—Irish twins! He'd had friends in school who were Irish twins—born within a year of one another, so close together that they got put in the same grade. These two were tremendous friends, and now that they were grown up and home from the war, they were in the car business together in Roanoke.

Timmy was active. What was he, exactly eight months today. Lillian had taped folded washcloths over the corners of the coffee table with masking tape, which wasn't supposed to leave marks, and Timmy was just sitting there, pulling himself to his feet and letting himself sit, and pulling himself up, and laughing. She wanted him to go down for his nap, but he was so excited that she didn't think he would do it. It made her a little anxious, but she decided to get out her Brownie camera and take some pictures to send to Rosanna. That was another thing—there was only one picture from their childhoods, one taken by Mrs. Frederick (poor thing) when Lillian was nine and Henry was three. None of Frank or Joe or even Claire, only one of Walter and Rosanna, on the day they were married. Lillian was deep into her first scrapbook already, with pages of pictures of Timmy, and more than a few of herself and Arthur taken here and there around town (though Arthur didn't like to be photographed, and in most of his, his hat was pulled down). He looked very sharp.

Lillian snapped six or eight pictures, making sure to get the sun behind her, and then set down the camera and picked up Timmy and kissed him all over. How another child was going to fit into their world, she could not imagine.

MAMA TOOK CLAIRE to the optometrist in Usherton because she had failed a test. It wasn't a regular test, it was one where the kids had to go into the lunchroom, with all the shades down, and read from a lit-up square on the lunchroom wall, which was normally painted pale blue. There were letters in the square, big to small, and also things sitting up and lying down, and you had to say which direction they were pointing. It didn't take very long. Claire could read the two biggest lines of letters, but nothing below that without leaning forward and squinting. Mama was annoyed, because no one had ever needed glasses before in their family. "As far as we know," said Papa.

"Your family, maybe, but even Opa only needed reading glasses after he was sixty-five."

Claire wasn't quite sure what she was supposed to do at the optometrist's. There were things that she looked through and things that she looked at—mostly letters and figures, some of them filled in and some of them empty. The optometrist kept asking her questions, and after a while she was so bored that she just said anything that came into her head, or she tried looking at the things with one eye closed or squinting or something, which changed the way they looked. But she behaved herself. She always behaved herself. She did not fidget, and she spoke only when spoken to, and she kept her fingernails out of her mouth and also her hair. At school sometimes, she found the end of her left pigtail in her mouth, but only when the teacher was so boring that she made Claire forget what she was doing and where she was. Finally, while the optometrist was adjusting yet another machine, Claire put her head down on the table and dozed off. When she woke up, Mama was right there. She said, "What in the world is going on?"

"Well, she needs glasses, but I can't figure out . . ."

"Claire, are you giving Dr. Hicks a hard time?"

Claire shook her head.

She did, however, get glasses. Dr. Hicks had lots of styles. Claire sat in front of a mirror, and Dr. Hicks hooked them over her ears one temple at a time. He said, "Well, she has a round face, and so . . ."

"I don't think of her face as round. More heart-shaped," said Mama.

"Well, you see, though, this rounder frame is a bit more flattering. For the heart-shaped face, we like a wider frame. Perhaps if she wore her hair down rather than in pigtails."

Mama ignored this. "I think she looks fine in the rounder frame. But which is the sturdiest one? These are thirty dollars?"

"Yes, and that includes the frame, but for ten dollars more, I can give you a new type of lens that is really plastic. Much less easily broken."

"I'm sure Claire will be very careful with them."

In the end, they bought the new kind. Every morning, every afternoon after school, and every night before bed, Mama asked her where her glasses were if she was not wearing them. Claire got to be quite jumpy—when Mama used a certain tone, her hand would go straight to her face, not because she didn't know whether or not she had them on, but because she didn't know where they were. Didn't she care about being able to see?

Yes, she did, and there actually was quite a difference, but the glasses were a big responsibility. It was easier to sit in the first row and lean toward the blackboard and squint than it was to keep track of the darn things. And then, every time she didn't know where they were, it started an argument between Mama and Papa. Mama would say, "Is this child ever going to learn how to take care of her things?" and Papa would say, "She does fine. The problem is that you only have one to fuss over. Not enough chaos for you."

"Henry still lives at home."

"But if you fuss over Henry, he just walks away."

"She's eight years old. Eight-year-olds take a little fussing."

Walter shrugged, patted Claire on her hair, on the head that sat on top of her round face. At night, in bed, after taking off her glasses, and putting them carefully, temples down, never lenses down, on the table beside her bed, she lay on her back and set her palms beside her cheekbones and pressed. She pressed as hard as she could, counting to a hundred, three times, and then she fell asleep, pulling her chin down. Glasses were bad enough, and a round face was pretty bad, too, but glasses *and* a round face were hopeless.

NOW THAT SCHOOL WAS out, Henry had decided to rearrange his books. The day was hot, so he opened both windows and the door into the main part of the house. He smoothed his bedspread, and then took the books down, author by author. Right now they were arranged alphabetically, but, obviously, the better way was chronologically. The real question, which he hadn't yet answered in his own mind, was if they were chronological, should the chronology cross national boundaries or remain within a particular nation, and was a nation the same thing as a culture? Another detail concerned translations. At this point, Henry only read French and German. Granny Mary had given him some German books—the three Wallenstein plays by Friedrich Schiller, a well-read copy of *Die Leiden des jungen Werthers* and another of *Faust,* a book called *Das Erdbeben in Chili,* by Heinrich von Kleist that Henry had not been able to get through (nor had anyone else, it looked like). There was also a missal and a book of lieder. Of course, there were no German books to buy anywhere anymore, and Henry didn't dare ask for them at the library. He had only two French books, *Madame Bovary* and *Les Trois Mousquetaires,* which his French teacher, Madame Hoch, had given him, both in Bibliothèque de la Pléiade editions. He was her favorite student. These books, the

German and the French, he set against the end of the bookcase. Once he had done that, he decided to arrange the translations chronologically by author, and chronologically within authors.

The authors he had most of were Charles Dickens, Robert Louis Stevenson, and Wilkie Collins, but he also had a book of all of Shakespeare's plays, which he had read from cover to cover in the winter, without, he was willing to admit, understanding much. They had read *Twelfth Night* and *Much Ado About Nothing* at school, and they were due to read *Hamlet* in eleventh grade. He liked *Hamlet* okay. He set the Shakespeare book on the shelf above *Les Trois Mousquetaires*. The plays he had liked were the one called *Measure for Measure,* and another one called *Macbeth*. They were easy to follow, and what happened in them was kind of like what happened in junior high school.

As he placed the books on the shelves, rather happy with his arrangement, he wondered what he should do with the books he had stolen from the library. The evidence that they were from the library was right there on the binding, and obviously he could not cut the binding, which would deface them—he had already tried, unsuccessfully, to remove the numbers by erasing them, and even dabbing them with a little alcohol, but to no effect. The stolen books were under his bed, and they were his favorites—that's why they were stolen, and he didn't think anyone at school missed them. If there was another high-school kid in Usherton, at least in North Usherton, who gave a damn about *The History of Tom Jones, a Foundling,* a translation from the French of *Père Goriot,* a translation from the Russian of *Oblomov,* and another of *Dead Souls,* and a version in the original (which Henry could not make head or tail of) of *Beowulf,* Henry could not figure out who that would be. These books he had found on his own, wandering around the stacks, and none of them had been checked out since before the war. They were dusty and stiff, and Henry felt that he had rescued them. Except for *Beowulf,* he had read them all straight through, staying up late every night (and until morning for *Tom Jones*). They possessed him, and since he had stolen them rather than checking them out, those who did not miss them also did not know where they were. There was the remote possibility that Mama would find them, but Henry kept his own room neat, made his own bed every day, and gave Mama every appearance of total candor and no reason to pry.

Now he sat down on his bed and looked at the shelves. He liked the effect. Orderly, with books running left to right, like print. The shelves were not even or balanced, the way Mama would like them, and they had no doodads in place of books, something Mama also preferred. To the right, they had varying stretches of empty space, to be filled by more books, books that would be interleaved with the ones he already had. It was lovely, and gave him a wonderfully hopeful feeling about leaving the farm and seeing the world. Washington or San Francisco? The choice made him run his index finger back and forth over the scar under his lip. If he kept working as Dan Crest's stock boy, which he had done now since Christmas, he could earn his ticket to one or the other, his choice, but he couldn't for the life of him decide what his choice would be. Eloise was his favorite relative, wiry and funny and not so gapingly naïve as Lillian, but Washington was closer to France, England, and Germany. Once you got there, you might just step across. There was always that person, man or woman or fairy or monster, older or younger, or ageless, who would come up to you and ask you for a favor, or offer you a choice, and the reward would be your dearest wish. What was the name of that story Lillian had told him before he could read? "Lucky Hans." It was a cross between "Little Red Riding Hood" and "Puss in Boots"—the boy sets out through the forest, and since he has forgotten his napkin full of food, he gets very hungry. Pretty soon, he sees a small cabin, and the door is open, so he goes inside, calling out, "Hello! Hello!" A voice from the inner room calls out, "Come help me, my child!" And the boy tiptoes into the inner room. In the bed is a giant wolf, his mouth full of fangs and dripping with slobber, and as he sees Hans, he licks his lips. But Hans says, "What can I do for you?" And the wolf says, "Feel my brow." Hans is terrified that the wolf will bite his arm off, but he reaches out and strokes the wolf on the head. At that moment, the wolf gives a tremendous howl and leaps from the bed, and Hans thinks that he is going to be eaten, but instead the wolf changes into a prince, and the prince snaps his fingers, and the cabin becomes a castle, and Hans finds himself in a tower, looking out over the forest. It is a beautiful view, and all of it belongs to the prince, who asks Hans what he wants as his reward, and Hans asks for an old horse and a piece of gold, so he can see the world. The prince thinks this is a very small reward, but it is all Hans wants, so the prince makes sure that every time he spends the gold it is returned to him, and every time he saddles the old horse it grows younger. At the end of Hans's life, after he has seen (and this was Lillian's list) "China, Russia, Nashville, Chicago, the North Pole, Germany, London, and Florida," he comes back to the castle and lives in his room and eats tapioca pudding every day. Well, thought Henry, it could happen. You just had to decide—San Francisco, or Washington.

LILLIAN AND ARTHUR'S NEW HOUSE had two stories, in Woodley Park. There were three bedrooms, and they had fashioned a nursery for little Debbie out of the big closet in their room, so, when he visited, Frank had the back of the house to himself. He was almost asleep when he awoke with a violent start to find Arthur standing above him.

"Don't shoot me," whispered Arthur.

"I'm not armed," grumbled Frank.

"You wouldn't bring a gun into a house with children."

"I have," said Frank, "but not this time."

Arthur sat on the bed. The fluorescent hands on the clock read a quarter past midnight. Frank wiggled his shoulders, stilled his breathing, and sat up. Arthur offered him a cigarette and said, "Let's go for a walk."

Frank threw off the covers. Going for a walk with Arthur was always interesting.

They went down the stairs and out the kitchen door, which opened onto a nicely fenced yard (the reason they had chosen this house) and an alley (the other reason they had chosen this house—Arthur always liked an escape route). They turned right down the alley, toward a less traveled and not very well-lit cross street. Arthur paused once to look at the house. The light above the kitchen porch was on, but every other window was dark. The outdoors was a symphony of summer odors—dust and grass, roses. Layered under this was auto exhaust and fertilizer—Arthur's neighborhood was full of ambitious lawns.

It took Arthur about half a block to stop talking about the kids (Debbie was such a good sleeper, and Timmy was climbing the stairs and going right back down—he was careful but bold, a perfect combination) and ask Frank if he wanted to be fixed up with someone, a nice girl about his own age, good figure, said to be lots of fun, and fairly well known to be fast. "Who does she work for?" said Frank.

"She draws her paycheck from Justice. Who she works for is for you to find out."

"Is that right?" said Frank, in a tone of satisfaction.

"It's just a hunch," said Arthur, "and you're the man to follow it out. What happened was, last month, George Kennan was driving down U Street, and he had to stop for the streetcar at Fourteenth. A guy who got off the streetcar was someone he knew, a fellow from the Soviet embassy to the United Nations, named Valentin Gubitchev. These days, he works for the UN, as a translator, I think. Kennan recognized him and wondered what he was doing in D.C. He followed the streetcar down Fourteenth. A woman got off at Pennsylvania that Kennan thought he recognized, and when he got home, he realized that he did recognize her as someone he'd seen at the Justice Department. He even remembered her boss. So he sent her boss a message referring to a newly discovered source of uranium in Tunisia, a place where there is no uranium, and pretty soon, our own agents were picking up attempts on the part of the Soviets to find out who was mining uranium in Tunisia. She had handed it over. There was no other way for them to get that information."

Frank laughed. They had come to a park, and Arthur turned right along the sidewalk that skirted the darkness of the grass and trees.

"All you have to do is date her for a while. There is no reason for this girl to be a spy. She has no history of communist sympathies. Is she sleeping with this Russian guy? Is she giving him stuff because she's sleeping with him, or is he sleeping with her because she's giving him stuff? Or what? I'm telling you, it's like, if this girl can be a spy, then anyone can be a spy. We got plenty of suspicious characters who did this or that in the thirties and through the war, and believed something or other. But this gal, she has no reason at all."

"Arthur, am I being hired?"

"No, Frank. You are exercising your favorite hobby. You like pretty girls. Pretty girls like you. And I am curious. The thing is, guys that I work with are always running out and doing crap. Hillenkoetter will be a sitting duck for these guys. They want to start a war in Greece, they want to start a war in Italy. They believe everything they hear, as long as it gives them a reason to start a war. I'm not saying old Joe Stalin isn't a bastard. I'm not saying there aren't spies everywhere and commies in every broom closet—maybe there are. But if I knew something, I could do something."

"But you don't know what."

"But I don't know what."

Monday morning, Frank sent a telegram to his boss in Dayton, saying that he was down with the flu and would be home in a week. The girl's name was Judy—Frank wouldn't let Arthur tell him the last name—and the only other thing he knew about her was what she looked like (Arthur gave him a copy of her Justice Department ID photo). Frank followed her for two days, at such a distance that he started having the feeling that he was going to shoot her. He found out where her apartment was (Georgetown), where she shopped for groceries (not far from Lillian's), where she shopped for shoes, where she bought cigarettes and magazines. He followed her to a movie (*Life with Father*), and saw that no one met her there. She met someone for a drink, but afterward they went their separate ways. She turned out her bedroom light at half past ten on Monday, ten after eleven on Tuesday. She left her apartment building at 7:47 a.m. on Tuesday, and eight on the dot on Wednesday. Most important, she ate lunch at the same spot on Monday and Tuesday—on a bench to the west of the Navy Memorial. Frank was there when she arrived on Thursday, sitting with his egg-salad sandwich and his devil's-food cupcake and his Pepsi (she liked Pepsi). She paused for a moment, then, evidently deciding that he was harmless, sat down at the other end of the bench.

He gave her a sidelong glance. Up close, she was more buxom than he'd thought. Her face was one of those that looked plain sometimes and pretty sometimes. His assessment was that he was better-looking than she was, so he turned and gave her a big smile. She moved her handbag closer to her hip. He said, "Thanks."

She didn't say anything. He relaxed against the back of the bench, and pretended to doze off. She then relaxed, too, and began to eat her sandwich. She also had an apple—a pippin, Frank thought, from the rough skin. Four or five people passed—how many Frank couldn't really tell, once his eyes were closed. He counted down—three, two, one—and then sat up, looked at his watch, muttered, "Oh, damn!"

He leapt from the bench and ran toward 7th Street. His wallet fell from his pocket, and landed on the grass in front of the bench. As he disappeared around the corner of the Navy Memorial, he heard her shout, "Hey! Hey, you!" He peeked back at her just long enough to see that she was standing there with her arm out, holding his wallet in the air. Then, thinking he was gone, she opened it. Frank turned away. Part of the pleasure in this was seeing what she would do now.

He had put $113 in it—enough for someone who had a job and a non-criminal life, perhaps especially a woman, to hesitate over keeping. It also had the driver's license supplied to him (Francis Burnett) by Arthur, a library card, and an empty addressed envelope (with a list of groceries on the back) that had Arthur and Lillian's address on it. Arthur and Lillian were taking Timmy and Debbie to Charlottesville to visit his father. The house was his for two days.

She showed up about six. It was dark, and Frank had left the porch light on. He also made sure that the chair where he had been "reading a book" was well lit, that his martini was sitting on the side table beside the chair, that—a wonderful touch, in Frank's opinion—chicken soup had been warmed on the range. He came to the door in bare feet, with his shirt unbuttoned at the collar and his sleeves rolled up. Just before he opened the door, he ran his hand through his hair. When he opened the door and said, "Yes?" he beamed at her. She could not help smiling back. She held out his wallet. He took it, did not open it, said, "You were sitting on the bench! I noticed you. You were worried I'd steal your bag."

She blushed.

He said, "Come on in."

1948

⟨∾⟩

JUDY WAS MAKING HIM her special red velvet cake for his birthday, and they were having it for breakfast. She set a slice—bright red with white icing—beside his fried egg, and said, "Happy birthday, baby." Then she put her hands on her hips. "It's Hoover's birthday, too. But I don't hold that against you, personally."

She sat down. Her egg was soft-boiled, sitting in an egg cup—it made him uneasy to watch her eat it. This is what she knew: That he worked in Ohio and came to Washington every month for four days (that was fine with her—she didn't want him or anyone around all the time, anyway, she hated kids and was not the marrying kind); that he used to stay with his sister when he was in Washington, but now stayed with her. That he had served in North Africa, Italy, and the south of France. That he didn't care about politics one way or the other and wouldn't talk about it (a relief—all day at the office, all she heard was politics). That he grew up on a farm somewhere (she had never traveled west of Harrisburg, Pennsylvania, or south of Asheville, North Carolina, so her idea of where was hazy at best). That when they went to the Smithsonian, he preferred the anthropological exhibits to the historical ones. That he had been to New York City and New Jersey on the way to and from Europe, and he would go back with her sometime to see where she had grown up. That he read *The Saturday Evening Post* and sometimes *Time,* but nothing more taxing than that. That he didn't know the name of the secretary of state or the governor of Iowa, at least right off the top of his head. She thought this was hysterically funny. He also didn't know that a woman named Frances Hodgson Burnett had written a famous children's book, one of her favorites, called *The Secret Garden*.

She said, "What kind of birthday cakes did you have as a child?"

"My mother is a great believer in angel food."

"Ugh. So dry!" She leaned across the table and kissed him.

"Once in a while, a pound cake with burnt-sugar icing."

What she didn't know was that this was their last morning together. Frank didn't think she would mind terribly. He was going to say that he had decided to get engaged to a girl in Dayton. Supposedly, her name was Margaret, and they had been dating off and on for a year. That part would be insulting, but only insulting. After breakfast, when she got on the streetcar to go to the Justice Department, he was going to meet Arthur and give him his last report. Arthur was going to take notes, and then that would be that.

He didn't like the cake much, so he concentrated on his toast and the last of his egg, which was good—she knew how to get the edges crispy. They were fairly well suited to one another, neither capable of much in the way of passion. He had tried a couple of things over the two months since they'd started sleeping together—kind words, expressions of fondness (though not quite love). A couple of times, he had pinned her shoulders to the bed and not let her get up, just long enough to make her feel trapped and scare her a bit, but that didn't arouse her, either. He'd grabbed her wrist and twisted her arm behind her one time. After that, he didn't hear from her for two weeks, so he called to apologize and said he was drunk. In short, she was not susceptible as far as he could tell—she didn't even like gifts much. Two things he'd brought her—some Arpège and a couple of pairs of hose—she had exchanged for Chanel N° 5 and a bra. She was a practical young woman. Frank liked her.

She set the dishes in the sink while Frank shaved, and then they got dressed. It was just before eight when they stepped into the street. She put her arm through his. The streetcar stop was two blocks away. At first they walked in silence; then she said, "I hate having to go to the office today. It's supposed to be a holiday."

"Why are you going to the office?"

"I should have done some straightening up and file sorting before this, but I didn't. What are you doing?"

"Going back to Dayton."

She halted suddenly. "You are? You didn't tell me that."

He didn't say anything. When they had walked a few more paces, he said, "Judy, I'm not coming back."

She took her arm out of his.

It only took about five minutes. When she got onto the streetcar, she looked back at him. He smiled, and waved. He had described "Margaret." Fortunately, Judy had never met Lillian, so she didn't know he was describing Lillian. As he walked to where he was meeting Arthur, he thought that maybe this was the best relationship he'd ever had—mild and easy. Even so, he was glad it was over.

When he found Arthur, he did what he had to do to put him in the proper mood. He said, "So—how're my nephew and my niece?" If he asked, they could get it over with.

"Debbie took a bit of egg for breakfast. She liked it. She smacked her lips after she ate it." Arthur laughed. "But Timmy wouldn't sit up to the table at all. He got Lillian to set his plate on the floor, and then he got down on his hands and knees and ate like a dog."

"You're joking, right?"

Arthur shook his head.

"My folks must never hear about this."

Arthur laughed. "And he's wearing his cowboy outfit today. Canvas chaps, six-guns, and all."

Frank could only shake his head.

Arthur thought the best place for talking about Judy was the observation deck of the Washington Monument, and at nine, they were the first on the elevator, though because it was a holiday they weren't the only ones. They stood by the window overlooking the Tidal Basin, which was not frozen, but frosty, and watched the cars cross the 14th Street Bridge until the crowd got back on the elevator. Arthur said, "Slow but sure, right?"

"She's in the office today. She says she's getting organized. But it is a holiday, and no one else will be there."

"Okay," said Arthur.

"She answered the phone twice last evening. Once at eight and once at eight-twenty-one. She didn't converse either time. The second call, I wandered into the hallway, and I heard her say, 'Sorry. No one here by that name.'" Arthur wrote down the times. Frank said, "Still no discussion of politics, ever. When my aunt and her husband were commies in Chicago before the war, it never stopped. Never. They couldn't help themselves. I've never heard Judy use a single phrase, not even 'working class' or 'imperialist.' Not even 'bourgeois.' I don't think she knows what the Lumpenproletariat is. She went to New York for Christmas."

"Gubitchev was there around Christmas."

"When I asked her if she wanted to go to a production of *The Nutcracker,* she said she had to go to New York. I said I already had the tickets, could she postpone her trip? She said I could stay in her apartment."

"Did you look around?"

"Of course. But I didn't find a thing. Nothing in Russian, not even a translation of a Russian novel."

"I do not get it," said Arthur.

"She hates Hoover," said Frank. "Remember Melvin Purvis?"

Arthur nodded.

"I mean, she's my age, why would she care, we were kids. But I think she really hates Hoover. A month or so ago, she was furious that he had told one of the other women she had an ass like a mule and her face was twice as bad. The woman started to cry, and Hoover threw a wad of paper at her. Judy couldn't stop talking about that one."

"He is a jerk," said Arthur.

"I think if there's someone Hoover is after, then she thinks that person is by definition innocent, so whatever she's giving Gubitchev is somehow going to save that person. I think she thinks Hoover has crossed some line, and somehow she can get him punished. He's a tyrant. It's a vendetta."

Arthur stared at him, no longer taking notes. "Did he fuck her?"

"Not in a million years. But he offended her somehow."

"Uncle Joe is the real tyrant."

"But Hoover is the tyrant close at hand." Frank went on, "Well, she gets worked up about it, but why she then decides to pass secrets, if she does, I don't know."

As the elevator door opened again, Arthur said, "Not everyone has the same idea about a better world."

Frank replied, "Some people don't ever think about a better world."

ON HIS FIFTY-THIRD BIRTHDAY, Walter went to the doctor without telling Rosanna. He had cleaned the barn and trimmed the Osage orange, and, truthfully, now that they had no animals, the farm work wasn't much this time of year. You had to get out the equipment and make sure it was in good repair, but if you had put it away in good repair and oiled it and lubed it, which Walter always did, there was not likely to be much of a change through the months of cold. This year they had 500 acres to plant—140 of their own, 180 at the Fredericks', 100 for his father, and 80 for Rosanna's father. Joe was planting clover on his place and on part of the Fredericks' place. About a third of Otto's fields and a third of Wilmer's fields were going to lie fallow, which was a good thing, because Walter didn't like the idea of planting almost eight hundred acres. Even though planting both corn and soybeans stretched out the season somewhat, it was a backbreaking chore, and Walter didn't care as much for backbreaking chores as he once had—yes, sheep were a pain in the neck, and chickens were irritating, and when you were milking cows, you were always about two seconds away from some sort of accident, if only getting smacked in the face by a frozen tail. His old love of horses had subsided once he saw how "tractable" tractors were. But the place had been lively, hadn't it? He'd been running around, tearing his hair, never knowing how young he was or how good he had it. One thing he liked about Joe these days, though he didn't say a word about it, was that Joe knew what he was missing. He was a strong kid (young man now, really—he was twenty-six) with an appropriate air of faint melancholy. Rosanna was always saying to him, "What's wrong with you? Cheer up! Times are good!" and then shaking her head when he wasn't around and saying, "He needs to get over Minnie Frederick, is what he needs. She left him behind long ago, at least in her opinion. He's such a sad sack."

"He works hard" was what Walter said.

"Who doesn't?" returned Rosanna. "I need grandchildren in the neighborhood."

Dr. Craddock looked pretty old himself, and maybe, Walter

thought, it was the smoking. When he sat Walter down in his office after examining him, he lit up a Camel, and his fingers trembled when he flicked his ash into the ashtray. His voice was gravelly. "Walter, I'm saying you're about thirty pounds overweight at this point, though. You've gone up from one seventy-eight to one eighty-five in the last year."

Walter said, "I never weighed a hundred fifty after I got into the army. In boot camp, I weighed one fifty-five."

"Well, it's telling on you. Your blood pressure is one eighty over one fifteen, which is pretty dangerous. You're complaining of headaches and not being able to sleep. You say Rosanna gets up in the night and crosses the hall because you're snoring. I don't know that your aches and pains are plain old rheumatism, because there isn't such a thing as plain old rheumatism. You might have some osteoarthritis, or you might have a touch of gout, and if you have that, then you've got to cut back on rich foods and drink, anyway." Dr. Craddock's trembling hand reached toward the ashtray again, and the very long ash dropped on the desk. Craddock was as thin as a rail. He said, "You come back next week, and I'm going to do some more tests on you."

The two of them stood up, and Craddock closed the file as he walked him to the door of the office. He said, "You shouldn't have come on your birthday. It's always more depressing that way. Myself, I don't know whether, when you get to our age, the bad news is you might die or the bad news is that you might live." He stubbed out the cigarette. Walter didn't laugh just then, but he did when he was getting into his truck. He laughed right out loud.

ONE OF THE GREAT REVELATIONS of Joe's life, he thought while he was feeding the rabbits and the two new calves (this year's named Paulette and Patricia), and watching Nat run after Pepper, was soybeans. Before the war, there were farmers who grew soybeans instead of oats—once they were up, you turned the cows out into the field, and they were pretty good pasture. During the thirties, Walter hadn't planted soybeans because he had always expected enough rain to grow the crops he preferred, especially oats. Even that worst year— what was it, '36?—there had been so much snow and ice that Walter had finally rejected planting soybeans. What was he going to get for them? How was he going to harvest and store them? What could you use them for? If you were going to grow beans, then grow beans, was how Walter saw it—pole beans. Soybeans were like oats or clover or alfalfa, but not as useful. Joe, though, loved soybeans. When you planted them, because they were beans, they nitrogenated the soil, and did so much more efficiently than clover. Corn planted in a former soybean field nearly leapt out of the ground. Nor did they care much about rain, either way. The corn could be pale and short, and the beans would be green and thick. Cattle liked them, too. Joe didn't have a herd of milk cows or beef cows anymore, but farmers who did bought all the beans you could grow. Betty and Boop loved them ground up into meal, and beef raised on ground beans, it was said, had a good flavor—not too high for the city slickers.

But the day before, a guy at the feed store in Denby had walked right up to Joe and said, "How are you fertilizing your fields, Mr. Langdon?" And when Joe turned around to see if Walter had walked in, everyone standing there had a laugh.

Joe had been a bit irritated, so he said, "Why is that your business, Mr. . . ."

"Bob Reichardt, Mr. Langdon, from Middletown, down by Burlington. This year we are offering a product that we consider to be revolutionary in American farming."

Joe eased past him, saying only, "There've been a lot of those."

"Hey, Joe," said Mike Hatton, who'd taken over the feed store from his dad, and who Joe knew was pretty up-to-date (they agreed on a few things, including this Lincoln variety of beans). "He's not kidding. That Middletown plant was making TNT during the war. Now they're demobilized." Everyone laughed again.

"I got some pictures," said Bob Reichardt. "Down in the southeast corner of the state, we used it pretty extensively last year. A fellow from Iowa State ran a test. Look at these." He led Joe over to a table Mike had cleared, where he had laid out a set of ten pictures in two rows, right next to each other. Five fields, each photograph taken from a bit of a distance on the right side, and then close-ups of corn plants on the left. In the plant pictures, someone had set calendar pages between the rows—July 1, July 15, July 31, August 15,

August 31. The differences were clear, and so startling that Joe was instantly skeptical. The stalks on the right side in the last picture were a third taller than those on the left side, and the ears were bigger, too. The ears looked astonishing. There was one final picture, of two ears side by side, the husks pulled back. The one ear made the other ear look measly by comparison. Bob said, "Same hybrid, same seed stock, same planting date."

Joe stood still.

"You *can* afford it, Joe," said Mike.

"What else are we going to do with the nitro?" said Bob. "It's a gift from God, you ask me. Swords hammered into plowshares right before our very eyes. I'm not kidding. You know when I got back from Europe?"

"No," said someone.

"At Christmas."

"What were you doing all this time?"

"Delivering food. That's what I was doing. And they needed more than I had. This is the miracle that's going to feed them."

Bob looked like he really meant it.

Joe said, "I heard about those ammonium-nitrate pellets. I read about those."

"My dad wouldn't have those in the warehouse," said Mike. "Wasn't there an explosion on a ship down in Texas? About a year ago? I remember the paper said that was ammonium nitrate. Another ship exploded, too, and—"

Bob said, "And two planes fell out of the sky. Yes. Terrible loss of life. I think five or six hundred people. Yes, I have to admit that some of that cargo was manufactured in our plant, and was on the way to France as fertilizer. But we learned our lesson from that. I think everyone did. I have to ask myself, why did they let all those folks stand there gawking? The sea was boiling and the ship was expanding like a bubble."

Joe had to admire the way Bob Reichardt jumped in front of the story and seized it for his own. Bob exclaimed, "Yes! It was like an A-bomb. People said that, and you can see it. Some folks literally vanished in that explosion, the way they did in Japan. Houses and factories were leveled, and they felt it in Houston. I was in France at the time, and we heard about it there, because it was a French ship. The captain made a big mistake, but he wasn't familiar with our product—"

Joe said, "No, thanks." Men were beginning to walk away, with that uncomfortable look on their faces that the residents of Denby got when they thought they might be acting disagreeable. Bob said, "But that's not what I'm selling. I told you we learned some lessons. Now we've got a new product—that's the one we put in the fields for the pictures. No explosions, I promise." He paused. "That's not to say that the product is without dangers, but 'manageable' is the word. You fellows are used to managing, you sure are."

But people still walked away. Joe knew perfectly well that Rosanna was just the person to make a direct connection between the famous explosion in Texas and a potential disaster on the farm. He thought about it in the night, the way he sometimes did when Nat woke him up with his rustling, and he decided to stick with beans for nitrogenating his soil.

IT WASN'T OFTEN that Frank was taken by surprise, but maybe the right place for it was Chicago. He was walking down Wacker, about to turn onto Michigan, and he was simultaneously thinking three thoughts—that it was a cool day for September in Chicago, that the L above him reminded him of his ramblings around the city, and whatever happened to Mort? Mort, he had thought when they were in school, could take anyone—just clock him on the chin, and down he went. Mort must have survived the war. Of the others, he'd heard that Terry had been killed in Belgium, Bob had ended up down in Joliet for armed robbery, and Lew had come back from the Pacific, gotten married, and gone to work for the *Daily News*—on the presses, was that it? But he hadn't heard a thing about Mort. Just then, a body pressed against him and a hand slipped into his, and he nearly jumped out of his skin. He spun around, and here was Hildy Bergstrom. She was wearing a narrow-brimmed straw hat and a floaty flowered dress that revealed her shoulders. Her hand slipped out of his and went to her necklace, which was made of pearls. She said, "I've been following you for a block. I work at Marshall Field's, over there." She waved her arm. "How are you?"

She was good at it still, Frank thought—talking and smiling long enough to give him some cover while he reorganized himself and remembered he was in Chicago, and not, say, the European Theater of Operations. He said, "Hildy! Damn!" And she said, "But I shifted to my middle name, which is 'Andrea.' I don't think you can work at Marshall Field's as a Hildy unless you are about eighty." She looked good, Frank thought.

Frank said, "Where are you going?"

"I was supposed to be heading back to my office, but it's such a nice day that I thought I would walk around a block or two. Where are you going?"

"Back to my hotel. I was at a meeting."

"Where are you living now?"

"Dayton, Ohio. But I think I'm moving."

"Where?"

"Anywhere."

Hildy—Andrea—lit up. "Really? You're not in the tire business?"

"Not if I can help it."

Hildy slipped her hand into his again and pressed against his side. She said, "Let's move to New York."

Frank said, "Okay."

But first they went to Iowa.

She was really quite good at assuaging the suspicions of her parents—"I nearly choked on my toast when I saw the letter from Frank. We've been corresponding now for, what, about six months, darling? Just flying visits. I didn't want to say anything. You knew I wasn't really serious about Dan, I told you that at Christmas. Yes, I admit, I like to keep things to myself, it's a bad habit. I'm nearly thirty, Frank was always my first love, and now he's my true love— isn't that right, darling? Time to settle down. A girl can't spend her life on clothes forever and ever, you said that yourself, Mama. I can catch up to Sven in two years if I have two sets of twins. Well, of course I'm joking, Daddy." He let her do the talking.

In seven years, she had become the most sophisticated woman Frank had ever known, and he was a little intimidated; even the women he'd dated in Washington, including Judy, were frumpy by comparison. But she did it so naturally and quickly that he was fascinated rather than put off by it. Girdle, stockings, slip, blouse, skirt, jacket, hat, hairpins, makeup, heels, coat, corsage, gloves: she passed through the process automatically, usually talking, and then she was ready to go, and off they went. This led him to believe that she would pass through the complementary removal process as easily, though she hadn't done that yet with him. It was amusing to think about, and exciting, too. She intimidated her parents, and when he told her father that he planned to marry her, her father said to Frank, "You'd better have a good job, then, *min kjære gutt,* and steady promotions."

Frank paused and then said, "I do understand that she could get expensive, sir." He hoped the old man knew he was joking.

He said, "Ah, but her teeth are good and she's healthy. Never been ill a day in her life."

Frank thought Lars Bergstrom and Walter would get along quite well.

Rosanna seemed more suspicious than any of the other parents. She kept back when Hildy—Andrea—Andy—first got out of the car, and her facial expression didn't soften. But Andy was good with that, too. When Rosanna got up and went into the kitchen for the teapot, Andy followed her, and after they had talked, out they came, Rosanna carrying the pot and Andy carrying the pie, and Claire, who had come in the back door, clutching Andy by the skirt. When they had set the things down on the table, Andy said to Claire, "Come with me, honey. I brought you something." And they went out the front door. Claire came back in with two barrettes in her hand, silver filigree and shaped like bows. She showed them to Rosanna, who said, "Well, maybe these will keep your hair out of your face, Claire. For goodness' sake, Andrea, it's like her hair grows straight up in all directions. It will not lie flat for two seconds."

As well dressed as she was, she fit into the front room of the farm. She relaxed against the back of the sofa. She ran her hand over Rosanna's afghan, she admired the view out the windows, she said that the corn was as high as she'd ever seen it.

"You mean prices, right?" said Walter, and she nodded. When Frank carried her bag up to Lillian's old room, she did not recoil at the endless pink, but said, "How cute!" She admired Henry's bookshelves and said, "Name one that you really want."

Henry said, "*Illusions perdues.* In French."

"I'm sure that's expensive," said Rosanna.

"They always are," said Frank.

But they loved her. They considered her a prize. Frank watched as she deployed her charms, knowing every moment that he himself was the prize, as far as Andy was concerned. It was not only that he was flattered and entertained, though—he was also fascinated and seduced. Women were supposed to be mysterious, and most of the girls he knew did their best, but Andy truly was mysterious, in the way that only someone you had once known as a girl and now knew as a woman could be; he missed what she had been, and therefore loved it, and he marveled at what she had become, and so loved that as well.

ROSANNA COULD NOT HAVE SAID that she enjoyed making Thanksgiving dinner for twenty-three people (a turkey, a standing rib roast, and a duck that Granny Mary brought; ten pounds of mashed potatoes, and that not enough; five pies; sweet potatoes; more stuffing than could be stuffed; all the Brussels sprouts left in the garden, though they were good after the frost). She could not say that Lillian had control of those children, who were underfoot every time you took a step, though they were good-natured, to be sure. Henry scrutinized the dishes of food as though he were being asked to partake of roadkill, at least until the pies were served, and Claire burst into tears for no reason at all, but when they all had their plates in front of them, and a few deep breaths were taken, and first Andrea, and then Granny Elizabeth, and then Eloise said, "This looks delicious," she began to have a strange feeling. She should have sat down—Joe, who was sitting beside her, moved her chair in a bit—but she didn't want to sit down, or eat, at all (what with tasting everything, she wasn't hungry); she just wanted to stand there and look at them as they passed the two gravy boats and began to cut their food. It couldn't have happened, she thought. They couldn't have survived so many strange events. Take your pick—the birth of Henry in that room over there, with the wind howling and the dirt blowing in and her barely able to find a rag to wipe the baby's mouth and nose. Take your pick—all of them nearly dying of the heat that summer of '36. Take your pick—Joey falling out of the hayloft, Frankie driving the car to Usherton, Frankie disappearing into the Italian Campaign,

Frankie, for Heaven's sake, living in a tent all through college. Take your pick—Walter falling into the well (yes, she had gotten that out of him one day during the war, when he said, "Remember when I fell into the well?" and she said, "What in the world are you talking about?" and he blushed like a girl). Take your pick—Granny Mary with her cancer, but still walking around. Take your pick—Lillian running off with a stranger who turned out to be a clown, but a lovable one, and nice-looking, and weren't Timmy and Debbie just darling? Normally, Rosanna took credit for everything, good and bad (her eye flicked to the doorway, the very spot where Mary Elizabeth had slipped; it might be happening right this minute, that's how vivid it was), but now she thought, this was too much. She could not have created this moment, these lovely faces, these candles flickering, the flash of the silverware, the fragrances of the food hanging over the table, the heads turning this way and that, the voices murmuring and laughing. She looked at Walter, who was so far away from her, all the way at the other end of the table, having a laugh with Andrea, who had a beautiful suit on, navy blue with a tiny waist and white collar and cuffs. As if on cue, Walter turned from Andrea and looked at Rosanna, and they agreed in that instant: something had created itself from nothing—a dumpy old house had been filled, if only for this moment, with twenty-three different worlds, each one of them rich and mysterious. Rosanna wrapped her arms around herself for a moment and sat down.

1949

∽

I⎯T WAS ONE THING to decide to move to New York, and another
thing to find a job, but in the end, Arthur had an idea. What had
Frank been doing for two years if not reading those German papers
and passing them on to American companies? Arthur heard about
a fellow at Grumman Aircraft who needed an assistant to help him
organize and acquire government contracts. The company was in
Valley Stream, New York, and as for Andrea (whom Arthur liked
very much), Bonwit's was eighteen miles away, and they could live
on Long Island. Arthur told Frank confidentially that no one lived
in the city anymore—Manhattan was a nightmare with kids, much
more difficult than Washington.

Lillian put on the wedding, a Christmas affair, small but stylish. Andy's brother, Sven, and his wife and three children; the older
Bergstroms; Walter, Rosanna, Joe, Henry, and Claire all came on
the train to D.C. and stayed a week—the Bergstroms in a hotel and the
Langdons falling all over one another at Lillian's. Joe was out of the
house early every day. He wanted to see everything, and he covered
so much ground that no one offered to go with him, but Frank had to
admire the way he did it—he got himself a map of the city, divided it
into six parts, reconnoitered, and did a section each day. He also tried
new foods—Italian on Saturday, Chinese on Sunday, German on
Monday, French on Tuesday, back to American on Wednesday, then

Italian again on Thursday. What he liked best, he told Frank, was the lasagna, the minestrone, and the chow mein, with a nice crescent roll thrown in from time to time. Henry went to the Smithsonian and the Library of Congress, and Lillian and Rosanna took Claire to Garfinckel's to buy a dress for the wedding, but Rosanna was appalled at the prices there, so they went to Hecht's.

The wedding was Friday morning, the 24th, just a short service—and then the reception was that evening, at Arthur and Lillian's. Andrea had bought her gown at Marshall Field's, 40 percent store discount, and when Frank saw her in it, he almost forgot to say his part, but he did take her, indeed he did. Lillian looked good, too, as the maid of honor, and Timmy carried the ring, and Sven's daughter Marta was the flower girl; she and Debbie wore identical green velvet dresses. Claire wore red. Rosanna was a little insulted that she hadn't been asked to make the cake, but when she saw the one they got from the pâtisserie she changed her mind. Sven was the best man. When he gave his speech, he talked about how a man's greatest work in life was having a family. His kids sat quietly through everything, stair-step blond heads, big blue eyes. Timmy wore his toy holster and his toy six-guns the entire time, and no one, not even Rosanna, said a word. Lillian told him that if he drew on anyone the guns would be taken away. He understood perfectly. Frank wondered if the Bergstroms and the Langdons could be successfully hybridized, but he said nothing and hoped for the best.

It was February 1 when Arthur stopped by Frank's apartment in Floral Park for breakfast. He ate an English muffin and a couple of scrambled eggs. When Andy asked how he had managed to get there so early, he only told Frank and Andy that Timmy had climbed to the top of the living-room bookshelves to regain a toy truck that had been taken away from him, and had managed to climb down, but not before Lillian came in from outside and saw him about five shelves up. Frank laughed. "What did she do?"

"Well, she's learned by this time to stand there with her hands over her eyes and let him do it himself. If she doesn't, he'll try again when he gets the chance. I hear you were exactly the same way."

Frank glanced across the breakfast table at Andy and said, "Maybe it skips a generation."

As they neared the bus stop, Frank saw that the bus was pulling up. Arthur took his elbow and kept him moving. The next bus was in twenty minutes. Arthur headed across the street toward the park, even though the morning was bitter cold, and Frank followed.

The quarry this time was a very wealthy man, and Frank, and especially Andrea, were perfect for this. Arthur would get them invited to certain parties; Andrea would dazzle everyone and bit by bit Frank would get to know the man. He was a little older than Frank, and had spent the war as a bomber pilot, done good service, was now running an art gallery. He was very wealthy—had money, married money—and was very well traveled. That was what interested Arthur. If this fellow was not a courier for the Reds, then they were missing out on an excellent opportunity. But if he had a code name, there was no hint of it. If the transcripts of espionage traffic between Washington and Moscow from the war were complete, this fellow was clean. "He shouldn't be clean," said Arthur. "He was friends with the others. Good friends."

"What others?" said Frank.

"You'll find out," said Arthur.

"Will I?" said Frank.

"Maybe."

"Are you going to pay me this time?"

"Not in cash. I can't pay you in cash, because it's not part of my job to ask you to do this. I'm just asking you because you're good and you enjoy it." He stopped walking and looked Frank in the eye. "We're about to arrest someone, you know."

They stared at one another for a long minute, then Arthur said, "Look, brother, one side of my government agency is out of control—I would say nuts, though only right here, in the middle of the park in the howling wind, would I say that. They have all the money and all the excitement, and we have paper and pencils and some stuff to read and think about. The slower we go, the crazier they get. My seven dwarves and I are reading, reading, reading, twelve hours a day. When Lillian and the kids go to bed, I work for another three hours. How I am going to impregnate her again, I have no idea."

They started walking back toward the bus stop.

"But you helped me gain respectability around the agency with our last adventure, and as a result, when a certain fellow agent suggested that we go ahead and hire forty-two ex-Nazis to infiltrate the

Polish government, I was able to say that I didn't think this was a good idea. When your former quarry is arrested, it will be a nice distraction, and considerable resources will be devoted to hounding her. The very handsome gentleman that you will now befriend will cause an even greater brouhaha, so I pray to the Lord that he is busy as a bee sending information to someone in Moscow code-named, say, Binky. And"—Arthur gave him a little poke in the ribs with his elbow—"if he's on the up-and-up, you'll have gotten to know one of the biggest boys on the block."

By the time the bus came, Frank was ready to begin, and he only half understood why. He had meant to be paid. Was it that Arthur had a way about him, knew how to draw him in, knew how to say "Moscow" in a certain uneasy way (and was it that he owed Arthur a little something for the translation job and now the Grumman job—Arthur never made that argument, but maybe that was because he thought Frank's obligations were obvious)? Or was it that the adventure itself was the pleasure, that this was his path out of routine domesticity, back to his years in the tent, his years in the war, his years making trouble as a matter of course? Whatever it was, Arthur seemed to have his number.

THEY WERE DIFFERENT from the way they had been in college. It was almost enough to make Frank believe in that thing called maturity. He didn't try to talk to her—he just did talk to her. If she was in the room and he was thinking about something, he expressed it, whatever it was. He remembered Lawrence fondly, of course, but those boys they had been seemed terribly young to him now. He thought of them as little heads peering over the steering wheel of the giant Flying Cloud, their feet barely reaching the pedals. One night, he lay in bed with Andy before falling asleep and talked about Lawrence. Andy said, "You know, that was the first person I ever knew who died. Three of my grandparents were still alive at that point, and my grandfather died in the first war, so I was just so amazed. And I was the one who was supposed to comfort Eunice. I felt like a baby. She ended up comforting me."

"She seemed, I don't know," said Frank, "like she didn't care all that much. I hated her for that."

Andy took a drag on her cigarette and placed it carefully in the ashtray. She turned to him. Frank hadn't meant to say anything about Eunice. That the remark had slipped out was a sign of how different he felt with Andy from how he had with Hildy. She put her hand on his chest. A bright shaft from the streetlight outside slid between the imperfectly closed curtains to light up the top of her head and split her face in two. She said, "Honey, do you think we couldn't tell you were furious with her? But at that point she didn't care all that much for him. She was about to break up with him when he got that infection."

"You said they were going to get married."

"That's what she told me and his parents right then, but later she told me the truth." She took his hand. "Baby, I was fond of Lawrence, but you loved him best." Then she said, "I thought maybe, when you got into the army, you might make another friend like that."

When the storm started a few hours later and woke them both up, she was lying on her back, half uncovered, and Frank was pressed against her, his face in her hair. Thunder must have awakened him, but when the lightning struck, the first thing that he was aware of was her fragrance, a mixture of sleep and the L'Air du Temps he had given her for Valentine's Day. She turned toward him just then, and he was thrilled to the point of disorientation by the smooth weight of her in his arms. He kissed her all over her neck and in her hair, underneath her ears, along the ridge of her shoulders, everywhere. He slipped the straps of her nightgown down her arms while she lifted the elastic of his boxer shorts carefully over his cock. He could not wait to be inside her, Andrea, Andy, Hildy, this woman, that child. For once he needed no encouragement, no reassurance—was that what it was? Whatever it was, it was a relief to simply want her, to find her flesh and her scent and the wave of her hair and the sound of her voice magnetically alluring, first from the front, as usual, and then again from behind, which she was not quite prepared for but found ravishing. And then they were awake until the alarm rang, and as he turned it off, Andy said, "Well, my parents never told me about this sort of thing."

"What was that?" said Frank.

"That you could go to bed married and wake up remarried." After that, they got up and performed their usual routine, but, as if by common consent, they said nothing practical, made no plans. They had gone back to being strangers, and it was the most romantic thing Frank had ever known.

JAMES HAGGARD UPJOHN and his wife, Frances Travers Upjohn, were shaking hands in a receiving line at the Metropolitan Museum of Art when Frank first saw them. Frank was standing behind Andy, who had borrowed a Dior gown from a connection she had at Bergdorf's. Frank himself had invested in a tux, and, looking at Jim Upjohn, he suspected that he was going to give the thing plenty of wear. The cocktail party was for an opening, the biggest since the war, of a show of Greek and Roman art. Andy was now three people away from James Upjohn. Now two. Now one. Andy held out her hand, and Upjohn turned from the old lady he had been talking to and raised his eyes. Andy said, "Mr. Upjohn. Thank you so much. Lovely to meet you."

Upjohn's face, which had looked professionally good-natured, shifted through several different expressions just in the time that it took Andy to smile—they were confusion, surprise, pleasure. He said, "Thank you for coming. I'm sure we haven't met before." Frances Travers Upjohn's head swiveled to the right. Andy said, "Of course not. We are new in town. I'm Andrea Langdon, and this is my husband, Frank." Frank held out his hand. Upjohn's grip was brisk and manly—up, down, out. He also gave the tiniest bow, a flattering thing that acknowledged in its half-second of existence that Andy, and therefore Frank, could expect to see more of James Haggard Upjohn, Esq. Frank could not help looking a little extra merry as they proceeded down the line.

The entrance hall at the Met, now decorated with casts of all sorts of famous old statues (Frank recognized the *Winged Victory* and the *Laocoön*), was a far cry from Floral Park, but Frank had prowled all over the museum once Arthur had arranged the invitation. He had memorized the names of pictures and artists (Raphael, Picasso, Maillol), so that he could at least pretend familiarity. He didn't have a terrible eye—standing in front of the Maillol female nude, next to the cast of Aphrodite, he could get interested enough in the similarities so that when Jim Upjohn appeared next to him and spoke, he started a little. Upjohn offered him a smoke. Frank said, "Don't do that. Thanks, though."

Upjohn said, "Who are you two? I've never seen you before."

"Just hicks," said Frank. "Newly arrived in the big city."

"How'd you get into this party?" He said it not suspiciously but with true curiosity, like a kid. If this guy was a spy, Frank thought, he would eat his hat. Frank said, "Andrea knows everyone."

"I would like her to know me."

"That's what they all say," said Frank. "Thank you for stating your business so clearly."

Upjohn grinned. "That isn't my business. Mrs. Upjohn makes sure of that. But in a dull town full of dull people, when new prospects turn up, one gets a little excited."

"Are we still in Des Moines?"

"Even New York is a small town if there are only four hundred respectable folks and half of those have chips on their shoulders."

"I can't imagine you have offended anyone," said Frank.

"I haven't, but I have lots of relatives."

After the cocktails, during the dancing, Upjohn cut in on Frank and Andy twice. Frank went straight over and asked Frances to dance, and he was so good at leading her and spinning her and sweeping her around the room that she squeezed his hand when the music stopped.

Frank reported to Arthur that he had made contact, and that Upjohn would certainly be making a pass at Andy before the month was out.

"Think of it as your patriotic duty," said Arthur.

"I'll try," said Frank.

But the next time they met, at a gallery opening two weeks later, Upjohn followed Frank out into the street when Frank went to get some air, and they gabbed for fifteen minutes. In his report to Arthur, Frank said, "I think he's grooming me for something."

"Did you say anything about Eloise?"

"No. Why Eloise?"

"Well, we're watching her. Maybe they're watching her, too."

"Why are you watching Eloise? She hates Stalin with a passion.

She tells Rosa that Stalin and Mountbatten killed her father. On Halloween, they name two jack-o'-lanterns 'Joe' and 'Lou,' and the day after, they smash them with sticks."

"She talks to Browder. There's a file."

"Well, I guess you know more about her than I do. When I saw her last Thanksgiving, she didn't say a word about the Party. I assumed she'd quit and gone over to Shachtman's Socialists."

"I'm not worried about Eloise. But keep your eye on Upjohn. And—"

"Is there a file on Upjohn?"

"More than one," said Arthur. "It's chaos, all these files. Anyway . . ."

"Anyway what?" said Frank.

"You should be aware that she's been arrested."

Involuntarily, Frank thought of his last breakfast with Judy, the red velvet birthday cake, the look of her face, pale through the window of the streetcar, and maybe more dumbstruck than he had admitted at the time. He said, "How sure are you that she was passing documents?"

"Caught her red-handed in Union Square. Caught Gubitchev, too. She had papers in her purse."

"What papers?"

"Well, that's interesting. Not bomb-making information or anything like that. She spies on us while we spy on them."

Frank said, "Don't tell me any more. I kind of liked her."

"I don't think she knows that you spied on her spying on us spying on them. But if she did, she might enjoy it."

"She did hate Hoover," said Frank.

"Well, he has recorded just about her every move since I made my report, so he has had his revenge."

ON JUNE 11, when Andy talked him into taking her to the Belmont Stakes, they were standing in line at a betting window when the Upjohns came right up to them. Frances Upjohn even kissed Andy on the cheek and said, "I love your suit, darling! Do you have a box?"

And, easy as you please, Andy said, "A box of what?"

They all laughed.

Jim and Frances didn't have a box, either, but they had borrowed one from Frances's cousin, who had racehorses with a trainer named Hirsch Jacobs, right there at Belmont Park, though he had nothing in the big race that day.

The box looked down on the finish line from above, and Andy fit right in, sitting gracefully, half turned toward Frances, with one gloved hand on her knee and the other holding her program and her patent-leather handbag. She was wearing that hat Frank liked. Her skirt swept down from her tiny waist and floated above the ground. Behind her head, the vast emerald infield of the racetrack was seething with men in rolled-up sleeves who had pencils behind their ears and *Racing Forms* in their hands. Frank said, "This must be the biggest lawn in New York."

"You could set the Brooklyn Bridge in there, did you know that?" said Jim.

Jim and Frances peppered them with questions, and seemed gratified to learn that they were poor, that they rented their little apartment in Floral Park, that they had $751 in savings, that Frank worked at Grumman, grubbing for government contracts, that Andy was adept at remaking her clothes to keep them up-to-date, that Frank had seen two and a half years of steady action in the ETO—in the mud in the ETO, not the sky—that Frank had ended up with twenty-six kills (if you counted that German officer), that Frank didn't know how to read the *Racing Form* and had never been to a race before. The oddest conversation, Frank thought, was about farming. Had Frank driven a plow or a harrow? Had he actually castrated a baby hog? How many chickens were in a flock? Did anyone farm with horses anymore? If he, Jim, were to buy a farm, was Pennsylvania better, or Ohio, or Minnesota, or Nebraska? Frank said, "Have you ever thought about this before, Jim?"

Jim shook his head. "I never met a farmer before. I mean, other than a horse breeder who grows tobacco on part of his land." He thought for a moment, then said, "Oh, once I thought of buying an apple orchard in the Catskills." Frank couldn't figure him out.

In the race, Frank bet on Ponder, and Andy bet on Capot. She took home fifty dollars. On the way home (they waited until the Upjohns left, then walked the two miles), Andy declared that she was going to become a racetrack tout, and the fifty dollars was her investment fund. Frank said, "That's not very Norwegian. Did you say your mother's maiden name was Mahaffey?"

"My mother's maiden name was Carlson. But I do believe I've had a visitation." She opened her pocketbook and looked at the money. Frank tightened his arm around her waist, and they walked around the neighborhood until after dark, giggling and joking.

When Frank gave Arthur his final report in September, Arthur agreed with him that Jim Upjohn was a dead end. "He talks too much," said Frank. "He told me that he still gives money to the *Daily Worker* every month, because he just can't bring himself to stop, and then he offered to finance my down payment for a house in Levittown."

"He likes you."

"I think he likes everyone. When we got invited to a party at his house in Darien, there were a hundred people there. I told you I went around chatting everyone up, and everyone had a story of something Jim had given them or bought from them at an inflated price. He reminds me of a friend I had in college."

He reminded Andy of Lawrence, too.

OF COURSE he bumped into Ruben at the racetrack. Where else would Ruben be? Frank and Andy were at the rail, watching a race, and jumping up and down because Andy had a bet on the leader, and when the race was over and they turned around to go cash her ticket, she nearly fell over Ruben, who chortled at her and then noticed Frank. The funny thing he did was hop into the air and grab Frank's hat off his head, saying, "That you, Corporal? That you?"

When Frank introduced Andy to Ruben, he realized that he had completely forgotten Ruben's actual name—he hesitated over it so long that Ruben leaned forward and said to Andy, "Alex Rubino, ma'am. And this is my wife, Patricia De Oro Rubino."

And if Jim and Frances Upjohn were comfortable at Belmont Park up in the clubhouse with Whitneys and Vanderbilts, then Ruben and Patty were equally comfortable down by the rail, nattering on in Italian and Spanish (Patty had been born in Puerto Rico) with Giordanos and Sanchezes. Ruben walked with them to the betting windows, and then showed them his box—not so high up or close to the finish line as where the Upjohns sat, but well used. Ruben was in real estate now. He had used his GI Bill money to get a license. Frank and Andy sat with Ruben and Patty for the last two races. It got a little cold, and Patty put on her mouton coat, which Andy complimented. Yes, it was warm. Yes, it was the newest style. Andy said, "When I first met Frank, he used to shoot rabbits for their skins."

Ruben said, "Yeah, when I knew him, he was shooting things, too."

"Somebody had to do it," said Patty.

They all nodded.

By the end of the last race, it was a little too cold to walk home, so Ruben and Patty gave them a ride in their new Pontiac. It was comfortable, with a wide back seat and plenty of legroom. Frank wasn't sure that they would see the Rubinos again, but after all he got into the habit, as the year drew to a close, of going with Ruben when he looked at lots for sale. "The smaller the better," said Ruben. "Nobody wants a pile anymore. You get one of those big places, like if some old lady has died, and you might as well forget selling it. Nobody wants a basement or an attic, or even a goddamn staircase. The car and the house, they are getting to be about the same size." Frank could see that, he really could.

1950

JOE AND ROSANNA HAD several arguments about the Frederick
house, but Joe didn't take them very seriously, which Rosanna
considered to be a sign that he was getting just as stubborn as Frank.
Rosanna's beef was that Joe took better care of the Frederick house
than he did of his own house. Every time she went to his place (and
why was she bothering? said Joe), there were dishes in the sink,
crumbs on the table, clothes in a heap, beds unmade. Was that how
she had raised him? The barn was cleaner than the house. She found
it especially irritating because he had put in running water, hot running water, and never seemed to use it. He pointed out that he took
a shower every day, which was why he had installed the hot water in
the first place, but what especially got her goat was that he was over
at the Frederick place all the time (not all the time, said Joe), making
sure every last dust mote had been captured and shown the door. The
kitchen sparkled, the floors sparkled, all that oak woodwork sparkled.
Even the windows sparkled, and that was ridiculous, since the blinds
were always drawn, to keep the rugs and furniture from fading. Why
bother, was what she wanted to know. They hadn't heard from Minnie in three or four months, not since Joe sent her a money order for
her share of the corn and beans he had planted on her property. Joe's
side was that it was a nice place, the nicest around, and did she want it

to fall to ruin the way the Grahams' place had after they had to leave? Once a single window was broken, then it was all downhill from there to having to tear the place down, the way they'd had to tear the Graham place down because it got to be such an eyesore.

"You always have a reason," said Rosanna.

"Yup," said Joe, his hand tickling the top of Nat's head. "I always do."

"Well, you'd better contemplate the difference between a reason and an excuse. A reason is its own reward, but an excuse leads to disappointment every time."

Of course, they both knew what she was talking about. The other side of this coin was the way she said, "For goodness' sake, go into town and at least have a soda at the drugstore. You don't have to learn to dance in order to play a song or two on the jukebox." If he did say that he was driving into town, she would say, "Promise me that you will go to one other place besides the feed store."

"How about the garage?"

"When was the last time you spoke to a woman?"

"Yesterday, I asked the operator to put a call through. Her name is Lynn."

"Yes, it is, and she's nice. She's Maggie Birch's youngest niece, and a practical girl if ever there was one."

"I'll tell her you said so the next time I see her."

"Joe, you can't—"

But he snapped his fingers to Nat and walked out of the house. He never allowed her to tell him what he couldn't do.

In the fourteen inches of snow they had, the Frederick house looked like a Christmas card. He had cleared the front steps, but the railings still had frozen little caps all along their length. Once upon a time, Roland Frederick had done an odd thing and painted the house yellow. It was now faded, but it stood out against the snow, bright and inviting, though of course as cold inside as it was outside.

In the letter he got from Minnie saying that she was returning as a replacement for the assistant principal at North Usherton High School, she wrote, "Don't be too impressed. I think my main job is counting heads and overseeing detention. Mrs. Ellington got pregnant, and they can't let the kids see that, so I have a job!" She didn't say that Lois was coming with her, but when she showed up four days later, it was Lois who was driving the car. Joe was well prepared—he had fired up the basement furnace, and Rosanna had made the beds. Lights were on upstairs and down, and the big cubical house shed its welcoming glow in every direction. Minnie would not let him drag her suitcase up the steps outside or the staircase inside. She thanked him by shaking his hand. Her hair was in a bun, and she wore a warm felt hat. But Lois, who was wearing fur-trimmed boots and a fur-trimmed hat, stood back while he carried her bags in. She said, "Oh, you should have seen the dump where we've been living."

"It was not a dump," said Minnie. "It was perfectly respectable and clean."

"And the window of my room looked over an airshaft. I was suffocating."

"There are worse things than airshafts," said Minnie.

"Yes!" asserted Lois. "Crowds!"

Minnie turned to Joe and said, "She thinks ten people is a crowd."

"Isn't it?" said Joe.

Lois walked into the dining room. It was cleared now of Mrs. Frederick's bed and sickroom paraphernalia. Joe and Rosanna had tried to remember how it had once been, and pushed the table and chairs back into some semblance of that. Rosanna had actually waxed the floor. The dining room had always been the nicest room in the house, a paneled and glass-cased showplace where parties were meant to be lit by candles. The house, as Walter pointed out, was a city house shipped to the country for some reason. Lois came back joyful, and said, "Home, sweet home."

Minnie unpinned her hat and set it on a shelf beside the fireplace. She said, "Well, my girl, you'd better figure out something to do here, that's all I've got to say."

"Mama canned and baked and made brandy-soaked peaches and sewed and knitted and embroidered pillowcases. She was always singing to herself and trying things out."

"Sweetheart, you don't know how to do any of those things."

"So I'll learn. Better than bookkeeping."

When Minnie wasn't looking, Lois took Joe's hand and kissed him on the cheek. She also invited Nat in, and let him up on the sofa.

Joe didn't get home until after nine, and when he did get home, he washed his dishes and put them away.

ON THE FIRST OF MAY, Andy got a letter from her mother saying that her mother's uncle Eugen had died, the last person alive during the life of her great-great-uncle Jens. Jens had died in 1890, and had hated all of his living relatives so much that he designated in his will that his estate was to be preserved until they were all "out of the way and could do no further harm," even the babies. The estate, invested in bonds of some sort, had grown as prolifically as the family, and each member of each generation was to get the same amount, twenty-five hundred dollars. Two days after that, Alex Rubino called Frank and asked if he wanted to buy into a house for sale in Elizabeth, New Jersey—well, not really a house, but a whole block. Frank, remembering all those knickknacks that Rubino had picked up in Germany and sent home, conscious of Patty's mouton coat and of Rubino's blue Pontiac, said, "Maybe." Rubino laughed.

It was a drop-dead perfect deal. This guy Rubino knew was getting together a group of investors to buy up a block of Bond Street in Elizabeth. They had maybe four weeks to do it before the state got there. Governor Driscoll had sworn to get that turnpike done by November '51, eighteen months. Because he had given himself such a short deadline, the state didn't have enough manpower to get to every farmer and every shop owner and every home owner in the right of way, so a guy with some pull could get there ahead of time, make a deal or two, and then turn it around. Some of those home owners on Bond Street had expected to be bought out when they expanded Newark Airport, and were a little ticked off when the thing stopped and went the other way, so they had the planes coming in and going out all day and now all night, and no way to get out of there. That irritation was gold to an investor. All those folks, at least the ones who weren't deaf, would take cash and be glad of it.

"How much do you want?" said Frank.

"How much you got?" said Rubino. Frank gave him twenty-two hundred, not without thinking that Walter might have sold the farm for that twelve years earlier.

....

ON THE FOURTH OF JULY, Joe gave a party. When Rosanna got the invitation—in her mailbox ("Mr. and Mrs. Walter Langdon, Box 32, RR 2, Denby, Iowa"), she didn't at first recognize the handwriting on the envelope, it was so neat, and when they got to Joe's house at the designated time, 2:00 p.m. ("Claire, stop kicking the back of my seat, please. You girls are very giggly"), she didn't at first recognize the place—Joe had put up a fence that confined the heretofore wandering driveway, and planted grass along it. The main part of the driveway went back to the barn, as always wide enough for a tractor and whatever implement it might be pulling, but the branch went off at a right angle now, crossed the front of the house, and stopped at the stand of lilacs that had been out of control but was now cut back. The effect of the fence was to turn the slope in front of Rolf's old house, which had once dribbled down to the drainage ditch beside the road, into a front yard. Sure enough, there was some lawn growing there, and not just the same old bunchgrass and foxtails. Well, he had planted fescue, it looked like.

Walter stopped the car and came around to open her door. She got right out with the peach pie and said, "You bring the rolls, Claire. Girls, Joe must be around somewhere. Go say hi."

And the porch was cleared of junk; you could walk right into the house, which was also cleared of junk, and somewhere he had bought a piece of green flowered carpet that he had laid over the linoleum in the living room—covered it almost to the four walls. No curtains on the windows, of course, but the shades were straight and half drawn, and the place was cool and dim. The two cats were lying around when Rosanna walked in, the one on the back of the sofa and the other one on the heat register, but they skittered past Joe as he came through the kitchen door. Rosanna said, "My, my, the place looks better than it ever has, Joey, and you . . ." Well, she couldn't say that, but he did look handsome at last. Tall, and dark, and with a nice haircut, his cuffs straight, and his nails trimmed. He looked, in fact, like Walter had when she met him so many years ago and decided that she was going to show her mother and all the others how to be a real farm wife. She kissed Joe on the cheek. Oh, he did look happy. She walked through into the kitchen. And why not? Through the screen door, you could really get a look at his seed-corn field, and it was the best she had ever seen. Knee-high by the Fourth of July, except not here—the corn was hip-high, and the field was as flat and neat as a patchwork quilt. There was one Oma had made—where was that?—called "rail fence," a simple pattern, green and blue with black accents, as Rosanna remembered. Anyway, Joey's back field somehow brought that to mind. Between the cornfield and the house (the yard was also cleared, and even the doghouse looked as though it had been painted) he had set two picnic tables, and put cloths on them, and tacked the ends under the tabletops so they wouldn't flap in the wind.

And then the others started coming in, Mama, and then Minnie and Lois, who was wearing a very handsome black-and-white-checked skirt, and a red scarf around her neck. Minnie was carrying a pan of something covered in a dish towel, which she set on the table, and Lois had a chocolate cake, which she set beside Rosanna's peach pie, and it was a fine cake, only a little dip on one side.

Rosanna stepped out onto the back porch, and nearly fell over her own ice-cream maker, filled with ice and covered with a towel, which she lifted. Strawberry. He would have bought the strawberries in Usherton, since strawberry season was over. She stuck in her finger, just the tiniest bit, and put it in her mouth. Delicious. Well, he was full of surprises, and it was about time. Claire was right beside her. She said, "Can I have a taste?"

After a moment, Rosanna said, "Well, okay, but go get yourself a teaspoon."

Claire came back with a spoon, and Rosanna dipped it into the pale-pink coolness. She said, "Don't tell anyone."

Walter stepped out onto the porch. He said, "You're the hostess, Clairy, so go be with your friends," and she hugged her arm quickly around his waist and then ran after Nat, who had come around the house with a stick in his mouth. Walter said, "Best-looking corn I ever saw."

"You said that about ours."

"I did. I was wrong."

Rosanna smiled.

"I guess that anhydrous is the real thing."

"Until it blows up."

"Hell, it's not going to blow up. Might freeze you to death if you fell in the tank, or suck the moisture right out of your body. They say—"

"Ugh," said Rosanna.

"Joe is a careful young man. He knows the steps, he says the steps out loud to himself, and he follows the steps. He even says, 'Put on your gloves,' and then he does it. I don't know if I could be careful like that, but he is."

"Good thing he's in charge, then," said Rosanna.

"I'm not disagreeing with that," said Walter. "I do wish Frankie and Lillian were here."

"We can go there once the babies are born."

"When's that again?"

"I guess October for Andrea and November for Lillian. We can wangle an invitation for Christmas."

Walter chewed his lip for a second, looking out at the glittering field. Rosanna forbade herself to ask yet again why he wasn't content. Who was, after all? At last, Walter pointed to the ice-cream maker. "What's in there?"

"Don't you want to know," said Rosanna, as she turned him toward the house.

They ate about four-thirty, when it was cooling down a little. Joe had set up a sprinkler for Claire and her friends. The two girls were also a little young for their age, eleven; they jumped around, shouting in the arc of water, more like eight-year-olds, which was fine with Rosanna. Henry put on some trunks he had (he had learned to swim down in Iowa City) and jumped around with them, then threw on a shirt and played fetch with the dog for at least an hour. And he didn't make the dog do all the running—Henry had turned into something of an athlete. He had canvas shoes, and he ran with the dog, getting him to leap and race around the yard and down the road and back. Minnie remarked that North Usherton High School was installing a swimming pool, too, if you could imagine that, and might even get a swim team together.

"Who's doing the farm work?" said Rosanna.

Walter said, "Joe, I guess. Joe is just going to farm every place around Denby by himself."

They all smiled.

Joe had cooked pork shoulder. The conversation about the table started with Frank and Andrea and Lillian and Arthur and the children, then moved on to Korea. Rosanna hadn't known that the North Koreans had captured Seoul, but she wasn't surprised. Then everyone, by unspoken agreement, backed away from that subject, but not before Lois said that a man she knew at the feed store had enlisted. Walter asked who was going to the fair this year, and Minnie said she was helping with the 4-H-ers and she expected Lois to go along.

"Well, I'll take a pie."

"Wait a year," said Minnie, but Rosanna thought the girl should be encouraged. Minnie was always after her to make something of herself and get off the farm, but while Minnie was at school, Lois came to Rosanna and asked to be shown how to do everything—she didn't know how to cook or sew or even clean, really clean. Oh, she could wipe down a table and wash the dishes in hot running water and put the washed clothes through the wringer. She could crochet but not knit, and Rosanna had taught her how to knit—made her learn the German way, not the English way. But no butter churning, no egg candling or egg gathering or chicken raising, no carding or spinning of wool (even Rosanna barely knew how to do that, but Oma had done it for years). They did dye some wool blue with chopped red cabbage, red onion skins, and white vinegar, and the color was pale but attractive. Lois was knitting it into a vest. Like her mother (poor thing), Lois wanted only to bake—cookies, cakes, pies, hardly even bread. Well, maybe she would reopen that bakery—what was the name of that fellow? Those baumkuchen he had made were about the best thing Rosanna had ever tasted in Denby. She was a nice girl, Lois, and just because she jutted out her jaw every time Minnie said anything to her didn't mean she was uncooperative. Kids go their own way.

Walter limped in from inspecting that field again. His limp was pretty pronounced some days, not so pronounced other days. Wouldn't go to a doctor, now that Dr. Craddock had passed on. At the funeral, Walter had whispered in Rosanna's ear that he was sure there was a carton of Camels in the coffin. The doctor who had bought the practice was named Schwartz, and Rosanna had even said, "You liked Julius. Jews are smart. Good doctors." Walter had replied, "That's not it." But he still wouldn't go. Rosanna looked away. He made his way around the table, put his hand on the back of her chair as if he really needed the support, then pulled out the chair beside hers and sat down. He said, "I can die now."

"Oh, for goodness' sake!"

"He knows everything I know, and more."

"Then it's time to enjoy it, not to die. Stick around and let him know you admire him."

"He knows that. He was such a whiny child. Drove me bananas."

"Well, you drove your ma bananas, too."

"She told you that?"

"She did. She said you couldn't take 'no' for an answer. She might say, 'No, you can't do that,' a hundred times, and you didn't do it, because you knew you'd get a whipping if you did, but you'd wait about five seconds and then ask again, in the exact same voice, if you could do it."

Walter burst out laughing. Then Claire ran up to them and said, "Joey says we can serve the ice cream."

"Ah," said Walter, "the real supper begins."

THE WHOLE TIME that twenty-two hundred dollars was out in the world, Frank thought about it every night, and the time seemed to pass with infinite slowness. It was accompanied by another feeling that Frank didn't understand at all, something that came to him just before he fell asleep, or just as he woke up—something new, much deeper and more pervasive than mere fear of losing money that six months ago they hadn't known existed. The feeling had nothing to do with nightmares; once he was dreaming of trying to get to the grocery store, and had this sensation and awoke panting. It had nothing to do with his life. He felt it at work only as a shadow, he felt it at home only as a reason not to go to bed. It didn't locate itself—he did not look at Andy and imagine her getting hit by a car, he did not look at his hamburger and think of food poisoning. His mother would have said, and had often said, that Frank didn't have the sense to be afraid. So maybe this was a visitation of some sort—senseless and inchoate, but colored orange, and peopled with small figures. What was frightening about them was nothing that his conscious mind recognized. But he felt it. Some nights he felt it so strongly that he got up and poured himself a shot of whiskey.

He didn't say a word to Andy, though if he woke up from one of these episodes he took her hand. When he mentioned it to Arthur, Arthur was too literal about it—Stalin had the bomb now, people in the know (did he remember von Neumann, who worked at Los Alamos?) were convinced he would use it, and Arthur himself was thinking of relocating to Maryland, because if a bomb hit D.C. the nuclear plume would be carried by weather patterns away from some towns and toward others. A friend of his whom he trusted had moved to Frederick, but it was a forty-mile commute. . . .

If Andy noticed anything wrong, she didn't say a word. Frank doubted that whatever it was had to do with the war, and he had nothing around the house that reminded him of the war—his one piece of memorabilia, if you could call it that, was a picture of his father and two of his World War I buddies, so faded that the three young men were almost indistinguishable. Sometimes Frank peered at it, trying to feel something about this boy, his father, or to make a connection between the day the picture was resurrected and what he himself had been doing at the time—at boot camp, scrambling around in the underbrush in the Ozarks. But nothing clicked.

In the summer, with all the windows in the duplex wide open and them sitting in whatever breeze there was, dripping with sweat, the baby seemed to be developing at about a cell per second. Andy declared that she would never have a fall baby again, but what was the proper season? She hated being as big as a house in the hot weather, but did you really want the throwing up all summer and then to have to buy a whole hideous wardrobe for the winter? It was a conundrum. Sometimes she stood in front of her closet and said, "I can see everything going out of style while I am watching it." On the whole, though, Frank thought she looked good—she was tall, and from behind you didn't even realize that she was pregnant until the last month. Her ankles didn't swell, like Lillian's, and she got around fine. She took walks around the neighborhood. There were pregnant women and new babies everywhere; the discussion of their every need and desire went on day and night. They talked about the investment only once, when Andy said, "It was funny money. I never heard of Uncle Jens. We've still got our savings and the GI Bill." There were houses in Levittown that now came with not only a carport but also a television and the antenna. They went to see the models twice.

When Rubino called him up around the first of October and said he had seven grand for him, Frank couldn't believe his ears. Rubino was living in Washington Heights for the time being, so Frank met him at a bar not far from the old Sperry plant in Lake Success. As he entered the bar and peered around for Rubino, Frank decided that probably Rubino was in the neighborhood because he had some plan for the Sperry plant, which was now housing the United Nations while that building was under construction. If Rubino could screw a dime out of each of the United Nations, Frank thought, he would consider it his greatest victory.

As soon as Rubino saw Frank, he patted his jacket, over the pocket, but Frank knew anyway that he was going to have to talk the little wop out of his money. Rubino was in a good mood, and deep into his third Scotch and soda. Frank ordered a martini. Frank said, "What's going on here at Lake Success? This whole neighborhood is wearing little hats. I didn't think it was your kind of place."

"Yarmulkes. They're called yarmulkes, and you're gonna learn to say that word and a dozen others if you're going to stop sounding like the rube you are."

"Like what?"

"Like 'schmuck.' "

"I know what a schmuck is. Private."

They both took another sip of their drinks. Rubino patted his jacket again. Then he said, "I've got another idea."

"I want to see the fruits of the first idea."

Rubino leaned on the bar and looked up at Frank, then slipped his hand inside his jacket and pulled out an envelope. The envelope was fat. He set it on Frank's knee and said, "You lucked out, Corporal."

"I should hope so."

Rubino shrugged, finished his drink, and said, "Not everyone did. The turnpike could have gone another way. We bought some property along that right of way, too." He lifted a finger; when the bartender came over, he ordered another Scotch. Frank had never seen him drink this much, and guessed that was why he had let it out about the other investment.

"I'm not going to count it right now."

"Do what you want, Corporal. But I'm telling you, this place around here, you have a look at it. You know what? It's moving closer to the city, and for that reason, it's filling right up. Good air. View of the bay. Sid Caesar lives here. You know who that is?"

Frank shook his head.

"Funniest guy now living. You've heard of the Marx Brothers, anyway."

"Maybe."

"They live here, too. I'm looking at four lots. Big ones. Enough for six houses, anyway, because they're all contiguous. We hold on to those for a year, and we triple our dough."

"How much dough are we tripling?"

"You put in your seven, you triple that."

"How much are you putting in?"

"Ten, more or less."

"I'll think about it," said Frank.

"Well, stop thinking about it tomorrow, because I got to make the offer."

"One of those Levittown houses is eight grand. Free and clear."

"You don't make money on where you live," said Rubino.

Frank wouldn't have said that he was actually angry when they walked out of the bar fifteen minutes later. It was another one of those feelings he had that he didn't understand—he had the envelope safely in his own inside jacket pocket, and because it was cold, he had buttoned his jacket and wrapped his scarf around his neck. They walked along. Down the street, Frank could see the blue Pontiac parked alongside a blank brick wall, the streetlight glaring across it turning it the color of sand, and maybe that was what triggered him. His own Studebaker was around the corner.

Rubino put his hand in his coat pocket and pulled out his keys. A moment after that, Frank had him pinned against the brick wall, with his forearm at his neck, the way Rubino himself had once pinned Lieutenant Martin at Monte Cassino (was that really only six years ago?), and, as Rubino had done then, Frank felt his pockets for a weapon, which he did not find. He said, "I don't want to be one of those investors who lost their money because you put it into the wrong piece of property, Rubino. Alex." Rubino struggled. Frank pressed harder; Rubino gagged. Frank was six inches taller, and certainly outweighed the other man by thirty or forty pounds. Frank said, "I've learned a lot from you, Private."

Rubino's arm flew out, but Frank caught it and pressed it against the wall. He said, "I just want to be clear about my intentions. If everyone loses, I don't mind losing, too. I understand that. But if you gain, I gain. Got it?"

Rubino gagged again, and Frank let him loose, just a little. Rubino coughed, and then said, in a hoarse voice, "I would never screw you, Corporal. You should know that."

"I will never forget you said that, Private."

Rubino put his hand to his neck and stretched his head upward, then nodded. Frank said, "You okay to drive?"

Rubino shrugged, but got into his car. He didn't seem all that surprised by what had happened, but he did seem a little more sober. Frank watched him pull away. Maybe there were two lessons Rubino was going to take away from this encounter, and one of them was to reduce his liquor consumption. The next day, Frank called to say that he would put six grand into the new project. Rubino sounded normal. He estimated nine to twelve months before they realized their investment, but no more than that. Frank thanked him. That feeling he'd had before falling asleep dissipated, didn't even kick in when the baby was born. Frank put it out of his mind.

ANDY NAMED her daughter (seven pounds, five ounces) Janet Ann, and Lillian named her son (seven pounds, seven ounces) Dean Henry. For Thanksgiving, Frank, Andy, and Janet, now six weeks old, took the train to Washington. Lillian had gotten a second bassinet for Janet. They would keep the bassinets downstairs during the day, and then carry them upstairs after supper. (Dinner—in Washington it was called dinner, but Lillian kept calling it supper, and Andy did, too. In that one way, Lillian thought, you knew she was from Decorah, Iowa, not Bedford Hills, New York.) They got there late Wednesday night, so Lillian didn't really have a look at the baby girl until Thanksgiving morning. Dean was two weeks old, but Lillian felt fine. Once she came home from the hospital, Timmy and Debbie had her so on the go, anyway, that she hardly had time to rest. A three-hour labor, from the first pain to the birth, was nothing. She was getting to be like Mama, except that she didn't get up the day the baby was born and go milk six cows before breakfast.

Arthur laughed. "She never did that."

"No, but she did give birth to Henry all by herself, in Frank's room, during harvest. Joe was the first one to see him when he went in to get a handkerchief. I guess he stood there blowing his nose. Frank and Papa were out harvesting corn, weren't you?"

Frank said, "I don't remember."

"You do," said Lillian, poking him.

"Nothing," said Frank.

The weather was fairly good, so, before Lillian served the turkey at five, not so terribly early, Arthur and Frank took Timmy and Debbie for a long and, everyone hoped, exhausting walk about Georgetown, and she and Andy got down to seriously comparing the babies. They sat side by side on the sofa and laid the babies on their knees, facing upward. Bit by bit, they opened the blankets. Dean was too young to mind, but Janet was old enough to get a little fussy.

Such a comparison, Lillian thought, might have been unfair to Dean, but he was about a week late, and had plenty of hair—Arthur's hair, since it was dark. His nose had not been flattened in the quick birth, and he wasn't terribly cross-eyed. He had long fingers and long feet, and slender arms and legs, just like Timmy, and look at him (if you dared—half the time he was getting into something). Like all blonds except Lillian herself, according to Mama, Janet had fine hair that would come in late, but she had a little crown of gold around her head, and two beautiful dimples. Andy said, "I'm not sure dimples are the wave of the future." Janet's eyes were bluer, and her lips were already full and distinct. Her birth length had been twenty-one and a half inches. Lillian, who wasn't tall, said, "She is going to be tall," and Andy, who was tall, said, "There's a mixed blessing for you."

"But you've already lost the weight, and look at me. I have so far to go."

"My mother said it always drops off faster with the first one."

"Maybe. I don't know. I have this feeling that it will be hard this time, and Arthur will not be helpful, since he likes butter, butter, butter and cream, cream, cream for every meal."

Andy turned and kissed her on the cheek. She said, "But I'm so flat-chested, even with nursing. If you go to that Dior boutique in New York, which I did every week from the seventh month on, just for inspiration, you see what it's going to be—hourglass."

"If I ever get a waist again."

Lillian sighed and lifted Dean against her shoulder. Andy unself-consciously opened her blouse and put Janet to the breast. Lillian didn't say anything. Dean had finished his bottle a half-hour before. He was not a fussy baby, and took all of his formula every time. Andy said, "My mother said nursing takes the weight off. But she only had two."

Lillian could not help watching—she had never nursed any of the three, even for a day. The hospital where they were born seemed to find it distasteful and unhealthy. As she watched, she carefully suppressed a little pang of regret, until Andy said "Ouch!"

"What's wrong?"

"Oh, you know, the nipples are so tender. But supposedly that goes away." Lillian didn't say anything.

When Arthur, Frank, and the kids came in, Frank said, "The weather is really strange out there. Don't you ladies hear the windows rattling?"

"It's very dark to the west," said Arthur. "I'm glad I reglazed the windows this summer."

Lillian said "Brr," then, to Frank, "Remember that winter you went to Chicago in the blizzard? I didn't know whether to be more afraid for you or more afraid for us. The snow was to the eaves."

"We did get stuck somewhere. Where was that? Before the river. Must have been around DeWitt. Some old ladies got me a berth so I could stay warm. It felt like a . . . a foxhole, I guess. Gave me nightmares."

Andy said, "We had such deep drifts in Decorah that my brother made himself a ski jump out a second-story window into the backyard. He would squat in a couple of shoeboxes and sail down."

Dinner was fine—the turkey only a little dry. Andy set the table, and the pumpkin pie she had brought was delicious, and so they yawned and dozed and went to bed.

On Friday, the storm hit while they were sitting at breakfast—there was a shattering, crashing sound, and at the very moment Lillian said, "What's that?" Timmy ran in from the living room and said, "Mommy, wind came through the glass!"

They ran in, and there it was—glass all over the floor, a big branch cracked against the front of the house, and rain gusting through. Frank moved the bassinets into the dining room, and then he and Arthur went out and nailed a board over the window. Andy kept Timmy and Debbie in the kitchen while Lillian swept up the glass.

Once the antenna blew off the house, there was no television of any kind (Lillian enjoyed television—not so much for the programs, which she was running around too much to pay attention to, but for the friendly demeanor and the nice clothes of the stars), and shortly after that, no electricity. Arthur wrapped the refrigerator in a blanket and pinned it with clothespins, which made everyone laugh. They were warm enough—the furnace was coal—and Lillian had steril- ized and filled her bottles for the day, but what if it lasted through tomorrow? She could fill them, since the stove was gas, but she would have to set them outside to keep them cool. Well, she wasn't going to think about that. It did remind her of some of those weeks on the farm, stuck in the house with the whole place rattling. It was cozy, but there was an edge of threat, just as the rooms were warm but with the knife of a draft sailing through from time to time. Andy had two sweaters on, and was smoking about twice as much as she had the day before, carefully turning her head away from the baby, who was cradled in her left arm, half asleep. Lillian, who thought that babies were better off in their bassinets, said, "Was she up in the night?"

"Oh, yes. But I just put her between me and the wall, on the other side from Frank, and nursed her off and on most of the night. Keeps her quiet, anyway." Lillian did not approve of this, either, but she was not the sort of person to say anything. Andy said, "How about you?"

"Twice. Two a.m. and six. Arthur took the two a.m." She leaned forward and lowered her voice, careful to avoid the cigarette and the smoke. "I hope, for your sake, that Frank is just like Arthur. He's not, you know, a father, more like another mother. I trust him completely, and the kids adore him."

Andy stubbed out her cigarette in the ashtray beside the sink and, also in a low voice, said, "So what are he and Frank talking about all the time? Whisper, whisper, whisper."

And, without thinking, Lillian said, "Oh, that must be Judy. They always talk about Judy in low voices, but I don't see why."

"Who's Judy?"

It was then that Lillian realized she should have kept her trap shut. Stalling, she laughed once and said, "Oh, he hasn't told you about Judy?"

Andy visibly bristled. Her eyebrows lifted, and she put her other arm around Janet and laid the baby's head against her neck. There was a sudden gust of wind against the side of the house that startled Lillian, but it didn't distract Andy. She said, "Tell me. I knew he had girlfriends, but he's never said a word about any of them."

Lillian bit her lip and wished that Dean would cry or something. Even Timmy and Debbie were inconveniently quiet. She made herself say, "Well, honey, Judy was not a girlfriend, in the sense you mean. You know who she is."

"I do? I don't know a single Judy."

Lillian leaned over and whispered the name in Andy's ear, and Andy said, "No! He dated her? She's the one who was convicted for spying for the Russians, and now they let her off again."

Lillian would have said later that she thought long and hard about her next remark, but she really paused for only a second or two. She said, "Arthur put him up to it. They—we—were suspicious of her, and Arthur got Frank to check her out, and Frank decided that the suspicions were valid. And then they got her. Hoover hates her with a black passion. But in the end, that's why she got off, because he tracked her every move without a warrant."

"Hoover who?"

"J. Edgar."

"Oh, good Lord!"

"Frank didn't like her much," said Lillian. "She baked him a cake for his birthday, and then he broke up with her twenty minutes later." She thought this would be reassuring for Andy. "It was all business for him."

Andy didn't say anything.

Lillian said, "I don't think you should hold it against him. Do you hold it against him?"

"I don't think anything about it right now. It's too . . . But, Lillian, Arthur works for the . . . ?" She waited for Lillian to answer, and so Lillian finally said, "Doesn't everyone? At least around here. Anyway . . ."

But there was no "anyway." When she was feeding Dean up in her room, an hour or so later, and feeling deeply embarrassed for being such a babbling idiot, Lillian decided that it was the storm that got to her, the storm that was getting louder and more violent by the hour. You never knew what you were going to do in a big storm. After Dean finished the bottle, she lay down in the bed and pulled the comforter up, snuggling with him, closing her eyes, and giving thanks that they were in Georgetown, not Usherton; if the house blew away or something bad happened, at least people would know it right away.

1951

〜

Henry hadn't told Mama or Papa yet what he was majoring in. As far as they knew, he was going to be a doctor or a dentist. Or he could go on to Davenport and go to Palmer. All Mama knew was that there wasn't a doctor within thirty miles of Denby who had any up-to-date training at all, so a bookish boy like Henry, who had lived for eighteen years on a farm and still didn't know how to drive a tractor, could make himself more than useful in some sort of medical profession.

But science did nothing for Henry. He had seen more fetal pigs in his day than any of the other biology students, and he had never seen one that he wanted to slit down the belly. He also had to go to the dental school and have four cavities filled by student dentists, one of whom talked incessantly while drilling, and then, when the professor came over to inspect the fillings, he let out a little cluck. Henry knew that the student would be getting a D. But there was no offer to replace them. If Henry had felt any desire to take up dentistry, it vanished completely.

Of course he liked his English-literature class, and of course he wrote his papers with speed and enthusiasm. The first semester, they read "The Miller's Tale" and "The Wife of Bath's Tale," *Everyman,* Book Three of *Le Morte d'Arthur,* about Sir Lancelot, *Doctor Faustus,*

Othello, King Lear, Twelfth Night, The Duchess of Malfi, 'Tis Pity She's a Whore, Pilgrim's Progress, and, in the last two weeks, the first half of *Paradise Lost.* Over Christmas break, he finished that and went on to *Robinson Crusoe* and *Pamela.* By the end of the year, they were to get to Oscar Wilde, which was fine with Henry. The real benefit of the class, though, was that he met Professor McGalliard, and now, in the second semester, he was having a private tutorial in Old English, or Anglo-Saxon, or whatever you wanted to call it. After Christmas, he had brought that stolen copy of *Beowulf* back to Iowa City with him, and he kept it under his mattress. (He did not think his roommates would care if he had a book from the North Usherton High School library—their room was decked with street signs, girls' underwear, ripped banners from other Big Ten schools—the Ohio State banner had been defaced in several ways—and even two hubcaps from the homecoming game against Northwestern.) He got along with his roommates fine, but neither of them knew something that Henry was proud and fascinated to know, that "foot" had originated in the Caucasus as *ped* and was of course related to the Latin *pes, pedis,* the Greek *pous,* the Sanskrit *pád,* and German Fuß, that the "p" turned into an "f" by means of Grimm's law. "Ball" had originated as *bhel,* meaning "to swell," and was related not only, of course, to "bellows" but also to "follicle" and "phallus." The Grimm in question was Jacob Grimm himself, who was also responsible for "Little Red Riding Hood" and "Clever Hans," those stories that, in time-honored fashion, Lillian had only half remembered, and so had told to him in mixed-up and made-up versions (during one of their sessions, he related to Professor McGalliard the story of the wolf prince, his favorite).

Professor McGalliard was kind and encouraging. He had gone to Harvard, and seemed a bit perplexed about finding himself in Iowa City. He only let Henry do etymologies for part of the session—the first job was to learn to read basic texts like *The Anglo-Saxon Chronicles* and "The Seafarer." *Beowulf* was to be saved for next year, when Henry had a better ear for the rhythm of the line. In the meantime, Henry was also taking German, and in the fall he was going to sign up for Latin. Eventually, there would be Greek, too, once he got hideous wastes of time out of the way like calculus and American history. You could only take medieval history as a junior, but there were plenty of books in the library that he could read on his own, such as *Medieval Cities: Their Origins and the Revival of Trade* and *A History of the Franks* by Gregory of Tours. It was pretty clear that he was going to have to improve his French, too, not because French itself was a language he was interested in, but because all of the best work was in French—Marc Bloch, that sort of thing. Professor McGalliard seemed rather amused at his enthusiasm, especially when Henry mentioned that he'd been raised on a farm. "I hardly ever went outside," said Henry, to reassure him, but he just laughed at that.

As for the other freshmen, Henry could not quite figure out why they were at college. His roommates, Forrest and Allen, were from Council Bluffs and Fort Dodge. They ate and slept Hawkeyes, and were furious that the president of the university would not or could not hire a decent football coach. Iowa hadn't won the Big Ten title in thirty years. Henry was taller than Forrest and outweighed Allen by fifteen pounds. Neither of them would ever play football (*pes bhel*), but they talked about it every day. Forrest thought he was going to major in business, and Allen had no idea. They slept through classes as a matter of course and talked about girls all the time, though they never actually talked to girls. As for the girls, Henry liked girls well enough. Did he not get along perfectly with Lillian and quite well with Claire? He knew how to talk to girls, and he often watched them, but college girls were not like girls he'd known before. The particular problem was one of vocal timbre. His skin prickled when they made certain squawking or screeching sounds, and in bars and in the commons, they seemed to make these sounds a majority of the time. He went out sometimes with girls who were a little calmer than most, but, unfortunately, when they asked him what he was studying, he forgot and told them. Inevitably, their jaws dropped, and that was the end of that. Henry didn't care. When he told Mama and Lillian that he loved college, that he was perfectly happy with his part-time job reshelving books in the library, and that he was dating off and on (he did take a girl from Davenport to the Christmas dance, and they looked great in the photograph), he knew they were imagining a life that he was not living. But that was fine. There was a ghost in him that would someday emerge from those books that he could not yet read, and that, he knew, would be the real Henry Langdon.

THE RETURN ON their Rubino investment had been nineteen thousand dollars, plus the original six. In a single year, old Uncle Jens had rolled over in his grave twelve times, but that was not what Frank was thinking of when he looked at Andy and Janet and said, "Yup. So if we buy me an MG TD with a little of the payoff, what can we buy you?" Jim Upjohn had an MG TD—left-hand drive, very exotic, and not something Frank wanted—but there was nothing that he really wanted.

"Oooh." She glanced at him, and Janet, and then surveyed their small kitchen. By rights, she should say, "A house." But she said, "I saw a navy shantung skirt with its own petticoat that was nine yards around the hem the other day. I even sat Janny in the corner of the dressing room and tried it on with the contrasting jacket."

"How much was it? You should—"

She glanced around again. "I don't think it would fit inside this duplex." She reached for her pack of Luckies that was lying on the table. "Nutria is always nice. It can be quite blond, with lovely highlights. A nutria jacket with a nipped waist?"

"Why not the skirt and the house to wear it in? Those Levittown houses are twenty-five feet by thirty-two feet now."

"Oh, Frank!" Andy laughed. "But I'm not ready for a house yet. Just a very large skirt is fine."

It turned out, though, that what they bought was a television, so that Andy could watch the news. Dinner would be on the table when he got home—tonight it was minute steaks and mashed potatoes, some salad, and some red cabbage, which Andy was fond of. They ate quietly, and Andy was pleased because Janet actually took a bit of the cabbage. Andy said, "It's sweet underneath. Bitter is the first flavor you taste, but if you take your time, it's nice. She understands that, don't you, *lille elskling*?"

"We should try her on some schnitzel."

"We should try *us* on some schnitzel. I love that. I keep forgetting to find a recipe."

They moved into the living room, Frank carrying Janet and Andy carrying the last of her lemonade and her Luckies, for her after-dinner smoke. And then the news came on. Frank settled Janny in his lap and picked up a magazine. Andy's preferred news show was John Cameron Swayze's *Camel News Caravan*. Swayze had a circus-barker delivery style that made Frank laugh, so he didn't mind it, though he found the "news" always to be a few days behind things, if you were keeping your eyes and ears open. The news show was only fifteen minutes long. Frank was about a page into the article he was reading, and Janet was sitting quietly, when Andy started yelling at the TV.

Setting Andy off, he had once thought, was nearly impossible. Was there anyone as agreeable and accepting as Andy? They had never had an argument, and Frank liked it that way—Mama, not slow to tell Papa what to do, had given Frank a distaste for domestic noise. So maybe, startled at Andy's tirade, he squeezed Janet a little too hard, but there she was, screaming, too.

"Hey!" barked Frank, and Andy whipped around in her chair. She said, "He was right!"

"Who was right?"

"MacArthur was right! We should have gone into China right then and done in those Chinese communists, and Truman fired him, and now we're all going to have to pay, because Stalin is going to give them the bomb!"

Frank didn't completely disagree with this assessment—no one did—so he only said, "But that was April or something—"

"And he got away with it! I thought they would impeach him, but they chickened out, and now . . ."

"Now what?"

She reached for the baby—Frank paused for a moment before he handed her over, but decided it was safer in the end to do it—and took her in her arms. Janet's crying subsided.

Frank stroked Andy's hair. Everything was quiet for a moment. There was a Tide commercial, and the music started for *You Bet Your Life*. Andy turned the TV off. Janet struggled to get down, so Andy put her on the floor, and she crawled to her toy box. Andy got up and came over, sat in Frank's lap, put her head against his shoulder. She said, "I'm sorry. I snapped. But you know what? Every day, I sit in this duplex, and all I think about is bombs."

"You do?"

"I do." Andy sat up. She said, "Don't you? Every single thing we do is on the surface. Every single thing we do is just a pretense that we all aren't going to be blown to bits by the Russians."

"We aren't going to be blown to bits by the Russians, Andy."

"Yes, we are." She said this with icy certainty.

"They don't have a delivery system. They have a bomb or two, but—"

She scowled and said, "We don't know what they have, but they know what we have."

"We know what they have."

Janet came crawling back and reached toward him. Frank gave her his hand, and she pulled herself up.

Andy did an odd thing—she picked up her skirt and ran the edge between her thumbs and forefingers, back and forth—then said, "Why did we bomb Nagasaki?"

"I don't know," said Frank.

"Does Arthur know?"

"He might, but he's never mentioned working on anything to do with the Manhattan Project." Frank knew Andy had read the John Hersey book about Hiroshima. It was on the bookshelf across the room. He avoided looking at it so that her gaze would not follow his.

"Was it showing Stalin something he needed to know?"

"I don't know," said Frank.

Andy put her face on his shoulder again, and after a while said, "You'll tell me when they can blow us up, right?"

"Right." Then he said, "Honey, maybe this is an effect of listening to the news too often. It's just a show, like any other show."

Andy nodded.

After Janet went down and they were reading, though, the argument resumed. Andy looked up from her issue of *Vogue* and said, in a surprisingly bitter tone, "Everyone in the State Department is just busy as bees making sure the commies know all about us."

His mistake was saying, "Us?" He had picked up the morning paper, but in fact was remembering that night in Strasbourg when they discovered that the Jerries had vanished.

"Yes, us!"

He turned and looked at her. Alight with indignation, she was beautiful. He said, "I don't think the commies care about you and me. Arthur and Lillian, maybe, but not—"

"What about Judy?"

"Judy?" He put down the paper. But of course he knew whom she meant.

"You knew her! She knows you! You work at Grumman! Don't you think she's keeping track of you?"

"Well, I would be flattered, but—" That was his second mistake. She leapt off the couch. "You would be flattered!"

"Anyway, she doesn't know who I am. She never knew who I was. She thought I was Francis Burnett from Dayton, Ohio. Baby, I've covered my tracks." After making this flat joke of the thing, he reached for her hand, tried to pull her back to the couch and kiss her.

Andy said, "Did you love her?"

"No, Andy. I did not." She stayed over by the arm of the couch.

"Did she know that?"

"Know that I didn't love her? Yes. I saw her once a month. It was a very cool relationship."

"Did you tell her that you loved her?"

"No."

"What did you tell her?"

"I told her the usual things—that she was nice, that she was fun, that she was special, that she looked good tonight, that I liked her outfit, had she changed her hairdo, had she lost weight, had she been to the dentist, had she, I don't know. I never said 'I,' I always said 'you.'"

"That's the way you treated me in college."

"Is it? But I told you I loved you."

"Once."

"More than once." But Frank felt his heart start to beat more quickly, the way he always did when they approached the memory of Eunice. He said, "Anyway, I was a jerk in college. We've agreed on that. You, Andy, are the person I love. You are my wife. How Frankie felt about Hildy nine years ago has nothing to do with how I feel about you now. Nothing." She stared at him, and he held her gaze. Inch by inch, she eased toward him on the couch, and then they kissed, and he led her to the bedroom. There, he helped her unbutton her shirtwaist dress, and then take off the pearls and the girdle and the bra and the hose and the panties. He helped her slip her silk nightgown over her head, and then he kissed her good night. When she was breathing steadily and deeply, he turned out the lights, and regarded the moon through the window to the right of the bed. A half-moon. A good moon for hunting rabbits.

Everyone he knew was afraid of the Russians. Arthur and Lillian muttered about the Russians all the time. At work, there was this constant sense of being prodded to stay ahead of the Russians, because the Russians, if they got rockets and long-range bombers, would have no scruples about using them, and even if regular Russians did have scruples, Stalin did not. The standard view at work was what Arthur had said months ago, that unless Stalin understood his every waking and sleeping moment that he himself would be blown up within an hour of sending out the first A-bomb, blown up for sure and without fail, then Stalin would not hesitate to send out that bomb. Was that not the lesson of everything Stalin had done since the death of Lenin and the exile of Trotsky? Frank's own experience in the war confirmed this. Who were the French and the Brits and even the Americans afraid of? The Germans. Who were Germans afraid of? The Russians. Why were they afraid of the Russians? Because the Russians were afraid of Stalin, and so would do anything. But Frank was sure that Stalin did understand what he was supposed to understand.

Frank still had his shirt on, though he had taken off his khakis. Now he eased off the bed and slipped them on again. His loafers were at the bottom of the steps. He opened the front door and went out into the darkness, closing the door while feeling his key in his pocket. Maybe it was ten, but their residential neighborhood was quiet. Frank headed down the block, toward the park. Since the birth of Janet, he had stopped taking as many walks, but he still went out on hot nights, like this one, looking for a breeze or something. He wondered whether anyone else they knew would call what they'd had tonight a fight. He didn't know. No blows, of course, no yelling back and forth (he heard the next-door neighbors but one do that fairly often), no thrown objects. (One family story had Granny Elizabeth throwing the coffeepot at Grandpa Wilmer once, when she finally got fed up with his overseeing her every move in the kitchen. Coffee grounds stuck to the wall for months, a reminder to him to watch his step.) Frank unclenched his teeth, and then unclenched them again.

The air was thick with humidity and the smell of cut grass. Every house he passed had geraniums in pots and tiger lilies in rows and children's toys scattered in the yards. The streetlights made the night a little stark and bleached out. The park, he thought, would be gloomier and more reassuring. He took some deep breaths. He was shaking, maybe not with anger. There was no reason to be shaking with anger. She was afraid of the Russians, she had heard about Judy, probably from Lillian, and anyway, Judy was free again—Hoover was as much of a screw-up in the end as Fredendall, Clark, and Eisenhower, wasn't he? Frank unclenched his fists. Here was how he felt, walking in his quiet neighborhood in Floral Park, New York, now the most average of men—he felt more frightened than he had ever felt before in his life. There had been a fear he'd known in the army, even after he was used to the explosions: a sudden nearby boom would make his balls jump, and seem to shoot an electric charge right up his spine. This was not like that. This was vaster and higher, the same feeling he'd had in dreams, but now he was awake—he had been walking down the road, and the road had turned into a tree limb across an abyss, and he was out in the middle, surrounded only by air. His scalp prickled. But he hadn't felt this fear in months, and now it was as if Andy had shot it into him like a bullet. Or had he shot it into her? Maybe, he thought, that was what love was. He opened his step and headed for the high school.

When he got home, Andy and Janet were both sound asleep—of course, he had not been afraid of their waking up, the very thing he should have been afraid of. It was after midnight, and cooling a little bit. He closed Janet's window and got into bed beside Andy. The walking had tired him out, so that, when she got up at dawn and left the room, he didn't stir. At breakfast, she apologized—she only now realized, cleaning the kitchen, that she'd had too much to drink, she wasn't even going to say how many, but—she put her arms around him—never again. How stupid of her—it was so dumb to put gin in your lemonade, it disguised the flavor, she'd just poured it in without thinking, and, Frank agreed, that was that.

ON WARM DAYS, Claire liked to go over to Minnie and Lois's house and lie on the floor of the upstairs hallway, right on the wooden floor, and stay cool that way. She always took a book—right now, she was reading one she got from the library about a girl named Trixie Belden. She was to the part where the two friends, Trixie and the rich girl, Honey, find the redheaded boy sleeping. It rather pleased Claire that she was lying quietly in the only house around them that could even remotely be called a mansion. The windows were closed on the west side, and the shades were drawn, but sunshine skated through the south-facing windows and spread over the red-gold boards of the floor around her. This hall was her favorite place in the world, not only because it was cool, but also because the color of the doors and the doorways and the set of drawers across from her was so deep and comforting. She liked the book, but she turned it on its face, took off her glasses and set them across the spine, then closed her eyes.

She dreamt of the book, of course. Trixie and Honey were in a small room by themselves. They looked a little like Mary Ann Adams and Lydia Keitel at school. The Claire in the dream was looking down at them, and they were trying to get something out of the corner of the small room, a kitten or a chicken or a picket—Claire couldn't understand the word. As she looked down at them, the room got smaller, and Mary Ann (Trixie) started to cry, and then she said, "I made lunch for you."

When Claire woke up, her hip was stiff—she had started sleeping on her back, but had turned onto her side, and the floor was hard. She yawned and sat up. The voice said, "With cupcakes." The voice was Lois's, and Claire got up on her knees and pushed her hair out of her face. The voice was coming from the dining room, which was to the right at the bottom of the stairs. The staircase, which was not carpeted, was funneling it up to her. She yawned again. Then Joey's voice said, "You are sweet." Claire closed her mouth and opened her ears.

Mama had said to Papa the night before that Joe had better get going, because she had seen Dave Crest making up to Lois at the market the day before. Dave had a crew cut, and wore nice clothes, and worked around the market like he owned the place, "Which he does," said Papa.

"Well, Dan owns the place, but Dave is an only son," said Mama. "He walks down the aisles like he's seen too many John Garfield movies. Can't you say something?" said Mama.

But they all knew that Papa wouldn't say anything.

"I do love pea soup," said Joe.

"This is fresh pea soup, and cold. Because it's a hot day. And I made cornbread and some chicken from last night."

And then Claire heard the sound of a kiss, a small kiss, but definitely a kiss. At this very moment, there was a flurry and a scratching on the stairs, and here came Nat, wagging his tail. Claire grabbed his nose before he could bark, and started petting him. He flopped into her lap and rolled over. She pushed the book and the glasses across the floor so he wouldn't roll on them.

Two chairs scraped, and then scraped again. Joe said, "Oh, this is good."

"These are the last of the peas."

"They were good this year."

"The lettuce topped out early, though."

Silence while they ate. Thinking of those cupcakes, Claire had made up her mind to do something noisy and then trot down the stairs when Lois said, "Let's get married."

Joe said, "You and me?"

"Mm-hm."

"Oh, Lois . . ." His voice tapered off.

"It's a good idea."

"Lois, you're twenty-one years old and I'm twenty-nine, that's such a . . ."

"Eight years is not a big difference."

They must have gone back to eating, because after a moment Joe said, "The cornbread is really good."

"Do you like the chicken?"

"Of course."

"I rolled it in the breadcrumbs twice."

"It's crispy."

Lois's tone of voice hadn't changed during this whole conversation. She had proposed, and Joe was going to say no, and Lois just kept on talking. It was not at all like, say, *Little Women*. Lois said, "I know you're in love with Minnie. I don't care."

"I . . ." said Joe, but then he chickened out.

"She's never going to get married. I asked her last night to tell me for sure, and she said that she wants to have her free time to herself, and after Mother and Pop, she's had enough."

"She told me that," said Joe.

"Well, then," said Lois, still in the same tone, as if the conclusion they should come to would be self-evident.

Joe said, "There's something wrong with me."

"What?" said Lois, so brightly that Claire almost barked out a laugh.

"I get fixed in my mind on something and I can't let it go. You want to know something?"

"Of course."

"I think I was about five when this stray came to live in the barn, and she had puppies. I guess there was a lot of rabies around back then, and Mama made Papa drown the puppies and shoot the dog, and of course they had to do it, because we had sheep and cows and horses. But I thought about those puppies every day until I got Nat. That was seventeen years. A couple died and I wrapped them in handkerchiefs and buried them. I named the bitch 'Pal.' Look at me."

"You have tears in your eyes?"

"I don't get over things."

To Claire, this somehow felt like it was a pretty definite no to her asking him to marry her. Claire very carefully shifted her position and reached for her glasses. Her back was starting to hurt.

"You add things. You added Nat. Add me."

"Lois! Why do you want that? Why would you want that?"

"Joe, I want this! I want this exact thing. Making lunch for you. Living here. Having some babies, and *them* living here. Right here. Anybody else, and I would have to do what he wants to do, go where he wants to go."

Now there was a long silence, then a scraping chair, then foot-steps. Lois would be carrying the dishes back to the kitchen.

Joe said, "What would we do if it didn't work out?"

"You'd move back to your house and it would be just like this. There's no bad thing that would happen."

"What if you fell in love with someone?"

"I am in love with someone. You. And I don't think you're in love with Minnie, either. I don't think you know how to be in love yet. I want a chance. It's like an arranged marriage, except that I am arranging it."

Joe laughed.

Claire crawled over to one of the bedroom doors, then through it into the bedroom, through the bedroom onto the sleeping porch; then she stood up and half walked, half stomped through the bedroom into the hallway. She picked up her book and ran down the staircase. Joe and Lois looked up, sat back, startled. She said, "I was reading on the sleeping porch and I dozed off. What time is it?"

They fell for it. Lois said, "Want a cupcake? Lemon icing."

Claire reached for one.

JIM UPJOHN CALLED Frank at the office and asked what he was doing that afternoon. Frank looked at the clock. He had skipped lunch. It was a quarter to one. He said, "I am reading descriptions of rockets."

"American or Soviet?"

"German."

"Old hat," said Jim.

"You wish," said Frank. "They had something so much bigger than the V-2 in the works that we still haven't totally figured it out."

"Mm," said Jim, and Frank remembered to shut up. He said, "Nice day."

"Yes, Corporal Langdon, it is. And that's why I'm calling."

"Yes, sir," said Frank.

"Meet me in half an hour at Anderson Field, building one. We're going to take my new plane for a spin."

Frank was out the door in less than a minute.

It was beautiful—bright but calm. The breeze was southerly, straight from Florida, it felt like, light and warm. The apple trees that edged the parking lot of his building were heavy with fruit, and the grass was thick, the way it got before the first frost. He didn't get into the car, though—Anderson was only a quarter-mile from where he was standing. He left his jacket and his briefcase in the Studebaker, and sprinted. Jim was waiting for him. The plane was already outside of the hangar, and the two of them pulled the blocks away from the wheels. Frank said, "What's this one?"

"It's a Fairchild Argus. I've been wanting one of these for years, but with four seats. I finally found one. With the see-through canopy. Just wait."

It was as pleasant as Jim had predicted—buzzing down the Anderson runway and then lifting over Jamaica Bay and turning south toward New Jersey. Frank had been having an especially tedious day, but now his spirits lifted with the plane, and he said, "A pilot's license seems like a good idea right about now."

"Wait till we come in for a landing, then decide. I flew the first time when I was twelve. I was too stupid to think that anything could go wrong, so, obviously, the Army Air Force was the place for me. Ever ridden a horse?"

"Only a plowhorse." They were shouting, but they didn't seem to be.

"Well, when you ride horses really fast, you learn to never look down. Same with a plane. What draws the eye draws the body."

But Frank knew that he could be good at this, that it was the natural culmination of every step forward that he had ever taken. They flew on—along the Atlantic coast of New Jersey, low enough to look at Sandy Hook, then the thinly peopled length of the boardwalk at Asbury Park, then down along the coast to the Barnegat Lighthouse (according to Jim), then farther south, over the flat green of the Pine Barrens. Jim turned north, and they flew past Trenton, along the Delaware River. Here and there, the leaves were beginning to turn. Moment by moment, Frank ceased looking at every spot as a potential home-buying opportunity, and began seeing the earth again, the way he had on the farm, when he was living in his tent, when he was marching through Africa and then through Italy, France, and Germany. He said, "You know, this reminds me that I've never spent so much time in one place as I do now. It's either the apartment or the office or the bus between them."

"You don't go for rides in your car?"

"Only to look at open houses on Sunday."

"How's the baby?"

"She's got hair. She's almost walking. She and Andy have matching outfits."

Jim laughed, then said, "Well, you tell me what's worse, Corporal. Looking obsessively for a place to live—"

"Which is a lot like looking for the perfect spot for a foxhole."

"Or knowing that you will always live where you are supposed to."

"My heart weeps for you."

"Too big is as bad as too small."

"You should meet my friend Rubino the real-estate magnate. You would see eye to eye."

"Corporal, here's what I learned in the war. There's nothing more haunted than a house. Doesn't matter where, how grand, how small, made of brick, straw, stone, or gingerbread, whether perfectly cared for or blown to bits. Beings gather there. Every house is a planet, exerting gravitational pull. Every house is in a dark wood, every house has a wicked witch in it, doesn't matter if she looks like a fairy godmother . . ."

Jim's words seemed to nestle beside the roar of the two engines, perfectly clear and impossibly so.

"A plane doesn't have that kind of existence. It's like a thought. It's either flying or it's vanished. It doesn't linger to haunt you, to make you wonder what you did wrong, to make you ponder your sins."

"I can sense that," said Frank.

"A house gradually lowers itself into the earth."

"And a plane?"

"Gradually dematerializes."

They stopped talking, and the Argus swept onward, looping around Scranton, and then crossing the patchwork green and yellow of the Catskills, dotted here and there with lakes that shone in the sunshine like electric lights. Then the city was before them. Jim flew south along the Hudson, low enough so that the banks on either side seemed far away, and then he turned out over the dark ocean and headed for Anderson. In spite of their conversation, Frank's spirits were as expansive as the empyrean that was revealed through the see-through canopy of the plane.

He was home by six, his usual time. Andy and Janet had slept most of the afternoon—they looked disheveled but beautiful, especially since Andy was back to her old weight and wearing her old clothes. She looked good and still managed to serve up macaroni and cheese that she had put together that morning, and some green beans and a salad. Janet sat in her high chair with a spoon in her hand, pressing the bowl against bits of macaroni that Andy set on her table. Every so often, she said, "Ha! Ha!" A breeze, the same breeze that had invigorated him at the office, blew through the open window. Andy said, "I'm so glad fall is here."

"I went up in the plane with Jim Upjohn today. For a couple of hours. I think I'd like to get my pilot's license."

Because she was Andy and not any of the other women he knew, she didn't say, "Why?" She said, "Good." She leaned toward Janet and touched her cheek with one finger. Janet smiled. "Flying baby."

Looking at her, Frank felt his paralysis seep away.

1952

DEBBIE MANNING KNEW as soon as she woke up that it was Easter morning and that the Easter Bunny would have been there in the night, and left some candy and presents—Mommy had been talking about this for a long time, and she had even taken Debbie out and bought her a new green dress for going to church. The dress had its own slip, which bunched at the waist and pricked her, but the skirt stuck out so that she couldn't see her white Mary Janes, and so she didn't mind it very much. Timmy had a new suit with a blue tie, and Dean had a white shirt and blue shorts that buttoned to the shirt. The problem, of course, was that there was no way for the Easter Bunny to make his rounds. Santa had reindeer and Halloween witches, who, according to Mommy, were actually very nice, just pretending to be mean, and had broomsticks, but no provision had been made for the Easter Bunny, and Debbie could not figure it out. Timmy said that he had a flying convertible made of glass, very much like Cinderella's carriage—but when he said it, he was laughing, which with Timmy always meant that you couldn't believe him. She lay in bed, even though the sun was bright in the window, because she knew that she was supposed to wait for Mommy and Daddy to get up, but just then she heard running feet outside her door, which was half open, and she slipped out of bed and went to peek. She was wearing her Alice in Wonderland pajamas, which always made her feel very happy.

The running feet were Dean's, and she saw his head disappearing down the stairs. She went to the top step and whispered, "Stop, Dean!" but he just looked up at her and kept going down, half backward, his hands on the upper step as his feet felt for the lower step. Debbie hadn't realized that Dean could climb out of his crib. Otherwise, the house was silent. Dean had also managed to get out of the lower half of his pajamas, and his diaper was hanging, heavy and wet, below his bottom. Debbie put her hand on the banister and followed him.

The Easter baskets and whatever else there might be were on the dining-room table, three tall pink-and-green arches for handles. Dean didn't even look at them—he was running around going "Hooo-hoo-hoo"—and Debbie realized that he was just up, Easter had nothing to do with it. She went over to him and took his hand, then said, "Want your bottie? Let's look in the figerator."

Dean said, "Bottie!" He let her keep holding his hand. His diaper smelled bad. Debbie couldn't actually reach the handle of the refrigerator, but she managed to stick her fingers into the rubber edge of the door and pull the thing open. There was one bottle on the bottom shelf. She took it out and took the cap off the top, and handed it to Dean, who sat down with a thump on his wet diaper and put it into his mouth. He was big enough now so that he held it with one hand and stared at her while he sucked and played with the edge of his pajama top. Timmy came through the door of the dining room, carrying an Easter basket. He was wearing cowboy pajamas and cowboy boots instead of slippers, and he looked as though he was about to get into trouble.

Debbie said, "What time is it?"

Timmy looked at the clock, then said, "Two hairs past a freckle, eastern elbow time." He bit the second ear off his chocolate bunny. Then he said, "Let's do something."

"What?" said Debbie suspiciously.

"Let's hide the eggs."

"The Easter Bunny did that."

Timmy, who could reach the handle of the refrigerator, opened it and pointed to the bowl of eggs on the bottom shelf. Debbie said, "They're white."

"So?" He removed one from the bowl and handed it to Dean, who balanced it on his palm. He said, "Come on, Deano, let's hide the egg!" Dean threw down his bottle, which Debbie picked up, and gave his hand to Timmy. Debbie followed them into the dining room and then the living room with a sinking heart. Timmy pointed to the corner of the sofa and said, "There's a good place."

Dean carefully set the egg in the corner, and backed away. Timmy said, "Let's get another one!"

They disappeared into the kitchen. Debbie put her fingertip on the egg but was afraid to grab it. They came back with two eggs this time. Dean put one in the toy box and the other one by the leg of the bookcase. When they went back to the kitchen, Debbie removed her Raggedy Ann doll from the toy box.

Pretty soon, the boys had set more eggs than Debbie could count around the living room, some in better hiding places than others. Timmy had finished most of his bunny, and had dropped the rest on the floor in the kitchen. He had also spilled some of his jelly beans, but Dean had sat down on the floor and eaten those—had colored bits in the corner of his mouth. When Mommy and Daddy appeared in the doorway between the living room and the dining room, Timmy was kneeling on a dining-room chair, sifting through the paper grass in his Easter basket, and Dean was sitting on the table, the smallest of the baskets across his bare legs. He had taken some of the foil off the bunny and tried it, but he didn't like it. It lay next to him. Debbie had removed her basket from the area entirely and put it in the closet. She had not touched any of the candy, but she had claimed the stuffed bunny, and was holding it. Mommy said, "Goodness, what a mess!"

It was Daddy who sat on the first egg, the one in the corner of the sofa. Debbie saw him, but didn't say anything until he said, "What the—?" and sat forward. Yellow gunk was stuck to his shorts and dripping over shards of eggshell on the couch. Mommy started laughing. Dean sat up on his knees and started laughing, too. Daddy leaned forward and stepped on the egg under the coffee table. "Uh-oh," he said, "minefield."

Mommy went into the kitchen, opened the refrigerator door, closed it, and came back. She said, "They're all gone. There were nearly a dozen." She lifted Dean off the table and set him on the floor. Timmy said, "I didn't do it, Mommy."

Mommy turned to Debbie, who said, "Not me." Daddy said, "We're to assume that Deany laid the mines?"

Timmy nodded.

Daddy said, "Who opened the refrigerator door for him, Timothy?" Timmy was frank, as always. "I did."

Mommy said, "Who brought him downstairs?"

Debbie said, "He got out. He went down. I saw."

Mommy got down on her hands and knees and crawled around the living room, picking up the eggs. She got every one except the one in the toy box, which Debbie handed her.

After everyone was cleaned up, and Mommy pulled a chair up to the stove and helped Timmy make the scrambled eggs, and Daddy set Dean in his high chair "to keep him out of range," then helped Debbie set the dining-room table, they had breakfast: eggs, ham, toast, and pink sugar bunnies. When Daddy finished his eggs, he lit his cigarette and said, "Do you sportsmen and women know the story of Uncle Frank and the Canada goose?"

Debbie shook her head. Timmy shook his head. Dean whapped his spoon on his tray.

Daddy said, "Well, you know, Uncle Frank was a great hunter as a boy, and he used to go out into the fields with his long long shotgun, looking for rabbits and beaver and bears and even geese, and one day in the fall, he is lying in the grass, and he hears honking, so he looks up, and here comes a flock of Canada geese, black and white, looking for water, and Uncle Frank thinks that they are going to settle in the creek, which is a half a mile across. And he thinks that when they do that he is going to shoot one, and take it home for supper."

Debbie looked at Mommy, who was smiling.

Daddy said, "So—the geese begin to come in for a landing, and Uncle Frank raises his shotgun and takes aim at the biggest one, and just as he's about to pull the trigger, something falls out of the sky and bops him on the head, and he falls over, half knocked out." Daddy's head flopped to the side and his eyes rolled; then he sat up. "When he wakes up a few minutes later, there is a golden egg lying next to him. He picks it up. The geese are all honking like mad and running toward him with their wings up, hissing, and you know geese are pretty scary, but Uncle Frank was the bravest boy ever, and so he just sits there, clutching the golden egg, and a very big goose comes up to him and says, 'That's my egg.' Like this." And Daddy leaned toward Debbie and loudly hissed, *"Dassssss my eggggsssss."* Debbie sat back in her chair.

"And she reaches out and opens her beak around the egg and starts pulling. Uncle Frank pulls, too, but then he says, 'What will you give me for it?' because Uncle Frank knows how to make a deal. And he leans over and hides the egg. What do you think the geese offered?"

Timmy said, "A dollar?"

"The geese didn't have any money."

Mommy said, "Maybe they offered a couple of ducklings."

Daddy said, "Just to rid the world of those pesky ducklings, right? But Uncle Frank had no use for ducklings."

Debbie's gaze was wandering around the room, and she happened to see the famous golden feather, which Mommy kept in a glass cabinet with some nice dishes. She said, "A golden feather."

Daddy said, "Did they have a golden feather?"

Debbie said, "They had one. It was old and they took very good care of it." Debbie saw Mommy glance at the golden feather. "They thought that something bad would happen if they lost it."

"So why would they trade it?" asked Mommy.

"Because there was a golden baby in the egg," said Debbie. "They had to."

"Yes!" said Daddy. "That's exactly right. All of the geese got together and they brought out the golden feather from the little purse they kept it in, and the biggest goose carried it over to Uncle Frank, and they traded. And then a score of years went by, and something happened to that feather."

"What?" said Timmy.

"One day, Uncle Frank was walking down the street in Chicago with that feather in his hand, and Aunt Andy, the love of his life, came walking by, and he gave her the feather, and they lived happily ever after."

"They did," said Mommy.

Later on, at church, right when the minister started talking about yet another thing that Debbie could not understand, Debbie turned her head toward the window and thought about the golden feather, and she knew that someday the golden feather would belong to her.

ROSANNA SIMPLY DID NOT say a word—not one word—about the fact that Minnie was living in the big house with Joe and Lois, and showed no sign whatever of moving out, or even thinking of moving out. It was easy enough to say that a thirty-three-year-old woman who wore her hair in a bun and never a brighter color than maroon was a dyed-in-the-wool old maid, and would certainly come in handy when this child was born who was coming in February, but Rosanna thought it was something out of her grandparents' generation. In those days the countryside was full of old maids and widows and no one thought a thing of it, what with the Civil War and the cholera and the smallpox, but these days it looked strange and it was strange. However, not a word. Here she was, she had gotten everything she wanted and, as Walter said, "You're still not satisfied." They were finishing supper; Claire had already gone upstairs to do her homework.

"It's not a question of being satisfied or not." Rosanna stood up to clear the dishes.

"What, then?"

But she didn't know what it was a question of. The expression that came into her mind was 'Well, I made my bed, so I might as well lie in it,' but she didn't know what that meant, either. She said, "Did I have my fiftieth birthday yet?"

"Yes, you had that two and a half years ago."

"Dear me," said Rosanna.

Walter patted her hand when she reached for the potato dish.

"Anyway," said Rosanna, "my mother has had to put up with much more than I have, and your mother, too, and they just tut-tut and keep going. Every so often, my mother tosses her hand and rolls her eyes, and that's as close as she ever comes to getting fed up."

"My mother's got more of a temper," said Walter.

"And more to put up with, or at least she used to. But she never strangled him with her bare hands or poked him with the bread knife."

"Or not so it showed, anyway."

"They never complain when things are going well."

"No, they don't," said Walter.

"But that's when I want to complain. When things are going badly, I'm afraid to complain."

"I don't think of you as a complainer," said Walter. "I think of you as a suggester."

"Then we've had a happy marriage?"

"Doesn't your mother sleep in her own room with the door locked?"

Rosanna said, "She always says that once she's waked up she's up for the night, so she has to lock her door."

"That's what she says."

"Well, six children is six children." And then, "One of her cousins had ten in ten years."

"You had better tell Lillian how it works," said Walter.

"If she doesn't stop after this one, I will," said Rosanna.

"When's it due?"

"Lois is February, so Lillian is January, and Andy is March."

"I keep expecting Henry to pop in and say he's found the girl."

"In the library," said Rosanna. "Sleeping on a shelf and waiting for the prince to kiss her, and Henry's the only person to enter that section in a hundred years."

"Sounds about right," said Walter.

So it was a pleasant conversation. A bit later, Claire came down and asked if she could play the tune she was practicing on the recorder, and she did—Rosanna barely made out that she was getting at "Amazing Grace," and then there was another one by Bach, and she and Walter clapped. The recital, Claire informed them, was in two weeks. Then Walter finished reading the rest of the *Saturday Evening Post* that had Eisenhower on the cover, and Rosanna finished the row she was knitting in the sweater she was making for Lois's baby—she had already finished the one for Lillian's baby, and would do Andy's next.

They went up the steep stairs. Joe had put a railing on either side, and they both held on. Walter seemed to haul himself from step to step. Yes, she knew she was fifty-two and a half, and that made him fifty-seven and a half. Up was easier than down—some days her right knee hurt so that she had to bob down the steps, holding the railing and sort of lurching right and left. No running up and down looking for this little thing and that anymore.

In the bedroom, Rosanna sat on the seat of her dressing table and took the pins out of her hair, then brushed it and braided it loosely for the night. Walter sat on the edge of the bed, rubbing his feet and separating his toes. Then he put his hand behind his neck and held it there while he opened his mouth and twisted his head, right, left, up, down. Then he blew his nose. Well, maybe there was a reason her mother locked her door, and it had only to do with the sad noises that old married people made. At least they had their, or most of their, teeth. Rosanna's grandmother (not Oma, but Grandma Charlotta Kleinfelder) had an itinerant dentist take out all her teeth, because they were too much trouble, and she ate soups for the rest of her life.

"Oh my," said Rosanna. She turned out her little light and stood up. Funny to think that for years she had gotten ready for bed by kerosene. Those lamps they had used were lined up in the barn, as if they might use them again. "Someday," she went on, "this house will have an upstairs bathroom."

"We can move our things down to the boys' old room."

"Chilly in there," said Rosanna.

"Chilly in here," said Walter.

They did what they did every night, which was roll toward the lowest part of the mattress, the center, and arrange themselves as comfortably as they could. Every night, Rosanna swore she was going to buy a new mattress, and every day, she forgot about it. She pulled up the sheet, and then the comforter she had made. Walter had on a nightshirt, and she could feel his hairy calves and bony feet move over and clamp her inside her flannel nightgown. It wasn't yet time for bedsocks, but soon it would be. She pulled the sleeves of her nightgown down over her hands and pushed her head into the feather pillow. It was cold. Walter began to snore, and she shifted him onto his side.

When he came under her nightgown, it was in the usual way—more as if he was looking for warmth than looking for satisfaction—but as she rose to wakefulness, she realized that he was trying to kiss her, an unusual thing, and that his member was stiff, pressing against her side and then her thigh. The room was so dark that the moon must have set. She said, "Walter! Walter! Are you awake? You're lying on my arm."

He continued to lift her nightgown, and then he kissed her smack on the lips, a pushy but cushiony kiss, and, well, she reciprocated, which just made him worse. Moments later, he had her nightgown unbuttoned and over her head, and she had to disentangle her own arms. But she wasn't so cold anymore, and neither was he. She pressed her breasts and stomach against his hairy chest and shoulders, and it was comforting, as it always had been. His hand came around and opened at the small of her back. He kept kissing her. He might or might not be awake. Sometimes he insisted that he was much more passionate in his sleep than awake, though why he would tell this story, Rosanna didn't know. She lifted her leg up over his hip, and he found her and pressed into her. Now he was kissing the base of her neck, where it met the shoulder. Rosanna tingled. The hollow in the mattress seemed to deepen enough for them to break through and hit the floor, but it didn't, though the bedstead creaked and complained.

It went on for a minute or two. At the end, Walter was coughing with the exertion, and finally had to sit up and take a sip of water. Rosanna put on her nightgown again and smoothed it over her hips and legs. She handed Walter his nightshirt, which had draped itself over the headboard. She straightened the pillows and the quilt. Walter had stopped coughing and blew out a large breath. "Oh me," she said.

When they'd rearranged themselves in the center of the bed, and Walter had fallen asleep, Rosanna yawned a couple of times and then, secretly, just for herself, touched her husband's forehead, gently, affectionately, amused at that expression about making her bed and lying in it. Yes, indeed. It was a strange thing, eight or nine hours day after day, every day they were alive. So many things that took place during the day drew them apart, and then there were these nights in this room, this very bed, warm and almost wordless, that had kept them together.

ELOISE AND ROSA SHOWED UP in Iowa City the morning Henry had a big exam in his Eighteenth Century Novel class, and he was so busy finishing *Clarissa* (fifteen hundred pages) that he hadn't thought much about either cleaning up his room or where he could take Eloise and Rosa for lunch before they drove him back to the farm for Christmas break. *Clarissa,* of course, had not been assigned, nor had *The History of Sir Charles Grandison*—only *Pamela*—but Henry enjoyed rounding out his exam essay on *Pamela* by referring with casual savoir faire to the other two novels, and he made sure to refer to a passage at the end of *Clarissa,* just so Professor Macquart would know that he had read the whole thing. He had also, of course, read many other unassigned works of the eighteenth century, including *Justine* and *Juliette.* And all the boys read *Fanny Hill,* even if they had no idea what they were reading. He rather liked eighteenth-century literature, though it was awfully easy to read, and more suited to enjoyment than to scholarship. His preferred text was the type that was missing a lot of lines, one where you had to infer what the faceless author might have been getting at rather than having it all sitting there before you. And he liked poetry more than prose.

Rosa was at college, too. Maybe she was at Berkeley. Wherever it was, it was someplace enviable, but at least it wasn't Harvard. He hadn't seen Rosa in four years or more, not since they came that Thanksgiving—Andy's first Thanksgiving, when the house was jammed with people and he had to sleep on the sofa so Frank and Andy could have his room. And so it was surprising to see her coming toward him down North Clinton and then cutting across the lawn in front of Schaeffer Hall (where he had just taken his exam). That would be Eloise beside her, talking, of course, just like Mama, but taller than Mama, and better dressed—Eloise waved when she saw him. Rosa was slender, in slacks and boots and a jacket like a navy peacoat. She was dark; her black hair fell in a thick wave down her back, as if she didn't care a thing about it. She had a long, thin face and a large, mobile mouth, and was eye level with him, and he was considered to be tall (though not as tall as Frank—that wasn't allowed in their family). Eloise put her arms around him and said, "Darling Henry! You are so grown up now!"

"I am." He let her hug him tight.

He couldn't take his eyes off Rosa. She stood very upright, and held out her hand. He said, "I remember you."

"Oh dear. That's such a bad beginning. I was impossible when I was fifteen."

"I guess I was so impossible myself that I didn't notice."

"You only ate pie," said Eloise.

"I'm sure I had my nose in a book."

"That, too," said Rosa. "But I pretended not to care."

Henry put his arm around her shoulders and said, "It's nice to see you now."

Eloise said, "Where shall we eat? Are you finished with your exams?"

Still, he could not take his eyes off Rosa.

They ate at a café on Iowa Avenue at the corner of Dubuque, and Henry ordered what Rosa ordered, which was dollar cakes with sausage and apple compote, orange juice, and a cup of coffee. Eloise had only the coffee and an English muffin. It was good that Henry was so practiced at keeping his thoughts to himself while carrying on a conversation as if he cared about it, because Eloise seemed satisfied that they were having a nice meal, while all the time Henry was taking inner snapshots of Rosa, smiling, frowning, rolling her eyes, laughing, eating, glancing out the window. Everything about her was plain and unglamorous—she wore no makeup, her shirt was like his, and she had a thrift-shop men's vest from the twenties over it. Her gestures were graceful. If there was such a thing as love at first sight, Henry thought, this was it. He only remembered when they got in the car that the girl was his first cousin, that he had known her off and on his whole life, that after a week in Denby Eloise and Rosa were going back to San Francisco, exactly the wrong direction.

When they got to his room, just to see it for a moment and so that he could pick up his suitcase, his roommate Mel was there, sitting on his bed in his pajamas, drinking milk from a bottle, and rubbing his chin. He glanced up, said hi, groaned, set the bottle on the floor, and fell back in his bed. Eloise stood in the doorway; Rosa came in and surveyed his bookshelf, her hands in the pockets of her peacoat. Mel didn't even seem to see her.

The car was from Hertz—Eloise had rented it in Chicago, a roomy Ford. Henry put his suitcase in the trunk, with theirs, and got right into the back seat—he wanted to watch Rosa for the couple of hours that it would take to get to Denby, but to do so naturally. Eloise asked him if he wanted to drive. He did not. He said, "So tell me all the bad stuff that Mama doesn't want to know before we get home."

Eloise laughed, but then got serious. She said, "Well, it's a nightmare, Henry. You must know that. I had to testify before the California Un-American Activities Committee for four days in November."

"What did you say?" said Henry.

Rosa said, "Take the Fifth, take the Fifth, take the Fifth. I think she should have said 'fuck you.'"

Eloise said, "Thank you for that, darling. But it's pretty clear. You have to just take the Fifth, because if you give them any excuse at all, even saying that you will tell about yourself but not about anyone else, that's an admission that you have things to tell, and you can't admit that or they will make you say them."

"Are you going to have to go to Washington? You could stay with Arthur and Lillian."

"I wouldn't do that to them," said Eloise. "If I go there, I will just keep to myself."

Henry sat forward. "What are you saying, Aunt Eloise?"

Rosa said, "She's saying that she can damage Arthur, but he can't help her. We had to make sure that they weren't going to be here before we came here. We did." That she looked elegantly furious as she said this, Henry found entrancing. "People we know in Oakland said that I should change my name, because it's so obvious who I was named for."

"Who were you named for?"

"Rosa Luxemburg and Sylvia Pankhurst."

"Who were they?"

Rosa said, "Oh, for God's sake."

Eloise said, "Rosa Luxemburg wrote 'Leninism or Marxism?' and Sylvia Pankhurst was a suffragette."

Henry looked out the window. They were past Marengo now, going through the snowy black-and-white woods that would soon give way to the open prairies along Highway 30. He found himself touching the scar where Mama had sewn his lip with a length of silk thread, him screaming in Lillian's lap. He imagined it turning red (it was actually whiter than the rest of his skin, and smaller in the mirror than it sometimes felt), and put his hand in his lap.

Rosa said, "I'm certainly not going to change my name."

Henry watched the way she reached back and rolled her hair around her hand, then tossed her head.

"We're not movie stars. We aren't important enough to be black-listed," said Eloise. "I'm not a teacher. I'm not working for the government anymore. And Rosa's father was a war hero. I think we're safe enough, personally, but that's why it's best to keep ourselves to ourselves for the time being. Rosa consorts with outcasts, anyway, so no problem there."

"Who do you consort with?" said Henry.

She said, "Poets. I babysit for Kenneth Rexroth. He has a little girl."

Henry did not say that he hadn't heard of this person. He said, "I wish I did that."

"You do?" said Eloise. "That's funny. There was an Iowa professor who sponsored a leftist peace conference I went to a couple of years ago, McGalman, something like that."

"McGalliard?" said Henry.

"Yes, I think so."

"I see him almost every day. We're reading *Beowulf*. I'm going to do my senior thesis with him."

"Are you surprised?"

"I don't know."

"Well, everyone sponsored that conference. Judy Holliday sponsored that conference. Albert Einstein sponsored that conference. Smart people were fighting to get on the list."

"May I come visit you after I graduate?" said Henry. "I bet I can get into Berkeley." His hand moved toward the scar again—a habit he thought he'd broken. That was how he knew that Rosa was affecting him.

"I bet you can," said Eloise.

"Oh," said Rosa, "you should."

That was enough for now.

1953

WALTER SLIPPED OUT of the house before Rosanna was awake and headed east, toward the rising sun. The air was clear and bracing, and he just wanted to look over the fields before planting commenced and the fields turned into a task that maybe he was no longer up to. There were so many acres they had to plant now that he was resolute about doing his share. The big house and the barn showed no signs of life, so even Joe wasn't up yet. They had injected the anhydrous, at least—that was the nerve-racking part, and the fact that they themselves hadn't yet had an accident wasn't much solace. Rosanna's brother John had accidentally disconnected the hose and released a white cloud of the stuff, and it was a good thing he was fast and the breeze took it away from the house. No real damage done, just a scare, and a warning.

Walter had to admit that the Easter trip to see the babies had taken more out of him than he'd expected, and it was not the train ride that did it (Frank paid for a roomette, and that was pretty comfortable). They'd gone first to Washington and seen Tina (Christina), who was quite a large child—nine pounds if you could believe it—and reminded Walter that any ancestor could crop up in a family, and if you kept crossing Angus and Herefords, sometimes you got a pure Hereford and sometimes you got a pure Angus, and sometimes you got a combination of the two. In this case, Lillian and Arthur had gotten a Cheek, and no doubt about it—thick, straight dark hair, pale-blue eyes, white skin, and intense gaze. But at least she was healthy. The same could not be said for Frank and Andy's twins, the larger of whom was Richard, five pounds five ounces at birth, and then the surprise—the doctor had said, "And what do we have here?"—that was Michael, five pounds even ("And fortunate to be that," said the doctor; "you must have eaten a lot of ice cream, my girl, and be glad you did"). The twins were in incubators still, after a month, and not expected to come home for another week. Walter didn't know what to think of that. He had only seen them once, during a brief visit to the hospital. Rosanna kept saying she was sure they would be fine.

Of course, the real surprise was Ann Frederick Langdon, born February 14, and a valentine by any measure. She didn't look like Lois and she didn't look like Joe, she looked like Lillian, and was just that same sort of child—"angel" stamped all over her, said Rosanna. "Lois loved Lillian as a child," said Joe, and Walter said, "Well, you know, back in the old days, when my father was breeding horses, he used to bring his best-looking yearling out of the barn and walk it in a circle around every mare right after the stallion bred her, just to give her the proper idea of what to produce." Now Miss Ann was two months old, gazing at everything in animated fascination, and that other thing was true, too, that your grandchild was much more of a treat than any of your children could ever be. Joe changed the baby—something that Walter had never done, but the sort of thing that Joe would do.

Walter had passed the barn and the Osage-orange hedge, but now he headed back in that direction. Ah, the damn thing was thriving. The leaves were pushing their way out on every one of the spurs that had grown where he'd clipped the thing the year before. The leaves were the brightest green in the world, maybe in the universe—flat and waxy and full of themselves, protected by the thorns. Every year, Joe said, as Walter always had, that he was going to pull it up, but he never did—the roots had probably spread everywhere, and taking the thing out would be a major pain in the neck. There was always a reason not to bother. Walter touched one of the thorns. He was used to the hedge, but the thorns still seemed menacing.

JOE WAS in his own barn, behind the big house, when Rosanna entered. She was wearing her robe, her nightgown, and a pair of rubber boots. Her hair was hanging in a gray, disheveled braid, and her eyes were wide. She didn't say a thing, she just came to him and grabbed his hand. He dropped the wrench he was holding and followed her out. He said, "Mama! Mama! What's going on?" But she still didn't answer, and that was how he knew. The only mystery was that he expected her to take him to the house, and she took him to the barn, and beyond there, around the Osage-orange hedge, and there was Papa in his overalls, folded on his side, his arms crossed over his chest, his back to the hedge. Rosanna said, "I don't know why he left. I was asleep. He just left. He just left."

Joe stood still for a moment, and then they both knelt, and he could think of nothing to do other than to put his palm over Walter's forehead. It was cool. His mother said, "I looked all over the barn, and then I came out here, and some crows were in that tree there, making a lot of noise, so I—" She stood, crossed her arms over her robe, then said, "Goodness gracious, Walter!" Joe took off his jacket and laid it over Walter, but did not, in the end, cover his face. He had to pretend that his father was merely sleeping one last time. Rosanna said, "Walk me to the house. I'll call the undertaker. I guess we'll use the same one we used for Grandpa Wilmer. I'm so sorry your grandmother lived to see this." She held Joe's arm and they stepped carefully.

Joe said, "Do you think it was his heart?"

"I think it was something he knew was coming, which was why he refused to go to the doctor after Dr. Craddock died. Oh, dear me. What a stubborn man!" She put the crook of her robe-clad elbow up to her eyes, then said, "No, Joey. Don't walk with me. I know the way. You go back and sit with him till the undertaker comes. I'll call Frank and Lillian and Henry. Claire can stay home from school today, too." Joe let her arm go and watched her walk away, hunched and busy, plopping through the field in those mucky boots. Then he turned and went back to Walter. He stood for a moment, and sat down. From here, he could see the last thing his father had looked at—the long stretch of plowed land to the east, the gently curving, flat horizon, and just the tops of the Grahams' old windbreak—they had planted blue spruces, but only a few survived. He had seen birds, Joe hoped—at the moment, there were a couple of red-tailed hawks floating on a draft. Off to the right, maybe he had seen the upper story and the roof of Joe's house, Lois's house, Minnie's house, Ann's house now, where Lois was certainly wondering where he was and Minnie was getting ready for school.

It was too bad, Joe thought, that this present quiet had to give way to the movement and bustle of a funeral and a burial, but that was, of course, what Walter would expect. Joe thought the better thing would be to sink into the earth right in this spot, to be here where everyone in the family could run past each day and offer a greeting or a memory. Joe took a few deep breaths and edged a little closer to Walter one last time. He closed his eyes and listened to the air scudding along the surface of the earth, and as the day warmed, fragrance rose to envelop him.

AS SOON AS Claire woke up, she thought of the biscuits. Over the weekend, when Claire was supposed to be babysitting for Annie, Lois had let Claire make three batches, each time mounding the flour, cutting in the butter, sprinkling on the salt and the baking powder, then, as quickly as possible, with a few pats and prods, pushing the dough together, rolling it out, and—pop, pop, pop—cutting it with the biscuit cutter. The difference between Lois and Mama was that for Lois there was no picking up the leftover dough and prodding it into a less delicious second batch. Lois cut the outlines into randomly shaped biscuits and set them on another baking sheet; when those came out of the oven, she said, "Here's what you need to know about geometry. Taste this."

They were crispy, flaky, and buttery—all edges, no centers. Claire walked into the empty kitchen, dressed and ready for the school bus. It took her five minutes to get out the flour, the butter, the baking powder, and the salt. Her batch would be a surprise for Papa. The night before, she'd been reading *Jo's Boys*—late, just the little light on beside her bed—when he'd knocked on the door and peeped in. His hair was standing on end. He smiled and came in, sat on the bed. When he saw what she was reading, he laughed and said, "Well, at least that's something I can make head or tail of," and then, "Your mama is a hare and I am a tortoise, and, Claire, I sure hope you can find another creature to be, because I don't think either of those works."

She had given him a little kiss on the cheek and said that she would be a cat.

He said, "That's a good one, sweetie," and went down the stairs to the bathroom.

The oven was always lit for warmth, so when she tested the temperature by sticking her hand in (it was plenty hot), she didn't wonder where Mama was. Mama couldn't stay away from Annie, and she was always tramping across the south field to Joe's house, wondering if they needed anything. Papa, of course, would be in the barn, the first place he went every morning. Claire had heard him, almost before dawn, going down the stairs, coughing, talking to himself. That was how she knew that the day had begun: when she began to wake up and think—what was she going to wear, what did she have to do, what was there to put up with, what was there to look forward to. She had started her day like this for as long as she could remember.

Her hands didn't work as quickly or as lightly as Lois's, and she had to push her glasses up her nose with her wrist, but the biscuits looked handsome as they went into the oven, round and tall, three across and four down. As she was closing the oven door, Mama blew in and exclaimed, "What in the world are you doing?"

"Making bis—"

"Oh, good Heaven! Oh, good Heaven!" said Mama. "Who's going to eat them?"

"Papa will."

"No, no, no!" exclaimed Mama.

It was long after the moment when Claire knew that Papa was dead (though what she imagined was not him lying under the Osage-orange hedge, but him lying in the middle of the road, flat on his back) that Mama actually said the words. Mama started crying and coughing, then sniffling and blowing her nose, and as long as the words were not said, Claire didn't have to react, didn't have to feel that thing that she was going to feel, that thing that was like an empty house with the windows smashed and the paint peeling and the pillars of the porch broken and the porch roof itself collapsing, which was something she had never seen, but became something she would never forget.

If you enjoyed *Some Luck* don't miss the second book in the
Last Hundred Years trilogy

EARLY WARNING

1953. When a funeral brings the Langdon family together once more, they little realize how much, over the coming years, each of their worlds will shift and change. For now Walter and Rosanna's sons and daughters are grown-up and have children of their own.

Frank, the eldest – restless, unhappy – ignores his troubled wife and instead finds himself distracted by a face from the past. Lillian must watch as her brilliant, eccentric husband Arthur is destroyed by the guilt arising from his secretive government work. Claire, too, finds that marriage is not quite what she expected it to be.

In Iowa where the Langdons began, Joe sees that some aspects of life on the farm never change, while others are unrecognizable. And though a few members of the family remain mired in the past, others will attempt to move beyond the lives they have always known; and some will push forward as never before. The dark shadow of the Vietnam War hangs over every one . . .

In sickness and health, through their best and darkest times, the Langdon family will live and love and suffer against the broad, merciless sweep of American history. Moving from the 1950s to the 1980s, *Early Warning* is epic storytelling at its most wise and compelling from a writer at the height of her powers.